Victoria in the Win

Due to illness, Jean Plaidy was ┄┄┄┄┄┄
taught herself to read. Very early ┄┄┄┄┄┄┄┄┄┄
'past'. After a shorthand and typing course, she spent a couple of
years doing various jobs, including sorting gems in Hatton Garden
and translating for foreigners in a City café. She began writing in
earnest following marriage and now has a large number of historical
novels to her name. Inspiration for her books is drawn from odd
sources – a picture gallery, a line from a book, Shakespeare's
inconsistencies. She lives in London and loves music, second-hand
book shops and ancient buildings. Jean Plaidy also writes under the
pseudonyms of Victoria Holt and Philippa Carr.

Also by Jean Plaidy in Pan Books

Jean Plaidy

Victoria
in the Wings

Pan Books London and Sydney

First published 1972 by Robert Hale & Co
This edition published 1980 by Pan Books Ltd,
Cavaye Place, London SW10 9PG
© Jean Plaidy 1972
ISBN 0 330 25958 X
Set, printed and bound in Great Britain by
Cox & Wyman Ltd, Reading

Contents

for Mary Barron

Bibliography

Aspinall, A. (edited by) *Mrs Jordan and her Family*
The Unpublished Correspondence of Mrs Jordan and
the Duke of Clarence, later William IV
Aubrey, William Hickman Smith
National and Domestic History of England
Boaden, James *Life of Mrs Jordan*
Boulton, William B. *In the Days of the Georges*
Croly, the Rev George *The Life and Times of George IV*
Fitzgerald, Percy *The Life of George IV*
The Good Queen Charlotte
Fulford, Roger *George the Fourth*
Fulford, Roger (edited by) *The Greville Memoirs*
Hasted, Jane-Eliza *Unsuccessful Ladies*
An intimate account of the aunts of the late Queen Victoria
Hopkirk, Mary *Queen Adelaide*
Huish, Robert *Memoirs of George IV*
Life and Reign of William IV
Leslie, Doris *The Great Corinthian*
Leslie, Shane *George IV*
Long, J. C. *George III*
Melville, Lewis *The First Gentleman of Europe*
Malloy, Fitzgerald
The Sailor King, William IV, His Court and His Subjects
Petrie, Sir Charles *The Four Georges*
Redman, Alvin *The House of Hanover*
Richardson, Joanna *George IV*
Sandars, Mary F. *Life and Times of Queen Adelaide*
Stephen, Sir Leslie and Lee, Sir Sydney (edited by)
Dictionary of National Biography
Thackeray, W. M. *The Four Georges*
Thompson, Grace E. *The Patriot King Life of William IV*
The First Gentleman
Wade, John *British History*

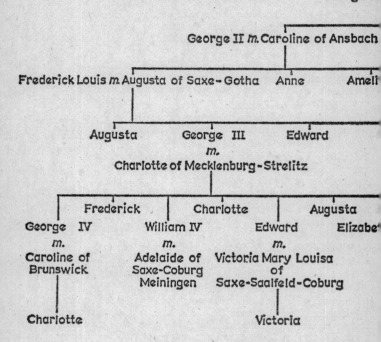

George I

George II *m.* Caroline of Ansbach

Frederick Louis *m.* Augusta of Saxe-Gotha   Anne   Ameli

Augusta   George III   Edward
m.
Charlotte of Mecklenburg-Strelitz

Frederick   Charlotte   Augusta
George IV   William IV   Edward   Elizabe
m.   *m.*   *m.*
Caroline of   Adelaide of   Victoria Mary Louisa
Brunswick   Saxe-Coburg   of
Meiningen   Saxe-Saalfeld-Coburg

Charlotte   Victoria

Sophia Dorothea of Celle
|
Sophia Dorothea
|
Caroline   George   William,   Mary   Louisa
                              Duke of Cumberland
|
William   Henry   Frederick   Caroline Matilda,
                                               Queen of Denmark
|
Ernest   Adolphus   Sophia   Alfred
      Augustus   Mary   Octavius   Amelia

The momentous year

It had been a momentous year. Napoleon had been sent into exile, his power broken. No longer could mothers quieten their children with the threat 'Boney will get you!' because Boney was an ineffectual exile whose grandiose dreams had been shown to be nothing more than such, and the smallest child knew it. He was a figure of ridicule, hatred or pity – one could decide according to one's nature; but all agreed that there was nothing to fear from him. He had been beaten at Waterloo by the invincible Wellington and the bewhiskered Blücher, and Boney's days of glory were over.

'Boney *was* a warrior, Jean François,' sang the children derisively.

England had never been so rich nor so powerful. Led by the exquisite taste of the Prince Regent the arts flourished; rarely in the history of the country had so much encouragement been given to creative genius. Nowhere in the world – now that French glory had departed – was there a mansion to compare with Carlton House; the Pavilion at Brighton, that oriental extravaganza, was unique though it might owe its conception to Chinese artists.

So much splendour; so much glory. There was no other country in the world so powerful; yet there were people not far from Carlton House, in the hovels of Seven Dials, dying of starvation; the national debt was overwhelming; the weavers of Manchester were in revolt against the installation of machinery and the hungry crowds marched to London, burning hay-ricks as they came, ominously singing the Marseillaise. Never far from the minds of every member of the royal family was the memory of the terrible fate which had befallen their cousins across the Channel: bestial violence, murder, the collapse of a régime and resulting chaos, the most bloody revolution the world had yet known.

The Duke of Clarence had said in one of his fatuous speeches that the people of Europe had a habit of cutting off the heads of their kings and queens and soon there would be many thrones without kings and kings without heads.

Clarence was the fool of the family. He had not been educated as well as his brothers because his father, determined to make a man of him and remove him from his brothers' demoralizing influence, had sent him to sea when he was thirteen; and although a tutor had accompanied him, the Duke having no inclination for learning and circumstances being understandably not conducive to study, he had become a better sailor than a scholar.

The Prince Regent was dissatisfied with life. He longed for the one thing he lacked; the approbation of his subjects; but no matter what he did he could not win this. They hated him; his faults were exaggerated; his virtues minimized. Prince Charming of his youth had become Prince Ridiculous of his middle age.

Driving to open Parliament on a bitter January day his carriage had been surrounded by a hostile mob who had broken the windows; and someone had taken advantage of the tumult to fire a shot which missed him by an alarmingly few inches.

The Regent was not as physically brave as his father who had faced similar acts of lese-majesty with calm. 'There is One who disposes of all things and in Him I trust', George III had commented when a would-be assassin had fired a shot at his carriage; and picking the bullet from his sleeve where it had lodged he had handed it to Lord Onslow, who was sitting with him, and remarked: 'My Lord, keep this as a memorandum of the civilities we have received this day.' The Prince Regent lacked his father's faith; and the only part he failed to act with conviction was that of the man indifferent to death. He was worried about his health; he was not ready to die; and, being more cultured than his father, an unwashed, illiterate, unreasonable mob filled him with greater distaste.

What have I done to make them dislike me so? he asked himself. I have done everything I could to make this country great. I would have stood beside Wellington if it had been permitted; but as this was not to be I have honoured Wellington and made him my friend. I have brought beauty and culture to this country; I have even given them an heir to the throne, though what this cost me they will never understand. And yet they hate me.

His brother Frederick, Duke of York and Commander-in-

12

Chief of the Army, was not hated as he was, although he had given the royal family one of its biggest scandals when his mistress Mary Anne Clarke had been accused of selling commissions, and Frederick's letters – banal, illspelt, revealing in the extreme – had been read in court. Frederick had necessarily been dismissed from his post in the Army, though he had regained it on his brother's accession to the Regency. For a time Frederick had been the victim of lampoon writers and the cartoonists, but somehow he had crept back into a certain contemptuous favour.

Why can't I do the same? wondered the Regent. He was cleverer than Frederick; he was the King in all but name; he had done his repulsive duty in marrying Caroline of Brunswick and had had a daughter by her. All this – and they showed no gratitude. They depicted him in their cartoons as twice the size he was; they wrote disgusting things about him; the writer Leigh Hunt had been fined and imprisoned for libelling him; they called him 'fat' – an adjective which made him shudder whenever he heard it; they exaggerated his extravagances; in fact they showed in a hundred ways that the most unpopular man in the kingdom was its ruler.

Often he remembered a long-ago conversation with Lord Malmesbury who had been his friend – although he would never forgive him for not warning him of the vulgarity of Caroline of Brunswick; for Malmesbury, as the King's ambassador who had gone to Brunswick to make the arrangements for the marriage, had been fully aware of Caroline's crudeness, her unsuitability and her lack of cleanliness. Whenever he thought of her his slightly retroussé nose which had been so charming in his youth twitched with disgust. If he could have married Maria Fitzherbert openly, all this would not have happened. He would have been a happy man, a monarch beloved of his people; and where could he have found a woman more worthy to be his queen than Maria?

So he remembered Malmesbury's words when he was trying to persuade him not to commit himself with Maria. 'You will never hold your subjects' affections until you marry and have children. That is what they ask of you and that is what they expect.'

But life had been cruel.

The Regent believed that if he could rid himself of that woman, marry again – a woman of his choice this time – he would beget a male heir very quickly. That would be an end of his daughter Charlotte's hopes of the crown which would please him. Charlotte was popular with the people who gave the impression that they were waiting impatiently for his departure, so that she might become their Queen. The English, it was said, preferred queens to kings. There was a superstition that the country prospered under them because it had under Elizabeth and Anne.

And now they were waiting for Charlotte to be their Queen, cheering her whenever she appeared, and she was well aware of this and did everything she could to encourage it. She was seen in public with her arm lovingly through that of her husband Leopold; the press wrote kindly of her; and now that she was awaiting her confinement at Claremont she was the idol of the public.

The Regent's mother, Queen Charlotte, had said that the family was more in favour than it had been for a long time and this was entirely due to her granddaughter who was also her namesake. There was nothing the people liked better from their royal family than marriages, unless it was births – in moderation of course; her own happy events had been too frequent; fifteen was after all a large number of children to give to the nation, particularly when each must be endowed with titles and income. Two had died before needing these expensive necessities but thirteen was a goodly number – and seven of them sons!

Life was so perverse. The King and Queen had had fifteen children; and the Regent had but one – and that one a girl.

It was no wonder that all eyes were on Claremont, where the Princess Charlotte, heiress-presumptive to the throne of England, awaited the birth of her child.

And before the end of that memorable year the Princess was brought to bed of a still-born son.

So there was no child to be a future king or queen of England. More calamitous, shortly after the birth, Charlotte herself, only young heiress to the throne, was dead.

It seemed as though the House of Hanover would be extinct if speedy action was not taken.

14

There must be an heir. The ageing sons of the King – himself living in the retirement his mental aberrations made necessary – must marry without delay.

The Queen and the Regent

Queen Charlotte was at Bath where she had gone to take the waters when the news of her granddaughter's death was brought to her. She fainted when she heard it. Her women took her to her bed and when she had recovered a little she lay there thinking of what this calamity would mean to the family.

'Who would have thought it,' she murmured to her daughter Elizabeth, who sat dutifully at her bedside. 'I had no notion that anything could go wrong. Charlotte was so young.'

'It was a *long* pregnancy, Mamma,' Elizabeth reminded her. I think the doctors were beginning to get a little anxious.'

'Poor George! His grief must be overwhelming. We must return at once. It will be necessary for us to make plans.'

'Mamma, you should rest awhile.'

The Queen looked surprised that her forty-seven-year-old daughter, even in such circumstances, should presume to tell her what she should do; but because of these circumstances she decided to ignore the lapse. Elizabeth, conscious of her indiscretion, added quickly: 'Your physician advises it.'

The Queen closed her eyes. I'm an old woman, she thought. There is not much time left to me and something will have to be done very quickly. So many of them and none of them has given us a legitimate heir. They are no longer young. It is almost like a blight on the family. Who would have believed it possible that with seven sons there should not be one legitimate child of the young generation!

George was the only one who had done his duty. Poor dear George, fastidious and elegant in the extreme, who had been

15

obliged to marry That Woman. Of course he could have had *her* niece, Louise of Mecklenburg-Strelitz, instead of the King's niece, Caroline of Brunswick; and that was where George had made the biggest mistake of his life. But she condoled with him; she loved him, and no one else in the world had ever touched her cold nature as he did, her first-born, her clever, beautiful George, whom she had had modelled when an infant; and she still kept that delightful baby form on her dressing-table. She must see George without delay.

He would be prostrate with grief. He and Charlotte had always been in conflict, but then – though not wishing to think ill of one so recently dead one must be truthful – Charlotte had been difficult. A hoyden, no less; no true sense of royalty, too ready to mix with the common people and somewhat disrespectful to her aunts referring to them as the Old Girls and to her grandmother as The Begum. Once she had bracketed the Queen with apple tart – or was it boiled mutton? – as the only two things she really disliked in the world. Then there had been all that trouble with her mother, running away to join her and causing a most unpleasant contretemps, arousing public opinion against the Regent and sympathy for his wicked wife. And then refusing to marry the Prince of Orange when her father had made it expressly clear that he wished her to, and breaking off her engagement as though she were some ordinary young girl to be permitted wild fancies, instead of a Princess and heiress to the throne.

But she had shown signs of improvement when she married Leopold of Saxe-Coburg, the man of her choice; she had been in love with him and Charlotte never did anything in moderation. They had lived at Claremont together quite modestly and the Princess had often been seen walking in the neighbourhood clinging to her husband's arm. It really was most un-royal; but the people liked it; and heaven knew the family needed public approbation badly. Charlotte the hoyden had done more to bring popularity to the family than any other member of it; so that was something to be grateful for. One had charming reports from Claremont of the harmony of the royal pair; how Prince Leopold sang to her, read to her and wisely impressed on her the need for dignified behaviour; and how she listened to him as she had never

16

listened to anyone else; and declared that she adored him and that the magnitude of her love could only be compared in its enormity with the national debt.

Even the Regent had become slightly less unpopular and treated to silence in the streets instead of abuse while the whole nation waited for the birth of their darling Princess's child.

And now . . . It was difficult to grasp what had happened. She felt old and ill and all that she wanted was to shut herself away and forget the tragedies of her family. But she was not the woman to do that. She had had crises enough in her life. She considered it; coming to England a plain little German princess, unwanted by the King who was in love with someone else, unable to speak the language, learning very soon that being the Queen of England meant a perpetual state of giving birth or waiting to do so. Fifteen children in a little over twenty years. All must agree that she had done her duty. It was only now that she was beginning to wonder whether she had done it too well. But her eldest son had made everything worth while . . . now, though it had not always been so. The only emotion in her life had been her feeling for him; true, it had come near to hatred at the time of the King's first lapse from sanity – or at least his first public lapse – when there had been all that conflict over the Regency and she and Pitt had stood against the Prince and Fox.

Happily that was over; she had only hated him because he would not love her; he merely had to show some affection and she was at his side. She thanked God that now they had come to an understanding; they were allies; she had admitted that George had always been the most important one in her life, and he, sentimental in the extreme, overflowing with affection – providing it did not interfere with his pleasure – accepted her devotion and in return made her his friend and confidante. So as she advanced in years she had gained some comfort. The King, her husband, whom she had never loved and who had put her into a subservient position from the day she arrived in England, making of her, as she often thought resentfully, a prize cow whose only task was to produce a calf every year – was recognized to be insane; adored George was the Regent; and they were friends.

All had seemed, though not as well as it might have been if the

17

others had done their duty, at least reasonably acceptable while Charlotte lived and showed herself able to bear children.

And this brought her back to the terrible calamity which the family had to face.

She had lost her only legitimate grandchild – and with her the baby who would have secured the succession.

Action was imperative. What were a few rheumatic pains, recurring dizzy spells? She must return to London and see George without delay.

The Regent was in Suffolk with a shooting party when the news reached him that Charlotte's labour pains had begun. It was seemly that he should be at Claremont at the birth of his grandchild who would be an heir to the throne so he left at once.

He arrived too late to see Charlotte alive.

Like his mother he could not believe this could have happened. Charlotte had been so vital; that she should have lost the child was a minor tragedy but that she herself should die stunned him. He wept; he embraced the bewildered Leopold who was dumb in his grief, and rode back to Carlton House with the blinds of his carriage drawn.

The whole nation mourned; the people in the street spoke of Charlotte as though she had been a saint. Verses were written of her:

Daughter of England! For a nation's sighs
A nation's heart went with thine obsequies.

The darling of the nation was dead. There was nothing to be done but mourn.

When the funeral was over the Queen came to Carlton House to speak very seriously to the Regent.

He received her with a show of great affection and wept affectingly while he talked of Charlotte; he had spoken of little else since her death.

'My dearest George,' said the Queen, 'this is a terrible ordeal for us all and you in particular.'

'No one can know,' murmured the Regent. 'Not even you.'

'I can imagine,' said the Queen quickly. 'But the nation's affairs must go on and there is little time.'

The Regent was not listening. He said: 'I have decided to go to Brighton. I want to shut myself away for a while and I am asking Gloucester to spare me Mary for a few days.'

The Queen nodded. Mary, his favourite sister, had married her cousin the Duke of Gloucester last year. Mary had been forty then and had been eagerly desiring to marry her cousin for years, but the King had been so firmly against any of his daughters marrying and in fact there were few possible husbands, the qualifications of being both royal and Protestant proving so hard to fill. Mary had gleefully married 'Slice' as those dreadful cartoon people had christened Gloucester (comparing him with a slice of Gloucester cheese) and although Slice was proving quite a martinet of a husband Mary preferred any husband to none at all, so was not dissatisfied.

'Mary will be an excellent companion and you always have enjoyed her company. My dear George, I understand your reluctance to *think* of anything but your unhappiness, but I do believe this to be an urgent matter of State. I may not be here much longer . . .'

He placed his hand appealingly over hers. 'I forbid you to say such a thing.'

Dear George! Always so charming. How much did he really care? she wondered. But he had such a charming way of pretending that he did that it did not seem to matter. She would rather have George pretending to care than the genuine devotion of any of the others.

'Your brothers must consider their obligations,' she said.

'How I agree with you.'

'Immediately. There must be no delay. They must marry and produce legitimate children before it is too late.'

'You are right, of course. Our recent loss makes this necessary.'

'Unless our branch of the family is to become extinct. It is so extraordinary. All these sons . . . and not one child among them.'

'Their duty should be made known to them.'

'As I said, without delay.'

'When I return from Brighton I will put the case before them.'

When he returned. It should be now. There was not a moment to lose. But one did not argue with the Regent. He had such a sense of the rightness of everything. First he must mourn the daughter for whom he had not greatly cared during her lifetime; he must shut himself away at Brighton with only Mary to comfort him. He must play his part of bereaved father, before he gave his thoughts to reminding his brothers of their duty.

The Queen decided that there was no need for her to wait so long. She would intimate to her sons that the Regent had certain propositions to put before them; and even the least intelligent of them must realize what they were.

York

The Duke of York drove down to Oatlands, the country mansion at Weybridge which was more his wife's home than his. When they had realized, long before, that their natures were not compatible they had decided to live apart and the Duchess had consoled herself with her animals, the Duke with his mistress. The years had mellowed their relationship and once they had decided to make no demands on each other they had become good friends.

The Duke had his career in the Army and between that and his ladies he enjoyed life; the Duchess was happy indulging her eccentricities at Oatlands. The house and garden were the home of numerous animals – any stray was welcome; monkeys climbed the banisters and hung from the curtains; she had even added ostriches and a kangaroo. There was an animal cemetery, where each corpse was treated to a separate burial and an inscribed stone was placed above the beloved creature's last resting-place. Her life was spent between caring for her menagerie and her good works, for she made the welfare of Weybridge her concern and the poor had reason to be grateful to her; she liked to sit on the lawns of Oatlands in summer sewing garments for the poor with a cat in her lap, a dog at her feet and a monkey perched on the arm of her chair. She was fond of the society of people as well as that of animals, though not so passionately, and gave weekend parties, which her husband often attended. She hated going to bed and seemed to need little sleep; she roamed the grounds of Oatlands by night with her protective army of dogs around her ready to tear to pieces anyone who attacked her.

When the Duke arrived at Oatlands he found his wife very sad, for she had genuinely loved Charlotte and the Princess had paid many happy visits to Oatlands. There were no visitors this weekend; Frederica, Duchess of York, was in mourning.

But she was pleased to see her husband. Poor Frederick, she thought, he was showing signs of wear. Who could wonder, considering the life he led. Once she had thought him so handsome; she remembered when he had presented her to his parents – he so tall, she so short. What an ordeal that had been, for she had no illusions about her appearance and her new family were so critical. Smallpox had spoiled her skin and her teeth were brown and uneven but her fair hair and blue eyes had been pleasant. She had been over-elaborately dressed, with her hair piled too high and set with diamonds, and what she remembered most from that occasion were the cold eyes of her mother-in-law, Queen Charlotte, and the silver foil frills on her sleeves which were uncomfortably itchy.

But that was years ago, when the revolution had been raging in France and they had come near to being killed as they passed through that country and were recognized by the mob for royalists. Only the calm courage of the Duke had saved them. How she had admired him then! He was at his best at such moments – the true soldier, indifferent to danger. But ordinary domestic life oddly enough was more difficult than facing a mob of revolutionaries and she had quickly realized what a failure the marriage was.

They had quarrelled; she had failed to produce the desired heir; they had parted, they had lived their own lives and in time come to friendship.

This had been strengthened at the time of the Mary Anne Clarke scandal when she had left Oatlands to stand by him; and while he was facing a serious charge and was dismissed from his post it was his wife who had been with him, comforting him,

21

disappointing the lampoon writers – for of what use was a faithful wife to them?

Now Frederick embraced her in the usual cool but friendly manner and they went into the house together.

'The poor child,' said Frederica, 'the poor, poor child!'

'I would not have believed it possible,' murmured the Duke.

'It is always possible. But she was so young, so full of vitality. How is the Regent taking it?'

'Badly.'

'Ah, poor George. Perhaps he reproaches himself.'

The Duke looked surprised. He, who always took his cue from his brother, was now ready to believe that the Regent had been devoted to his daughter and she to him. Frederica was more realistic. Everyone knew of the stormy conflicts which had raged between the Regent and his daughter. Death did not change that.

'At least,' went on the Duchess, 'she married the man she loved. Oh, it was good to see them together. She was happy . . . at the end. Perhaps it is the way to die . . . at the peak of happiness. My dear, dear Charlotte! It grieves me that she will no longer come bounding across the lawns in the way she did. What a mother she would have made! I always used to think of her with many many children, though not as many as your mother had . . .'

'God forbid,' interrupted the Duke, remembering the necessity to curb Frederica's flow which if allowed to would go on for an hour. It was one of the traits which had made it impossible to live with her. 'But, Frederica, what I have come to talk to you about is my brothers.'

'Ah yes, yes. They will have to marry now. They will understand this. They will not need to be told. It is obvious. Our darling Charlotte gone . . . No hope of the direct line. It is the duty of one of your brothers. If the King died and the Regent became King George IV and he died, you, Frederick, would be King.'

'God forbid,' said the Duke again, for his conversation was inclined to be repetitive and he relied to a great extent on overworked expletives.

'It would break your heart, poor Frederick, because you could only be King if George died and you have always loved him dearly. I have heard him say often that you are his favourite brother. No, you would not be happy as King. And what of me? I should have to leave Oatlands and all my darling, darling children. What would they do without me?' She patted the head of one of the darling children – a soulful-eyed spaniel which had leaped on to her lap when she sat down. 'Oh no, no, it must never be. You, because of George . . . me because of my children here.'

He let her talk; it was less exhausting to listen than to attempt to break in. She had always been animated and that had been part of her charm in her youth and at first of course one did not realize that a virtue could so soon be seen as a vice. She laughed frequently – on happier occasions than this – and that too had begun to grate.

But that was in the past. Now he knew her for a good woman and as long as he was not expected to live with her he could be fond of her. A pity she had been unable to bear a child. If they had had a son that son would now have been third in the succession and it would have been almost certain that he would have been a King. But it was not to be and fortunately Frederica was too old now to bear children so their existence need not be disrupted.

He broke in on her talk then: 'You know what this means. It's what I came to talk to you about. The Queen is hinting that my brothers should prepare themselves . . . my unmarried brothers.' He smiled grimly. 'All those who are not married now have to think about getting wives.'

'Clarence has been trying . . . unsuccessfully for some time.'

'Now he will have to succeed.'

'And Kent and Sussex and Cambridge. Cumberland is the only one who so far has obliged.'

'Obliged! The Queen would hardly call it that. She still refuses to receive his Duchess.'

'Poor Frederica, my namesake! How difficult it makes it when so many of us have to share each other's name! But I do not think she cares . . . that she is not received, I mean. I believe she and Cumberland are devoted to each other.'

'It's strange to think of my brother Ernest being devoted to anyone. But love works strange miracles, they say. It would not surprise me if Charlotte's death brings them back to England.'

'I heard she had given birth to a daughter.'

'Still-born. But that does not mean they won't have more. Frederica has had children in her adventurous life, and as she is still young enough there is no reason why she should not present Ernest with a son. And now that Charlotte is no more . . . it might seem very important to them that they should.'

'Ah yes, but none has become as important as you, my lord Duke.'

'Every one of us has taken a step nearer to the throne.'

'It will be interesting to see who reaches it,' said the Duchess. 'But I shall not be here to do so.'

'What makes you say that?'

She lifted her shoulders. 'My dear Frederick, I am nearly fifty years old.'

'That is nothing.'

Again she lifted her shoulders. No need to tell him that she believed herself to be very ill. Would he care? Yes, she thought. A little. In any case the subject of marriage was so much more entertaining than that of death.

'I think,' said Frederick, 'that I'll go and talk this over with my brothers. When George returns from Brighton they'll be summoned and presented with an ultimatum. They must prepare themselves.'

'They will know this.'

'Clarence, yes; and it will not displease him. I am thinking of Kent.'

'Ah poor Madame de St Laurent! Do you think he will abandon her?'

'I think it will be impressed on him that he must do his duty.'

'The Regent is very sentimental where such affairs are concerned.'

'It's true, but I believe that it is the Queen who will decide what should be done; and I do not think for one moment that she will allow sentiment to cloud her judgement.'

'If she did it would be for the first time in her life.'

Frederick nodded. He was next to George but the thought of a world without George who had been his idol since they shared the royal nursery at Kew was distressing. He was, he reflected, the only one of the brothers to be unaffected. He was already married to a barren woman so they could not think of marrying him to anyone else; he could not long for the crown when to receive it would mean losing his best friend and beloved brother.

Charlotte's death had made less difference to Frederick, Duke of York, than to any member of the family – in spite of the fact that it had brought him nearer to the throne than any of them.

Clarence

The Duke of Clarence was driving down to Brighton to propose to the lady whom he had decided to make his wife and he was certain of the outcome this time. He had to admit that he had been very unlucky so far. No Prince could ever have been so constantly refused. He could not understand it. Sometimes he thought it was the ghost of Dorothy Jordan mocking him from her obscure grave across the Channel.

'Nonsense,' he said to himself. She would be the first to wish for my happiness. Had it not always been so? She had always thought of him. Why, when she drew her salary at the theatre she would write to him and say: 'Do you want it? Please let me know before I spend it.'

Dorothy had invariably understood as soon as he had explained his motives to her.

'Dear Miss Wykeham.' He rehearsed the speech he would make to his prospective bride. He enjoyed making speeches and the proposal of a Prince who was third in the line of succession was surely the occasion to make one. 'Dear Miss Wykeham, I have something of the greatest importance to say to you. I have not a farthing to my name. I owe sixty thousand pounds. But if you would like to be a Duchess, and perhaps a Queen, I should have great pleasure in arranging it.'

There! A rough sailor's wooing. That was after all what he was.

He was fifty-two – not an ideal age to become a bridegroom

but still able to beget children, he would explain to her, as she would discover. She was young; and if they could get a son that boy would most certainly be a King of England. Unless, of course, the Regent realized his ambition to divorce Queen Caroline, re-marry and have a son of his own, which was very unlikely. George was three years older than he was, and hadn't worn so well. In spite of his gout and asthma he was in better shape than George. The life at sea had been a healthy one; it had hardened William and he had lived quietly and respectably for twenty years at Bushy Park with Dorothy Jordan and their ten children, whereas George had indulged himself far more.

Not such a bad figure of a man, thought William, considering himself. Why had the women refused him? It was a mystery to him. Had it had anything to do with Dorothy?

He frowned remembering her. He wished he could forget her; he couldn't help feeling ashamed of the way in which he had treated her. They had been good days when she had agreed to set up house with him and they had been together – a husband and wife in all but name – and the children started to arrive; he, a young man of twenty-five, Dorothy a year or so older, clever, piquant, charming, the finest comic actress on the stage; and how deeply he had loved her! He had thought it would have lasted for ever and it would have done but for the fact that they grew older and Dorothy put on weight and he had his gout and asthma; and there was always the vexing question of money between them. Dorothy was always trying to save up money to give a good dowry to the girls she had had before she met him. That had rankled; and of course they had been the subject of considerable comment and ridicule in the press.

Moreover, he was after all the son of a king and a king's son was expected to do his duty to the State as his mother was con-stantly reminding him, and one of his most unpleasant duties had been to remind Dorothy of this.

Poor dear Dorothy! How stricken she had been at that last meeting. He could see that she hadn't believed it was possible. 'It's only because I have to do my duty . . .' His voice had been a little more high-pitched than usual, and *false*.

That was the dreadful thing. It had been false. He need not have deserted her. The Queen might complain that he did not do his duty but his brother George, the Regent, would have stood firmly behind him if he had refused to leave Dorothy.

But he had wanted change. That was the plain truth. He was weak; he was vain. He would not accept the fact that he was an ageing man; and how better to prove that he was not than by taking a young wife. If he married he could expect the government to settle his debts and increase his income. It had happened with George and Frederick. And if he married a woman with money, the unfortunate pecuniary difficulties need not arise again.

Miss Wykeham was an heiress to estates in Oxfordshire – pretty enough, young and rich. He asked no more. This time he would succeed.

He could not understand why he had failed to do so before for he had made several attempts since he parted with Dorothy. Was it because he was no longer young or because he had ten children named FitzClarence whom he acknowledged as his own, or because the press ridiculed him mercilessly and immediately involved the lady he was wooing in that amused contempt as soon as it was known his fancy had alighted on her. That was it, he assured himself. It was the ridicule of the press which had persuaded Catherine Tylney-Long, one of the richest heiresses in the country, to choose Wellesley Pole instead of him. He remembered now the humiliation when she refused his offer; she a commoner to refuse the proposal of *marriage* from a duke; whereas Dorothy, a leading actress, a woman of high principles, had become his mistress for love of him.

The refusal of Miss Tylney-Long might have been lived down had not another heiress, Miss Mercer Elphinstone, refused him too.

By that time he was becoming a laughing-stock. He would offer to elevate no more commoners; next time it should be a princess and then perhaps the Misses Tylney-Long and Elphinstone would begin to realize what they had missed.

His brother Adolphus, Duke of Cambridge, who was some nine years younger than William, had been sent to Hanover to act as Viceroy there. Adolphus was one of the most endearing of the brothers; there was an innocence about him; his manners

27

were charming and he was good looking. One could trust Adolphus.

William wrote to him: 'My dear Adolphus, I want you to look for a suitable bride for me. She must be a princess, young enough to bear children, charming, one who could, if the occasion arose, grace the English throne. She must be a Protestant, as you know, and you may well run across her at one of the German Courts, the stables from where our princesses come. Where else could they come from, since they must be Protestant? The family needs another German princess for England. Find her for me, my dear Adolphus.'

As he had told himself repeatedly, one could trust Adolphus who had immediately set to work and found the lovely Augusta Wilhemina Louisa, daughter of the Landgraf, Duke Frederick of Hesse-Cassel.

No sooner had Adolphus set eyes on this lady than he *knew* she was the most perfect woman he had ever met; and who better suited to the throne of England than such a paragon? Adolphus, not addicted to the use of the pen, turned it now to express his admiration. He must write of the perfections of Augusta. She had lived through the hazardous years of the Napoleonic occupation which had increased her understanding; she grew in beauty every day. She had the most glorious dark eyes and brows – a bewitching contrast to the flaxen-haired blue-eyed princesses who were commonplace in Germany. Life had tended to make her a little serious but this merely added to her charm; she could sing exquisitely and to see her with a piece of embroidery in her fine tapering fingers was to see Grace personified.

'I know of no one who would make a more ideal Queen of England,' wrote Adolphus.

William read his brother's letters, picturing the joy of receiving such a beauty in England, and all that would follow on his marriage: the government grant, his heir to the nation.

Adolphus continued to write, and his letters consisted of nothing but praise for the perfections of Augusta, until at last, reading one of these letters an idea flashed into William's head. Surely no woman could be quite as perfect as Adolphus painted Augusta. 'He's in love with her himself,' cried William.

This amused him. He laughed aloud. His laughter had become louder, his oaths more frequent since Dorothy died.

Adolphus, a young bachelor of forty-three, was in love with a young princess whom he was wooing on behalf of his brother! And she, how did she feel? It was almost certain that she was in love with the charming, nine-years-junior prince who had discovered her perfections.

William resembled his brother George in that he was sentimental in the extreme and enjoyed making a fine gesture. He was also fond of Adolphus. He now made the gesture.

'My dear Adolphus, tell me the truth. Are you by any chance in love with the lady?'

What could Adolphus answer but that it was not possible to be near Augusta of Hesse-Cassel without loving her?

'I resign her to you,' wrote William.

He was rewarded by Adolphus's gratitude. When Augusta agreed to marry him he wrote: 'I believe that on the surface of the globe there is not a happier being than myself. She is everything in heart, mind and person that I could wish for.'

Charming! Affecting! William took the letter to the Regent and they wept together over William's sacrifice and Adolphus's happiness.

But that did not find a bride for William.

He was determined on royalty, though. He tried the Tsar's sister, the Duchess of Oldenburg, who after pretending to consider his proposal and even visiting England and being lavishly entertained there, decided against the match. Another humiliation! After her, the Princess Anne of Denmark.

He *must* succeed. He was becoming known as the Prince who could not find a wife. It was a situation beloved of the cartoonists and naturally they made the most of it.

He engaged the poet Southey to write poems for him to send to the Danish princess but before he could dispatch them she refused the match.

Another chortle of glee from the press! Poor Clarence! And whenever he appeared in the cartoons – which was with distressing frequency – Dorothy Jordan was there in the background with the ten FitzClarence children clinging to her skirts.

What had William, Duke of Clarence, to offer? Nothing but a vague possibility of becoming King of England, having two brothers to come before him. He was past fifty and no longer a Prince Charming, if he ever had been, was somewhat rough in the speech and manners which he had acquired at sea, and he was overburdened by debts. 'Small wonder,' said the press, 'that when William offers the ladies decline.' Worst of all they recalled Dorothy. He had deserted her after twenty years; she had died in poverty in France; she was buried in an unknown grave. Not a very good recommendation for Husband William, for he had been husband to Dorothy Jordan in all but name.

There had been a distressing crop of rumours about her.

Her eldest daughter by Richard Daly, who had been a source of trouble to Dorothy and William all her life, declared that she had seen her mother in the Strand, and that she had been so startled for some seconds that she had allowed her to pass. When she had sought to follow her, Dorothy had disappeared.

The theatre critic, James Boaden, who had been a great friend of Dorothy, declared he saw her looking in a bookshop in Piccadilly. He was certain it was Dorothy because of the strange way she handled the eyeglass she had invariably used to aid her short sight. Like Dorothy's daughter he had been too startled by the vision of one whom he believed to be dead to speak for a moment; and the vision lowered a thick veil over her face and hurried away.

This gave rise to two rumours: Dorothy Jordan was not dead but had come back to London from which she had fled to avoid a debtor's prison. Dorothy Jordan, unable to rest in her grave, had come back to haunt the man who had treated her so badly.

William declared he did not believe either of them. Fanny Alsop, Dorothy's daughter, had always hated him and would tell any tale that might harm him. As for Boaden, he had been mistaken. The whole thing was a fabrication.

But was it one of the reasons why no one seemed anxious to become his wife in spite of a promise – a vague one it had to be admitted – of a crown?

He had, however, great hopes of Miss Wykeham. In his pocket he carried Southey's poem to the Princess Anne of Denmark which a little adjustment had made applicable to Miss Wykeham. He would forget past failures and concentrate on success.

He joined George at the Pavilion, where he was staying with their sister Mary. George embraced him with great affection.

'So you have come, William, to be with me in my sorrow.'

George always acted so well that one immediately took one's part in whatever drama was being enacted. Mary, who was now Duchess of Gloucester, wept with George for the loss of his daughter; and as they talked of Charlotte William could not recognize in his niece the young woman whom death had endowed with qualities she had never possessed – or at least her father had not admitted she possessed – in life.

William was thinking of his wooing. A sailor learned to be practical. But even he realized that this was not the moment to speak to his brother and sister of his intentions.

But Miss Wykeham was staying in her house at Brighton, for like most of the rich and fashionable she had a house there; and William took the first opportunity to escape from the gloom of the Pavilion in mourning to Miss Wykeham's house.

She received him a little archly. She was fully aware of why he had come. He needed a bride and Miss Wykeham – who was no fool – knew that the death of the Princess made the need imperative and, from her point of view, the match more desirable.

'How *good* of you to call.'

'Oh, I had a purpose.'

He was very lacking in the graces of polite society. Was it due to all those years of bourgeois existence with the easy-to-please Dorothy Jordan? wondered Miss Wykeham.

'A purpose? Now I wonder what that could be.'

She fluttered her eyes at him. She had been told they were very fine. As fine as her fortune? she had wondered, for she was a somewhat cynical young woman.

'You shall see. Here read this. Or would you like me to read it to you?'

'You read it to me. But pray first be seated.'

She led him to a couch and they sat down together while he read Southey's poem to the Princess Anne of Denmark.

'What flattering words. Did I really inspire them?'

'No one but you, my dear Miss Wykeham. And you must know why.'

'In case I have misunderstood, don't you think you should explain?'

'It's as simple as this,' he said. And he repeated the speech he had learned by heart. 'Dear Miss Wykeham I have not a farthing to my name, but if you would like to be a Duchess and perhaps a Queen, I should have great pleasure in arranging it.'

She laughed. Plain Miss would certainly like to be a Duchess; she would like even better to be a Queen. An exciting prospect.

'That is what is called a rough sailor's wooing, I suppose,' she said.

'You can call it that, but I mean every word of it. Well, what's the answer?'

'Please arrange it,' she said.

He laughed with her. He kissed her. She was young, she was not unhandsome; she was very rich, and at last he had found a woman to accept him.

Kent

There could not have been a more domesticated couple than the Duke of Kent and Madame de St Laurent.

It had been said that the Royal Marriage Act countenanced adultery and fornication in the royal family. An Act which forbade the sons and daughters of the King to marry without royal consent until the age of twenty-five and after that without the consent of the Parliament made a choice necessary; princes and princesses must either marry the partner chosen for them or not at all; and if no partner was offered they must either live in celibacy or in sin.

What could men – lusty Hanoverians at that – be expected to do?

If they were young and romantic they married secretly and

morganatically as the Prince of Wales had married Mrs Fitz-herbert, or openly as Augustus Duke of Sussex had married Lady Augusta Murray. The Fitzherbert marriage had caused endless conflict and few people were sure whether or not it had taken place; it was one of the reasons for the unpopularity of the Regent at this time; and had caused suffering and humiliation to Mrs Fitzherbert. As for Augustus, when he had married the Lady Augusta the King and Queen had refused to acknowledge the marriage and there had been a case to decide whether or not the marriage was legal, although it had been celebrated before an English priest in Italy and later in St George's, Hanover Square. The verdict, however, was that although the Duke of Sussex might have been married in the eyes of the Church this was no true marriage in the eyes of the State because it flouted the Royal Marriage Act which was a law of the land. So Sussex and his Augusta set up house together, supported by his brothers who deplored the Act as much as he did. Sussex had since left her as the Regent had left Mrs Fitzherbert, but both believed that if life had been made less difficult for them, if the women they looked upon as their wives had been able to share their social as well as their private lives, they would have been happily married to this day.

The Duke of Kent, the serious military man, cared passionately for his career; twenty years before he had met in Canada and fallen in love with Mademoiselle Alphonsine Thérèse Bernardine Julie de Montgenet, a beautiful young refugee from the French revolution.

He would have married her but he knew that the King would never have given his consent to his marriage with any but a princess – preferably German and certainly Protestant – of his choosing. So they too set up house together, and had lived a life of great happiness and devotion to each other for more than twenty-five years.

Edward Duke of Kent was a martinet in the Army; he was a man without humour and in every way different from his brother the Prince Regent. He had suffered acutely when he had been recalled from the Governorship of Gibraltar where his stern methods had not been appreciated; he had been jealous of the

Duke of York's Command of the Army, considering him to be but an indifferent soldier; it was said he had played some part in bringing the Mary Anne Clarke scandal to light and had hoped – in vain – to become Commander-in-Chief of the Army when York was forced to resign. But through all his troubles Julie, who had taken the name of Madame de St Laurent after the St Lawrence River on whose banks they had met, had remained with him, to comfort him, to love him, to nurse him when he was sick and to restore his belief in himself when he felt himself to be unappreciated and overlooked.

When they had come to England the Regent with his usual charm and sympathy had received Julie as though she were the Duchess of Kent; and they had bought Castle Hill Lodge at Ealing from Maria Fitzherbert who, being a Catholic like Julie, was drawn to her; they acquired a house in Knightsbridge for Julie, and Edward had his apartments in Kensington Palace. These establishments were costly to keep up and Edward, like all his brothers, was soon deeply in debt.

He and Julie lived in a pleasantly domestic atmosphere. There were young people constantly in and out of the houses. Julie was fond of children and had become godmother to several when she was in Canada and these paid frequent visits. It had been an exceptionally happy household – more domesticated than that enjoyed by Dorothy Jordan and the Duke of Clarence because Dorothy's frequent absences at the theatre had meant that the occasions when the family could be all together were rare. Not so with Edward and Julie. They, as Julie often told Maria Fitzherbert, lived for each other.

Julie's charm offset the rather morose character of Edward – not that he was morose with her, but in company her gaiety was the charming antidote to his seriousness. He liked everything to be done at precisely the time assigned to it. His servants must be on duty all the time; a manservant must remain awake all night to come into Edward's bedroom during the night and light the fire so that the room was warm by morning; another servant must bring in his coffee at the stroke of six; another, exactly half an hour later must come to take away the tray. In this he resembled his great-grandfather George II who had, it was said, even made love by the clock. In fact Edward was fascinated by time-pieces; in his bedroom it was impossible to escape from their chiming and ticking.

Like all his brothers, Edward was in debt, but he did not take the matter as lightly as they did. With his precise methods of keeping accounts he deplored the fact that his expenses were more than his income.

He talked this over with Julie who was concerned to see his anxiety. 'Castle Hill,' he pointed out, 'Knightsbridge and my apartments in Kensington Place! That is three homes. Do we need three?'

'I need only one if you are in it,' Julie replied.

'And as I am of like opinion,' he replied, 'why should we keep up these three homes? Why don't we settle for one? Do you know, it's three times cheaper in Brussels than it is in London.'

'Brussels!' Julie's eyes gleamed at the thought. She would be closer to her family who were in Paris, and now that the war was over it was safe to travel on the Continent.

'I have an idea,' said Edward. 'We'll take a house there. We'll sell Castle Hill and the Knightsbridge place and I'll give up my apartments in the Palace. That would settle some of the debts and we'd be more or less free to start again.'

Julie was clearly delighted, but she was eager that he should be sure that he wanted to make this move.

'Your family . . .'

He shrugged them aside. He had been unpopular with the Duke of York since the Mary Anne Clarke scandal and that had meant to some extent with the Regent, for George believed firmly in family loyalty; and in any case he and Frederick had always stood together. The Queen did not approve of the irregularity of life; and he and Ernest had always been the outsiders in the family.

'You are my family, Julie,' he said. 'Your godchildren could come and visit us there, and you could see your family frequently.'

Julie was delighted, so they rented a mansion in Brussels and Julie, who loved flowers, immediately began planning the gardens while Edward made a few improvements to the house, for why should they not settle here where they could live on a quarter of

35

his income and the rest could be used to pay off his debts?

It seemed to be an admirable arrangement, and they settled down to a peaceful existence, visiting Paris, entertaining Julie's family, playing cards and chess together, giving parties in the gardens of which Edward was growing very proud.

Then the Princess Charlotte died.

When they heard the news they could not believe it.

'Not that great bouncing girl!' cried Edward.

'Poor, poor Leopold!' sighed Julie. 'I have heard that he was so devoted to her. I can't get him out of my thoughts.'

What Edward could not get out of his thoughts was the fear of what this was going to mean. He would have to go to England, he supposed. Sooner or later he would receive a summons from the Regent and there would be a family conference. He wondered what suggestions the Queen would make.

He watched Julie covertly. Was she remembering how often they had congratulated themselves that he was the fourth son of the King, for had he been the first or second he would have been forced into marriage as the Regent and the Duke of York had been. And with what disastrous results in both cases! He kept thinking of Julie's distress over poor Dorothy Jordan when William had abandoned her. 'I should not have believed it of William,' she had said. 'I do not admire him for it.'

And she must have been thinking of him and herself, for were not their cases similar?

He wondered if pressure had been brought to bear on William by the family, and if that were not the reason why he had suddenly deserted a woman with whom he had lived for more than twenty years and who had borne him ten children.

He had soothed Julie. 'You should put the thought that it could happen to us out of your mind.'

'I think I should die if it did,' Julie had answered.

What he could not get out of *his* mind was that conversation.

And Dorothy had died. He did not believe those stories of her walking down Piccadilly and in the Strand. Nor did he believe that her ghost had appeared there. Poor Dorothy Jordan!

He could not sleep for thinking of what lay in store for him. He waited for the message. The peace of Brussels was shattered. He knew the summons would come; and when it came he would have to obey it.

He had had a sleepless night; he had lain still afraid lest Julie should be aware of his lack of ease. He did not want her to suspect just yet. He wanted her to enjoy every hour to the full. It was important now that they both did.

He was tired when he went down to breakfast. His letters with the papers from England were awaiting him at the breakfast table as they always were. They were placed there precisely five minutes before he appeared.

He picked up the letters and Julie held out her hands for the papers.

He gave them to her and settled down to the letters.

She did not speak but he was aware that something dreadful had happened. He looked up. She was lying back in her chair, her face the colour of the cloth on the table, her eyes closed.

'Julie, my darling, what's wrong?'

She opened her eyes and her fingers caught at his sleeve.

The paper! Of course it was the paper.

He looked down. There it was in large print on the front page. 'Dukes of Clarence and Kent to marry now. The death of the Princess Charlotte has made it imperative that her uncles do their duty by the State. There are rumours that . . .'

So it had come.

He threw the paper to the floor. He laughed. 'Oh come, Julie. Newspaper talk. You know what the press is like.'

She opened her eyes and looked at him. She was begging him to reassure her, and he went on talking. His lips told her what she wanted to know, but in his heart he knew he was lying. He could hear those words she had spoken beating like a malicious tattoo in his head. 'I think I should die.'

Cumberland

In her bed in the Berlin mansion which she shared with her husband Ernest, Duke of Cumberland, fifth son of King George III, Frederica, the Duchess, was resting. She had taken to rising late since the birth of her still-born daughter, for the fact was that she was no longer very young. It was thirty-nine years since she had been born in her father's dukedom of Mecklenburg-Strelitz; but her vitality, her flamboyant good looks and a certain magnetism which she had possessed since a young girl made her – and all about her – forget her age. She would be the fascinating Frederica until she died.

She stretched luxuriously. Life was good. She was in love with the man she had married – her third husband – and that seemed to her not only an idyllic but also a rather comical situation. She, Frederica of the lurid reputation, and Ernest, the wicked Duke of Cumberland, the sinister member of the British royal family who had been suspected of most sins – as she had herself – had met, and found their match.

She laughed every time she thought of it; and so did Ernest.

She was particularly pensive this morning and was thinking of her old Aunt Charlotte, Queen of England, who, one would have thought, would have been delighted to accept her niece as her daughter-in-law. Not so old Charlotte. Charlotte did not approve of her niece's reputation, she would not receive her at Court, and if it had been possible she would have stopped the marriage.

Poor old Charlotte! laughed Frederica. Surely one of the most *un*attractive women in the world. Didn't they always see evil in those members of their sex who possessed the charms they lacked!

Oh God, she thought. I wish Louise were here.

If Louise, sister and friend who had scarcely been parted from her until her death, could be with her now she would ask nothing more of life. In moments of happiness she would remember Louise. She would see herself sitting at her sister's bedside at the last, talking to her, trying to divert her mind from pain, recalling the early days of their triumphs when they had been fêted and courted and had shocked the Court of Berlin by being the first to dance the waltz there.

Louise, Queen of Prussia, had borne ten children and she had only been thirty-four when she died. They ask too much of us, thought Frederica angrily. We are bred to breed. Ten children and only thirty-four! Beautiful Louise – born only to breed and to die doing it!

No wonder she felt angry.

But before all that how wonderful life had been in Grand-mamma's house in Hesse Darmstadt, where Grandmamma was the Landgravine. They had gone there because their stepmother had died giving birth to little Charles. Their mother had died two years before, also in childbed, and the child had died with her.

Charlotte, their eldest sister, had married the Duke of Hild-burghausen, so she did not accompany the younger ones to Grandmamma Landgravine. There were just Thérèse, Louise, Frederica, George – who was a year younger than Frederica – and now stepbrother baby Charles.

They were happy carefree days which had perhaps helped to make her what she was. The Landgravine was a clever woman. She wanted the children to be happy so she gave them a certain amount of freedom, but at the same time she introduced them to music and the arts and saw that they were endowed with all the social graces. Recognizing the outstanding beauty of the girls, she decided that as they grew older no opportunities should be missed. Thérèse immediately found a princely husband, and the Landgravine then turned her attention to Louise and Frederica.

Life went on gaily, full of trivial excitements, until the carefree existence was brought to a sudden halt. Revolution had crippled France and from the ruins had risen the Corsican adventurer whose dream was to dominate Europe. The Landgravine was alert as each day came news of Napoleon's successes and every hour brought his invading armies to their home.

It was unsafe, the Landgravine decided; and the girls were sent off to their sister Charlotte.

They were young and lively and the war seemed far away from lovely Hildburghausen in the sweet-smelling pine forest. Char-lotte gave balls and banquets to launch her sisters whose beauty had become a legend; Louise and Frederica were the two loveliest girls in Germany, it was said; and they were clearly looking for husbands.

How happy they had been – she and Louise! Everywhere they went they were together. They spoke of each other as one person. 'Louise and I do this.' 'Frederica and I think that.' They had never thought in those days that separation must inevitably come. Their brother George, who was as gay and vivacious as his sisters, was their staunch ally; he adored them and they him; but in the case of Louise and Frederica they were as one.

Snatches of conversation came back to Frederica now as she lay in bed in Berlin. 'But, dearest Freddi, when we marry we shall have to part.' 'Then I won't marry. I'll stay with you! I'll be your companion. Your dresser. Your lady-in-waiting. I'd rather be with you than marry a King.' 'Always so wild,' chided Louise. 'If they decided you'd marry, you'd have to. But when I marry I shall invite you to stay with me and you must invite me to stay with you.' 'I don't want to be a guest in your house, Louise. I want to belong.'

And then came that night in Frankfurt through which they had passed on their way home with the Landgravine who had come to collect them from Hildburghausen; there was great excitement because the King of Prussia with his two sons was in the town and it would be unthinkable for two such highly-born ladies not to pay their respects to the monarch. Besides, with him were his two unmarried sons.

The inevitable happened. Or had it been planned? The sons of the King of Prussia needed brides; and the Princesses of Mecklenburg-Strelitz needed husbands.

After that first meeting, the King told the Landgravine that her granddaughters were as beautiful as angels, and that his sons had fallen in love with them at first sight.

Although, thought Frederica ironically, it was not clear with whom the Crown Prince had fallen in love – herself or Louise. As for his brother Prince Louis, he was immersed in his own private love affair, and was unimpressed by either of the beautiful girls who were paraded for his approval.

He had told her afterwards, when they were married, that he knew he had to take one of them and it hadn't mattered to him a jot which, and the Crown Prince felt the same but as he had to make a choice he took Louise, who talked less and apart from the fact that her neck was too short which gave her a humped look, was quite beautiful.

But then Louis had disliked her because she had been a necessity. But not more than she disliked him, of course. And if Louise's neck was a little short it was her only imperfection and was easy to disguise by the lovely gauzy draperies she affected.

But the sisters were ecstatically happy because if they married the brothers they would live at the same Court and their fears of separation were groundless. For the rest of their lives they would continue to say: 'Louise and I think this.' 'Frederica and I do that.'

Who cared for husbands? Louise did a little. But that was Louise, gentle, sentimental, and when she started bearing his children she felt a strong affection for the Crown Prince and he for her. Frederica was different. She was more proud, more eager to go her own way and not so docile as Louise. Louis had done his duty by marrying her; he had got her with child; his duty was completed until the time came to produce another child so he could return to his mistress.

Let him. What did she care? She could dance, amuse herself, surround herself with admirers.

I am, she thought, picking up a mirror from the table beside her bed, the kind of woman about whom there will always be scandal – even now.

What had she cared? She had danced through the night, made assignations with men; lived wildly and feverishly, but the happiest times were when she was alone with Louise, while Louise was waiting for a child to be born; then they were at peace, listening to music or making it themselves, talking of the children, laughing over the old days.

She had her beautiful baby, Frederick William Louis, and she loved him; but she had never been a domesticated woman. It might be different now, she believed. She was mature where she had been young, serious where she had been lighthearted; she loved one man, whereas in those butterfly days she had been humiliated by her husband's indifference and perhaps determined to prove that he was the only man who did not find her attractive.

While awaiting the birth of her daughter, Frederica Wilhelmina Louise, she and Louise had lived their quiet completely satisfying life together; but the time came when she was rejoined by her husband, and soon after that he died. It was said to be a fever, but the whisperings had begun then. Everyone knew that she disliked him; they were unfaithful to each other; and he was so young to die. What was this fever? What had caused it? No one could be sure.

She was a widow of nineteen with two babies and her reputation for frivolity had changed a little. There was a sinister tinge to it.

She laughed thinking of it. What had she cared. She would rather be thought a wicked woman than a fool. Louis had treated her shamefully – and Louis had died. Perhaps that would be remembered if anyone else decided to treat her badly.

It was not to be expected that she would remain unmarried; and if a husband was found for her she might have to leave the Court of Berlin.

'I won't do that,' she had declared.

But she knew they would force her to it.

Her family was very proud of its connections with the Court of England, which was natural when one compared little Mecklenburg-Strelitz with that great country. All her life she had heard references to 'your Aunt, Queen Charlotte of England'. It was a legend in the family – the story of how one day news had come to her grandfather that his daughter the Princess Charlotte was sought in marriage by King George III.

And that same Charlotte had many sons and one of these, Adolphus, the Duke of Cambridge, was four years older than Frederica, entirely eligible, and of course the English royal family could have no objection to his marriage with a niece of the Queen.

Adolphus came to Berlin. No one could dislike Adolphus; he was too mild and pleasant. Dull, was Frederica's comment. And if I married him I should have to leave Louise.

She talked the matter over with Louise. 'We'd be parted,' admitted Louise, 'and that would make us most unhappy. But you have to marry, Freddi, and Adolphus is very kind.'

'I wonder what it's like at the English Court with that old legend Aunt Charlotte in command.'

'There is a king, you know. And the Prince of Wales is said to be the most exciting Prince in Europe.'

'Ah, the Prince of Wales! Why didn't they offer me him instead of Adolphus?'

'Adolphus will be good to you.'

'And what of us?'

'You must ask him to bring you here often. Perhaps you could settle here. Why not? He could live in Hanover. They might give him a position there.'

'That's true. I see I could do worse than Adolphus.'

And so she had become betrothed to him, and was becoming moderately reconciled to marriage when she met Frederick William, Prince of Solms-Braunfels, a Captain of the King's Bodyguard, who had seemed at that time devastatingly attractive. Was it because he was so different from Adolphus – gay and dashing and determined to seduce her?

'But I am betrothed to the Duke of Cambridge,' she protested.

'Do you think I should allow that young man to stand in my way?' demanded Frederick William of Solms-Braunfels.

Frederick William certainly had a way with him, and perhaps she was in rebellion against those who would choose her husband for her, and against the legend of Aunt Charlotte.

It was not enough to make her his mistress. That was a secret affair. He wanted to flout the Duke of Cambridge, to throw his defiance at the English Duke; he wanted the world to know that the beautiful Frederica was so enamoured of her bold captain that she would turn from mighty England to little Solms-Braunfels. And she had believed it was due to his passion for her! She married him secretly, and made one of the biggest mistakes of her life.

She shuddered even now to recall the storm that arose when it was discovered that she had married. She had brought about a coolness between England and Prussia because she had jilted a son of the King of England; she had married unsuitably and behaved in a manner which could only bring discredit to herself and the family.

She did not want to think of the years that had followed when she learned slowly and bitterly what a fool she had been. Being banished from the Court meant that she had lost Louise, and Frederick William was soon showing himself for what he was – a bully even capable of physical violence towards her. What unhappiness for herself and for Louise! And of course there was the war. Nowhere was safe from Napoleon's troops; and soon she was pregnant and her daughter was born. She called the child Louise – which seemed some consolation.

She could not bear to think of that time, although there was reconciliation and she and Louise were allowed to be together again. But the disaster of war threatened continually and when peace came Louise was about to bear her tenth child; and soon after that . . .

No, she would not think of it. It was over. She now had Ernest and although they had lost their first child there would be others.

She had sat by Louise's bed; she was the one who was with her to the end. She could feel the pain in her heart now. 'Louise, Louise, we were to have been together for the rest of our lives. And now you are leaving me.'

But Louise had gone and she had been alone in a world of hostility, dominated by a husband whom she had come to hate; but she was not the woman to sit down and cry over her troubles. Instead she snapped her fingers at Fate and sought a way out of them. She had lost Louise, the one she loved best in the world, and she was left with a husband whom she had grown to hate. She took one lover, two lovers. Her reputation was becoming tarnished – even worse, for there were many who remembered what had happened to her first husband; but she did not care.

And then she met Ernest.

What was there to attract her so strongly in the brother of that Adolphus whom she had so shamelessly jilted? He was scarcely handsome – at least he was not to others; but to her there was something completely fascinating in his somewhat sinister face. He had lost an eye at the battle of Tournay and his expression was sardonic. One could believe the stories that were told of him. His reputation matched her own. He was said to have murdered his valet who discovering his master in bed with his wife had attacked

44

him with the Duke's own sword. Ernest's retaliation – so it was said – was to cut the valet's throat. Was Ernest a murderer? It was a question which was constantly asked.

It was said of Ernest that there was no vice which he had not practised and looking at him one could believe this. He had lived as dangerously as she had herself; she was immediately attracted by him and he by her. They were of a kind – different from other people. They took what they wanted from life and were prepared to pay for it.

A new excitement had come into her life such as no man had ever given her before. It was inevitable that they should become lovers. Inevitable too that the Prince of Solms-Braunfels should discover this. How indignant unfaithful husbands could be when they learned that their wives were playing the same game! This amused her; she laughed at him.

'I will divorce you,' he had cried.

'Nothing would please me more,' she retorted.

'Do you realize you will be an outcast in Europe?'

'I realize that I shall be free of you, which gives me so much pleasure that I can think of nothing else.'

In a fury he set divorce proceedings in motion; he produced evidence of her adultery; she did not deny it and the divorce was granted.

Immediately afterwards he died . . . mysteriously.

She laughed now remembering the storm. To have one husband who had died of an unidentifiable fever was scandalous enough, but when a second did the same, then conjecture must become a certainty.

'How strange that he should die at that time,' it was said.

'Of course she had her divorce but it would have been awkward having him alive if she planned to marry again. Did she arrange for him to die?'

'Did I?' she asked of Ernest. 'You were suspected of murder once, my love. From the moment I met you I wanted to share our experiences. I had to be your equal, you know.'

He was amused. He did not ask her if she had murdered her husbands; she did not ask him if he had murdered his valet. Each liked the aura of mystery which surrounded the other. They knew that they were two strong-minded people, that they were capable of murder. That was all they wished to know.

They delighted in each other. The passion between them was unquenchable.

'I always meant to marry you,' she told him. ' I was determined on that.'

'Not more determined than I.'

Her delight in the death of her husband, her pleasure in her approaching nuptials with Ernest set the gossips talking. It was said that there was only one other with a reputation evil enough to be compared with that of the Duke of Cumberland and that was his future wife, Frederica, recently Princess of Solms-Braunfels.

Shortly after the divorce Frederica gave birth to a son, Frederick William; he was reputed to be the child of the Prince of Solms-Braunfels but that, said rumour, was a matter of which only Frederica could be sure.

She laughed now thinking of Queen Charlotte's welcoming her into the English royal family. Charlotte had always wanted to get one of her nieces married to one of her sons. She was not aware, at first, of the shocking history of Frederica though she did know that she had been widowed twice; but since the lady's birth was acceptable so was she.

It was only natural that the old Queen should want detailed reports of her prospective daughter-in-law, and when Charlotte's envoys returned to her with these what a different picture she was presented with! Frederica had been giddy in her manners and light in her morals before the death of her first husband . . . somewhat mysteriously. And then she had not been faithful to the second husband who had divorced her for immorality and then had died . . . also mysteriously.

Frederica could imagine how her Aunt Charlotte would have received the news. She would not have raged and stormed; it was not in her nature to do that. Her anger would have shown itself in the tight lips and the cold snake-like eyes. Poor old Charlotte, thought Frederica almost indulgently, she came to power too late not to want to enjoy every minute of it.

Frederica might be a niece of hers but she was not the kind of woman she would choose for one of her sons and Charlotte wished to make it clear that the marriage would not have her approval.

Ernest laughed. His mother was far away; and nothing was going to stop his marrying Frederica. They had had a brilliant wedding in Strelitz, her father, old Charlotte's brother, gave her away, and for the first time in her life she had been happy – happy with Ernest of the evil reputation, who looked as though he were capable of anything for not only had he lost an eye but his face had been badly scarred in battle which added a malevolent touch to his features. His appearance gave credence to that rumour that he was capable of all and every vice.

We are a pair, she thought.

But how interesting he was! His mind was sharp and probing; he was the most intelligent man she had ever met; she admired him as she could admire no one else; and he was the only person in the world who could make up to her for the loss of Louise.

She was happy. She could say: To hell with Queen Charlotte. To hell with the world – while I have Ernest.

He had taken her to England soon after the marriage. He wanted to make sure of the allowance which Parliament granted to the sons of the King when they married, and that the Queen did not poison the Regent's mind against Frederica. The Regent was charming to her, but the Queen refused to see her; and the Parliament refused to increase Ernest's allowance. Frederica had created trouble in the royal family because while the Regent received her and the Duchess of York entertained her at Oatlands, the Queen refused to and forbade her daughters the Princesses to.

There had only been one dignified thing to do. She and Ernest returned to Berlin.

And here they were.

Ernest came into her bedroom and sat on the bed; he was holding a letter in his hand and she knew that it contained news of a startling nature.

'News from England,' he told her.

'Yes, Ernest?'

'Charlotte . . .'

'A son or a daughter?'

Ernest shook his head. 'A boy born dead. But, Frederica, that's not all. Charlotte herself . . .'

'Dead?'

He nodded.

'My God, think what this will mean?'

'I am thinking.'

'If our daughter had lived she could very likely have been a Queen of England.'

Ernest said: 'You know what this will mean.'

'It means that my dear mother-in-law and aunt, Queen Charlotte, is very busy making plans.'

He nodded. 'There'll be marriages now, you see. Clarence and Kent will have to get busy.'

'Busy breeding!' said Frederica with a laugh. 'But the gentlemen have left it a little late. And you come next, Ernest. *Our* sons and daughters...'

'Yes,' he said, his eyes gleaming so that he looked like a satyr.

'You look adorably wicked at this moment,' she told him. 'I believe you're ambitious.'

'Wouldn't you like to see your son King of England?'

'I would, and the thought that perhaps I shall, fills me with exultation. If it were only to have my revenge on Aunt Charlotte ... but it's more than that. Yes, I should love to see our son a King of England, Ernest. That would be good for England ... if he were like you. Tell me about those who stand between.'

'George will never live with Caroline again.'

'What if he should divorce her?'

'He'll try but he forgets how old he is.'

'What is he ... fifty-five? It's not so old.'

'When a man has lived as George has, it's not young. He has indulged himself too much for his health's sake. And he is married to Caroline, who is at the moment making an exhibition of herself all over Europe. Of course she may well give him grounds for divorce but even so these matters take time. And George grows older. A divorce ... a marriage ...! Oh, I don't think there's anything to fear from George.'

'And the Duke of York?'

'Married to a barren wife. No, nor him either.'

'And Clarence?'

'Well, of course he's the danger. They'll marry him off without delay and he's proved with Dorothy Jordan that he's capable of begetting children.'

'Unless of course he gets a barren wife.'

'That's a chance he'll have to take.'

'And after Clarence?'

'Kent. He'll have to say goodbye to Madame de St Laurent and he won't like it. But he'll be forced to it.'

'And then Ernest, Duke of Cumberland, and his devoted fertile wife, Frederica.'

He leaned over and kissed her.

'And how is my love this morning?'

'Full of health . . . and hope . . . considering the news. We must have a child, Ernest. I am going to snap my fingers at my wicked old Aunt who refuses to receive me at her court. She will be obliged to receive the mother of the heir, will she not?'

'I doubt she would. And while Clarence and Kent lived she would always hope that they would forestall us.'

Frederica threw off the bedclothes.

'It is wise for you to get up?' he asked anxiously.

'My dearest Ernest, I am recovered. I am well. I am ready now. We go into battle.' She was thoughtful suddenly. Louise often seemed to come back to her to reproach her. Louise had been different from her – the gentler one, sentimental, kindly. Now it was as though Louise reminded her that her elation was due to a tragedy. A young woman had died in childbed and her child with her. And this was the cause of her excitement.

But she dismissed Louise. Life was a battle. It was something Louise had never realized. Perhaps if she had she would be alive today. But Louise had submitted; she had, knowing her health was failing, gone on bearing children.

No, her way was best. There was only one person who truly mattered to her: Ernest. And if she bore him a child that child would be her delight. Life was good, she decided, as she had thought it never would be when she had lost Louise. She was married to the man she loved and they had a chance of bearing a King or Queen of England.

49

'In the circumstances,' Ernest was saying, 'I think we should set out for England as soon as possible.'

Frederica laughed aloud. As usual she was in complete agreement with Ernest.

Victoria, the widow

The Queen had asked the Regent to call on her at Kew.

She sat in her chair, her back to the light, that he might not see her face. She felt very ill; her rheumatism was so painful that she could scarcely move; she was so irritable with the Princesses that they were afraid to speak to her. She deplored this but as she did not wish to complain of her pains she must give vent to her feelings somehow.

She was tired and a little resentful with life. Now she had come to enjoy power and had gained the confidence of her dearest son, she was too old to enjoy it.

'My dearest Madre.'

He had taken her hands and kissed them. As usual his delicately scented person, his elegance and charm delighted her.

'My dear George, I cannot rise. My limbs are too painful today.'

'I shall not *allow* you to rise, Madre dear. I shall seat myself beside you and you shall tell me what it is that troubles you.'

He brought a chair close to hers; he took her hand and caressed it lightly. What beautiful hands he had! And how gracefully he used them! She wondered then as she often had in the past how she and George III had produced such a man. He was so different from them – so much more erudite, endowed with excellent taste, a lover of the arts, the theatre and good manners; she looked with adoration at her beloved Regent.

'My dear,' she said, 'could you bear to talk of our tragedy? Are you sufficiently recovered to bear it?'

The Regent took a perfumed handkerchief and held it to his

eyes. A charming gesture, but his eyes were dry, of course.

'I must,' he said, 'since there has arisen this matter of some urgency.'

'You are so brave. I knew you would understand. Dear Charlotte is gone and that is a great bereavement in the family. But because Charlotte was the only legitimate child you and your brothers produced it made her of such importance. We have to marry off your brothers . . . without delay.'

'Perhaps haste at such a time would appear to be a little unseemly?'

'That may be. Then we must act in an unseemly fashion if it is wise to do so.'

'We'll have no difficulty with William.'

'That is if we can get a bride to take him. He has been making a laughing-stock of himself after making a scandal with his actress.'

'Poor William. One cannot blame him.'

'You are too kind, George. You have always sided with your brothers. I wish to discuss William with you. I think you should without delay give orders that feelers be put out in certain places. Ernest is married to that disgraceful woman, so we can do nothing about him. Adolphus is about to be married; that could be hastened. Augustus committed the folly of going through a ceremony with Augusta Murray and therefore is best left alone. But William and Edward must marry at once.'

'Have you anyone in mind?'

'My thoughts have been ranging all over Europe, but the religious question makes it so difficult. There is the Princess Victoria of Saxe-Coburg.'

'Leopold's sister?'

'Would that matter? She is the widow of the Prince of Leiningen and has proved that she can bear healthy children. She has a boy Charles and a girl Feodore. I have discovered that they are lively, attractive, bright and intelligent. She will do for one of them. And for the other there is the eldest daughter of the Duke of Saxe-Meiningen – Adelaide, I think they call her. Well, I have found our two princesses, Adelaide and Victoria.'

'You have been your usual wise self, dear Madre.'

'I knew action had to be taken and speedily. There are few

princesses available who have the necessary qualifications. The point is that William and Edward must be married without delay. Perhaps you will decide that you should summon them and make this duty clear to them.'

'I see that it is imperative to do so.'

The Queen sighed with relief. 'I knew you would. There may be some opposition from Edward.'

'You mean because of Madame de St Laurent.'

'I do. But I do not think that even he will want to turn his back on the possibility of giving us the future ruler of England.'

'Perhaps not.'

'The two Princesses will have to be considered carefully. While Adelaide is unmarried – and no longer so young for I believe she is twenty-five or twenty-six – Victoria is a young widow and as such accustomed to a little freedom. Victoria I think may have to be wooed a little; with Adelaide it will be the normal procedure – a match arranged between us on one side and her parents on the other. In the circumstances I suggest Adelaide for William and Victoria for Edward.'

The Regent nodded. He saw the point. William had proved himself rather frequently to have little charm as a wooer and had won a reputation as the most rejected Prince of his time. It would be unwise to send him wooing the Princess Victoria. Therefore quite clearly he must have Adelaide and Edward Victoria.

'I see, Madre,' said the Regent, 'that you have settled the matter as I would have done myself.'

'My dear son, then you will lose no time in setting these matters in motion?'

'I shall do so without delay. We are all growing so old, alas, that there is little time to be lost. But I will tell you something.'

Her cold face was touched with sudden warmth and she looked almost handsome for a second. His confidences were the delight of her life.

He put his head close to hers. 'Caroline is behaving in quite a shocking manner. I don't despair of ridding myself of her. And if I did ... who knows, *I* might present the nation with the heir myself. What do you say to that?'

52

'I would say,' said the Queen fervently, 'that Heaven had granted my dearest wish.'

They were silent for a moment contemplating that happy event.

But they both knew that the House of Hanover could not continue to exist on the hope of a granted wish however dear to them both.

William, Duke of Clarence, called at Kew and asked for an audience with the Queen.

When he was brought to her Charlotte looked at him quizzically. He was not very attractive, she had to admit. He had never had half George's looks; none of them had, but the others had more *presence* than William. She had always known it had been a mistake to send him to sea at such an early age. It had certainly not developed his *royalty*. She had told the King so a hundred times; but he had never taken any notice of her. Now of course he was shut away and had no say in matters at all; and it was hardly likely that he ever would.

It was too late to brood on William's upbringing now that he was a man of fifty-two; at least he was a Prince, a son of a king and very likely would be the father of one. He had the family's jaw and protuberant eyes – all the faults of the family which she fondly assured herself George had missed – and she had heard it said that his head was the shape of a pineapple. She could see what was meant by that. No, poor William was not the most attractive of her sons; but the death of young Charlotte had made him one of the most important, due to the unfortunate matrimonial difficulties of his two elder brothers.

'William, my dear son,' she said perfunctorily.

'How are you today, Mamma?'

'Not as well as I would wish to be. But who of us is? My rheumatism was not improved by the Bath waters. But that may have been due to the shock of Charlotte's death.'

'It grieves me to hear it.'

'I think we are all grieved by this terrible calamity.'

'I was referring to your rheumatism, Mamma,' said William.

'Thank you. But that is a small matter compared with our loss. I believe George will have something very serious to say to you.'

'I have something very serious to say to you, Mamma. And that is why I have come here to see you.'

'What is this?'

'You have always told me that I should marry.'

'It was your duty to have done so years ago. If you had and those children of yours were legitimate Parliament and the people would be better pleased with the family.'

'My son George would make a fine King.'

'The son of an actress! Don't be ridiculous. The illegitimate son at that!'

William flushed a little. 'Your Majesty would find it hard to name a more handsome fellow and better soldier.'

'I've no doubt the young man is admirable, but he happens to be your bastard son and his mother was a play actress.'

The Queen looked coldly at her son. William had always been such a fool. He was a little abashed at the reference to Dorothy. It was not that he wanted to forget her; he merely wanted to forget his treatment of her. He wished that he had waited a little until she had died naturally; then there would have been nothing with which to reproach himself.

But he had good news to tell his mother so he said: 'I am engaged to be married.'

'What did you say?' said the Queen.

'That I have decided to marry. I have chosen my bride.'

'Then the Regent has spoken to you?'

'I have not yet told him of my decision.'

'I did not know that the arrangements had gone so far. So you are pleased with the prospect.'

'It delights me. I shall go ahead with arrangements as quickly as possible.'

'It is my fervent hope – and the Regent's – that you will.'

'Have no fear. We'll have the child before the year's out.'

He really was a little crude. The rough sailor attitude could be carried too far. She wondered what Adelaide was like. But German princesses were brought up to be docile.

'It should not take long to make the arrangements. I am sure the Duke will have no objection. I believe he would have welcomed the suggestion before.'

'The Duke?' asked William bewildered.

'Adelaide's father, the Duke of Saxe-Meiningen.'

'Adelaide!'

'The lady's name.'

'I don't understand, Your Majesty. Miss Wykeham's name is not Adelaide.'

'And who is Miss Wykeham?'

'The lady I have asked to marry me and who has accepted me.'

'William, are you mad?' In spite of her agitation she wished she had not used that word which was one she rarely allowed to intrude into her vocabulary. It was a constant fear of hers that one of her sons should have inherited his father's illness.

'Mad! Indeed not. It is to tell you of this that I called here today. I have asked Miss Wykeham to marry me and she has accepted me, and I see no reason why the marriage should be delayed. Can Your Majesty name one?'

'I can name several; but I will content myself with giving you one why it should not take place at all.'

'Not . . . take . . . place!'

'You are going to marry Adelaide, the daughter of the Duke of Saxe-Meiningen. Envoys are being sent to the Duke now. Who is this woman with the ridiculous name?'

'If you mean Miss Wykeham, I must protest. Her name is not ridiculous and she happens to be a considerable heiress. I gather that is not considered to be an obstacle.'

'We know your debts are shamefully large; but the possession of wealth does not qualify a commoner to become the mother of a future King of England.'

'If she has a child she nevertheless will be, for I am going to marry her.'

'That is where you are mistaken.'

'I have offered marriage and been accepted. I cannot step out of it now.'

'You can and you will, for the simple reason that you are going to marry the Princess Adelaide.'

'I am sorry to disagree with Your Majesty, but I have given my word.'

'Have you forgotten the Royal Marriage Act, which makes it a

55

law that a member of the family cannot marry without the King's consent?'

'Under the age of twenty-five, Mamma. I am a little older than that.'

'And after that, without the consent of Parliament. Now do you think that the Parliament is going to allow this young woman to be the mother of the future heirs?'

'I think that when the Parliament realizes that I have given my word it will give its consent.'

'This cannot be allowed. Leave me now. You have upset me very much.'

William bowed. 'I am sorry for that,' he said, 'but it does not alter the fact that I intend to keep my word to Miss Wykeham.'

When William had left the Queen summoned the Princesses Elizabeth and Sophia.

'My snuff-box,' she commanded; and Elizabeth immediately brought it.

Having taken a comforting pinch the Queen said: 'I am most distressed. It is William again. What a fool your brother is! When I think of his behaviour from the time he was a young man, I cannot remember one occasion when he has acted with the slightest wisdom. He was constantly promising marriage to this one and that. Miss Fortescue, Miss Somebody else . . . I've forgotten the names; and then of course he settled down with that actress and produced all those children. And after that we had to watch his ridiculous efforts to get married. Now he has proposed and been accepted by a Miss Wykeham.'

'She is a very considerable heiress, Mamma,' said Elizabeth.

'So she may be, but she is not going to be William's wife. I must write to the Regent immediately. I can see that we are going to have trouble with William. Bring my writing materials and call the messenger. He should take my note to Carlton House immediately.'

The Regent had asked the Duke of Kent to visit him at Carlton House. Edward was not one of his favourite brothers; they were so different. Edward was too serious; George was prepared to admit that he was a good soldier, but he had never really forgiven him after the Mary Anne Clarke scandal, and he had been secretly pleased that the post of Commander-in-Chief to the Army, which Edward had hoped would be his when Frederick was forced to resign, had not fallen to his lot.

But the Regent had no desire to quarrel with any of his brothers. He liked to be outwardly at least on good terms; so now he received Edward with a show of affection and when the greetings were over he allowed a mask of concern to fall over his face. It was not entirely false; he was thinking of Madame de St Laurent, a charming woman, who had been Edward's faithful mistress – for twenty-seven years was it? He disliked hurting charming women; but Madame de St Laurent, he was sure, was a sensible woman, as Dorothy Jordan – another of his favourites – had been. She would have to understand.

'Well, Edward,' he said, 'I'll swear you know why I've sent for you.'

'Does it concern marriage plans?'

The Regent nodded. 'The Princess Victoria of Saxe-Coburg . . . Leopold's widowed sister. She is young, good looking and by all accounts very charming.'

'I see,' said Edward gravely.

'I can guess your thoughts, Edward. You are thinking of your . . . commitments. Poor Julie! But she is a brave and clever woman. I am sure she will understand.'

George always made other people's troubles seem so light, thought Edward resentfully; but the smallest cloud in his own blue sky was a matter for great tribulation in which everyone was expected to participate. Edward asked himself as he had many times before why a grudging fate had not made him the eldest son.

'It will be a great blow to her.'

'I know, Edward, but she must already be aware . . .'

Edward thought of Julie at the breakfast table. Poor sad Julie! She was going to be broken-hearted. But he must do his duty. There was no evading it.

He said: 'Has the Princess Victoria made her willingness known?'

'No. That's the point. You should visit her at Wald-Leiningen and persuade her how advantageous it will be to become the

Duchess of Kent. The fact is it is not easy to find Protestant princesses who would make suitable wives. We have fortunately found two.'

'And the other?'

'Adelaide of Saxe-Meiningen.'

'Should I not be allowed to select one of the two?'

'One is for William. He would doubtless say that he should have first choice. The fact is, Edward, Victoria must be wooed and we don't trust William as a wooer. That is why Adelaide is for William. We fear that if he went to court Victoria, the courtship would end in failure. You'll make a better job of it.'

The Regent watched his brother covertly. Edward was rising to the flattery.

'What do you know of Victoria?'

'That she is delightful – beautiful and intelligent.'

'All marriageable princesses are.'

'You have become cynical, Edward. I daresay Victoria is as attractive as most young women. She will not be stupid either for she is a mother and has two charming children, so I hear.'

'So I am to have a ready-made family?'

'My dear Edward, the only family you have to concern yourself with is the child the Duke and Duchess of Kent will have. You should be grateful that Victoria has already proved her ability to bear children. How frustrated you would feel if you discovered after marriage – as William may well do – that he has married a barren woman.'

'And I am to visit this Victoria?'

'As soon as possible.'

'And what am I to tell Madame de St Laurent?'

'I should tell her nothing as yet. It is possible that the Princess Victoria will reject you. She is able to make her own choice. As I told you that is the reason why we have decided on her for you. She will find you irresistible I am sure, Edward, but in case she should not, you will not want to lose Julie before you have gained Victoria.'

'You make it sound so unromantic.'

'The marriages of princes always are. It is the extra-marital affairs which bring such joy. No, do not worry Julie. Tell her that you are going on a mission for me to Leopold's family. I think that would be the best. And then ... if things went wrong she need not know. There is no need to alarm her before it is necessary.'

'Thank you, George,' said Edward. 'And when shall I leave?'

'At once. Don't lose any time. An attractive young woman like Victoria will doubtless be much sought after. Go at once.'

'I will,' said Edward.

As soon as he had left a messenger arrived with a letter from the Queen. The Regent read it and frowned. William was being difficult. He had proposed marriage to and been accepted by a Miss Wykeham. If he could not get royal assent, he was going to Parliament.

The Regent passed his hand across his brow.

If only Charlotte had lived! It was odd that at the time of her birth she had been so important because her coming had meant that he need never go near her mother again; and now her death had thrown them all into this state of panic. Her birth and her death had been so important; it was only during her lifetime that they had been able to ignore her.

William was a fool. Of course he could not marry his Miss Wykeham. How fortunate that the decision did not rest with him. He would tell his ministers that the marriage between the Duke of Clarence and Adelaide of Saxe-Meiningen must be brought to its satisfactory conclusion no matter what objections were made by the Duke of Clarence.

Julie was delighted to see Edward back.

As they went together into the house and she showed him the new improvements which had been completed since his absence, she clung to his arm.

'Edward,' she whispered, 'is all well?'

'Er ... yes, yes. All is well.'

'I thought you would come back and tell me that a marriage had been arranged for you.'

'No ... no, no.' It was true. Nothing had been arranged yet.

'I suppose they just wished you to be there because of Charlotte's death.'

'Because of that,' he said.

'I have so missed you.'

'And I you, my darling.'

'I've been longing for a game of chess, of all things. That seems so trivial . . . and yet . . .'

'I know,' he said. 'I know. I have in fact been sent on a mission . . . for George.'

'A mission?'

'Yes, to Germany.'

'I see.' She did not ask what. She was discreet enough for that. A mission could be anything. She would not associate it with courtship. He should tell her, but he could not. The words would not come. He who could face the most barbarous enemy could not face her. It was cruel but he must do his duty.

'And you will be away long?'

'Oh, I don't suppose so.'

'Then you'll come back to Brussels, I suppose.'

'I shall have to report to London first.'

'Just briefly,' she said. 'And then you'll be back.'

He had to let it rest there. He could not be so brutal. Besides, this Victoria might refuse him. They might not be able to find a bride for him.

He had asked George to keep the matter secret so that she did not hear through the press. George would do what he could. He was always gallant to women and it would grieve him to make Julie suffer more than was necessary.

He would stay here for two days before going on to Wald-Leiningen, and who knew perhaps he would never have to tell her how near he had come to deserting her.

The Princess Victoria was thoughtful. She had always known that she was too young to remain unmarried for the rest of her life, for she was only thirty-one years of age. She had two delightful children, healthy and good looking; it was natural that there should be suitors.

Her brother Leopold, now mourning the Princess Charlotte at Claremont, had written to her. He believed that nothing could be more suitable than a marriage with the Duke of Kent. He desired it and he hoped that as his dear sister had done him the honour in other important matters of taking his advice, she would in this one.

Victoria considered.

There were certain things a widow must give up if she married again. Freedom was rather pleasant and so rarely enjoyed by German princesses; but since the death of her husband, Prince Emich Charles, she had enjoyed it; merely in her household of course, but the castle of Wald-Leiningen was her little world and she was complete mistress of it.

There were the children to consider. Charles and Feodore. She adored them and they her, in spite of this discipline she enforced. She was a woman who liked to have her own way, but, she always reminded herself, it was for the *good* of others.

Leopold was her favourite brother, although younger than she was. There had been great rejoicing in the family when he had married Princess Charlotte, heir to the throne of England. Young Charlotte had loved him passionately, which was small wonder for Leopold was handsome and attractive in every way, although very serious; but that in the Princess Victoria's eyes was a virtue. The Princess Charlotte must have thought so too for by all accounts Leopold was the only one who could subdue her – and she loved him for it.

And then the bitter tragedy! The death of Charlotte in childbirth and the misery of poor dear Leopold who had loved his wife so tenderly and had believed that he was to be the father of a future King of England.

And it was due to Charlotte's death that she was facing her present problem now. The loss of Charlotte meant an imperative need to marry and produce an heir quickly among the King's sons; and the Duke of Kent was one of them.

She heard the sound of children's voices and looking from her window she saw Charles and Feodore riding into the court-yard with their grooms. Little Feodore was ten years old and was going to be a beauty, and Charles was a boy to be proud of. He was now waving the groom aside and helping Feodore out of the saddle. He was very courteous, her young Charles. They would change from their riding habits and present themselves in her drawing-room, for the Duke of Kent was due within the next hour and she wished him to see the children before he committed himself.

Victoria turned away from the window and sat down looking into the fire.

He will have to take a widow and two children, she thought. And I shall have to take a reluctant man of fifty.

Reluctant? Well, of course he would be reluctant. She had asked Leopold for all details of the Duke of Kent and he had not spared her.

'He has been living for the last twenty-five years or so with Madame de St Laurent, a woman to whom he is devoted. She was received by the Prince of Wales who is notoriously lax where his brothers' indiscretions are concerned.' (Dear Leopold, *he* would never be lax over such matters!) 'But of course it was a relationship of the left hand and she was not received at Court. Recently they went to live in Brussels where they intended to settle, until my dearest Charlotte died and so changed all our lives.'

She could imagine it well. The Duke's being forced to abandon the mistress whom he would regard as his wife and marry a strange young woman who could not speak English – although he could speak German she supposed; and in any case his mother Queen Charlotte could not speak English when she first arrived in England.

The language presented no difficulty. It was Madame de St Laurent. But she would be old compared with herself, and she who was plump and handsome was attractive to men, she was fully aware. If she did not take the Duke of Kent there would be other offers.

'The Duke of Clarence is older than the Duke of Kent, but he has made himself rather ridiculous lately,' wrote Leopold. 'First by deserting the actress with whom he lived for twenty years and by whom he had ten children, who live with him in his house at Bushy. Then by proposing marriage to several people, some most unsuitable, and being rejected by them. At first I was put out that you were not to be offered Clarence because any children he had would come before any you might have. But it is almost certain that you would prefer the Duke of Kent, who is more serious-minded and in every way more suited to become the father of the heir to the throne.'

One could always trust Leopold. He had the family welfare so much at heart.

There was a knock at the door and the children came in. Feodore curtsied; Charles bowed. Her expression softened. How delightful they were! If they should have a stepbrother who was Prince of Wales brilliant marriages would be arranged for them.

'Did you enjoy your ride, my children?'

'Yes, Mamma, thank you,' said Charles.

'We rode so far we could see Amorbach in the distance.'

'That was quite a distance. I am expecting a visitor, from England.'

'From Uncle Leopold, Mamma?' asked Charles.

'No, not exactly; but he would be a friend of Uncle Leopold.'

'Then he must be a good man,' said Feodore. 'When will he arrive?'

'At any moment, I believe.'

'As he has come from England,' said Charles, 'he will be able to give us news of our uncle.'

'I shall ask him when Uncle Leopold is coming to see us.'

'You must not ask questions,' said their mother, 'but wait until you are spoken to.'

'Is he very important, Mamma?'

'He is the son of the King of England.'

The children's eyes were round with wonder.

'Even Uncle Leopold's Charlotte was only the daughter of the Prince of Wales,' said Charles.

His mother laid her hand on his arm. 'You talk too much, Charles,' she said severely. 'And when the Duke arrives I want you to remember that you are in the presence of a very important man.'

Thus when Edward arrived he found Victoria with her children.

I can't do it, thought Edward, as he made his journey across Europe to the castle of Wald-Leiningen. It will break her heart. Clarence will have to be the one. Why not? He's older than I. Then there's Ernest; he's very likely to have a child. Just because

63

my mother won't accept his wife that's no reason why his child should not inherit the crown. She's even royal – my mother's own niece. And what of Adolphus? He's betrothed. Why should I disrupt my life when I have so many brothers?

I will behave in such a way that she refuses me. She might refuse me in any case. But would a young widow who had probably made up her mind she must marry at some time refuse the Duke of Kent to whom she could bear a king or queen of England?

But I can't hurt Julie, he kept telling himself.

And yet ... the prospect was glittering. Life in Brussels was cheap; there was a pleasant social atmosphere; Julie was happy there. But England was his home. He hadn't told Julie how homesick he was. He had been all those years in Canada; and his career in the Army had often taken him away but now that he was getting older he did long to be at home. If he married his debts would be settled; he would get a grant from Parliament, a larger income. And suppose he had a child? He did regret that Julie had never had his child. There was William with those ten FitzClarences, and although some might deplore their illegitimacy, William took great pride in them and there was no doubt that he derived a great deal of pleasure from them.

They had come to an inn in the heart of the forest and there were to stay the night. In a few days now he would arrive at the castle of Wald-Leiningen and he would have to make up his mind. He would not admit it to himself because he refused to consider the fact that any woman but Julie could attract him, but he was eager to see whether the Princess Victoria was as handsome as she had been made out to be.

Princes were so often deceived in these matters. He only had to think of the Prince of Wales' own marriage to Caroline of Brunswick. There could not have been a greater disaster than that.

'Your Highness!' It was his equerry come to conduct him to the room he was to have in the inn.

The innkeeper was delighted at the prospect of being host to a royal Duke. He was preparing the finest meal he had ever offered to guests and the smell of sausages and sauerkraut filled the parlour.

It sickened Edward who was too concerned with his affairs to think of food.

He kept seeing Castle Hill, the home he had loved in Ealing, the house in Knightsbridge where he and Julie had lived together, and his apartments in Kensington Palace which he had left, but which had been home to him. He wanted to go home and if he married this young woman there would be no question of it.

He looked about the room – the best in the inn – and said to himself: 'I can never do it.'

He imagined his mother's face cold with fury. He couldn't do his duty! Did he realize that he had been receiving an income from the State so that when the moment came for him to do his duty it should be done.

He could imagine George's apologetic shrug. We all have to do these things, Edward. I myself had the most unfortunate of experiences. No one could suffer more than I did.'

A prince must do his duty.

His equerry was at the door. The meal was ready. Would His Highness honour the host by coming down to partake of it?

The meal was over when the gipsy came in. She had been passing, she said, and she had felt an impulse to enter because she knew there was an important guest under the innkeeper's roof that night.

She had no doubt seen the equipage, thought Edward, but everyone else was eager to let her talk.

She could foresee the future, she told them. If they would cross her palm with silver.

The bright alert eyes were on Edward. She had selected him immediately as the important personage; it was his future she was anxious to foretell.

He shook his head and she took the hands of other members of the party and spun her tales of glory and disaster while Edward looked on and thought it was as good a way as any to pass the time.

'And my lord?' she pleaded.

He held out his hand and she chuckled gleefully.

'Here's glory,' she cried. 'My lord is going to marry.'

'What, at my age!' cried Edward.

'Ah, my lord is young at heart. He will marry and be the father of a great queen.'

Edward's heart had begun to beat faster and he was anxious that none of the company should know it.

'You might have given me a king,' he reproved her.

She shook her head.

'A queen,' she insisted.

'A higher price for a king,' he tempted.

But she shook her head and said with dignity, 'I am an honest woman your lordship should know. I cannot sell what is not here.'

'So it has to be a queen,' he sighed.

'There is nothing your lordship should regret in that,' she answered.

The gipsy told no more fortunes. She left the inn; and Edward retired to his room to rest before the morning's early start.

And he kept thinking: A queen. How strange that she had said that. A *great* queen, she had insisted.

And a few days later he came to the castle of Wald-Leiningen and there was received by the Princess Victoria with her children.

She was plump, handsome, fertile, desirable: and he could not get the gipsy's words out of his mind.

A queen. A great queen.

He knew that he wanted to marry the Princess Victoria. If it were not for Julie he could be completely reconciled to his position. And what could he do? He had come to court the lady; it would be churlish not to do so.

She was charming; so were her children; she was serious and made no secret of the fact that the marriage would be one of convenience.

She told him quite frankly that she would forfeit a considerable income if she married. The Duke must understand that she would be giving up her independence.

He saw this clearly; at one moment he was anxious to urge her not to give up her freedom; in another he was almost imploring her to. He was unsure what he wished for. She was very attractive; he liked the children; and he kept hearing the gipsy's prophecy.

Did she sense his hesitancy? Was that why she gave voice to her own? They were both mature people, she pointed out. They had sacrifices to make. She thought they should not make up their minds in a hurry.

He was relieved by the delay.

He returned to London but he did not call at Brussels on the way.

When he reached London a letter from the Princess Victoria awaited him. She had decided to give up a life in which she had enjoyed independence and comfort; but she hoped to find compensation in the Duke's affection and the children they would have.

So he was committed. But he would keep secret . . . just at first. He would make sure that everything was made as comfortable for Julie as possible. She must be looked after. She must have an adequate income. She must be allowed to live with dignity. He must impress on everyone that Julie was no ordinary mistress. Theirs had been a marriage in all but the legal sense. Julie had never lived with anyone else. It was merely the fact that he was a royal Duke who could not marry without the consent of the King and Parliament that had prevented his marrying her.

They *must* understand this. She must have a dignified life, servants, carriages . . . He would accept nothing else.

He could not understand his feelings; they ran in opposite directions. Complete desolation at the thought of what he was doing to Julie; exultation at the future with Victoria.

Julie wrote to him. He must not grieve. It was inevitable. They must be thankful for all the happy years they had enjoyed together.

She wished him success in his new life. She herself had decided to go into a convent and he must think no more of her.

'So,' said the Queen, 'Edward is *happily* settled. He could not have a better bride than the Princess Victoria. Now we must get William's affairs arranged without delay.'

The Regent agreed.

'Now that Parliament have made it clear that he cannot have his Miss Wykeham, he is reconciled. Parliament have supplied his reasons to the lady for him. He couldn't have a better excuse.'

'We must bring Adelaide over as soon as possible,' said the Queen.

'I don't anticipate any difficulties.'

'I shall not rest until they are married,' said the Queen, moving stiffly in her chair. And she thought: I hope I live long enough to see the unions fruitful. But she did not mention this to the Regent who hated references to death.

'It would be pleasant if we could arrange a double wedding,' he was saying. 'William's with Adelaide, Edward's with Victoria.'

Adelaide

When Adelaide was born to the Duke and Duchess of Saxe-Meiningen there was great rejoicing throughout the Duchy, for after ten years of fruitless marriage it had been feared that their efforts to provide the heir were destined to fail.

A princess, it was true, when a prince would have been more welcome, but at least the baby proved that the Duchess was not a barren woman and a girl-child was better than none at all.

'*Nun danket all Gott*,' sang the choir at her christening; and the Duke gave orders that there were to be concerts and similar decorous celebrations throughout Saxe-Meiningen. In the mountain chalets and the inns of the Thuringer-Wald the people danced, sang and drank the health of the child who had been christened Amalie Adelaide Louise Thérèse Caroline.

The small Duchy of Saxe-Meiningen was north of Coburg and Bavaria, a land of rich green forests and mountains; since the Duke had come to power farming had flourished. The Duke was a man who had the good of his people at heart; he liked to mingle with them and discuss their problems – not in order to win popularity but to discover how they could be solved. When he had married Princess Eleanor of Hohenlohe there had been great rejoicing, for she was of the same mind as her husband; her great desire being to further the good of the people and to produce a son who would continue with the work she and the Duke had set in progress. Thus while the Duchy flourished there had been the shadow over it. What would happen when the Duke was no longer with them? Into whose hands would the Duchy pass?

And then had come the great news that the Duchess had given birth to a living child. And if the baby was a girl – still it was a child; and every man and woman in Saxe-Meiningen rejoiced for their Duke and Duchess and themselves.

The Duchess devoted herself to her daughter while she prayed that her union might be further blessed.

She was not disappointed. Fifteen months after the birth of Adelaide she was once more pregnant.

With what excited anticipation was the birth of this child awaited. Surely the prayers of the people would be answered.

'Let it be a boy,' prayed the people in the churches.

'Let it be a strong healthy child,' prayed the Duchess.

The Duchess's prayers were answered but not those of the people and the Princess Ida joined Adelaide in the nursery.

The two little Princesses were the Duchess's delight. She wanted them to be wise and good. Nor did she despair of providing them with a brother for she now seemed to have entered into a productive rhythm; two years after the birth of Ida she was ready to give birth again. This time there was a disappointment. Her daughter was still-born.

The two little girls were devoted to each other. Ida looked to Adelaide to lead the way and Adelaide was always conscious of the responsibility of looking after her younger sister.

Her mother had talked to her very seriously. 'You are a princess, my dearest child,' she told her. 'You must never forget that. You are *born* with responsibilities.'

Adelaide looked in some alarm about the schoolroom as though she expected to see them there, but her mother smiled and laid a hand on her shoulder. 'You will recognize them when they come,' she said. 'And then you must let nothing stand in the way of your duty. And you must help Ida to do the same.'

Ida was just a little frivolous. It was due to her being the younger.

'You must always lead Ida in the right direction,' said the Duchess.

And Adelaide was faintly worried, wondering whether she would know which was the right direction when the time came to lead Ida.

But of course it happened continually. She had to stop Ida stamping when she did not get her own way; she had to tell her how wrong it was to kick their nurses, to throw the milk over the table, to stare out of the window when she should be studying her books.

Adelaide recognized those responsibilities; and as the best way of teaching Ida was to set a good example she became a model of decorum herself. 'Adelaide is such a *good* child,' they said in the nursery. But Adelaide discovered that they were more amused by Ida and it was Ida who received the caresses, the smuggled-in sweetmeat. It was Ida who was the pretty one.

Their father frequently came to the nursery with the Duchess. He was often thoughtful on account of the burdens of State, but he wanted to see what the children were doing and he questioned their tutor Friedrich Schenk very closely and heard them read to him in French and Italian.

The Duke would take the inattentive Ida on to his knee and put an arm about Adelaide while he talked to them of the importance of learning. It was the gateway to knowledge. They must never forget it. They must listen attentively to everything Herr Schenk told them and they would discover how much more exciting it was to acquire knowledge than to play idle games.

He was starting a girls' school in Meiningen. Was that not an excellent thing? He did not believe that the education of girls should be neglected. Perhaps he had a special affection for girls – because he had two of his own. Ida, watching the smile on his lips started to laugh, and Adelaide permitted herself to smile with him.

Yes, he wanted his girls to be an example to all the girls of the Duchy. In this school they would be taught Latin. So *his* girls must work hard at their Latin, for they did not want to be outpaced by his subjects, did they? Ida did not care in the least, but Adelaide could see that this must not be so and made a vow that she would try to work even harder and listen even more carefully to Herr Schenk.

Education and work, said the Duke, were the most gratifying things in the world. One must not forget work. That was why he had commanded that young people when they were not learning should work in the gardens or be taught trades. They earned money, and the Duchy had prospered in the last years because of work and education. He wished it to remain like that.

Adelaide listened gravely while Ida played with the buttons on his jacket.

Afterwards he said to the Duchess: 'Adelaide is such a dutiful child. She will make someone an excellent wife when the time comes. I want good matches for them both.'

'I am sure they will marry well. There are not many Protestant Princesses in Europe.'

'Oh, you are thinking of England.'

'The King has so many sons and they always come to Germany for their brides.'

'I should like to see them marry into England.'

'We shall hope,' answered the Duchess, 'and in the meantime look to their upbringing.'

'I doubt the system of education in England compares with ours,' said the Duke proudly.

'I doubt it, too, now that you have introduced your schools, and the Duchy is becoming so prosperous.'

'How I wish we could have a son.'

'We shall not always be disappointed,' replied the Duchess.

Adelaide remembered vividly the seventh year of her life. That was when the weather was so cold and the snow lay in drifts about the castle. She and Ida knelt on the window-seat looking out at the white-encrusted firs and listening to the wind whistling round the castle walls. Ida thought of ski-ing down the mountain slopes; Adelaide thought of the poor people who might not have enough fuel to warm their houses and keep out the cold. She asked the Duke how the poor managed to keep warm and he told her that

71

he had given an order that they might help themselves to wood in the forest providing they did not take green wood. 'For you see,' he said, 'our forests provide a large part of the Duchy's wealth and to cut down striplings would be folly.'

Everything her father did was wise and just, Adelaide knew. He was a very stern and righteous man; and although his edicts sometimes meant a certain hardship, his people realized that everything he did was for their own benefit and they accepted this.

'It is for your own good,' it was a phrase Adelaide had learned to use to Ida.

There was a sadness in the castle too because it was three years since the Duchess had had her still-born daughter and it seemed as though the two-yearly happy event was not to be repeated.

It meant that the little girls were even more important than they had been before, because if the Duchess Eleanor was to have no more children Adelaide as the eldest daughter might take over the reigns of government.

It was an anxiety. But Adelaide was a serious child, pointed out the Duchess. It was true, but she must become even more serious and be made to realize the enormity of her responsibilities.

A new tutor was introduced to the schoolroom, Herr Hofrats Schmidt Buckeburg, and there were even stricter rules to be obeyed. There was to be no singing or dancing on Sundays.

'It is a rule I have made throughout the Duchy,' said the Duke, 'and what we ask our people to do we must perforce do ourselves.'

Life was very serious. When the snows of that winter were cleared away the Princesses must drive through the country with their parents and see for themselves how the people lived; they must bring relief to the hard-working poor by taking them blankets and clothing – which they had helped to make themselves. Oh, those coarse shirts over which Ida wept tears of frustration and anger while she pricked her delicate fingers and spattered them with blood! Adelaide did not like to sew them either but she remembered her responsibilities.

The next winter was less severe and to the Duchess's great joy she was once again pregnant.

There was great rejoicing throughout the castle and the Duchy; and on a cold December day it seemed to Adelaide that the whole

72

world must be wild with joy for Bernhard Erich Freund, Crown Prince of Saxe-Meiningen, was born.

Adelaide could not help but be relieved. Attention was no longer focused on herself. Now she might be allowed to be a normal little girl of almost nine because she was merely a princess daughter of the Duke; she had been shorn of her responsibilities.

'How they spoil Bernhard!' grimaced Ida.

But Adelaide pointed out that they should. He was a boy and as the Crown Prince he was naturally the most important person in the nurseries. He would one day have to rule Saxe-Meiningen whereas they . . .

'What shall we do?' Ida wanted to know.

Adelaide was suddenly sad. 'I think we may have husbands and go away.'

Go away from this castle stronghold in the beautiful forests with the Rhine Mountains in the distance, and the cold snowy winters and the warm summers, and dearest Mamma who loved them in her cool restrained way and Papa who was so good and wanted them to be the same. Adelaide shivered slightly; but Ida had started to dance, seeing herself as glittering with jewels as Mamma was on State occasions.

She was, after all, barely seven years old, and she had never had to be serious like her sister.

Adelaide would have liked to be gay like Ida. To dance round – though not on Sundays, as Ida sometimes disobediently did – to laugh and refuse to do her lessons, but the habit of obedience was strong in her. She was set in her ways.

Even shorn of her immense responsibilities Adelaide continued to be the good child of the nursery.

The happy days came to an abrupt end when Bernhard was three years old.

It had been a bad winter. The snow had started early and the Duke, who never neglected his duty, had gone among his subjects as was his usual practice, advising them, helping them, and being the good ruler he prided himself on being.

One day his sledge was overturned and he was almost buried in a snowdrift but soaked to the skin he had continued his journey. When much later he returned to the castle he was shivering with the cold and although the Duchess herself got him to bed and brought him one of the possets she had prepared herself, during the next few days he had developed a very bad cold; this would not be cured and in a week had turned to bronchitis and from that to a congestion of the lungs. On the most dismal day of Adelaide's life her father died.

There was grief and consternation not only in the castle but also throughout the land.

The new Duke was but three years old; the Princesses Adelaide and Ida eleven and nine; the Duchess Eleanor must become the Regent until her son was able to govern.

But to the children this was more than the loss of a ruler; they had loved their father who, in spite of his sternness and the strict rules which he had insisted should be obeyed, had been the benign arbiter of their lives.

'What shall we do without him?' cried the Duchess Eleanor.

She called a meeting of her husband's ministers and told them that she was to some extent at their mercy. She needed their help. It was fortunate that her husband had consulted her, kept her informed of his plans, and indeed sometimes had asked her advice. She believed that now, with their assistance, she could be their Regent until such time as the little Duke could take on his duties.

She was warmly applauded. Everyone was eager to do what the late Duke would have wished. They had seen how the Duchy had prospered from his wise rule and they knew that his wife, who had been beside him throughout their married life, was the one who could best take on his mantle until her son was old enough to wear it himself.

When the ministers had gone Duchess Eleanor sent for her eldest daughter.

She was grateful for this calm, serious girl.

'My dear Adelaide,' she said, 'you know that nothing will ever be the same again. We have lost dearest Papa who was so wise and good. We have to think now of what he would have wished, and until little Bernhard is ready I have to rule in his place.'

They wept together and it was Adelaide who comforted her mother.

'You have always been a good child, my dearest Adelaide, but now you must be even more serious. We must remember all the time what Papa would have wished. I shall rely on you to help me. You will do that by being good, by guiding your sister, by loving your brother. I want Papa when he looks down from Heaven to see his good little Adelaide behaving just as he would wish. It is a great responsibility.'

So after being briefly relieved of her duties Adelaide found herself once more burdened with them.

It was doubly necessary now to work hard, never to disobey, to be an example to her sister and brother.

One could grow accustomed to anything, Adelaide supposed. As the months began to pass, life in the castle settled down. The Duchess Eleanor tried to be as calm and wise as her husband had been; and she succeeded by following the laws he had made; nor did she neglect her children.

The days were full and as their grief receded they began to be happy again.

Ida was gay and attractive, growing prettier every day. Adelaide believed she herself grew more plain. Her skin was not clear and fresh like Ida's; her nose was too long. 'I shall never be a beauty,' she said ruefully.

'Never mind, darling Adelaide,' cried Ida. 'You will always be the good one.'

They had grown closer together after their father's death; and Ida, though still loving to sing and dance and amuse herself, recognized the qualities of her sister and loved her for them, just as Adelaide adored Ida; and while she knew that it was necessary to consider one's responsibilities she frequently wished that she were like the gay and volatile Ida.

She often wondered when they would have to leave the castle; for it was the inevitable fate of all princesses to leave their homes. She could not bear the thought of it and was sometimes glad when she looked in her mirror.

'I am too plain for anyone to want to marry me,' she told Ida.

At which Ida declared that marriages were arranged for people such as they were and neither bride nor bridegroom knew what they were getting until they were presented with their partner. So looks were not all that important.

'They always will be important,' said Adelaide sadly. 'And even if marriages are arranged pictures are sent and a bridegroom would have to approve of the picture before he accepted his bride.'

Ida kissed her sister. 'How you exaggerate! You are really quite good looking. I mean *good* looking – and that is very unusual. Your eyes are nice and your hair isn't bad.' Ida studied their faces side by side in the mirror and she could not hide the look of satisfaction as she studied her own pretty one.

Perhaps, thought Adelaide, it is only in comparison with Ida that I seem so plain.

Nothing remained the same for long. Soon there was a shadow looming across the castle. The whole of Europe was trembling in fear of the man who had determined to dominate it. Napoleon was on the march.

Nearer and nearer came the terror as one small State after another fell into his hands.

'If only your father were alive,' cried the Duchess Eleanor.

But she knew and so did everyone else that even the Duke would not have had the power to stop Napoleon's armies.

The French soldiers were in the streets of Meiningen, which fortunately was too small a Duchy to interest Napoleon, who was on the way to bigger objectives. But the Duchy was no longer free; the people must receive the soldiers in their houses; they must cook for them and work for them during their stay.

Their commander had sent a message to the castle. Providing the people fed and housed the soldiers no property would be destroyed and no one harmed.

There was nothing to do but comply. It was occupation of a sort.

The French passed on and the Prussians came; and although they were not enemies, their demands were the same.

War had come to Saxe-Meiningen and it brought with it all its terrible consequences.

The good old days when the Duke had ridden out into the forests to learn the needs of his people were gone.

Such days, it was said, would never come back.

Meanwhile the Duchess Eleanor lived in the castle, the Crown Prince growing into lusty boyhood, while his sisters left their childhood behind them.

There were long afternoons when Adelaide and Ida sat together making bandages for the wounded soldiers, sewing garments for them and sometimes attending the wounded who were brought to the castle.

Even Ida lost some of her gaiety; the sights they saw were so depressing; and since there was this war which devastated the land and from which no one was safe, how could there be those balls and festivities at the castle which in ordinary times would have been considered necessary for two young women who were about to be launched on the world? How could there be visits to other Duchies where they might have found suitors?

War put an end to such activities. Instead they must sit making their bandages, waiting for messengers to arrive with news of the fighting, asking themselves when there was going to be a halt to the wicked Napoleon's conquests and life was going to return to normal.

They were growing up. Adelaide was twenty-three; Ida was twenty-one; even Bernhard was fifteen. They were no longer children and still the dreary war went on.

And suddenly there was change. The bells were ringing all over Europe. The soldiers of Saxe-Meiningen who had gone to fight in the Prussian Army returned home and there were victory parades through the streets. What had seemed the impossible had become the possible; it had in fact actually happened.

Napoleon had been beaten at Waterloo by Blücher and Wellington. England and Germany had rid the world of that megalomaniac and the world was free again.

No more bandages. No more occupation. The war was over.

'This,' said Ida, 'is an end to the dull existence. Now they will find husbands for us, you see.'

*

She was right. So much time had been lost, mused the Duchess Eleanor. The girls were no longer very young. She consulted with her ministers. They must make up for lost time. They must find husbands for them without delay.

The Duke of Weimar was young, handsome and not ineligible. He was Governor of Ghent and from this post derived the greater part of his income. They would invite him to the castle and there he could meet Adelaide and perhaps if he were agreeable the marriage could be arranged.

If it were not the most brilliant of matches it would be a comforting one, at least, mused the Duchess, for Weimar was not so far distant from Saxe-Meiningen that there could not be frequent visits and Adelaide was a girl who loved her home and family dearly. Eleanor would not wish her to be too far away.

There was excitement throughout the castle. The seamstresses were busy. There were beautiful gowns for the Princesses and particularly for Adelaide.

She felt nervous and shy.

He will be very disappointed when he sees me, she thought; but she did not mention it even to Ida.

Those rooms in the castle where soldiers had been billeted were repainted and refurnished. The Duke of Weimar's suite must be adequately housed.

'What an important visit this is!' cried Ida with a chuckle. She was excited because she knew that her turn would come.

The Duchess seemed happier than she had since the death of her husband; she was sure they had left the dark days behind. Bernhard was now sixteen – in two years' time he would be of age; then there would be no need for a Regency and Saxe-Meiningen would have its reigning Duke. And the girls would be married – Adelaide first and then Ida – both into neighbouring dukedoms, so that they need not be distantly separated.

The girls were watching from the turret windows; soon the cavalcade must come into sight and at the head of it would ride the Duke of Weimar. 'Do you remember how we used to look from this window and see the soldiers coming?' said Ida.

Adelaide nodded.

'This is rather different, eh, sister?' Ida was chuckling with excitement. 'Suitors are more fun than soldiers. Ugh! That awful war. Those bandages! I shall never forget them. I wonder what he will be like.'

'Who?'

'The Duke of Weimar, of course. His name is Bernhard the same as our brother's. I long to see him. Do you think he will be handsome?'

'I hope not . . . too handsome.'

'Why ever not? People should be as handsome as it is possible to be. The more handsome the better.'

Not when they have a plain bride waiting for them, thought Adelaide.

She could scarcely bear to look, yet she was as eager to see as Ida was. Let him be kind, she prayed. Let him not ask too much.

'Do you know,' said Ida, 'I fancy I can see something in the distance. Is it? Yes . . . I'm sure. Look, sister.'

They strained their eyes to see. It was indeed the outriders of the cavalcade in the livery of the House of Weimar – brilliantly colourful among the trees.

Ida gripped her sister's hand in excitement.

'Adelaide,' she cried. 'They're here. They're here.'

Her eyes were brilliant; there was a faint colour in her cheeks; she was beautiful.

One of their women was coming up to the turret.

'You know what this is,' said Ida. 'Mamma has sent for us to go down. We must be ready to greet the Duke when he arrives. Am I presentable?'

'Very. Am I?'

'You always are. Always neat. Always tidy. Dear Adelaide, you are such a pattern of virtue. What shall I do when you are gone? I shall deteriorate . . . rapidly, I fear. There will be no good example for me to follow.'

The woman had entered.

'I know! I know!' cried Ida. 'We are to come down and be ready to greet the Duke when he arrives.'

He had leaped from his horse, a commanding figure, six feet four inches tall. He came forward to greet the Duchess Eleanor who gave him her hand to kiss.

'You must allow me to present my son to you.'

The Dukes of Weimar and Saxe-Meiningen bowed.

'And my daughters,' went on the Duchess.

They stood on either side of her – Adelaide the plain and Ida the beautiful.

The Duke of Weimar looked from one to the other.

'The elder, the Princess Adelaide,' said the Duchess.

Again that bow.

'And the Princess Ida.'

Once more he bowed and his eyes rested on Ida and lingered there.

The Duchess took his hand and led him into the castle, and it was as Adelaide had known it would be. He could not take his eyes from Ida, nor she from him.

The Duchess Eleanor called her ministers to the castle.

'The Duke of Weimar is asking for the hand of the Princess Ida,' she told them.

'Would it not be more agreeable if the Princess Adelaide married first?'

'It would have pleased me better, but the Duke of Weimar asked for Ida. It is a good match and we cannot with wisdom refuse it.'

It would be the utmost folly to, since if the Duke of Weimar could not have Ida he would certainly not take Adelaide.

'It is an excellent match for a younger daughter,' said the Duchess; 'and what pleases me is that neither the Princess Ida nor the Duke would have to be persuaded to it. They are more eager than we could hope. In fact they declare they are in love.'

In the circumstances it seemed that there was only one thing lacking to make the young couple completely happy and that was the consent of the Duchess and her ministers.

That consent was readily given, although every one of them believed it would have been more fitting for the elder princess to marry first.

*

'Adelaide!' cried Ida, throwing herself at her sister.

'What is it? You're crying.'

'Such odd tears. I'm so happy . . . and yet I'm so sad.'

'How can that be?'

'Oh, Adelaide, dearest Adelaide, I don't know what to say to you. They . . . they have given their consent. Bernhard and I are to be married.'

'Well, what is that to cry about?'

'Oh, sister, my dearest Adelaide, you really don't mind?'

'Mind . . . but I am delighted to see you so happy.'

'I . . . I shall marry before you.'

'And so you should because you are so pretty.'

'But he was to have been for *you*.'

'Being very sensible he fell in love with you instead. I can't say I blame him. As a matter of fact if he had not done so I should have thought there was something lacking in him.'

'Oh really . . . Adelaide . . . you are not . . . furious!'

Adelaide laughed. 'Did you really think I should be?'

'No,' admitted Ida. 'Even if you had loved him, which I trust you don't.'

'No, my dear Ida. I do not think I should fall in love so easily. I should need to know someone for years and years.'

'Yes, I believe you would. You are so calm and wise and good. And I am wildly happy, Adelaide, if you are not unhappy about this I am the happiest woman in the world.'

'Then you are indeed the happiest woman in the world.'

Ida had pressed her face against her sister's. She was always so impulsive.

'Now, I shall ask your advice . . . about my wedding dress, my jewels . . . everything. Because you always tell the truth. So if you were really unhappy you would have to say so. But then you might not because you are also unselfish and you might think you would spoil my happiness. Oh, Adelaide, do you really mean this?'

'I mean it. I don't want to marry. I hope I never do. I hope I stay here with Mamma and Bernhard – my Bernhard not yours – for the rest of my life. I begin to think that is what I really want. I am sure no man would really want to marry me any more than your Bernhard did.'

'It's nonsense. He would have fallen in love with you if I had not been here. I'm sure of it, because someone will love you one day – very much. I am the sort of person they fall in love with – you are the sort they grow to love. One day someone will love you as I do and Mamma does and our Bernhard does. That's because we *know* you.'

'Ida, you are growing hysterical.'

'Dear Adelaide, you are always so calm, so good.'

The wedding was to take place immediately for there was no point in delay, said the Duchess. Ida was intoxicated with happiness; the seamstresses were working at full speed in that room at the castle which had been set aside for them and the whole of Saxe-Meiningen was talking about the wedding.

The great day came; the bells rang out; the bride was a vision of beauty in her shimmering gown and jewels and even Adelaide looked handsome on that day with the jewels in her hair and the gown which had been made for her to wear at her sister's wedding.

'Your turn next,' said her brother Bernhard; and she laughingly shook her head.

The Duchess told herself that they must busy themselves with finding a husband for Adelaide; it was not right that the younger sister should marry before the elder.

The wedding celebrations continued for two days with festivities in the town, fireworks and illuminations; it was as exciting as the victory celebrations. When Ida and her husband left for Weimar Adelaide ran to the turret to watch them until they were out of sight.

How she missed Ida! She could not remember ever being separated from her before. The castle seemed quieter; she would often think: I must go and tell that to Ida, and then remember that Ida was not there.

The Duchess watched her daughter anxiously. Adelaide was twenty-four. It was not really very young and she looked her age. That cursed Napoleon! thought the Duchess. Precious years had been wasted because of his selfish desires for conquest.

'My dear Adelaide,' she said. 'I know you miss Ida sorely – more so than any of us. I am sorry that she should have been the one to go first.'

'It was inevitable, Mamma.'

'Well, she is married, and it will be your turn next.'

'Perhaps not. I am not eager for marriage. I should be happy at home here with you and Bernhard.'

The Duchess shook her head and smiled, but she did not press the matter.

'My dear,' she said, 'I need your help. The prosperity we gained under your father's rule has disappeared. These terrible wars have impoverished us all. I am most concerned for some of the poorer classes. There is starvation in the villages such as there never was in your father's day – nor would there have been now but for the war. The beggars have multiplied. I want you to help me look into these matters. They are most urgent.'

Helping to relieve cases of hardship she was more contented than she had been; the Duchess gave her permission to found a group of ladies like herself who would join with the Poor Law Institution, and she worked eagerly at this.

When she rode out into the streets the people cheered her. Good Princess Adelaide, they called her.

She was pleased because she was of some use. Perhaps, she assured herself, it was better to be useful than decorative.

One day there were visitors at the castle.

One of the women came running into Adelaide's apartments to tell her that a band of riders was approaching.

She hurried to the window; her heart began to beat fast; then she went down the great staircase and out to the hall and the court-yard.

Ida threw herself into her sister's arms.

'Ida. You have come home.'

Ida was laughing. 'Don't be alarmed. I have not run away. My husband had to go away on a mission for a short while and I got his permission to visit you for a few days. So here I am.'

There were fond embraces and they went into the castle where

Ida could not stop talking. She must tell them all about Weimar and her husband's castle and life there and how happy she was – particularly as she was not too far away to pay visits like this. She had a secret. She was almost certain that she was pregnant. She wanted nothing more than this to complete her happiness.

It was wonderful to have Ida back home even for a short stay and when she left the Duchess Eleanor and Adelaide accompanied her part of the way back.

And so a year passed. Ida had given birth to a daughter whom she called Louise, and Adelaide and her mother had been to Weimar to see Ida and the child.

There were no suitors for Adelaide. It seems there never will be, she thought. No, the Duke of Weimar saw me and preferred my younger sister. All the eligible bachelors in Europe will know that by now, and they will not want to take what Weimar refused.

She did not care. She was twenty-five – growing old fast. She was often with her mother; the Duchess discussed State affairs with her; when her mother was sick, she nursed her; they were as close as she and Ida had been.

One day while they sat together over a batch of accounts which Adelaide was helping her mother to balance, the Duchess said: 'There is news from England.'

'England?' said Adelaide, but mildly interested. It was very far away, although there was a link between the German States and England; the Kings of England were of the House of Hanover and many of them had been unable to speak English without an accent – and George I had not been able to speak it at all. Herr Schenk had taught her history which he said was the subject most important to royal people.

'The Princess Charlotte is dead. There will be consternation for she has died giving birth to a child who would have been heir to the throne.'

'Poor child . . . to be without a mother.'

'The child died too. That is what makes it so important.'

Adelaide nodded. She knew of course that the Princess Charlotte of neighbouring Mecklenburg-Strelitz had married King George III and they had had several sons and daughters and none of the sons except the Prince of Wales had had a legitimate heir. And that heir was dead. Princess Charlotte and her baby.

'There will have to be some hasty marriages in the English royal family now,' said the Duchess, looking speculatively at her daughter.

Every ducal house in Germany had its eyes on England. There were two marriageable dukes who would be looking for wives; and one of these wives could, in certain circumstances, be the Queen of England.

Little Mecklenburg-Strelitz had never ceased to give itself airs because one of its daughters was now the reigning Queen. England always looked to Germany for its Queens. All the wives of the Georges had been German; though no parents could wish their daughters to be treated as the wives of George I and George IV had been. But perhaps that was partly the fault of Sophia Dorothea of Celle and Caroline of Brunswick themselves.

True, neither of the two dukes was very young, and although the Duke of Kent was the younger and therefore a step further from the throne than Clarence, he was the favourite among aspiring parents of marriageable daughters. Clarence's liaison with Dorothy Jordan was common knowledge; so was the fact that he had ten illegitimate children whom he regarded as his family and with whom he lived on terms of intimacy.

He had also made himself look rather foolish by proposing marriage in several quarters and being refused. There was something undesirable about Clarence. Kent was another matter. True he had never married and there had been a liaison with a French woman to whom he had been faithful for many years but he had lived discreetly – unlike Clarence – and was a good soldier. And he was two years younger – not much it was true; but at their time of life two years could make a difference.

The Duchess Eleanor could not help being affected by the excitement.

She did not want to lose Adelaide but she was a good enough mother to be concerned about her daughter's future; and because Adelaide was so sensible it was possible to discuss the matter with her.

As they sat over their sewing – for the poor of Saxe-Meiningen – she discussed the situation with her.

'I think it very possible that you may be in the field,' she said.

Adelaide closed her eyes and inwardly shuddered. How she hated to be considered in this way. 'In the field.' As though she were a horse who was about to be put through its paces.

'Of course,' went on the Duchess Eleanor. 'It would be a wonderful opportunity. Either of the two chosen could be a Queen of England.'

'Why should I be chosen?'

'Because, my dear, there are not so many who fill the qualifications. Young enough to bear a child and Protestant.'

'I should hate to leave home.'

'All of us do, but it's something we have to face. And, my dear, think of the alternative, which is staying here all your life. I shall die in due course and Bernhard will marry . . . and what will your place be? It is never very satisfactory to be the unmarried daughter.'

'No, I suppose not,' said Adelaide.

'And you would have children. What a consolation they can be! Why, my dear, what should I do without you and Bernhard? My life would be wasted. I know what I'm talking about. For ten years your father and I had no children. We were happy together. He was the best of men. But when you were born . . . when I had my child . . . well, then I knew I had not lived in vain. Then there were Ida and Bernhard. Why, my dear, I knew then that I could never have been so contented if I had not married . . . and yet when my marriage was arranged I cried for days and nights because I was leaving home. I was younger than you and . . . and not nearly so sensible in those days.'

Adelaide said: 'I can see that if one had children everything would be worth while.'

'And that would be the purpose of this marriage, as it is of all marriages but even more so in this case – to have children.'

'Ida has become much more serious since Louise was born.'

'Exactly. Our frivolous Ida has become a woman. I have seen you with Louise. I think it is the only time I have seen you envy your sister.'

'Yes, it is true. I should love a child of my own.'

The Duchess Eleanor laid down her work and gazed at her daughter.

'You would be as good a mother as you have been a daughter and sister. How I wish that I could let the Queen and Regent of England know how admirable you are. Then I am sure they would not hesitate for a moment.'

'It was different with Ida,' said Adelaide wistfully. 'Her Bernhard came here and saw her . . . and wanted to marry her.'

'It rarely happens to people of our rank. Besides, Adelaide, we are not speaking of marriage with the ruler of a small Duchy but alliance with the reigning House of England. The child you would have could be a king or queen.'

'If I had a child,' said Adelaide, 'that would be enough for me.'

The Duchess Eleanor smiled. If the great opportunity came their way, there would be no difficulty in persuading her docile Adelaide to accept it.

The Duchess Eleanor was bitterly disappointed.

The Duke of Kent had fallen to the widowed Princess Victoria of Leiningen.

'It's only to be expected,' said Duchess Eleanor to Adelaide with some chagrin. 'She's the sister of the Princess Charlotte's husband Leopold – and you may be sure that he had a hand in arranging this. Besides she has proved that she can have children. She has two already. So . . . we have lost Kent but we can still hope for Clarence.'

Clarence! thought Adelaide. The father of all those children! The man who had offered himself to several women and had been refused!

She shivered. It was alarming to consider herself going to a strange country which would be so different from anything she had known in Saxe-Meiningen – and more alarming than anything else was the stranger who would be her husband.

The Duchess Eleanor was constantly receiving news. She had sent messengers in all directions to discover what they could.

The Duke of Clarence, it was said, had proposed to a Miss

Wykeham who had accepted him and with whom he declared himself to be enamoured. She was a somewhat brash young woman who spent her life riding about the countryside on spirited horses, but she was very rich and this was her great attraction for the impecunious Clarence.

'They will never allow that marriage to take place,' said the Duchess; and she was right.

But a further disappointment was waiting for her.

The Duke of Cambridge, shortly to marry his adored Augusta of Hesse-Cassel whom he had discovered for Clarence and with whom he had himself fallen in love, had suggested that Clarence should marry a cousin of his bride-to-be, Princess Caroline of Hesse.

'So this is the end of our hopes,' said the Duchess.

'The Princess Caroline is very young,' said Adelaide. 'It is small wonder that she is considered suitable.'

'She is eighteen,' replied the Duchess. 'Far too young to be the wife of a man of fifty-two. And as Ida has had Louise so soon after her marriage it shows we are not a barren family.'

Adelaide smiled at her mother's indignation. She was relieved. She would love to have a child, but she could not contemplate with equanimity marriage to a man of fifty-two who had the reputation of the Duke of Clarence.

So, she thought, I shall be left in peace.

But it was not to be. The Duke of Hesse had declined the proposal on behalf of his daughter. She was so young, and although the Duke was conscious of the honour done to his house he must decline.

'Who else is there?' asked the Duchess Eleanor. She was elated. Adelaide was only twenty-six; there were many years ahead of her during which she could bear children; and the choice of a princess young enough to be a mother who was a Protestant was very, very narrow.

'We have a chance,' she cried; and every day she hopefully awaited the messenger.

At last it came.

William Henry, Duke of Clarence, asked for the hand of the

Princess Amalie Adelaide Louise Thérèse Caroline of Saxe-Meiningen.

The castle was in a ferment of excitement. What was Ida's marriage compared with this? There were messengers arriving every day with despatches from England.

'How delighted your father would be if he were alive today,' declared the Duchess fervently.

Adelaide supposed he would. She supposed she should be too. It was a brilliant marriage, not because her bridegroom would be the Duke of Clarence but because a young woman had recently died with her baby and neither of the Duke's brothers had a legitimate child.

'It is a certainty,' said the Duchess Eleanor, 'that your child will be a King or Queen of England. Think of it. How proud you must be.'

Proud, thought Adelaide, to go to a stranger, to an unknown land! To be the bride of a man who had been rejected by so many! But I myself was once rejected, she reminded herself.

And she would leave her home, her mother, her brother. But she saw clearly that her mother believed any marriage to be better than no marriage at all.

She thought about her future husband. A man of fifty-two, a royal Duke, a man who had spent his early years at sea, who had lived with an actress for twenty years, had had ten children by her, and then deserted her. He was overburdened by debts; it was for this reason that he would marry, she knew, and because he was forced to do so by his family and the English Parliament, and the reason was that if the House of Hanover was to be preserved the urgent necessity was an heir to the throne.

In such circumstances should she be proud?

There was a new respect for her in the castle. The Princess Adelaide could be the Queen of England. Two ageing and not very healthy men stood between her and that exalted position. Ida wrote to her: 'Dearest Adelaide, what great good fortune! Who would have believed this could happen to you!'

Yes, who would have believed it? Adelaide asked herself. And did she want it?

Yes, in a way. She had known ever since she had held her little niece in her arms that above everything on earth she longed for a child.

Whatever unpleasant experience lay between her and that goal must be endured.

Adelaide had never asked for the impossible, so she must be prepared.

She had tried on the gowns which had been made for her, and the Duchess dismissed the dressmakers which was a sign that she wished to talk confidentially.

'My dear,' she said, 'one must be wary of the English royal family. I have decided that I will accompany you to England. I have talked this over with my advisers and we all agree this to be best. The royal family of England has not always treated those who join it with the respect due to them.'

Adelaide smiled with pleasure. 'Oh, Mamma, that will make everything so much easier.'

'Yes,' said the Duchess. 'I can leave Saxe-Meiningen for a few weeks and travel with you. I should not wish to leave you in England until I see you safely married. I have declined to have a proxy marriage ... which I consider to be of very little use. Besides, that would have entailed a great deal of expense. Caroline of Brunswick was treated very badly when she arrived in England. She was greeted by the mistress of the Prince of Wales. Can you imagine anything more shocking?'

'You think I shall be greeted by my future husband's mistress?'

'My dear Adelaide. You speak too frankly. There is no evidence that he has a mistress. There was, of course, that disgraceful affair with the actress Mrs Jordan but at least it lasted for twenty years and she is now dead, although there are all those children. Heaven knows what complications there will be over them. But that you will discover. The point is that the family is not always gracious to those who marry into it. The Queen refuses to receive the Duchess of Cumberland. Not that I am surprised. That woman's reputation is quite horrifying. But all the same I should like to see you safely married before I left you in England. I

90

have heard that the Prince of Wales almost refused to marry Caroline of Brunswick at the altar. Think of that.'

'Do you think that the Duke of Clarence will refuse to marry me once he has seen me?'

'What nonsense! Why should he?'

'I am not what is called an attractive woman.'

'And he is a man of fifty-two! He will find your youth ... your comparative youth ... delightful. No. It is the family I am thinking of. And I am determined to come with you.'

'Well, Mamma, your decision gives me great relief.'

'My dear child, don't think I don't realize what an ordeal this is. You are so sensible that you don't display your fears but I realize that they are there none the less. I have no qualms about your future, my love, because you are yourself. Your dear father used to say Adelaide will never cause us any anxiety, and I have always known it to be true. We were fortunate indeed to have such a daughter; and I am desolate at losing you, but I know this is right for you.'

'Yes, Mamma.'

'It is your duty ... and such a glittering future!'

'I know, Mamma. I know.'

'Well, then, we must not allow our emotions to take control of us. We shall travel inconspicuously. We could not afford to do otherwise. Nor do we want to make a show of having what we have not. I believe the Regent's manner of life to be most elaborate. But you have been taught that it is better to live modestly than in ostentatious state which you cannot afford; and for all their grandeur the Princes of England live beyond their means. But no matter. You will manage your household with care, I know, as you have been taught to do. I was saying that we shall travel in accordance with our means. You shall have two ladies-in-waiting and I will take von Konitz and von Effa to counsel me. I shall need their services.'

'I think that this is an admirable arrangement, Mamma.'

'And there is one other thing. How are you getting on with your English lessons?'

Adelaide smiled. 'I am working hard, Mamma.'

'You will soon master it. But I daresay your husband will speak German. Or perhaps French. And in time of course you will master the language. There is nothing like living among the natives to do that. Queen Charlotte could not speak a word of English when she arrived, but she seemed to get on very well. But I believe the poor King was very different from his sons. How I wish that we had had you taught English. If only we had known ... but who would have thought such a glittering possibility would come our way. We should rejoice, should we not, that it has.'

The Duchess Eleanor was looking anxiously at her daughter. She wished romantically that the Duke of Clarence could have come to Saxe-Meiningen and fallen in love with Adelaide and she with him – as with the case of Ida and Weimar.

She was being absurdly romantic, but she did hope that Adelaide was not too fearful. She did not show her feelings, admirable girl.

Let her be happy, prayed the Duchess.

Every day the Duchess Eleanor fearfully awaited a message. She was terrified that there might be some hitch.

But preparations went on and nothing happened to stop them, and one warm July day the party set out for England.

The bride took her last look at the castle and wondered whether she would ever see it again. Adelaide, soon to be the Duchess of Clarence – and perhaps in due course Queen of England – was on her way to the new life.

'The Humbugs'

Queen Charlotte fervently wished that she did not feel so ill. At this important time she needed all her strength of purpose. She awoke every morning with the realization that the family's existence was in danger and that none of them seemed to be urgently aware of it.

She was not a woman to magnify her ailments, but she was fully aware what the dropsical state of her body meant and doubted whether she would live long enough to see the birth of the new heir to the throne. Who would be first, she wondered, Clarence or Kent – or failing them there was Cumberland (God forbid that it should be that woman's child) or Cambridge. The marriages took so long to arrange, and her sons were not the most ardent of wooers; there was Kent with his French woman and he seemed to be more concerned about *her* future than that of the woman who was to be his wife. That somewhat independent widow, the Princess Victoria, might become aware of this and change her mind. As for Clarence, when had he ever behaved with wisdom?

He had been furious to have to jilt Miss Wykeham. Jilt! What a ridiculous expression! He had never been properly betrothed to her in any case and if she had had any sense she would have known it.

And then all that fuss about the marriage allowances. Really Clarence had a perfect genius for getting himself into absurd situations.

She sent one of the women for her daughter Elizabeth for she wished to talk to her about the marriage which was being proposed for her.

Such a crop of marriages, she thought. Necessary for brothers but why for the sisters? There was something rather pathetic about an ageing woman marrying – and being so eager to do so.

Elizabeth came to her call. She was forty-eight. Indeed, she should have more dignity.

'My dear Elizabeth, my snuff-box.'

Elizabeth hastened to bring it to her mother.

'It has not been filled,' complained the Queen.

Elizabeth thought: How irritable she is! Her rheumatism, I suppose. What joy to be free of it all!

'Thank you. I am surprised that you forgot to fill it, Elizabeth.'

'I am sorry, Mamma.'

'You had other things on your mind.' The ugly mouth curled to a sneer. 'This . . . marriage of yours, I'll swear.'

'I suppose when she is about to be married a woman could be excused for being a little absent-minded about a snuff-box.'

93

'Oh dear!' sighed the Queen. 'How you have changed!'

'I am sorry, Mamma,' said Elizabeth. 'I shall not forget again . . . as long as I am here.'

'So you have determined to accept this proposal.'

'I have already accepted, Mamma.'

The Queen laughed unpleasantly. 'I have heard he is little better than an animal.'

'That could apply to so many,' retorted Elizabeth blithely.

'Elizabeth, I do not think you have considered this sufficiently.'

'I did not have to consider it, Mamma. I always knew that I would prefer any marriage to none at all.'

'I cannot understand you . . . any of you.'

The Queen's mouth shut like a trap. She would have liked to oppose the marriage but George was for it, providing, he said, Elizabeth wanted it. He was sorry for his sisters. They had never had a chance, he affirmed; and it was unnatural for them to be shut away as they had been all their lives. The King had behaved towards his daughters as though they were birds to be kept in cages. He forgot they were human beings although they were princesses. George had always sworn that when he came to the throne – and the Regency was the same thing – his first act would be to do something for his sisters. And for once George had kept his word. He had given them all allowances and if any of them could find men to marry them, he was not going to withhold his consent.

So when the Landgrave of Hesse-Homburg offered for Elizabeth the Regent declared that it was Elizabeth's affair and if she wished to accept the fellow she might do so. And she had accepted with unbecoming alacrity.

What she would do without Elizabeth, she was not sure. Elizabeth had been her favourite daughter – because she was the most useful. Mary had married her cousin Gloucester, that ridiculous 'Slice' as the papers called him or 'Silly Billy' as the Regent had named him, and she was no longer available to wait upon her Mamma. There would be only Augusta and Sophia left when Elizabeth had married, and Sophia was so often ill that she had to keep to her bed.

And just at the time when I most need them! thought the Queen irritably. Surely they could have waited a little longer before rushing off with the first man who asked them.

Elizabeth guessed the Queen's thoughts. How unfair! She was forty-eight. How could she be expected to wait! Already she was too old to have children and when she thought how they had all been treated she could hate the irritable ugly old woman in the chair for having condemned them all to live as they had. Although perhaps Papa was more to blame. But how could she hate that poor shambling old man who was nearly blind and completely deaf and lived shut away from them all with his doctors who were really his keepers?

But the door of the cage was open at last and no matter what the Landgrave of Hesse-Homburg was like she was going to have him.

'Sit down. Sit down,' said the Queen. 'You fidget me standing there looking so . . . so helpless. What is the news? Have you heard any?'

'Nothing I daresay, Mamma, that you would not have heard already.'

'Pray take your embroidery. I do not care to see you sitting idle-handed.'

For the time it was easier to obey, thought Elizabeth. But the tyranny was almost over. Soon the Landgrave would be in England. What was he like? She had heard some reports that were not very flattering but then people were so unkind. They loved to poke fun. And anything . . . just anything would be better than this slavery.

Elizabeth was thinking of her sisters. Charlotte the eldest who had married twenty years before. Strangely her bridegroom had been the husband of the Regent's wife's sister who had disappeared mysteriously and was said to have been murdered. She remembered how ill poor Charlotte had been when she had thought the wedding might not take place because of a rumour that her bridegroom's first wife was still alive. She had suffered from jaundice, poor girl, and had been quite yellow at the ceremony. But she had achieved marriage, the only one of them to do so at that time. Mary had married last year. She should have married Gloucester years before. Augusta was doomed to remain a spinster and that left Sophia who had not been without adventures. She had at least had a lover – old General Garth – and there had been the boy to prove it. What a time that had been when they had discovered Sophia was pregnant and had had to get her down to Weymouth 'for her health's sake' where she had successfully given birth. Garth adored the boy – and so did Sophia. She saw him whenever she could and Garth was still at Court. The scandals in this family were almost beyond belief. It was because the King had been so strict with the boys that as soon as they were free they rushed off wildly to make up for lost time; and the girls did what they could in their prisons to brighten the monotony of their lives. Even the dead, sainted Amelia had been in love with Charles Fitzroy and had had to keep it hidden from Papa.

And now here was freedom coming towards her in the person of the Landgrave of Hesse-Homburg.

Was she going to seize that freedom? She certainly was . . . with both hands; and she had quoted an ancestress of hers to Augusta: 'I would marry an ape rather than no one at all.'

And nothing is going to stop me, she determined.

'Of course,' the Queen was saying, 'when you see the Landgrave you may change your mind.'

Elizabeth plied her needle steadily.

The Queen sighed. 'At least your brother Clarence is being sensible at last. He was in quite a tantrum. First about that woman with the odd name.'

'Miss Wykeham.'

'That is the creature. And then declaring that he would not marry at all because Parliament only offered him an additional £6,000 a year.'

'He has decided against that now, Mamma. He is quite ready to take the Princess of Saxe-Meiningen.'

'I should think so. Such a waste of time. I shall not rest easily until these marriages take place. And when I hear that they are fruitful I shall be really at peace.'

'Yes, Mamma.'

'I cannot think why there always has to be *fuss* about these matters. And why your brothers seem to do everything they possibly can to make themselves unpopular.'

Elizabeth shrugged her shoulders. That freedom which was almost within her grasp made her reckless.

'I heard that the Duke of Wellington has said that the royal dukes are the damnedest millstone round the necks of any government that can be imagined.'

'That man uses the most coarse language. I am surprised at your repeating it, Elizabeth.'

'I thought Your Majesty wished to hear *all* I had heard.'

The Queen closed her eyes. 'Bring me the higher footrest. And hand me my snuff-box.'

Elizabeth obeyed and, looking at her mother lying back in the chair, her eyes closed, that yellowish tinge to her face, thought how ill she looked and even uglier than usual.

She felt sorry for her. She would not repeat the latest quip about George. 'Prinney has let loose his belly which now reaches to his knees.' A comment on the fact that the Regent no longer belted his waist. They were coarse and unkind; and they liked to ridicule them all. She could imagine what would be said of her and her Landgrave.

But I don't care, thought Elizabeth. All I care is that I escape.

She looked at her mother and believed she had fallen asleep.

How unlike her! And how grey and old she looked in sleep!

Poor Mamma! thought Elizabeth. She is as ill in her way as Papa is in his.

And she thought of her father, and how it was sometimes necessary to put him into a strait-jacket, and her cold-hearted mother, who had helped to ruin so many of their lives, and George with his wild affairs and the other brothers with their matrimonial difficulties.

What a family!

The Landgrave of Hesse-Homburg had arrived in England and the public was amused. What was this creature who had come to marry the Princess? There was something ridiculous about a woman of forty-eight behaving like a coy young bride which, it was insisted, was what the Princess Elizabeth was doing. She was over-plump, somewhat unwieldy in fact; and when her bridegroom appeared the cartoons came thick and fast.

When he arrived in England, it was said, his face and body were so caked with dirt that no one could see his features. He had never washed in his life. He did not think washing necessary. He smoked continuously and the smell of his smoky unclean person sent people scurrying away from him.

They had had to insist that he take several very hot baths one after another to make some inroad into the grime; and to take his pipe away from him, which made him peevish.

The truth was that hygiene at the English Court had become something of a fetish owing to the Regent's habits. He himself bathed every day and he expected everyone who came into contact with him to do the same. Thus the bathing habit was taken up throughout the Court but baths were rarities in Hesse-Homburg; and remembering the disastrous meeting of the Regent with Caroline of Brunswick when the odour which emanated from her person so sickened him that he turned away calling for a strong brandy, the Landgrave was advised to bath and change his linen before being presented to his future bride.

He seemed to be an easy-going fellow and submitted to the baths with a good grace; and when he was presented to Elizabeth she blushed deeply with pleasure. He was extremely fat but she was no sylph. They might appear to be a most unromantic-looking couple but he was willing to marry her and more than anything else on earth she wanted to be married.

So the bride and groom were satisfied with each other.

The press was delighted with its Landgrave. He was such a good subject for caricature. Because he was from Hesse-Homburg he was quickly christened the Humbug; and the bridal pair were known as The Two Humbugs.

Their wedding gave rise to coarse comment and much that was caustic too.

Naturally the Princess was lavishly endowed.

'A fresh attack on John Bull's Purse,' commented the papers.

The Regent offered to lend the pair one of his houses for the honeymoon, but the bridegroom declared ungraciously that he did not care for the country; however, no one took any notice of this except the Queen who expressed her surprise that Elizabeth could consider marrying such a creature. To which Elizabeth retorted that she was completely content.

The Queen took to laughing at him – at his manners, at his lack of cleanliness and most of all his clumsy attempts to speak English.

'Many foreign princes – princesses – have to learn a new language when they marry,' retorted Elizabeth. 'There is nothing unusual in that.'

They all changed, thought the Queen sadly, once they married. Look at Mary! Now she was the Duchess of Gloucester how different she was from when she had been plain Princess Mary – and all because of her alliance with that Slice of Gloucester Cheese whose mother had been a milliner and had no right to marry into the royal family at all.

At the wedding ceremony the Queen could not control her laughter at the strange manner in which the Landgrave spoke English. It was too comical; and the whole wedding was a farce. So said the Queen. But it was not so much amusement that made her laugh as the desire to ridicule her daughter's bridegroom. She hated losing her daughters. She wanted them all at her side, waiting on her as they had done in their youth.

The Regent was kind to his sister. After the ceremony he embraced her warmly and wanted to know if she was happy.

'I am completely content,' she told him.

'Then I am happy, too.'

Dear George, he didn't really care, but he always pretended to so charmingly.

And she was married at last. She would not be the old maid of the family. That would be Augusta. For in view of her adventures no one would ever be able to call Sophia an old *maid*.

Shortly after the marriage of Elizabeth and the Landgrave, Adolphus, Duke of Cambridge, was married to his lovely Augusta at her father's Belvedere Palace in Cassel.

Adolphus, the forty-four-year-old bridegroom, was happy. He was marrying for love; he could not forget his great good fortune in coming to Hesse-Cassel to seek a bride for Clarence and finding one for himself. He was gentle, rather naïve; and they were very happy.

Even the Queen of England approved of the bride and had sent her warm messages of welcome and an invitation to come to England.

'We must,' said Adolphus, 'be married in England as well as here in Hesse-Cassel; and after the ceremony we'll come back here.'

Augusta was delighted; she had no wish to leave her beautiful mountain home where she had spent the happiest of childhoods with the kindest of parents and her brothers and sisters. Even the Napoleonic Wars had not greatly disturbed Hesse-Cassel, for Duke Frederick had successfully managed to remain in a sense neutral while he placated both sides.

He agreed with Adolphus that the marriage must be celebrated in England and announced his intention of accompanying the pair to England to assist at the ceremony.

Augusta herself was a little nervous of the visit. She had naturally heard a great deal about the happenings at the English Court. The affairs of that family had been the scandal of a Continent; for one thing no other family seemed to behave quite so outrageously and Germany was so closely linked with the English royal family, which was after all the House of Hanover, that all Germans were particularly interested.

'I am very nervous of meeting the Queen and the Regent,' Augusta told her husband.

'You need have no fears of the Regent. He is the most charming man alive – particularly to beautiful women.'

Adolphus looked complacently at his bride with her tall slim figure, her dark eyes, her abundant dark hair and thick well-arched brows; she was beautiful, entirely feminine; she could sing delightfully – which, Adolphus said, would please the Regent who fancied he had a very fine singing voice himself.

'But the Queen?' she asked.

The Queen? Well he was not sure of the Queen. She would admire Augusta's dexterity with the needle. Augusta was a very fine needlewoman and examples of her exquisite embroidery adorned her father's palaces; she could arrange flowers with true artistry. The Queen would find those pleasant accomplishments.

'The Queen does not disapprove of our marriage,' said Adolphus; 'and as she is disapproving of so much recently it may well be that she will be pleased to find something which she can like.'

And so they set out for England, and how rough was the crossing and how sick poor Augusta, tossing on her bunk and wishing she were anywhere on earth rather than on a frail boat in a malicious sea on a trip to see a fractious Queen of England.

But when the trip was over she looked very lovely with her white gown and lavender-coloured pelisse which accorded so well with her dark hair and bright complexion and her lovely eyes shaded by the white ostrich feathers in her hat.

The people thought her beautiful and cheered her. What a change from the fat, dirty Humbug from Homburg.

Adolphus was delighted by her reception but Augusta who could not understand what the people were shouting was a little alarmed. When she drove through the streets of London and grinning faces came close to the carriage windows she drew back in some alarm. These noisy streets were so different from what she had been used to in Hesse-Cassel where the people were orderly and disciplined and showed proper respect to their ruling house.

'They are admiring you, my love,' said Adolphus proudly.

She smiled faintly at the people and they began to think her aloof, so they did not care for that however beautiful she was, and Augusta, sensing a certain hostility, was longing to go home to Hesse-Cassel, although she dreaded another sea crossing.

The Queen, however, received her with the utmost affability. Augusta showed the proper deference to her; they spoke in German together, and Charlotte was less of an ogress than she had feared. The Regent was, as she had been led to believe, perfectly charming. Adolphus was the luckiest fellow on earth to have won such a beauty, he told her; and he sighed to imply that he envied his brother, and was faintly melancholy, in the most charming way, because the happiness of the newly married pair could not but remind him of his own sorry plight with the Princess of Wales.

Clarence and Kent were inclined to be suspicious. She felt they were weighing her up, assessing her fertility. Adolphus whispered that now the race was on they were all eager to have the child which would be heir to the throne.

'And we, my darling, have the start of them. Clarence and Kent are not even married yet.'

The meeting with the Duke of Cumberland was less successful, for she did not meet the Duchess who was not received at Court. He had a terrifying countenance and she could well believe all the stories she had heard of him.

The English ceremony was performed in the presence of the Queen. The bride looked charming, the bridegroom was clearly content, and even the Queen had no criticism to offer.

It was hardly to be expected that the press would not find something to ridicule.

Augusta might be a beauty and the royal family might be pleased with the match, but what of the cost to the nation?

Wellington was right when he said the family was a millstone round the nation's neck. Royal marriages were all very well, but these brides and grooms took government grants and an increase in income as their right. And where did the money come from but the taxes?

'More Humbugs,' announced the papers. 'Another attack on John Bull's Purse.'

And the activities of the two married couples were reported with glee – particularly those of Elizabeth and the Duke of Hesse-Homburg it was true; but they were known as the Four Humbugs, and Adolphus and his bride did not escape.

Frederica, Duchess of Cumberland, was furious. As she complained to Ernest, her husband: 'Cambridge's wife is received at Court. The Queen makes a great fuss of her. And yet *I* am beneath her notice. She behaves as though I don't exist.'

'My dear,' said Ernest, 'you know my mother. She is the most cantankerous old woman alive. She has made up her mind to disapprove of you and nothing will make her change it. I shouldn't fret. If you were dull and uninteresting she would approve. Remember that.'

'Like Madam, the Duchess of Cambridge? I hear she is a beauty.'

'Pretty but insipid.'

'I wonder . . .'

'What do you wonder?'

'Whether she is *enceinte* yet?'

'So soon?'

'They were married in Hesse-Cassel. The second ceremony was not really necessary. I wonder.'

'We shall know soon enough.'

'Not soon enough for me. I am determined that *we* are going to produce the King of England.'

'Of course. And it's a sobering thought that I have three brothers all with the same ambition.'

'Sobering! It's exciting. Who will be the winner? At least we and Adolphus are first in the field. Clarence and Kent haven't started yet?'

'No, but when they do, being the eldest they have the advantage.'

'It is not always the favourite that wins.' She laughed suddenly. 'Oh, Ernest, it excites me. This contest. Which of us is going to win? It's the race for a throne. And our chances are as good as any. But the Cambridges are formidable. She is young – twenty-one; he is forty-four, the youngest of the contestants. Somehow I feel that Clarence and Kent are too old. The Cambridges are our true rivals. And to think at this very moment your insipid – but extremely pretty – little Duchess may be with child.'

'We shall soon hear if she is. I must say Cambridge seems very pleased with himself.'

'He is very naïve. I knew him well once, remember. Imagine, I might have myself been the Duchess of Cambridge!'

'Are you regretting that?'

'My dear Ernest, it is not like you to ask foolish questions.'

'I have something to tell you. Leopold was very affable when I last saw him. I wonder why.'

'He is going to bring his sister to England to marry Kent. And he wants the family to approve of her.'

'But why concern himself with such unpopular members of it? What do you think? He is paying a visit to Saxe-Coburg and has offered us Claremont.'

'Excellent! When do we move in?'

'As soon as he leaves.'

'That's good news. Now if I only knew whether little Augusta was pregnant I'd be content. I don't mind telling you that I shall have no peace until I do know.'

'You must wait for an announcement like the rest of us, my dear.'

Frederica smiled slyly at her husband.

Augusta, Duchess of Cambridge, greatly enjoyed walking, and it was pleasant to escape from the crowds as one could in the gardens at Kew.

She took an hour's solitary walk there every day; and it appeared to be quite safe for on these walks she met no one but the members of the Queen's household who, respecting her need for privacy, often pretended not to see her.

She was walking through one of the shady paths close to the river when she heard footsteps behind her and turning saw a woman approaching her. Augusta was immediately aware of her beauty and regal carriage; and she was puzzled; she was not, to her knowledge, a member of the royal family and yet she behaved as though she were.

Augusta could not hide her surprise at being so accosted and to her relief the woman addressed her in German.

'I'm your sister-in-law, Frederica – Cumberland's wife. I know you are Augusta and the new Duchess of Cambridge.'

Augusta's face lit up with pleasure.

She's certainly pretty, thought Frederica. And yet ... somewhat insipid, but that may be compared with an adventuress like myself.

'It's such a pleasure to hear someone speak German,' said Augusta.

'I was thinking exactly the same. May I join you in your walk or do you prefer to be alone?'

'Please join me. It will be a great pleasure.'

'Tell me how do you like England?'

'It is very strange. There are so many people about. I find London ... terrifying. And the noise and the bustle.'

'Very different from Hesse-Cassel,' said Frederica. 'As it is from Mecklenburg-Strelitz.'

'You notice it too?'

Frederica nodded. 'I shall not be sorry to go home.'

'Nor I,' agreed Augusta.

'Although,' went on Frederica, 'I had a very sad time before I left. Ernest thought it would help me to forget if I went away. I lost my baby.'

Augusta's expression softened to one of great pity. Frederica was alert. Is she? she wondered.

'That must have been a terrible tragedy.'

'Only a mother can know how great,' said Frederica earnestly. 'You could not imagine . . .'

'I think I could,' said Augusta.

Significant? wondered Frederica.

'Do you really?' Her voice was warm, almost begging for confidences. But Augusta was not of a warm nature; she was also cautious.

'I suppose,' went on Frederica, 'now that you are married you are hoping . . . as we all do.'

'As we all do,' said Augusta. 'But you have other children.'

'Yes, I have other children.'

'From previous marriages.' The voice was a little cold. Oh, they have been gossiping about me, thought Frederica. What has prim little Augusta heard? If wicked old Aunt Charlotte has discussed me with her, I fear the worst. Augusta would at least know that Frederica was not received by the Queen.

'I have found happiness at last,' said Frederica in a voice she hoped sounded suitably soft and romantic. 'And I hope naturally that I shall bear a child.' And don't forget, Madam Augusta, that if we both bear a son mine will come before yours!

It was obvious that Augusta would not confide such a secret to her and she could not ask a direct question naturally. So she allowed the conversation to turn to their lives in their native countries which was clearly what Augusta enjoyed talking about. She would hope that unconsciously Augusta might betray what she wanted to know. So they talked pleasantly and

105

Augusta was clearly delighted to be able to chat easily.

But when they parted Frederica had not discovered what she wanted to know; and they had been seen and the fact that they had been together reported to the Queen.

The Queen was furious.

'Sophia! Augusta!' she cried. 'Why are you never here when I need you? Do you know what has happened? That woman . . . my brother's daughter . . . has been waylaying the Duchess of Cambridge in Kew Gardens and forcing herself upon her.'

'Well, Mamma,' said Sophia, 'I daresay they had a great deal to say to each other. And it must have been good to be able to speak in German together.'

How dared they bandy words with her! What had happened to her family? Mary had left her to marry that fool Slice and although she was constantly being called back to dance attendance on her mother one could not order the Duchess of Gloucester to do this and that as one could the Princess Mary. Elizabeth was making herself a fool with that Humbug. And now Augusta and Sophia seemed to think it fitting to Answer Back.

'It is disgraceful. Fetch my snuff-box. Sophia, I cannot understand why you cannot do a simple thing like remember my snuff-box. It was very different in the old days.'

'You were different in the old days, Mamma.'

They were forgetting the respect due to her. Everything was changing. She felt tired and there were pains all over her body.

'I am . . . incensed,' she cried. 'I gave orders that that woman was not to be received at Court and she has been . . . waylaying . . . Augusta.'

'Mamma, are you all right?' It was Sophia's voice coming from some distance it seemed. But Sophia was bending over; her eyes seemed enormous . . . full of secrets. What dreadful things were said about the children. Were they true? And they were turning away from her. They were all a disappointment to her . . . except . . .

'George?' she said, and the sound of her voice was like thunder in her ears.

106

'I think we should get Mamma to bed,' said Augusta. 'And call the doctors.'

The Regent sat by her bed. He held her hand tenderly; and in spite of the pain which racked her body she was almost happy.

He had come as soon as he heard she had been taken ill. How like him! Such perfect manners! But perhaps he was a little anxious. If he were half as concerned as he said he was she would be happy.

'It was good of you to come,' she murmured.

'My dear Madre, as soon as I heard you had been taken ill of course I came. Would you not expect that of me?' Tenderly reproachful, she thought. How well he did it! But never mind, he did it, and it was for her.

'My dearest son.' And there was no pretence about that. He was her dearest son, always had been and always would be. 'I felt so ill I was sure my last moment had come.'

'I beg of you do not distress me.'

She smiled. 'I will not. But I was so shocked. It was that woman ... Cumberland's wife. She is my own niece, I know ...'

'Yes,' said the Regent whose own troubles loomed so large in his life that he was easily reminded of them, 'as my wife is my father's niece.'

'A pair,' said the Queen almost viciously. 'I do believe the one is as bad as the other ... in their different ways. Immoral, both of them.'

'I don't despair of a divorce.'

'And she had the impertinence to accost Augusta. I don't blame Augusta. She speaks no English. She did not understand that I ... that we ... that you ... have forbidden her to come to Court.'

The Regent looked uncomfortable. He had not forbidden Cumberland's wife to come to Court. He had met her once or twice and thought her an exciting woman. It was the Queen who had refused to receive her. But he did not intend to raise controversial issues now.

The Queen said: 'That she had dared do this so ... upset me. It brought on this attack. It was such ... defiance.'

The Regent nodded sadly. He had been reminded of Caroline and once he got that woman into his head he could not get her out. He had sent his spies into her household on the Continent; there was an Italian, Bergami . . . a kind of majordomo. Was that man her lover? If he was there was every hope that he could divorce her; and then . . . he would marry again. Some fresh young princess, as exciting as Frederica, Duchess of Cumberland, as beautiful as Augusta, Duchess of Cambridge. Why should his brothers be married to women like that while he had the nauseating Caroline . . . for more than twenty years he had been tied to her. The years of my youth wasted! he thought dramatically.

'And,' the Queen was saying, 'I cannot allow it to pass. I want to show them my disapproval. I am sure you will approve of this. I am sure you will not wish me to be aggravated by the continued presence of that woman in the country.'

'Dearest Madre,' he said, 'anything that soothes you must be done.'

A triumphant smile gave a grotesque look to the Queen's yellowish face.

'I will let Ernest know that he is expected to leave England with his wife . . . immediately. And that is an order.'

'So,' said Frederica, 'we are ordered to leave.'

Ernest grimaced. 'And you have only yourself to blame for that, my dear. Your curiosity got the better of you.'

'But not of Augusta. The girl would not give away her secrets.'

'So your little encounter was a wasted effort.'

'Such efforts are never really wasted. I shall not be sorry to go back to Germany. Although, of course, this is the field of action and when the brides of Clarence and Kent arrive the battle will really begin.' She laughed. 'But one doesn't have to be in England to produce the future King. That is what your dear Mamma seems to forget. And although I should have enjoyed staying for a while in Claremont, which Leopold so graciously offered to us, I am not really sorry to go home.'

'In Germany we have to rely on news from England.'

'Don't worry, as soon as one of the contestants is pregnant we shall hear. But I intend to forestall them; and once I am to bear the future King of England even my wicked old aunt won't be able to keep me out.'

'Speed the day,' said Ernest.

'I have a feeling that it will not be long in coming. And Augusta . . . I think she was . . . or will soon be. But what chance will hers have against ours? How clever of you, my Ernest, to get born before Cambridge.'

'Cleverer still if I'd managed to outdo Clarence and Kent.'

'Never mind. It makes the fight all the more interesting when the odds are against you.'

But for all she said, Frederica was chagrined to be so dismissed from England by her malevolent old aunt.

Double wedding at Kew

Adelaide was apprehensive. This was a different marriage from Ida's. Ida had been in love and able to return home easily, whereas she was so far away that they could not visit each other comfortably. There was something final about crossing the sea.

The Duchess Eleanor was uneasy too. It was for this reason that she had refused a proxy wedding and was determined to accompany her daughter to England; she was glad that she had von Effa and von Konitz with her, for she was sure that she would need their services.

Adelaide was on deck when land was sighted. She stood, her eyes shielded, waiting for the moment when her new country would be more than a hazy white cliff in the distance. Her mother came to stand beside her.

'Very soon now, Adelaide,' she said, 'you will be stepping ashore . . . on to your new land. It is a solemn moment.'

'A very solemn moment,' agreed Adelaide.

'The Duke of Clarence will be waiting to greet you . . . impatiently.'

Impatiently? wondered Adelaide. She had heard rumours that

he had refused to marry because the allowance Parliament offered was not large enough. So could he be said to be impatient?

And he was fifty-two. He had been notorious for his love affairs – like most of his brothers. He had lived for twenty years with a charming actress. And there had been other women. What would he think of a plain young woman whose appearance had not been enhanced by a long sea voyage? She hoped he would not be there to greet them. A little respite would be desirable.

Now she could see the land more clearly. Away to the right were the treacherous Goodwin Sands where many a ship had foundered. She had heard that sailors on watch at night declared they could hear the cries of those long dead who had been swallowed by the Sands. And here were the white cliffs of Dover and St Margaret's Bay.

Nearer and nearer came the land. They came ashore at a little fishing village called Deal.

When she discovered that no member of the royal family was waiting at Deal, the Duchess Eleanor was annoyed. Was this the way to greet the princess who might be the mother of a king? She had heard that the royal family treated its new members churlishly; and they were having proof of this.

I am glad I insisted on accompanying my daughter, she thought.

Poor Adelaide. She looked pale, tired and in no mood to face a bridegroom who might be critical. As she might well be of him, thought Duchess Eleanor grimly.

How much better, how much more civilized if he had had the grace to come and woo her as the Duke of Kent had the Princess Victoria, who would be arriving in England at the same time. There was to be a double wedding. But she was not coming to a stranger, as poor Adelaide was. It seemed that there had been a courtship, and the Duke of Kent and his Victoria already had an affection for each other.

I would rather have had Kent for Adelaide, thought Eleanor, although Clarence undoubtedly has the first chance.

Out of the little houses which straggled along the front the people came to see the arrival of the Princess from Saxe-Meiningen. 'Another German,' they murmured. 'Always Ger-

110

mans.' But it was an exciting time with so many royal weddings; and Deal was pleased that Adelaide had first come to their town.

The dignitaries of the town were there to greet her – but no bridegroom, nor any member of his family. The speech of welcome was difficult to understand, but Adelaide had been assiduously studying her English since she knew she was to marry the Duke of Clarence and it was the Kentish accent which made the words unintelligible.

But if there was not a royal welcome there was at least a bed and hot food; and what Adelaide felt she needed more than anything was a good night's sleep.

They put up at an inn near the sea and although it was July the wind rattled her windows all night and she could hear the waves crashing on the shingle below. She slept fitfully and her mother came into her room soon after dawn and sat on her bed and looked at her somewhat fearfully.

'The journey has only just begun, Mamma,' she said.

The Duchess nodded. 'I wondered whether we should come ashore when I realized that they had sent no one to welcome us.'

'The people of Deal were kind.'

'That at least is something to be grateful for, but I'll swear they are astonished that we should be treated so churlishly. I have been informed though that they have sent two coaches in which we and our suite may travel to London.'

'At least we should be grateful for that,' said Adelaide.

That day they set out in the coaches for Canterbury where they passed a night and the next day left for London.

No one cheered them on their way; no one was aware that the young woman who was seated in the leading carriage with her mother and two ladies-in-waiting might one day be their Queen.

No lodgings had been assigned to them so they drove to Albemarle Street and there put up at Grillon's Hotel.

Von Konitz was angry; he discussed with von Effa what move should be made. It was an incongruous situation. The bride of a royal Duke to arrive and no one to greet her!

He would despatch a message to the Prince Regent without delay.

Meanwhile Adelaide was shown to a room in the hotel and

when she looked in the glass at her pale face with the somewhat muddy complexion she was relieved that there had been no one to meet them. There were shadows under her eyes which looked strained; they were never very strong at the best of times. Her hair was fair, though not golden or flaxen as Ida's had been but yellowish, almost lemon colour. She needed a little time to recover from the strain of the journey.

And even when I have, I wonder what he will think of me? she asked herself.

So she was here, thought Clarence.

He had heard that she had arrived in Deal with her mother and that was two days ago. She had spent a night in Canterbury and was now at Grillon's Hotel.

There was no turning back.

It was strange that he who had been trying to get married ever since he had said goodbye to Dorothy Jordan was now on the verge of undertaking that adventure – and had no great desire for it.

He was not anxious to see her for some reason. He kept thinking of Dorothy and that night when he had first seen her as Little Pickle on the stage of Drury Lane. What a delightful creature she had been! Many believed her to have been the most charming woman in England. She had grown fat and they had quarrelled – and all about money. That was the only real disagreement between them. How happy they had been in the early days of their association! Here at Bushy all the children had been born and grown up. His children, on whom he doted.

His new wife would have to understand that he had no intention of giving up his children. They were Dorothy's legacy to him; he loved them; he was proud of them; and they had been brought up to know that he was their father.

He hoped it had all been explained to her that when she married him she would have to accept his ten illegitimate children.

He believed she would; he had received one or two letters from her when they had been betrothed and he was impressed by the good sense with which she wrote.

He had said to George FitzClarence, his eldest son: 'I think we shall get along well with your stepmother. She seems a sensible woman. I don't think she'll be over-dazzled by the prospect of becoming the Duchess of Clarence.'

No, she would accept the family; she, who came from a tiny dukedom must be overawed at the prospect of marrying a son of the King of England. He often thought of himself as a future King of England, for neither George's health nor that of Frederick was very good – and if they died . . . without heirs . . . he would be King William, and Adelaide would not be unaware of that.

She was in her twenty-sixth year. It was quite young – at least when compared with a man over fifty. He should be looking forward eagerly to the nuptials. But was he? He was not sure. He had set his heart on Miss Wykeham. But of course that would have been unsuitable; but what a jolly, bouncing, healthy female Miss Wykeham was! He believed she would have presented him with a son at the earliest possible moment.

But he must forget her; he must do his duty. It was what he had said to Dorothy at their parting; and he would not forget that in a hurry either. In any case there was the family to remind him.

They would live at Bushy, dear Bushy, which was more like a gentleman's country house than a palace, but none the worse for that. Bushy would be their home then and the ten FitzClarences her stepsons and daughters.

We must start as we intend to go on, he told himself and going to the window and seeing his son George in the park with his brother, Frederick, bawled in the voice he had used at sea: 'George! Hi, George! Come here. I want to speak to you.'

If the servants heard they would shudder. That was not the manner in which the Prince Regent – that arbiter of good manners – summoned people to his presence. But William was a rough sailor and had no intention of changing his manners. People must get used to them. They should be by now.

George came and stood before him. William's eyes grew sentimental as he looked at his eldest son. He was very handsome in his military uniform. He had a look of Dorothy about him, and William flattered himself – for George was very attractive – he was not without a resemblance to his father.

'George,' he said, 'your new stepmother is at Grillon's. Go and welcome her.'

'You mean *I'm* to go?'

'Why not? You're her stepson.'

'Won't she expect to see you?' The FitzClarence children never stood on ceremony with their father although, regarding themselves as royal, they could be arrogant enough with others.

'It may be she will; but she will see her stepson instead.'

'What about her mother and the statesmen they've brought with them? Will they be pleased?'

'It's a gesture, you see. It's like saying to her: See, this is your new family. I want her to understand that she's to be a stepmother as well as a wife.'

George thought it a good idea that she should be made aware of the importance of the FitzClarence children in their father's life and said he would set out at once.

William watched him leave.

In due course, he said to himself, I shall put in an appearance. Poor girl, she must be overwrought. An ordeal to come to marry a stranger. She must be terrified of the impression she may make on me.

It did not occur to William to wonder what impression he might make on her. He was, after all, third son of the King, with a fair chance of wearing the crown.

George FitzClarence arrived at Grillon's and was conducted to a room where he was received by Adelaide and the Duchess Eleanor.

He announced himself: 'George FitzClarence, son of the Duke. He suggested I should come to welcome you.'

The Duchess Eleanor's face was a mask of disapproval, but Adelaide smilingly held out her hand.

'You are the eldest son.'

'Yes – and there are ten of us – five boys and five girls – even numbers, you see.'

'Yes,' said Adelaide. 'Even numbers will be easy to remember.'

'My father wants to present us all to you.'

'And I shall be eager to meet you all.'

114

'We're not all at Bushy at the moment. The girls are most anxious to meet you.'

'All five of them?' asked Adelaide.

The Duchess Eleanor could not understand her daughter. This was an affront. Was the Duke of Clarence deliberately trying to insult Adelaide? The idea of sending the son of his mistress to greet his future wife!

And Adelaide did not seem to see this. She was talking to this FitzClarence man – who could only be a year or so younger than she was herself – as though she found his conversation entertaining and there was nothing disgraceful in his being here.

'Tell me about your brothers and sisters,' Adelaide was saying.

'There's Henry, a year younger than I. He's in the Army now although he did join the Navy at first. Following in Father's footsteps, you might say. But he didn't care for it and transferred to the Army. There's Frederick – also a soldier and the handsome one of the family. Adolphus is in the Navy, and then there is Augustus. He's the youngest boy and is only thirteen, although Amelia is the youngest of us all, aged eleven.'

'And the girls?'

'Sophia, Mary, Elizabeth, Augusta and Amelia.'

'I feel I know something of the family already.'

'My father will be pleased. He said he wanted you to like us.'

'Did he say that?'

The Duchess Eleanor said: 'I believe someone is arriving. I should hope it is the Duke of Clarence.'

'I hardly think so . . . yet,' said George FitzClarence and strode to the window.

The manners of these people! thought the Duchess Eleanor. Is this what my daughter is expected to endure in England?

'Oh, it's Uncle George,' announced FitzClarence. 'My namesake.'

'Uncle George . . .' stammered Adelaide.

'The Prince Regent,' announced George.

Now the Duchess Eleanor could not complain of the lack of good manners.

He had entered the room – a glittering personage, his diamond star blazing on his mulberry velvet coat, his white buckskin

breeches gleaming, his chins carefully hidden by the swathed silk
of his cravat; his nut-brown wig was an elegant mass of curls; the
most delicate of perfumes came from him; and his bow was a
masterpiece of perfection.

He held out both hands – delicately white, discreetly flashing
with diamonds – in a gesture of informal friendliness.

'My dear *dear* sister. So you have come to us at last.'

The little nose was humorous, the eyes shrewd. He – that
connoisseur of feminine beauty was thinking: Poor William, she's
a plain little thing and her complexion is very bad.

Maria Fitzherbert's complexion had been the most dazzling in
the world – completely naturally so. He had noticed it the first
time he had seen her on the towpath near Richmond, years and
years ago. And her hair was golden like the corn in August. This
young woman reminded him of Maria by what she lacked.

Poor William!

But he said: 'Enchanting! Enchanting! And I trust you are
well looked after here?'

'Your Highness is gracious,' said the Duchess Eleanor. 'The
Duke of Clarence has not yet called but he sent his ... this
gentleman ... to welcome us.'

The Regent gave a surprised look in the direction of George
FitzClarence. What a tactless fool William was! If there was a
wrong thing to do William could be relied upon to do it.

Well, he would save the situation as he was well able to do; he
was delighted to see that even the mother was in awe of him. So
charmingly he set them at their ease and chatted light-heartedly
about the family, what they must see in England, how delighted
he was that they had come.

And while they were chatting easily another arrival was
announced.

The Duke of Clarence had at last arrived to greet his bride.

They regarded each other cautiously.

He was an ageing man; it was true his head was the shape of a
pineapple; he had the Hanoverian eyes, blue, protuberant, and
there was a hint of wildness in them; he was not nearly as tall
nor as glorious as his dazzling brother; but somehow the thought

of that ready-made family to whom she had been introduced by the eldest member of it – if only by hearsay – made her feel less alarmed than she might have done. There was something about him that was young, in spite of his age. She supposed it would be called naïve, and oddly enough this was comforting.

She had been brought up to believe that one day she would have to marry and very likely a strange Prince in a foreign land. Well, having seen him she was not as afraid as she had thought she might be.

He looked at her and felt a twinge of disappointment. She was no beauty. But he liked her gentle manner. And when she told him that she had already made the acquaintance of his son George and that George had talked to her of the rest of the family, he felt his spirits uplifted.

If she would come to Bushy and live there with them all, if she was ready to be a stepmother to the children, and if she could give him the child who would be the heir to the throne, he would be content.

They talked of her journey and he told her of the improvements he had made to the house at Bushy which was quite his favourite residence. He was looking forward to showing it to her.

It was almost a prosaic meeting. They had come nowhere near falling in love at first sight.

But she had decided that she might have had worse than her ageing Duke; and he perceived that although she did not possess the attractions of that brash young beauty Miss Wykeham, nor the exquisite features of Miss Tylney-Long, nor the handsome looks of Miss Mercer Elphinstone – all of whom he had tried to persuade to marry him – it might well be that she had qualities which those more flamboyant ladies lacked.

When they parted, although they could scarcely be said to be elated, they were not unduly dismayed.

When they were alone the fury of the Duchess Eleanor broke forth.

'I never imagined that you would be treated like this! I am going to suggest that we return to Saxe-Meiningen tomorrow. Or . . . or . . .' She faltered, but Adelaide smiled.

'Dearest Mamma, you know that it is the last thing you wish.'

'We should be objects of ridicule. It would be said that he had seen you and refused to marry you.'

'And I should never have another chance to marry. Think of that, Mamma.'

'But not to greet us! To let us come to an hotel. And then . . . insult on injury to send that, that . . . *bastard* of his to be so insolent to you.'

'I liked him, Mamma; and after all, he will be my stepson.'

'I should not use that word to describe your future husband's bastard.'

'But that's what he is, Mamma. They will all be my step-children . . . all ten of them.'

'You must refuse to see them.'

'I could not do that.'

'Why not? Why not? Von Konitz shall speak to the Regent immediately. We will make it a condition.'

'It is not what I wish.'

The Duchess Eleanor looked in surprise at her daughter. There had been one or two occasions in Adelaide's life when she had taken a stand and like all usually malleable people when she did stand firmly there was no shaking her.

'You can't mean . . .'

'I mean this,' said Adelaide, 'that my future husband already has a large family of whom he is obviously fond. What chance of happiness should I have as his wife if I refused to acknowledge them?'

'Your husband's family. The children of an actress . . . who by all accounts must have been a loose woman, for these ten children are not the only ones she has had.'

'They are nevertheless the Duke's children. You always knew, Mamma, that I wanted to be a member of a big family. I regretted that I had not more sisters and brothers. Well, when I marry the Duke I shall become a member of one. That is one of the things that please me most in this marriage.'

The Duchess Eleanor stared at her daughter.

'I shall speak to both Konitz and Effa in the morning.'

'Mamma, I am sorry to say this, but this is my marriage. I

think that I should be the one who decides how it shall be conducted.'

What had happened to Adelaide? She had become an autocrat already. Perhaps though, decided the Duchess Eleanor, one should rejoice because she had not given way to melancholy at the sight of her ageing bridegroom.

A very unbecoming welcome; and I tremble to think of leaving my daughter behind in such company.

Adelaide, oddly enough, seemed quite composed. It was strange to think that it was due to her future husband's family of bastards.

The Duke of Kent had brought his Duchess to England that the ceremony might be repeated there in the presence of the Prince Regent and the Queen. They considered themselves in fact, already married.

The Queen received the Duchess graciously; she liked what she saw of her; but as she said afterwards to Augustus and Sophia she was so disgusted by Cumberland's wife that any of her son's consorts seemed admirable in comparison.

But undoubtedly the Duchess of Kent was a discreet and worthy woman. She had left her son and daughter in Leiningen, whither she and the Duke would return for a while after their three weeks honeymoon in England.

Apartments at Kensington Palace were offered to the Duke and these he gratefully accepted. They rode out to Claremont to see Victoria's brother Leopold, who wept with joy and declared that nothing now could please him more than to see this match brought to fruition, for theirs was a union very near to his heart.

'I have not been so happy since my dearest Charlotte died,' he said.

Victoria, who was practical, asked him if he were wise to remain at Claremont, the scene of his last months with Charlotte.

'Wise?' he asked. 'I am nearer to Charlotte here than anywhere else.'

'Dearest Leopold,' said Victoria, 'you prolong your grief. You should get away.'

'You don't understand,' groaned Leopold.

'I too have lost a husband.'

Leopold looked at her in astonishment. How could she compare that old husband of hers with his young and vital Charlotte. But he merely covered his eyes with his hands and Victoria said no more.

He took them over Claremont. 'This was the room where she died. I have left it just as it was on that dreadful day. This is her cloak. After the last walk she took in the grounds, she hung it there. I won't have it moved.'

Victoria said: 'Dearest brother, it is time you took a holiday away from England.'

'It is what I propose to do. And when you are married you may borrow Claremont for your honeymoon.'

'That is excellent news, is it not, Edward?' asked Victoria.

Edward was forming the habit of agreeing with everything Victoria said and did, and he immediately concurred.

So it was decided that after the wedding the honeymoon should be spent here.

'And the first thing I shall do,' the practical Victoria told her husband, 'is take down Charlotte's cloak and rearrange that bedroom in which she died.'

The Duchess Eleanor was received by the Queen, who was feeling a little better on this day. She explained to Duchess Eleanor the nature of her complaint and how it varied with the days.

'Anxiety does not improve it,' she explained. 'And I have had plenty of that and to spare.'

Duchess Eleanor inclined her head sympathetically.

'I trust Adelaide will be happy here,' said the Queen.

'I shall feel that she has found a mother in Your Majesty.'

The Queen graciously inclined her head.

'William is not the most level-headed of the Princes, so I am particularly relieved that Adelaide seems to be a *sensible* young woman.'

'Your Majesty will find her so. She has a good heart. In fact there is a matter on which I would ask Your Majesty's advice.'

'Pray proceed.'

'On our arrival the Duke sent a young man, a George Fitz-

Clarence, to greet my daughter. He was in fact the first one to do so.'

'Surely this could not be!'

'Alas, Your Majesty, I assure you it was so.'

'Monstrous!' said the Queen; and Duchess Eleanor nodded in relief. 'Something must be done about it,' went on Charlotte, and added, 'Something *shall* be done about it.'

'How grateful I am to Your Majesty; but I knew of course that you would deal with this matter ... as it should be dealt with. The Duke plans that the honeymoon should be spent at Bushy. He proposes to take Adelaide there ... in the midst of this family.'

'It is not possible. I will see the Regent immediately. We could never allow such a thing to be. I fear that William has little sense of the rightness of things – although I am sure Adelaide will find him an indulgent husband. But pray leave this matter to me.'

When the Duchess had retired the Queen went to her bedroom and lay down for a short while. These internal controversies upset her now far more than they used to. She was afraid of having another turn like the last she had had. One of these days, she thought, and that soon, I shall not recover.

There was so much to be done.

She wanted to live to see the heir born, to know that all these marriages had not been in vain; and the affairs of Adelaide and William were most important for they could produce the King or Queen of England.

If only William were not such a fool!

She sighed, roused herself and sent for him.

'William,' she said sternly, 'you really must behave with more decorum.'

He raised his eyes, looking hurt. 'What have I done now?' he asked reproachfully. 'I have accepted this marriage you have arranged for me. I have made no fuss about it ... even though the Parliament has not met my demands. I ...'

The Queen held up a hand for silence. 'I beg of you cease, William. I am not feeling well and my strength threatens to give out. So pray let us get quickly to the point. You have that actress's family at Bushy.'

'I have *my* family there, Mamma.'

'Your bastards, William.'

William flushed hotly; sailors' oaths rose to his lips. He thought of his darling daughters, the pride of his life; he adored them. Gay and pretty Sophia just twenty-one; he liked to have her here with him, showing her off. Mary of twenty down to eleven-years-old Amelia. Nothing on earth would induce him to part with them. And if his new wife was asking that this should be done he would refuse to marry her even now.

The Queen saw the stubborn set of his jaw and sighed.

'You propose to spend your honeymoon at Bushy?'

'Where else? Leopold has offered Edward and his wife Claremont. I have had no such offers. In any case, I don't want them. I prefer Bushy.'

'The honeymoon should not be spent at Bushy, although you will wish to take Adelaide there in due course. There should be just you and Adelaide there . . . with your servants, of course.'

William looked surprised. 'My daughters live there. It is their home. And that of the boys when they are home.'

'So you propose to take your bride into the heart of this . . . this family of yours, all of whom are the illegitimate children of an actress.'

'I must remind you again, Mamma, that they are mine as well,' said William with dignity.

'You have no *sense*, William. This cannot be. It would be a scandal. You must move your children from Bushy. The Regent has in any case decided that you leave for Hanover three weeks after the wedding. What happens later could be a matter for you and Adelaide to work out between you; but you cannot take your bride to Bushy while those children are there; and as it has been arranged that you should spend three weeks in England before going to Hanover you should spend them at St James's. The FitzClarence family must leave Bushy.'

'They will not like it.'

'And *I* should not like it if they stayed. Nor would your brother, the Regent, nor the people, nor any decent thinking person.'

'Adelaide has raised no objection.'

'Her mother has raised it on her behalf.'

'I thought she was an interfering old woman.'

'William!'

'I'm sorry, Mamma, but this is my private affair.'

'It is an affair of the State when an insult is offered to visitors to our country even if they are shortly to become a member of the family. I have spoken to the Regent about this and he agrees with me. While he sympathizes with your affection for this ... this ... family ... he thinks the FitzClarence children should not make Bushy their home. You may leave me now, William, for I am very tired. But I shall expect you to consider my wishes.'

The Regent was sympathetic as the Queen had said, but he did urge on William the need to remove the FitzClarences from Bushy.

'It's what people would say, William. God knows how we always have to consider that. I've spent my life doing it.'

'What is so infuriating is that Adelaide has raised no objection.'

'She seems a pleasant creature ... docile, amenable. I think she will make a good wife. Edward seems to have been put into leading strings. Victoria is not unprepossessing in her way but she has her fixed opinions and she won't rest until those about her share them. An attractive woman, but not as *comfortable* as your Adelaide.'

'Yes, I think Adelaide will make a good obedient wife – and all things considered I prefer her to Victoria. But why should I disrupt the Bushy household when Adelaide doesn't object?'

'Because, William, the people would object.' The Regent was a little weary of the subject, so he yawned gracefully to show that the subject was closed as far as he was concerned and he expected William to comply with his wishes.

'Who was that woman you thought of engaging as a governess?'

'Her name is Miss Cooper. She is a very intelligent and capable woman.'

'There is your answer, William. Now I must ask you to leave. I have a long session with my tailor.'

William realized there was no help for it. He acquired a house in South Audley Street and amid the protests of his daughters moved them there and put the efficient Miss Cooper in control.

Then he prepared for his wedding. He must devote himself to his wife and the object of the marriage, which was to make it fruitful as soon as possible.

It was the day of the double wedding, which was to take place in the Queen's drawing-room at Kew. The Regent was due to arrive just before four o'clock in order to preside benignly over the proceedings and give both brides to their husbands.

The Duke and Duchess of Kent were less nervous than Adelaide and William. They had in fact already been married in Germany two months before and were quite satisfied with each other.

Victoria was attractive and domineering; and Edward in spite of a somewhat pompous exterior was a good subject for her domination. He had been able to salve his conscience concerning Julie by doing everything possible for her comfort and he was sure that she had found peace in her convent. He had to admit that he was such a man of habit that Julie had to some extent become a habit; and it was more exciting to have a young – or comparatively young – wife, who was gay, affectionate and charming – as long as it was accepted that she was always right. And she invariably was – a fact which might have been a little irritating to some, but not to Edward. He liked precision and efficiency; he liked Victoria.

As for Victoria she was enjoying her new life. Edward was dignified it was true; strictly religious, unimaginative; but she was satisfied with him. When she compared him with her first husband, the old Duke of Leiningen, she considered herself lucky. She had come satisfactorily through that first marriage because of her own sound good sense; but everyone had agreed that the old Duke was a trial. From him, though, she had her dearest Charles and Feodore, and for them she was grateful; and she looked forward to the time when she would have her children with her in one nursery with that all-important child who was to be the ruler of England.

She was sure *she* was going to be the one to produce the heir – and wasn't she always right? Only Adelaide and Clarence stood between the throne and the child she would have; and there was a certain ineffectuality about Clarence which she recognized – and as for Adelaide she did not believe she was a strong woman. She lacked the radiant health of Victoria.

Soon, soon, she prayed every night. I shall have my child – and that child is to be the *one*.

Edward had told her of the gipsy's prophecy, which she would have dismissed as rubbish if it had concerned anything else. But this prophecy was right – only she did not accept that it would be a Queen. She believed it would be a King.

But a Queen would do very well as the English did not regard sex as a bar to sovereignty.

So it was a very satisfied Victoria who stood before her mirror surveying her plump but seductive form. The dress of gold tissue was so becoming to a widow. Adelaide would be dressed in white no doubt. But the fact that she was in gold was a symbol that she was not a newcomer to marriage and she had already proved her ability to bear children. Her darling Charles and Feodore were living evidence.

It was a very complacent Victoria who made her way to the Queen's drawing-room.

Adelaide was less composed. The dress was charming. The insignia of a bride – silver tissue and Brussels lace. And the effect was enchanting.

As the diamond clasp was fastened about her waist she thought: Even I look beautiful today.

Duchess Eleanor clasped her hands with delight.

'You look lovely, my dear. No bride ever looked more beautiful.'

'It's the dress that's beautiful, Mamma.'

'Oh, why must you always denigrate yourself!' exclaimed the Duchess impatiently.

'I don't want to shut my eyes to the truth, Mamma.'

The Duchess clicked her tongue; but she was not displeased. That unfortunate matter had been comfortably settled and the FitzClarences moved to South Audley Street. A victory, she decided; and it showed that the Queen was ready to treat Adelaide with due respect even if William were not.

125

'It is time to go,' said the Duchess, studying her daughter intently to make sure that all was well.

'I am ready,' said Adelaide.

In the drawing-room members of the royal family were assembling. The Cambridges were already there – Augusta looking very beautiful – and Mary with 'Slice'. The Duke of York arrived, without the Duchess, who was ill and unable to attend. Though they had not lived together for years they were good friends and the Duke was melancholy on his wife's account. None of the other brothers and sisters were present and the Duchess Eleanor, noting this, thought how strange it was. There seemed to be so many rifts in this family. She knew that the Cumberlands had been dismissed from the country and the Duchess was not received at Court. The rumours she had heard over the years of the quarrels of the family were certainly based on fact.

But that did not matter. Her daughter's wedding was about to take place.

Adelaide looked composed and quite lovely; the Duchess of Kent, Eleanor decided, was too flamboyant in her gold tissue. How buxom she was, how healthy! Adelaide looked frail beside her. But Adelaide had more grace. She might not be beautiful but she managed to look elegant – far more so than Victoria. But Victoria did look as though she were bursting with vitality and very fit to bear children – which was, after all, what this ceremony was about.

But Eleanor refused to think of that, for the Regent was leading in the Queen, who looked very old and very ill, and the Archbishop of Canterbury was ready to preside with the Bishop of London, the Prime Minister and the Hanoverian ambassador as witnesses.

Leaflets were distributed among the company on which the service was printed in German and English. Victoria had found it very difficult to learn English and knew scarcely anything of the language; Adelaide had progressed much better; but it was comforting to have the German translation.

The Regent took his place at the altar which had been set up in the drawing-room and the ceremonies began.

Thus were the Dukes of Clarence and Kent married to their Duchesses in the presence of the Queen and Regent.

The ceremony over, the Queen looked as though she were about to faint and the Regent insisted on conducting her to her bed.

'I insist,' he told her playfully. 'Dearest Madre, if you had one of your attacks on such a day we should all be plunged into melancholy.'

'I know that as long as you are there everything will be conducted in the most fitting manner.'

The Regent inclined his head in acknowledgement of this; and having handed her over to her attendants and telling her that he would come back to make sure she was comfortable before he left Kew, he returned to his guests.

The company then adjourned to the dining-room where a banquet awaited them. The Regent at the head of the table, a bride on either side of him, conversed with grace and wit while he consumed large quantities of the most excellent turtle soup, delicious fish garnished with highly flavoured sauces and venison.

Victoria, who had a good appetite, did justice to the food and the Regent talked to her in some German and chiefly French (which he found a more graceful language admirably suited to his musical voice). He did not forget Adelaide whose quiet charm appealed to him. As he commented afterwards to Lady Hertford, she was a pleasant creature if one did not look on her face.

Clarence was at first a little sullen because he believed that the FitzClarence children should have been at the wedding and the Queen had firmly refused to allow this.

She's got to accept her stepchildren some time, he was grumbling to himself.

But grievances never disturbed him for long and he was at last married . . . a state he had never achieved before, although he had made many attempts.

And Adelaide – she was growing on him. He thought: I'd rather have her than Victoria. There is something about her . . . gentle and kind. The Regent likes her – and he knows a great deal about women. I fancy he is more taken with her than with Victoria who talks too much and is too sure of herself.

His eyes met Adelaide's and he smiled almost shyly.

She thought: He is young at heart. I believe he will be kind. It is not so bad. I really believe I am rather lucky.

The banquet was over and the company went back to the drawing-room from which the altar had now been removed. The Regent walked about among the guests and talked to them in his charming affable way.

Then Leopold's carriage which he had put at the disposal of his sister and her husband arrived to take them to Claremont for the honeymoon.

The Regent took a farewell of the Duke and Duchess; and the company went out to see them ride away for the first stage of their honeymoon in that house which so recently had been the scene of so much happiness and so much tragedy.

The Regent then led the company on a tour of the gardens which were such a feature of Kew.

He had taken Adelaide's arm and told her how he remembered these gardens so well from his youth. Here he used to make assignations with delightful young ladies. Happy, romantic days.

He sighed, thinking of occasions when he had crept out of his apartments to meet Perdita Robinson, the heroine of his first big romance. What joy that had brought in the beginning and what humiliation in the end when she had threatened to publish his letters. But he would not think of the end of that affair, only the beginning when they had met in the glades of Kew and later on Eel Pie Island.

So long ago and yet with this young bride beside him they seemed like yesterday. He looked at her with affection. Suppose he were the bridegroom instead of William. He would be content. If he were rid of that woman. Oh God, why had fate been so cruel as to burden him with Caroline of Brunswick!

And here he was back to an ever-recurring theme. His bondage with that woman; his desire to escape.

'I grow melancholy,' he said to Adelaide. 'You see, I am envious of William.'

At the Queen's cottage beside the Pagoda they stopped for a

dish of tea; and afterwards they returned to the palace and as they came across the gardens it began to rain.

The Duke's carriage had now arrived. It was time to leave; the ceremonies were over.

William had been hoping that Duchess Eleanor would have been invited to stay at Kew, but the Queen had not mentioned this. It was typical of William's affairs that he should find himself on his wedding night to be in a quandary about his mother-in-law.

He looked hopefully towards the Regent, but his brother was saying his farewells in that manner which was slightly ceremonious and could clearly not be broached on such a matter at such a time.

He had been hoping too that someone might have offered him a house for the honeymoon as Leopold had offered Claremont to the Kents.

But William had always been treated less royally than his brothers; it was an attitude he seemed to attract.

And here was his carriage – new for the occasion – with his coat of arms glistening on it – very fine, he commented; but where could he take his bride? If it were to Bushy, how easy it would have been; but everyone had set their minds against Bushy. He was beginning to think they were right; there would have been too many memories of Dorothy Jordan there; there might even be some of her possessions about the place.

The only place was his apartments in Stable Court at St James's. They were not large nor particularly grand, but they had been his headquarters when he was at Court – and in any case it was all he could think of.

And the Duchess Eleanor must accompany them!

So through the rain they drove to St James's and when they arrived there it was to find a little crowd of people assembled to see the bride.

There was a little laughter to see the mother-in-law as well, but they could trust Clarence to get himself into ridiculous situations.

Adelaide, however, appealed to them; she bowed and smiled and if she was not as beautiful as the Duchesses of Cambridge and Kent, she was more affable; so they cheered her.

The people still waited when they went into the Palace and Adelaide came out and stood on the balcony. That she should do this in the rain, won their hearts still further and it was some time before they would let her go in.

William had given orders for the Duchess to be conducted to a bedchamber – and then he and Adelaide were alone.

He waved his hand at the furnishings. 'They should have been renewed,' he said. 'I thought we should go to Bushy.'

'I know,' she said in her halting English.

The bed was rather grand; William looked at it and laughed.

'It was put here for the King of Prussia not long ago when he paid a visit. He used these apartments then. They were somewhat shabby so this bed was put in for him.'

Adelaide touched the deep pink silk bedcurtains and in some embarrassment traced with her finger the fluting on the pillars of the magnificent four-poster.

He smiled at her; then he took her hands; and as she lifted her face to his she thought gratefully: I need not fear him.

Royal death and Royal birth

The Duchess Eleanor, having seen her daughter safely married, decided that her presence was no longer needed in England.

She therefore prepared to make her departure. Her quarters in Stable Yard, St James's were cramped and dingy, and she did not consider them suitable for her rank and her position as the mother of the Duchess of Clarence and the sooner she was home in Saxe-Meiningen where her son would most certainly be in need of her advice, the better.

Adelaide and William gave a dinner party for her the day after their wedding to which members of the royal family came to bid her farewell. The Queen was too ill to attend, so Eleanor drove out to Kew to say farewell.

The next day she left.

Her departure, Adelaide realized, was not without its advantages for a situation arose the day after she left which would have caused her great concern and would no doubt have made a rift between herself and her daughter.

Adelaide had made up her mind that if it were possible she was going to make her marriage a happy one.

She did not expect William to fall in love with her. I am not, she told herself, the sort of woman with whom men fall in love. But one thing she had discovered was his devotion to his children, and while some might deplore this, she admired him for it and she believed it showed an admirable trait in his character. She was not going to refuse to meet the FitzClarence children; in fact in the short time since her wedding day she had asked all sorts of questions about them, and he had delighted to talk of them. He was proud of the bravery of his sons in battle. Young as they were they had distinguished themselves; he was delighted with the beauty and charm of his daughters. And he was grateful to Adelaide for wanting to hear about them.

So they had made a start towards understanding – which, Adelaide had to admit, her mother would have done her best to ruin.

It was on the second day of her honeymoon that one of the attendants told her that the Duke had left Stable Court in a state of great agitation. She had difficulty in understanding but it seemed that there had been an accident and Major FitzClarence was in a dangerous condition. The Duke had rushed out immediately the news had been brought to him and had not even stopped to explain what had happened to his newly-married bride.

Adelaide passed an uneasy morning and finally the Duke arrived in a special carriage. From this was taken a stretcher on which lay the young man whom William had sent to greet her at Grillon's Hotel on her arrival in England.

'It's George,' shouted William. 'He's had an accident.' Then he was giving orders. 'Lift it carefully. He's broken his leg. Now! Got it? Be careful not to jolt it.'

Adelaide said: 'I should put him on the bed . . . our bed. It will be more comfortable.'

So Major George FitzClarence was laid on the bed which had

been made for the King of Prussia. Pale and shaken he looked apologetically at Adelaide.

'I was driving my carriage,' he said, 'when the horse took fright and bolted.'

'You will soon be well,' she told him. 'You will stay here and I will nurse you.'

'You! That's impossible.'

'What do you mean? Do I understand? Not possible? My mother has been ill often. I always nurse her.'

She was happy suddenly. Now she would show William that she intended to be not only a good wife but also a mother to his family. It was true the young man on the bed was about her own age, but that did not matter.

'*You* will nurse him?' said William.

'Why are you surprised? I am a good nurse. You will see.'

And they did see.

'It's a strange way to spend a honeymoon,' said William.

'But it is not such a bad way,' she told him.

He was beginning to be quite fond of her.

It *was* a strange honeymoon. Everyone was saying how typical it was of the Duke of Clarence to take his son by Dorothy Jordan to his wife so that she might spend her honeymoon nursing him.

'Let them talk,' said Adelaide. 'It is, after all, our affair.'

The Queen thought it a ridiculous situation and quite undignified. She would have protested but she felt too ill. Now that all her sons were married she had done all she could and it was up to them. This acceptance seemed to have its effect on her. It was as though she were gradually relinquishing her hold on life.

She sent for Adelaide meaning to remonstrate with her but when her daughter-in-law arrived she was feeling so ill that she merely commanded her to sit by her bed and tell her how she was liking England.

'I did hear young George FitzClarence is with you.'

Adelaide told her in fluent German how he had had his accident and that he was progressing. The Duke had been very anxious about him and she was not surprised, for George was a son of whom anyone would be proud.

'And you are content to spend your honeymoon nursing him?'

'I am content,' said Adelaide.

'You are a strange young woman,' the Queen told her bluntly.

'Do you find me so?'

'I find you . . . unusual, shall we say,' said the Queen; and she was silent, thinking back to the days when she had arrived in England. Would she have been prepared to nurse a son her husband had had by another woman? She was not sure. But she had come to the conclusion that there was a strength of purpose about this quiet young woman which was admirable.

She said suddenly: 'I think you may do a great deal for William.'

Adelaide waited but the Queen said no more.

She had fallen into a doze and lay so still that Adelaide wondered whether she should leave. She rose quietly but the Queen opened her eyes and said: 'Don't go. Sit there. You comfort me.'

So she sat while Charlotte dozed and, half asleep, thought of the past and all its trials and the anxieties her children had brought to her and the King.

A Queen's life could be a hard one. Would she have been happier if she had stayed at home in Mecklenburg-Strelitz and remained unmarried? Would this young woman have been happier if she had not married?

But I became Queen Charlotte, she thought. Perhaps in time she will become Queen Adelaide. And if she has a child that child could rule England.

What are we – any of us – but links in the chain?

At the end of three weeks George FitzClarence and Adelaide had become the best of friends and George could not say enough in praise of his stepmother. William would sit listening while they talked together in German – and at Adelaide's attempts at English – with a smile about his lips. His marriage was going to be a success; he was sure of it. He had forgotten Miss Wykeham already; she would never have nursed young George as Adelaide had done.

But they could not stay in England, for in spite of the extra money his marriage had brought him, his creditors were pressing and a stay abroad was a necessity. Besides, it had been arranged that he and Adelaide should join the Cambridges in Hanover, where young Adolphus was acting as Governor-General.

Adelaide did not look forward to another sea crossing but she did not protest and as the time drew near for their departure she went to see the Queen at Kew to say goodbye to her.

She felt melancholy as the carriage carried her through Hammersmith; and the reason was that she was going to say her last farewells to her mother-in-law. It was a strange feeling, for the Queen had shown her very little warmth and yet there had been something between them – a certain rapport which Adelaide instinctively knew Charlotte felt with very few.

If we were together for a long time we might become friends, thought Adelaide.

When she arrived at Kew the Queen received her in her bedroom where she was resting. Adelaide found Charlotte lying in bed, and she knelt and kissed her hand.

'Sit down, my child,' said Charlotte gruffly. 'So you are shortly leaving for Hanover. I am sorry ... but it is best. William is surrounded by his family here. It is better for you to be away. There you will get to know him.' She smiled crookedly. 'You will find him a little ... ridiculous. But perhaps you will teach him ...'

Adelaide did not answer.

'It is sad,' went on the Queen. 'Sad ... for princesses. I remember ...'

But she did not say what she remembered.

Adelaide believed that she would never forget these moments – the dark bedroom, the curtains drawn to shut out the sun which worried the Queen, the faint musty smell of illness – and she thought: This is the last time I shall see the Queen.

'You nursed that boy,' said the Queen suddenly.

Adelaide replied: 'The Duke was anxious for him. He is, after all, his son. He could not be turned away. I think the Duke is pleased that we have become friends.'

'Ten children,' said the Queen. 'An actress's bastards! The scandal! It was all scandals.'

'Perhaps there will be no more scandals. I shall do my best to see that there are none.'

134

The Queen said: 'My heart-felt wishes go with you. But William was always ridiculous.'

They were silent for some time during which the Queen seemed to have forgotten her visitor.

'I tire you,' said Adelaide at length. 'I but came to say goodbye before we leave. I will go now.'

The Queen nodded without opening her eyes and Adelaide kissed her hand and tiptoed from the room.

At the door she took one look round the room and her eyes rested on that little shrunken figure on the bed.

I shall never see her again, thought Adelaide, once more, as she shut the door quietly behind her.

She stood outside the door. How quiet it was! She believed that Death was already in that room, waiting to come forward and say: Follow me.

An irresistible impulse came to her to take one more farewell of the Queen; she opened the door quietly and stood on the threshold.

Queen Charlotte opened her eyes and they looked at each other.

'You . . . came back,' said the Queen.

'To say goodbye . . . again.'

'A last goodbye,' said the Queen.

Adelaide felt tears on her cheeks.

'Come here,' said the Queen; and she went to the bed and stood there.

'My dear child,' said Charlotte, 'God bless you.'

'God bless Your Majesty,' whispered Adelaide.

'Go now, child,' said Charlotte. 'I shall remember that you came back. I shall remember that you wept for me.'

Adelaide went out to her carriage, bewildered and yet exhilarated, wondering what had happened between her and the unloving and unloved Queen of England.

The next day Adelaide and William embarked on the *Royal Sovereign* but despite the elaborate furnishings of the royal cabins on board it was an uncomfortable crossing.

The Duke had no desire to go to Hanover. He had travelled

the world, he told Adelaide, when he was a young man and was sent to sea and he had had enough of travelling. He wanted now to settle in England.

'That's my home,' he said, 'and that's where my family is.'

He referred constantly to the FitzClarences.

Adelaide tried to tell him of her last meeting with the Queen but he did not listen. William liked to talk rather than listen.

'My mother?' he said. 'Oh, I fear she is a disagreeable old woman. She led the King a nice dance before he was put away.'

So it was useless to try to explain to him. She realized that there would always be things which it was impossible to discuss.

'And what is it going to be like in Hanover?' he demanded. 'Cambridge is Governor-General and you will have to take second place to his Augusta because we shall have no official position there. How shall you like that, eh? And Adolphus is nine years younger than I.'

'It will be of no importance,' said Adelaide.

At which he laughed.

'You know, you are the most easy-going woman I ever ran across.'

That seemed to amuse him.

'I trust,' she said timidly, 'that this does not offend.'

'Offend. Now what husband is going to be offended by a docile and obedient little wife?'

She smiled with him; he had not yet learned that although she did not fret over details such as this matter of precedence she had a determination of her own.

But perhaps he never would learn this.

They set up house in the Fürsten Hof and here they were plunged into the social life of Hamburg.

Augusta soon realized that Adelaide bore no malice because she must take second place to the wife of the Governor-General and the two became great friends.

Adelaide was enchanted by Augusta's delicate needlework and they often sat together while working. Augusta loved growing flowers and arranging them in the most artistic fashion; another hobby she shared with her sister-in-law, and the two young women enjoyed each other's company.

'Adelaide,' said Augusta, 'you are the most reasonable woman I ever met.'

They laughed together over the pomposities of the ceremonies they were forced to attend; but they liked best to talk of their possibilities of having children.

Augusta would whisper to Adelaide that she had really believed she was pregnant only to be disappointed; and she was not going to tell until she was sure.

So as they sewed they were praying for the realization of their dreams.

'I shall feel like singing the Magnificat,' said Adelaide.

Augusta was a little shocked, but Adelaide went on: 'I should really feel that I was blessed.'

'One day,' said Augusta, 'one of us is going to come to the other and tell her of great good fortune. I wonder who will be first.'

Shortly afterwards there was no need to wonder.

Augusta was the fortunate one. She was pregnant.

But a few weeks later Adelaide had equally exciting news. This brought the sisters-in-law even closer together. They could talk of nothing but the child each was to have.

'I pray for a boy,' said Augusta.

'I shall pray for a healthy child,' said Adelaide. 'Perhaps my husband would be better pleased with a boy but for myself I shall not mind. I think the greatest blessing a woman can know is to bear a child. I believe I shall experience complete happiness when mine is born.'

And Augusta, her beautiful dark eyes beneath those finely arched brows soft and tremulous, agreed with her.

When the Regent came into her bedroom in Kew Palace Queen Charlotte focused her eyes on him.

'Dearest Madre!' He knelt beside her bed.

'George!'

He kissed her hand – old, wrinkled, misshapen with rheumatism.

'I wanted to talk to you, George.'

'It is my pleasure to listen.'

'George, we have loved each other, you and I.'

He nodded.

'From the first moment they put you into my arms you were everything to me.'

He put a hand to his eyes.

'I want you to know that that was how it was ... always ... Even when we had our differences. I want you to know.'

'Madre, you tire yourself. Do not speak.'

She nodded and kept her hand in his.

It was affecting. She had not long to live which was sad. His father the King lived out his clouded existence shut away from the world, and it was said that he looked through the windows of his apartment, which was really his prison, and grimaced at any who looked his way. How pitiful! And this was the man who had once governed the nurseries and beaten him and his brothers unmercifully for demanding pastry with their fruit and fat with their meat. He had not known how to rule his family nor his country; and now he was known to be mad. But he still lived and the Queen was close to death. It seemed ironical that this should be.

We are all getting old, he thought. Soon it will be the end for us all. There were times when he believed he himself was close to death and would be the first to go. Fred's health was poor. So was his Duchess's, and the Regent's own wife – the Princess of Wales – went on living scandalously on the Continent, giving him, he was certain, every cause for divorce, but no one seemed to be able to bring him the evidence. If only ...

'Madre,' he began, but she did not answer.

He stared at her and murmured: 'The Queen is dead.'

The Queen was buried with great pomp and the Regent went into abject mourning; he shut himself in his apartments at Carlton House and gave himself up to grief.

Adelaide heard the news without surprise and with a deep sadness; she wished that the Queen could have lived long enough

138

to know that both she and Augusta were pregnant. Because of her condition it was impossible to be melancholy. She longed for the child, and she knew that she was intended above everything else to be a mother. It was for this reason that she had been eager to receive the FitzClarence children, and hoped that her relationship with them could be that of a mother.

But a child of her own would fulfil all her longings.

She and Augusta gleefully calculated. Augusta would be first – at the end of March; Adelaide some weeks later.

William was delighted. He had done his duty and like Adelaide he loved children.

'Wait until our son is born,' he cried, rubbing his hands with glee.

Frederica, Duchess of Cumberland, heard the news of Queen Charlotte's death with dismay.

'I wanted my dear aunt to know that I was to present her with a grandchild. To think that she died before I could give her that pleasure.'

'She would have done her best to disown him.'

'She could never have done that. He will be her grandchild and in succession to the throne of England.'

'What of Adelaide?'

A cloud passed over Frederica's face. 'Until children are born one can never be sure of them. Adelaide has not yet given proof that she can bear healthy children. From what I hear she is somewhat frail.'

'And what of Madam Kent?'

'Ah! She's the danger. She has her two already. Plump and full of vitality. Just the type to produce her young like a gipsy at the roadside.'

'I doubt they will allow it to be born so casually.'

'I am sure they will not. They are very certain. Kent is putting it about that there has been some prophecy. Oh, Ernest, I have one complaint against you. You are your father's fifth son – and two are now in the running against you.'

'You once said the obstacles made it more exciting.'

'Now I'm not so sure. There are too many to come before us.'

'Caroline is making herself very well known on the Continent.'

'With this Bergami of hers. I wonder.'

'The whole world wonders.'

'Don't forget if it's proved, the Regent could beat us all. What if she went too far?'

'She has already done that.'

'What if adultery were proved? What if he married?'

'Too many ifs, my dearest. No, it is only the Kent child we shall have to fear.'

None could have been more sure of success than the Duke and Duchess of Kent.

Their child was due some time in May.

'We must go back to England for the birth,' said Edward.

Victoria had already made up her mind that this must be done and had in fact planted the idea in Edward's mind.

'We certainly should,' she said.

'There is plenty of time yet.'

She agreed with that also.

'She must be born in the country she will one day rule,' said Edward.

'How certain you are that the child will be a girl. That prophecy, of course.'

'I have a feeling that it will be so.'

'Edward! You are the last man for fancies and yet . . .'

'And yet of this I am certain.'

'Feodore was saying only the other day that she wanted a little sister.'

'She will have one.'

The Duchess of Kent smiled with pleasure. She did not accept the Duke's certainty that the child would be a girl; but she was certain that the child would rule England.

There was only the offspring of the Clarences in between and she did not believe for one moment that Adelaide would bear healthy children.

In her way she was as sure as her husband that she was going to produce the successful candidate in the race for the throne.

*

As Augusta's time grew near William became very excited.

'You see,' he announced to Adelaide, herself in a state of advanced pregnancy, 'this child could be an heir to the throne. If anything should happen to our child and Edward's and Ernest's, this child could be a King or Queen of England.'

Adelaide shuddered at the prospect of anything happening to the precious burden she carried but William was notoriously tactless.

'Strange things happen in royal families when there is a throne at stake.'

'Strange things?'

'There have been rumours of babies being smuggled in.'

'But why should Adolphus and Augusta want to smuggle in a child?'

'If theirs were still-born . . .'

'But why should they want another child?'

'That they might have the honour of being the parents of the ruler.'

'You think that of Adolphus and Augusta!'

'Well, no. But this is an official occasion. I am on the spot. I must be present at the birth of the child.'

'Do you think Augusta and Adolphus will mind?'

'Mind. It is not a question of minding. It's a question of procedure.'

William was, as his mother would have said, making himself ridiculous again.

As soon as Augusta's pains began William was close at hand; he watched all who went into her bedroom with suspicion. Adolphus was half irritated, half amused. But there was nothing to be done; and if there were going to be unpleasant rumours it was better that William should be watchful to make them an impossibility.

Augusta knew nothing of William's vigil; and in due course gave birth to a boy. Her delight was overwhelming.

Adelaide was one of the first to congratulate her. She held the child in her arms and marvelled at him.

Oh God, she prayed, let mine be as lusty as this one.

'We shall call him George,' said Augusta.

Adelaide smiled. George. A king's name!

'It is well,' said Adelaide's doctor, a man who had served with Wellington's army, 'to take plenty of exercise. It insures an easy birth. No matter what the weather, exercise should be taken.'

Adelaide followed his advice. She walked regularly in the palace grounds, William often with her and even when she tired, as she often did, he insisted on her carrying out the doctor's suggestions.

During one of these walks the rain was so heavy that Adelaide was wet to the skin for the shower had been sudden and she was unprepared for rain. William, however, was determined that she should walk the prescribed time and the walk was continued.

A few days later Adelaide had a cold which was followed by pleurisy. The doctor immediately ordered bleeding.

This left Adelaide very weak and a few days after the birth of Augusta's little George her birth pangs began, although they were not due to start for several weeks.

The result was the premature birth of a little girl.

The child should be baptized immediately, advised the doctors; and she was christened Charlotte Augusta Louisa just before she died.

Adelaide was desolate and there was no comforting her. Moreover the bleeding had left her very weak and had robbed her of the stamina she needed to recover from the birth.

William was distraught.

He had lost his child but what most concerned him – somewhat to his surprise – was his fear at the prospect of losing his wife.

They had known each other less than a year; theirs had been entirely a marriage of convenience; yet he found that he would be wretched if he had to face life without her. She was not beautiful. She did not arouse his passionate desire ... and yet how he would miss her if he lost her.

It was very strange.

He was constantly in the sickroom; he talked perpetually to the doctors; he made a nuisance of himself as, poor William, he could not help doing. But she was aware of him and she knew it was due to his affection and this did help to sustain her in her great sorrow. But she was unhappy. She knew that she had longed for her child, but only now did she realize how passionately. Those waiting months had been the happiest of her life, because she had so longed for their fulfilment. And now . . . it was finished. She was delirious and the doctors said she was on the point of death.

William was at her bedside. He would nurse her. Only he! She must get well, he told her. What would he do if she did not?

Vaguely she was aware of him and his presence, while it encumbered her nurses, did give her comfort.

Augusta longed to visit her but hesitated. How would Adelaide feel if she, the successful mother, appeared to parade her triumph before her? So she did not come to the sickroom and the festivities which had been arranged to celebrate her little George's birth were cancelled.

But with the coming of April, Adelaide's condition began to improve.

William stayed at her side and would not leave her.

'You must not fret,' he said. 'That doctor . . . those walks. That was what brought on your illness. And then the bleeding . . . and you lost our child. But you're so young. There'll be others. My sister, the Queen of Würtemburg, has written sending affectionate messages to you. She says you will not want to stay in Hanover but will want a change of scene. She suggests that as soon as you are ready to travel we go and pay her a visit. Would you like that, eh? Because if you would not, we shall not go. I am going to take care of you now. Don't you fret. The next time everything is going to be well. I can't lose my wife. The children can't lose their stepmother. Not when they're beginning to be fond of her, eh?'

It was a little crude – the bluff sailor who spoke his thoughts aloud. But it was genuine and she was comforted.

And because she had lost this child, it did not mean that there would not be others.

*

Neither the Kents nor the Cumberlands could pretend to feel great grief when they received the news of Adelaide's tragedy.

They reacted according to their natures.

'*She* presents no difficulty,' said the blunt Frederica. 'She's not the child-bearing type.'

'It's the will of God,' said Victoria with the complacent air of one who knows herself to be the elect.

'I think,' she went on, 'that it is time we returned to England.'

And as usual the Duke agreed with her.

They should, of course, have left before; but Victoria had been so anxious to remain in Germany as long as possible so as to have first-hand information of Adelaide's confinement. It was very *convenient* that the birth should have been premature; and although she would not go so far as to apply the same adjective to the infant's demise, it was in her mind.

But it was all part of the pattern of fate.

Money was a difficulty, of course. They had left England because of the Duke's debts and as they were still unsettled it was a little dangerous to return; but the important child must be born in England.

They must borrow money for their journey; the Duke could drive the coach to save a coachman's wages; and as it was an exceptionally large coach they could carry quite a lot of their baggage in it.

It was April when they left and the news had just reached them that Adelaide and William had started on a visit to Würtemburg.

'She will have another try,' said Victoria glumly, but the Duke so trusted his gipsy that he was sure nothing would come of that or any try.

'We must take no chances,' said the Duchess.

She would engage a midwife whom she had heard was the best in Germany and the woman should travel with them – in case of accidents.

Why, by all accounts, but for an accident, Adelaide might have a healthy girl to stand in the way of the child who was about to be born.

They must be prepared.

Fräulein Siebold was a most efficient woman. She told the

Duchess that she did not anticipate much trouble, that all was going well, and she had no doubt that the child would be as bonny as Charles and Feodore.

So they set out for England.

Apartments in Kensington Palace had been prepared for the birth; and on 19 May, with the utmost confidence of success, Victoria settled down to produce her child.

In the early morning the child was born.

'A girl!' The Duchess heard the voices about her bed.

The Duke was at her bedside. She smiled at him faintly. 'I'm sorry it was not a boy.'

But the Duke shook his head.

'No,' he said. 'It was to be a great queen, you know.'

Now she believed in the gipsy's prophecy as firmly as he did.

Three days after the birth of a princess to the Duke and Duchess of Kent, Frederica, Duchess of Cumberland, produced her child. To her great joy – and that of the Duke – it was a boy.

'We'll call him George,' declared Frederica. 'It's a good name for a king.'

So during that year three candidates for the throne had appeared – two boys and a girl; but the girl being the daughter of the Duke and Duchess of Kent, the fourth son of the King, was in the lead.

Only Adelaide had been disappointed.

'But there will be another,' she assured herself, 'and the next time nothing shall be allowed to go wrong.'

It was her only hope of happiness; just as it was the prevailing fear of the brothers- and sisters-in-law.

145

Christening at Kensington

The Prince Regent was feeling peevish. He was undoubtedly growing old; he was obliged to use a touch of rouge to give his cheeks some semblance of the delicate colour that had glowed in them in his youth. The gout worried him too frequently; he was prey to mysterious illnesses which the doctors did not understand and for which they prescribed perpetual bleeding, which made him feel weak.

His wife was behaving outrageously on the Continent and in spite of all his efforts he could not get the evidence against her he wanted. And now there was all this fuss about babies in the family.

He had one grand-niece and two nephews; and how much more fitting it would have been if he had had a son.

It was not too late. He insisted on it. If only he could rid himself of Caroline he could marry and produce an heir like the rest of them.

He was sorry that Adelaide had lost her child. If he himself could not provide the heir he would rather William did it. He had never liked Edward who was too self-righteous; and he had taken a dislike to Edward's wife. Madame de St Laurent had been so much more charming and Madam Victoria gave herself too many airs. She was a typical German, he decided; arrogant, sure of herself and eager to lead everyone by their noses. She might lead Edward, but there it would stop.

Aggravating indeed that the woman should now be behaving as though she were the mother of the heiress to the throne. It was almost as though she was saying to him and his father and to William: Hurry up. Die please, so that my daughter can inherit the throne.

Madam Victoria of Kent must be relegated to her place. If he were to remain as unlucky as he had been since he met Caroline of Brunswick, then there was Adelaide and William and their child to come before Edward's and hers.

Simply because he was tied to Caroline, and Adelaide's child had died, did not mean that this infant was heiress to the throne.

Far from it. Madam Kent was counting her chickens before they were hatched.

He mentioned the matter to Lady Hertford who was constantly in his company and who, when she had become his devoted companion, saw that her family was there too. Her son, the Earl of Yarmouth, popularly known as the Yarmouth Bloater, was reckoned to be one of the Regent's closest friends.

Lady Hertford, frigid, and eager that everyone should believe that the relationship was a platonic one, disliked the Duchess of Kent as much as the Regent did. The woman with her laces, ribbons and feathers was overdressed; she was constantly surrounded by a retinue of little dogs; and her hats with their drooping feathers were quite ridiculous. It was not to be expected that Lady Hertford, that leader of fashion and as elegant in her way as the Regent was in his, should approve of the flamboyant Duchess of Kent.

'That woman is too sure of herself,' she told the Regent.

'As usual, my dear, we are in complete agreement,' he replied. 'It tires me merely to think of her.'

'She is arranging the christening of her daughter as though the child were a young Queen. She is really quite impertinent. Do you know, she tried to humiliate me.'

'My dear, how insolent of her! I think it is time Madam Victoria learned that we will not allow her to rule now as she believes her daughter will one day.'

'The Duchess of Clarence is far more amiable.'

'Far more, my dear.'

'I hear they are going to call the child Georgiana, as near to Your Highness as possible, of course.'

'They have not yet consulted me.'

Lady Hertford laughed coldly. 'Your Highness, I do not believe they intend to. The Duchess of Kent is arrogant enough to believe she can dispose of all normal formalities.'

'She will discover,' said the Regent grimly.

His irritation had increased. They had desired him to be the infant's godfather and indeed he must be. He was, after all, her uncle. William's affairs always went awry. He even had to marry a woman who lost her baby, and since this was so, nothing could

147

alter the fact that, for the time being, the most important royal child was this girl of the Kents.

But not for long, he promised himself. Next time William must succeed. It would be a pleasant day for him when the Duchess of Kent's daughter was obliged to take a step backwards for the sake of William's child.

The Duchess of Kent was in a state of exultation. Her child was in the lead – her 'plump little partridge', as someone had called her; a perfectly formed little girl, with a lusty pair of lungs and a look of smug satisfaction with the world as though she had come to stay in it for a very long time. When she thought of poor Adelaide's failure she pitied her; but the very fact that the Duchess of Clarence had not produced a living child could only add to the glory of this little one.

She and the Duke stood by the child's cradle, admiring. It was wonderful how she had fascinated Edward so that he had completely forgotten – or at least he gave no sign of remembering – that woman with whom he had lived all those years. He was absolutely devoted to his new family; and now that she had their little daughter and Feodore and Charles were with her, the Duchess could admit that she had acted wisely when she had accepted the challenge to give up her freedom and become the Duchess of Kent, for she had relinquished little compared with what she had gained.

'Georgiana,' she murmured to the Duke. 'A queenly name for a queen.'

'William and Adelaide still have to be considered.'

'Nonsense,' declared the Duchess. 'Adelaide will never succeed.'

The Duke believed her, as he was beginning to believe everything she said. Besides there was the gipsy's prophecy.

'Named after her illustrious godparents,' went on the Duchess. 'Georgiana after Uncle George and Alexandrina after the Tsar of Russia.'

'It is always wise to choose names with care.'

The Duchess nodded.

148

It was while they were discussing the baby's names that a note arrived from the Regent. It concerned the christening of their child. He could not allow them to give the child the name of Georgiana, he wrote, because they were also naming her Alexandrina. Surely it would be a breach of etiquette for his name to appear before that of the Tsar of Russia – nor would he wish it to appear *after* that sovereign's. In the circumstances he could not allow the daughter of his brother Edward to be given the name of Georgiana.

The Duchess looked at the Duke with horror when he translated the note into German for her benefit, for she had progressed scarcely at all with her English.

'Not Georgiana!' she cried. 'But it is her name. I have always thought of her as Georgiana. It is the only name for her.'

'The Regent forbids it.'

'Oh, he hates us. He hates our little girl.'

'I would not say that,' protested Edward mildly. 'But there is no doubt that he hopes Adelaide and William will forestall us. He is not going to accept our baby as the heir if he can help it.'

'He will have to,' declared Victoria fiercely.

'It's true. If Adelaide and William fail he will have to.'

'They *will* fail and he *will* have to,' repeated Victoria firmly. 'But what of my little Georgiana's names?'

'He says he will talk to me about them at the christening.'

'At the christening! But then he will choose just what *he* wishes.'

'We must abide by his decision, of course.'

The Duchess stamped her foot. 'The Regent is no friend of ours,' she declared.

'I never thought I was his favourite brother.'

'It is your wife he does not like. Your wife and your little baby daughter.'

'Oh no, you take this too much to heart. It is only a matter of a name.'

'Too much to heart. This is my daughter! Never mind. I will fight the whole world for her . . . and that includes the Regent.'

The Duke took her hand and kissed it. She was magnificent in her anger against the Regent and her zeal for the child.

'No matter if she cannot have a grand-sounding name,' he said. 'She has the finest mother God could have given her.'

And the Duchess was somewhat mollified.

A font had been set up in the Cupola Room and those who were to attend the christening of the daughter of the Duke and Duchess of Kent had gathered there.

All were awaiting the arrival of the Prince Regent, the chief godparent; he was late in arriving and when he did come it was easy to see that he was scarcely in a benign mood.

Curtly he received the greetings of the child's parents and made a gesture which suggested that the ceremony should start immediately.

The look he cast in the direction of the child's mother was almost distasteful. Overdressed, he thought. No sense of the solemnity of the occasion. These German women! And his mood was not softened by the memory the woman brought to him of his own wife. She had always been overdressed; too colourful; they were all the same.

The Archbishop of Canterbury was ready to begin. He picked up the child who fortunately did not yell; and taking her to the golden font looked askance from the Duke of Kent to the Regent as he waited to hear with what names the child should be christened.

'Alexandrina,' said the Regent testily.

'Alexandrina,' repeated the Archbishop.

The Duchess of Kent opened her mouth as though to speak but her husband for once was able to silence her with a look. Alexandrina! she wanted to cry. This was no name for an English queen. Georgiana! Georgiana! That was what she wanted. It was an echo of Gloriana, the name which had been bestowed by her admirers on another queen. Elizabeth would have been a good name. A right and proper name. But perhaps better still Georgiana to follow the Georges. And the Regent showed his contempt for them by proposing Alexandrina.

But the child should have a second name.

Breathlessly she waited, but the Regent was still silent.

'Charlotte?' whispered the Duke of Kent. For queens need not be called by their first names and but for the recent family tragedy there would have been a Queen Charlotte on the throne in the years to come.

But the Regent would not have Charlotte.

His eyes were on the feathered hat of the Duchess and the face beneath distorted by passion; the woman looked as though she were going to burst into tears of anger and frustration at any moment.

'She should be called after her mother,' pronounced the Regent.

The matter was settled. The baby was christened.

Alexandrina Victoria.

The Duchess left the Cupola Room in tears. Alexandrina Victoria. Were those the names of a queen?

Adelaide's disappointment

To Adelaide's delight she was once more pregnant.

'I told you so,' said the delighted William. 'Why, you didn't think I could manage it! Dorothy Jordan had ten children – one following close on the other.'

Adelaide had ceased to wince at his lack of restraint; she had come to accept it and understand that it was due to a kind of naïveté which was not unattractive. He did not use so many oaths now as he had, and seemed eager to please her. Better, she often told herself, that he should say openly what was in his mind than attempt to deceive her.

'I believe,' she said, 'that our child should be born in England, for it is almost certain to be the future sovereign.'

'Excellent! Excellent!' cried William. 'We'll begin our journey back at once – and take it slowly, eh? We'll go visiting as we travel.'

And so they set out – first to visit Würtemburg where they were warmly received by the Queen of that land. This was William's eldest sister, the Princess Charlotte, who as Princess

Royal had married – to the envy of her sisters – twenty years or so before and even then she was thirty or even just past it.

She had changed a great deal, having developed an enormous stomach. Her face had grown so fat that her eyes had almost disappeared; she had lost most of her hair and refused to wear a wig. But she greeted her guests with pleasure, particularly Adelaide.

'I know what it is to lose a baby,' she said; and she looked forward to womanly chats, she assured her, so they discussed pregnancies and babies and the Queen gave Adelaide lots of advice which Adelaide could not help viewing with some suspicion as the Queen had lost her child. But she was kind and good and talked of the old days in England and how stern her parents had been; and how glad she had been to escape from the dreary lives led by the princesses who spent their days waiting on their mother, filling her snuff-boxes and walking the dogs.

'Marriage was our only escape but Papa would not let us,' she explained. 'He hated the thought of our marrying and was determined not to allow us to leave. But I was the lucky one. He had so many daughters he could not refuse to let one escape. Oh, my dear, how terrified I was that something would go wrong, for my husband had been married before and there was a scandal about his first wife. Some said that she had been murdered. In any case she had disappeared. She was the sister of my brother George's wife, Caroline, she who is causing such a scandal in Italy and wherever she happens to be. So what could you expect in *that* family. However, it was proved that she was dead, at least it was proved to my parents' satisfaction – and I was married, although I was terribly ill, while I waited. I remember my skin went quite yellow – and it still was when I married. And now I have lost my husband. Oh, it is a sorrowful life. But you have your husband . . . and your baby on the way. William is a good man, although a trifle foolish at times. But who is not? I believe he will be kind to you.'

The Queen could not stop talking but as she spoke in German was easy to follow; and when she spoke in English her accent was a decided German one, so long had she been out of England.

But Adelaide enjoyed listening to her stories of life at the English Court in the days before her marriage.

'I am delighted that you have married William,' she told Adelaide. 'It is good for him to be sensibly married. His manners have improved since I last saw him. That liaison with the actress was not good. And all those children! No, there is the family to consider with us royal people. And I hear that the Duchess of Kent is giving herself *airs* because of this child of hers. There is one nose which is going to be put out of joint.'

'But the child is strong and healthy. She must be a very happy woman, for she already has two delightful children. I don't suppose she will grudge me mine when it comes.'

'It's the throne, my dear. That's what she'll grudge. I wonder if they know of your state? And she is not the only one who is going to be just a little put out.' The Queen of Würtemburg looked really grotesque when she laughed; and it was no use Adelaide's trying to explain that it was not so much a crown she was thinking of, as a child. Her very own child.

When they left Würtemburg they passed through Homburg where Elizabeth had just arrived with her new husband.

Elizabeth greeted them warmly; she was eager to entertain them, and so delighted to have as she confessed 'escaped' from England.

'Although,' she said, 'it seems a little sad now that Mamma is dead. Perhaps I should have waited a while. But how was I to know? And when the chance of marriage came I had to take it, hadn't I?'

'Are you happy?' Adelaide asked her.

She was happy, ecstatically so. Her husband was kind; he never minded having to be reminded to take a bath and he very often agreed to do so. He was amused that she should think it necessary. It was a matter of custom, of course.

She often thought of poor Augusta and Sophia who had never married. But Sophia had had her little adventure in her youth and there was young Tom Garth to prove it. Oh, Adelaide would learn the family scandals in time. That had been a very alarming – though exciting – occasion, when Sophia had had to be smuggled down to the seaside to give birth to the child she was going to have. Who ever heard of a royal Princess giving birth to an

153

illegitimate child, though it was considered fair enough for Princes to have as many as they thought fit. She stopped herself in time from referring to William's ten FitzClarences.

'I am beginning to learn something of my new family,' said Adelaide.

'What a family!' cried Landgravine Elizabeth. 'I think there are more intrigues and scandals in our family than there ever could have been in any other.'

'I am beginning to think so,' smiled Adelaide.

'And more to come, I don't doubt,' added Elizabeth.

After Homburg they made their way to Ghent where it was pleasant to be reunited with Ida, who had become a happy matron. She had never regretted her marriage, she told Adelaide.

'Of course it is not a grand marriage like yours, but I am happy here in Ghent as the Governor's Lady. It's all I am, Adelaide, and we are not rich, and just think you may be a queen. *You.*'

'Very strange,' said Adelaide, 'that it should be the plain one.'

'You are not so plain when one sees your goodness shining through.'

Adelaide laughed. 'You make me sound so very unattractive, Ida.'

'Then I didn't mean to. You look lovely. Particularly with that new maternal look you're wearing. Will it be soon, Adelaide?'

'It's some months yet. But I can't wait for it. I can't tell you, Ida, how intensely I long to hold my own child in my arms.'

'Dear Adelaide, what a fortunate child it will be, with the best mother in the world and a crown waiting for it. I wonder whether it will be a boy or a girl.'

'Quite frankly, Ida, I don't care. I only want a child.'

'I see you do. You were meant to be a mother. I hear accounts of all these babies. It is like a contest. Now that you are to have one, the others will be disappointed.'

'I hope not too much so. I wish there were not what you call a contest, Ida. I am not thinking of a crown for my baby. I want him . . . or her . . . to be happy.'

'Sometimes, Adelaide,' said Ida, 'I think you are too good to be true. Let's come and see my daughter Louise, who I am sure will provide a contrast to Adelaide the Good.'

'You overrate me,' said Adelaide, 'I can see nothing unusual in wanting a child.'

Ida slipped her arm through her sister's and they went off to the nursery.

The summer was passing. September had come and they had still not crossed the Channel.

'Soon the gales will start,' said Adelaide. 'We shouldn't delay longer.'

William laughed. 'I like a bit of movement on deck,' he told her. 'I've been in some seas in my youth.'

She was sure he had, but she dreaded a rough crossing and they had left it rather late.

The weather had turned very bad; there had been heavy rains and on more than one occasion their carriage had to be hauled out of ruts in the ill-made roads. Often they were wet through.

'We should have left earlier,' admitted William. 'Still, we'll soon be home now.'

But this was not to be. One evening when they were jolting along the roughest of roads Adelaide was beset by sudden pains. She knew what this meant and despair filled her heart.

They stopped at the nearest inn, where she was hastily put to bed; but there was no saving the child and so on the way to England, where she had planned the future sovereign should be born, Adelaide had her second miscarriage.

William was distraught. He thought of Dorothy Jordan who had gone on tour until the last few weeks before the birth of her children. The delicacy of Adelaide was something quite new to him. It had not occurred to him that the rigours of travelling through the Continent over rough roads, sleeping in not always clean and comfortable inns, was scarcely the way to treat a delicate and pregnant woman. Dorothy had rattled round the country to play in provincial theatres, and had always casually given birth to healthy infants. But Adelaide was not Dorothy.

Adelaide was heartbroken. For the first time she began to doubt her ability to bear a child. Her great comfort was William who, essentially a family man, was always at his best during such occasions.

155

'Never mind,' he consoled her, 'there'll be others.'

She felt too weak to do anything but smile her assent. What had gone wrong this time? She knew, of course. She should have remained at her brother's court until the baby was born, or as soon as she knew she was pregnant left for England. She had not taken sufficient care and it was her fault.

Dunkirk was not the liveliest of towns. 'I always had a dislike for it,' said William. 'I never took to the French, either. When you think of all the trouble we had to beat them.'

There was something else that made him wish to leave this country. It was not so very long ago that Dorothy Jordan had come here to die. Her memory was more vivid than usual here. He kept thinking of her waiting to hear news from England and dying, so they said, of a broken heart.

It was all over, he assured himself; but how could he stop himself thinking of it all? Some people were whispering that he was unlucky with his legitimate children because he had treated the mother of his illegitimate ones so badly.

George FitzClarence wrote from England that he was going to be married.

'You and Adelaide must be there,' he wrote. 'It won't be right without you.'

William showed the letter to Adelaide.

'You see how affectionately he writes of you,' he told her proudly, and she was pleased because she looked upon the actress's family as her stepchildren.

'How different she must have been from me,' she said. 'She had her children without trouble.'

'Dorothy was a strong woman,' said the Duke shaking his head. 'She'd be on the boards until a week or so before, playing those romping parts. You ought to have seen her as Little Pickle and Priscilla Tomboy. I never laughed so much.'

It was strange for a royal Duke – possibly a future King – to be discussing his mistress so freely with his wife. But that is how I want it to be, thought Adelaide. And she sighed a little; she had to compete with that strong buxom woman whom she had heard referred to as one of the most charming in England – now dead, nothing but a ghost, yet she lived on in William's mind as she did in that of Adelaide, who had never even seen her.

'I should have liked to be at George's wedding,' said William wistfully.

How she longed to remain on terra firma for a few days, just until she felt a little stronger. But if they remained William would miss the wedding and that would upset him deeply. Whatever else William was, he was a devoted father.

'We must sail at once for England,' said Adelaide. 'It would never do for his father to miss George's wedding.'

The crossing was a violent one and she had not thought it possible to be so ill. Her relief when they landed at Deal was immense. But she had not realized how weak she had become and the prospect of travelling to London was unendurable.

The carriage rattled along the coast road. William sat beside her anxiously watching her, but she was scarcely aware of him.

She did not ask where she was going; she did not care; all she longed for was the comfort of a bed.

'It's all right,' soothed William. 'We'll soon be there.'

When she was carried from the vehicle she felt the cold sea breezes on her face and knew they had come only a few miles.

William was saying: 'Here you shall stay until you have re-covered your strength.'

She was carried within walls, undressed by her servants and put to bed.

William left her and rode on to London to be in time for George's wedding.

Adelaide's couch had been taken on to the ramparts and wrapped up in rugs she lay there watching the waves breaking about the shore, and on clear days looking across the sea to the coast of France.

She had learned that she was in Walmer Castle, whither William had brought her before going on to London; this was the home of Lord Liverpool, Warden of the Cinque Ports, and here she could be entertained and cared for until she was well enough to go on to London.

William returned to Walmer and excitedly he told her of

George's marriage – a most suitable one to a charming girl, Mary, who was the daughter of the Earl of Egremont. He was very happy with the union and was sure George had chosen wisely.

'He was sad that you were not at the wedding,' William told her. 'He is longing to present you to his bride, which he will do as soon as you return.'

'And when is that to be?'

'Not,' said William sternly, 'until you are well enough to travel.'

He was certainly changing, she thought. Perhaps in time he would abandon his sailor's oaths completely; perhaps he would cease to remind her that once he had loved a woman who was possessed of every attraction that she lacked – except one, which was royalty.

Lord Liverpool, the Warden, declared that they must make use of his house for as long as they wished to; and this they did. Adelaide taking walks in the delightful gardens and on the ramparts of the castle until she regained her strength, and William delighting in being so close to the sea; he would stand in the face of a strong wind and declare that he could almost believe himself to be on deck in mid-ocean.

But winter was almost on them, and the fogs of November were penetrating the castle. Clearly they could not take advantage of Lord Liverpool's hospitality for ever. Moreover, Adelaide's health was much improved and her hopes were high that she would soon once more be pregnant. They must return to London.

So one November day they drove out from Walmer Castle and took up their residence in the Duke's apartments in Stable Yard, St James's, which seemed dark and close after the airy ramparts.

Fulfilment of a prophecy

That winter was one of the worst in living memory. The Thames was frozen and the poor were dying in the streets from cold and hunger. The Regent had commanded that centres in London be opened, that those who had neither food nor shelter should go there and receive both.

The cold persisted.

In Kensington Palace the Duchess of Kent cared for her daughter, feeding her herself for she told the Duke this was natural, and therefore best and nothing but the best was good enough for little Alexandrina.

Every time she uttered the child's name she grew angry. It was quite clear, she said, that the Regent disliked both her and her daughter. And how a man could behave so unkindly to an innocent child, she could not understand. The Duke chided her gently; it was well that she spoke in German so that none of the servants could report her words and they reach his brother's ears. The Duchess snapped her fingers. What did she care for an ageing roué who was more dead than alive. The sooner he died, the better, and Clarence too, for then there would be no one to stand between Edward and in time, Alexandrina.

She adored her little Alexandrina; and so did Charles and Feodore. They were allowed to watch her bathed and dressed and even hold the child now and then. The Duchess wished everyone to realize as soon as possible that there was something very special about their little sister.

Fräulein Louise Lehzen had come over from Coburg to be her nurse – a very forthright woman, daughter of a Lutheran clergyman, she had already decided that Alexandrina was her special charge; and having great confidence in her, the Duchess encouraged this.

The Duke and Duchess discussed the child continually. She was healthy: she was bright: the Duchess never tired of telling everyone how bright. She should be seen in public as frequently as possible, said the Duke; and the baby carriage was wheeled to the most unsuitable places – so said the Regent; and after little Alexandrina had appeared in the Park during a military parade the Regent ordered that there should be an end to these public displays of the baby.

The Duchess laughed aloud at what she called the Regent's jealousy. Never mind. Nothing could alter the fact that *her* child was at the head of the list for the succession and only Adelaide and William could displace her.

'That old sailor-man!' she scorned. 'That fragile creature! She'll never bear a healthy child.'

'How can she,' agreed Edward, 'when the prophecy says that our daughter is to be the great queen?'

'My blessed angel,' cooed the Duchess, picking up her child and covering her face with kisses.

The baby uttered no protest, being accustomed to such displays of affection.

All might be well with the child but there were other matters to concern the Duke and Duchess of Kent.

'These bills,' groaned the Duke. 'These incessant bills!'

'But I thought you had settled them all.'

'You have no idea of the magnitude of my debts. My ideas for disposing of Castle Hill would have settled everything if it had worked. But it was not to be.'

'How tiresome these tradespeople are! But, Edward, you should have economized.'

'I am trying to, my love. I am trying to.'

'I will speak to Leopold,' said the Duchess.

She trusted her brother Leopold beyond all men, thought Edward grudgingly. And Leopold, it had to be confessed, was an extremely serious, capable young man.

He listened gravely to an account of their difficulties and offered them Claremont where they could live more cheaply than in Kensington Palace and where the country air would be so good for Alexandrina.

One could always trust Leopold, said the Duchess; and the family moved out to Esher and there lived comfortably for some weeks, while Alexandrina thrived; but tradesmen were not so contented. Claremont was a little farther away than Kensington, but the Duke was still accessible and the bills continued to arrive.

Since the gipsy had told him that he would beget a great queen and he had married his Duchess who had so promptly given birth to a daughter, Edward had become very susceptible to superstition.

Prognostications were constantly appearing in the papers and these he read avidly, almost always seeing something in them which referred to himself or his family. And as the royal family figured largely in these prophecies, he did not always have to tailor them to his fancy.

He was reading the papers one morning at breakfast, a habit he had kept up with the Duchess as he had with Julie, when he suddenly exclaimed 'Good God!' and turned very pale.

'What is it?' asked the Duchess, putting aside the letter she was reading.

'It says that two members of the royal family are going to die this coming year.'

'Well, the King is getting worse they tell me, and the last time I saw your brother George he looked as if he would not last long.'

'Death strikes in strange places,' said the Duke in a hollow voice.

'But they both look to me as if they are not long for this world.'

'I do agree. It's such a glittering possibility my dear. It dazzles me.'

'There would have to be three deaths before you were on the throne,' the Duchess reminded him.

'And then it would be Alexandrina's turn.'

'The darling!' murmured the Duchess.

'I know. But not yet. It would be disastrous if she came to the throne too early. I must take more care of my health. I must make sure that I live until she is eighteen . . . at least. She would be too young before that.'

The Duchess nodded complacently. *She* intended to guard her Alexandrina. And she was certain that she was as capable of doing so as the child's father was.

'Yes,' Edward was saying, 'I must take care of myself. You know my tendency to catch cold.'

'I know it well,' said his Duchess. 'And you must take care. Our baby will need you.'

'We shall have to live more simply. I must discharge my debts. It is somewhat expensive here, and the tradesmen are too close. The sea always agreed with me and the breezes would be excellent for the baby.'

161

'They would,' agreed the Duchess.

'Where do you suggest? Not Brighton. I am sure *he* would object if we went there.'

'No . . . not Brighton. That would be far too expensive. We must think of some little place . . . far away from the high fashion . . . and creditors.'

They discussed the matter for some days; and finally decided on Sidmouth.

The Duke's barber applied the dye to his hair and his whiskers. It was their secret.

I look like a young man, thought the Duke, and while I look like a young man I shall remain one.

He was thankful that he had not lived the kind of life that some of his brothers had lived. He had been abstemious in his habits; he had never become involved with women but had been faithful to Julie and now to his Duchess. He had been in control of his emotions so that now he had been forced to part with Julie he rarely gave her a thought, but had become devoted to his wife and daughter; he was fond of his stepchildren. He intended to live to a ripe old age and when he departed to hand over the throne – which by that time would be his – to a daughter who would have been taught that her destiny was to be a great queen.

Before Christmas they would set out for Devon; he had already made the plans in his precise way and decided where they would stop for the night during the journey. The Duchess would carry Alexandrina herself; she was too precious to be left to nurses.

Fresh air! he thought. What could be better? Alexandrina must be taught to appreciate it.

They left Claremont with as little ceremony as possible because he did not wish his creditors to know where he had gone. Not that he had any intention of not paying them; but they must learn to be patient.

The journey was long and tedious and the weather continued to be bitterly cold. The Duke, though, had set himself certain sightseeing tours on the way and no matter how bleak the conditions he would not alter his plans. As a result of one of these jaunts he caught a cold; the Duchess was angry with him, demanding to know what he would say if Alexandrina should take it from him?

'What is a cold?' he asked with a shrug.

'I don't want my child to catch it,' retorted the Duchess grimly; and she would not allow him to come near the precious infant.

He laughed at her and said it would not be for long. He was the strongest member of his family; he always had been. Fresh air would soon cure his cold. He was a great believer in fresh air, and sea breezes were the best in the world. Oh, they had been wise to come to Sidmouth.

But as the days passed and it grew clear that the Duke could not shake off his cold, the Duchess grew alarmed.

She discussed the Duke's health with his equerry, John Conroy, a man in whom she had great confidence. He had been an army captain but had decided that he could make a more exciting and profitable career in the Duke's household; and in this he seemed to be right for he was a favourite with the Duchess, which was essential to keeping the Duke's favour. Although Conroy did not look in the least like the Duke, they were of a type and many people noticed this similarity between them.

Conroy thought that the Duke should give up pretending that he merely had a bad cold which could be cured by doses of fresh air, take to his bed and see his doctors.

'I will persuade him to it,' said the Duchess firmly; but before she could do so Edward was so exhausted and unable to control his breathing that of his own accord he took to his bed. Before the day was out he was in a fever; and the doctors arrived to diagnose a congestion of the lungs.

The Duchess, alarmed, did what she always did in moments of stress – she sent an urgent message to Leopold who arrived shortly afterwards with his own doctor, Stockmar, in whom he had great confidence and who was his friend as well as his physician.

It was too late to do anything for Edward who was clearly dying. He should make his will without delay, said Leopold, and Dr Stockmar agreed with him.

The Duke feebly gave his assent and the will was drawn up and signed by him.

He lay back breathless on his pillows, a hint of whiteness showing at the roots of his hair and beard for he had been too exhausted to endure his barber's ministrations; he had become an old man in a few weeks and as the Duchess stood at his bedside, herself weary and exhausted for she had been up nursing him for five days and nights, she was asking herself what effect this was going to have on Alexandrina.

She had left the child with her nurses – fearful that she might carry some contamination from the sickroom. Fräulein Lehzen was a treasure. No English nurse could have received the Duchess's absolute trust, and little Alexandrina was safe with Lehzen until her mother could return to her and give her her full attention.

And as she sat by her husband's bedside she thought of her relations presided over by the wicked Regent, who did not like her and was not impressed by the charm of Alexandrina. What would become of them if they were left to battle alone? But there was one thing they could not take from her. If Adelaide and William could not produce a child, then her precious daughter must be Queen of England.

Nothing can alter that! It was her triumphant thought as she looked at the man in the bed who, such a short time before, had been strong and healthy.

He was dying. She knew it. He knew it too.

'Victoria,' he whispered and she bent over him.

'You will be alone.'

'I have friends. Leopold . . . my dear brother Leopold.'

'Listen to his advice. He will be a father to the child.'

She nodded.

'The prophecy . . . Who would have thought I was one of them? It should have been . . .'

She shook her head. 'Please don't talk. You distress yourself. You are going to get better. I know it,' she lied.

But he knew he was not going to be better. The prophecy had said that two members of the royal family would die and he was destined to be one of them. But there was that other prophecy. A great queen. Their daughter. It was something the Duchess must never forget now that he would no longer be there to remind her.

'I will never forget it,' she told him. 'Her welfare shall be my main concern. She has been brought up by myself . . . I will trust no other with her.'

'Oh, that I could have been there!'

'You may trust me.'

'There is no one else to whom I could trust our daughter.'

She nodded and pressed his hand firmly.

'Rest now,' she said.

He closed his eyes.

She thought of the day he had come to Leiningen, her indecision, their brief life together and the result of that union: her own adorable chubby precious child.

Everything had been worth while and soon once again she was to be a widow. She would never marry again. She now had her mission in life which was to prepare Alexandrina to be the Queen of England.

The Duke of Kent was dead and lay in a small house in Sidmouth.

John Conroy said: 'We must take the Duke to Windsor for burial.'

But how? the Duchess wanted to know. The journey would be expensive. She had no money, and it would be a costly matter to take her family and their attendants and the furnishings they had brought with them back to Kensington and the funeral cortège to Windsor.

'We must appeal to the Regent,' said Conroy. 'He will surely make himself responsible for the Duke's funeral expenses.'

Dear Conroy! She wondered what she would do without him.

The Regent's secretary wrote a cold note implying that his brother's funeral expenses were no affair of his, but fortunately Leopold was at hand.

'Leopold, what am I going to do?' she asked him in distraction. 'It's clear that the Regent dislikes me, that he is not going to help and that he refuses to give little Drina the place she should have. He is a hateful, jealous man. He was just the same with his own daughter Charlotte. He cannot bear anyone else to be popular and of course the people adore my child.'

'Let us be calm,' said Leopold. 'There is nothing anyone – even the Regent – can do to displace Alexandrina in the succession, except of course William and Adelaide, if they can produce a child. And that is a hazard we must face. However, it has not yet happened. The fact is that at the moment your daughter stands an excellent chance of ascending the throne being the first of the younger generation. The point, though, is getting the Duke buried, and you with your family and servants out of Sidmouth. But that is merely a beginning. How are you going to live? I believe you have very little money. The Duke left many debts which you will be asked to settle. Yours is not a very rosy prospect, sister.'

'I know it well. Oh, Leopold, how unfortunate we are! You to lose your wife, I to lose my husband.'

Leopold looked at her with faint exasperation. How could she compare either of her husbands with his lovely young and vital Charlotte. But their cases were not dissimilar. He had been married to the heiress to the throne; and his sister might well be the mother of a future queen. How badly these English treated their German relatives whom they had brought into the closer circle of the family. They were noted for their quarrels; and now it seemed one was brewing between the Regent and his sister Victoria.

He sighed. He had been fairly handsomely treated, having been given an allowance of £50,000 a year. He supposed he could not allow his sister to live in penury and it seemed that the Regent would do little for her. And if Adelaide had a child she would be reduced to no importance whatsoever.

'I shall go back to Germany,' the Duchess was saying. 'I will take up my life where I left it when I married Edward.'

'That would be a foolish step to take,' warned Leopold. 'Alexandrina must be brought up in England. It is a great mistake for those who may well rule one country to be brought up in another.'

The Duchess was secretly exultant for she was entirely of his opinion, her point being that she did not see how she could possibly continue to live in England without an income.

Leopold as usual came to the rescue. He would pay the Duke's funeral expenses; he would pay for the transport of the Duchess and her family to Kensington; and he would give the Duchess an income of £2,000 a year.

The Regent wept elegantly when he heard of the death of his brother. He told Lady Hertford that he was affected . . . deeply affected. Edward had not been his favourite brother, he admitted; but family ties were strong. He recalled so much from nursery days.

'Your Highness was most displeased with him over the Mary Anne Clarke affair.'

Oh dear, how tiresome! It was definitely not the time to refer to that. Edward had broken one of the rules of the royal brothers which was 'United for Ever' and, some said, deliberately worked against the Duke of York. The Regent preferred to believe it was only malicious gossip but his opinion of Edward had changed since. Most decidedly it was not the moment to refer to it.

Lady Hertford could be extremely tactless. He looked at her coldly. She had never really brought him comfort. And to think that it was on her account that Maria had left him. How often did he regret the loss of Maria! Of course her temper had been exasperating and she had not been particularly kind and understanding to him since she had left him when he did not wish her to go, but how often he wished that she were back! He had given up everything for Maria – and she had left him! He was most unfortunate in his relationships. He was tied to a woman he loathed; Maria had deserted him; and Lady Hertford who had always been frigid was of little comfort to him.

But there was one other who occupied his thoughts quite frequently. This was Lady Conyngham. There was something so comforting about her. She did not give herself airs like Lady Hertford; she appeared to have an easy-going temper, not like Maria. Whenever it was possible he summoned her to his side and bade her talk to him and this she did in a carefree artless way which he found extremely diverting.

She was plump – how he loathed lean women; she was handsome; no woman could attract him if she were not. She never gave herself airs. She quite frankly admitted that she was not of the aristocracy although she had married into it. She was at a comforting age – in her early fifties, a few years younger than he was himself. She was in good health and understood little of politics. Oh, these women, like Lady Hertford, who liked to dabble in state matters; how trying they could be! She would never be obsessed by her religion. It was Maria's religion, he was sure, which had broken their relationship. Elizabeth, Lady Conyngham, was in fact the most comfortable person at court and it gave him more pleasure to be in her company than that of anyone else. She had a complaisant husband. The Marquis Conyngham was no doubt pleased to see the favour his wife was finding with the Regent; she was motherly; she had four children to prove it; and she was rich in her own right, for it was money which had brought her her place in the peerage.

She had told him herself that her grandfather had been a clerk and her grandmother the daughter of a hatter. Her father had been a most excellent business man and had made a fortune in what the Regent could not remember. But his two daughters had married titles.

'Papa bought us a title apiece, Your Highness,' Elizabeth explained to the Regent, and he laughed with pleasure at her frankness.

'Politics, Your Highness,' she would say. 'I know nothing of politics. I am not clever like some. But I can tell a good diamond when I see one and I know how to be kind to my friends.'

An admirable woman. With her large languishing eyes and her comfortable maternal bosom, she offered just what he needed at this time.

He was thinking how much he missed the chats he had with his mother who had so adored him. He missed her more than he would have thought possible. There was something completely maternal about Elizabeth Conyngham; and at the same time she offered all the charm of a mistress. Comfortable, that was the word he would apply to her. It was something Lady Hertford had never been. Maria yes, at times; but there was Maria's devilish temper.

If he could go back to Maria . . . Ah, if he could! But he could not now. There would be too many recriminations. Besides, how could he, the Regent, live openly with a woman whom people believed to be his wife and who was a Catholic!

There was the crux of the matter. Maria's adherence to her religion. That was what was so comforting about Lady Conyngham. She had no stern principles which constantly ruined one's peace of mind.

He brought his mind back to Lady Hertford, sitting there elegant, it was true, like a porcelain figure, perfectly dressed, looking as though she were carved out of stone. An iceberg, rather. He wondered he had ever thought her attractive. There was no womanliness about her.

'I have never known the people so hostile to Your Highness,' she was saying. 'The mob threw stones at my carriage yesterday and called out the most uncomplimentary things about you.'

He shifted uneasily. Why was she always stressing his unpopularity? She herself was partly responsible for it. If he had stayed with Maria he would have been far more popular. Maria had always been a favourite with the people, whereas they loathed Isabella Hertford.

'No doubt they were intended for you,' he said coldly. 'And now I shall take my leave.'

She looked surprised for he had so recently come. But there would be more surprises awaiting Lady Hertford.

The poor old man, blind, deaf and lost to the world, who was the King of England, lay in his chamber in Windsor Castle. It had been little more than a padded cell. He did not know what events were taking place; he did not even know where he was, or sometimes who he was.

There were occasions when he would see a picture from the past of a young prince learning to be a king, of a young man in love with a beautiful Quakeress, visiting her secretly, suffering remorse for his treatment of her; sometimes in his muddled thoughts he saw lovely Sarah Lennox making hay in the gardens of Holland House and dreamed of marrying her; he saw his wife, the plain Princess Charlotte, who had become his Queen and borne him many children.

In the dark recesses of his mind he heard the defiant voice of a handsome boy raised in protest in the nursery demanding meat on the days when his father, the King, had said there should be no meat; then the handsome boy was an elegant young man . . . in trouble . . . always in trouble. Words formed on the lips of the poor blind, mad old man. 'Actresses, letters, wild living . . .' 'Ten sleepless nights I've had in a row thinking of those sons of mine . . .'

And there were no days, only the long endless night, with rough hands to tend him – and sometimes laughter at the foibles and follies, the childish inanities of a man who had once been their King. No light . . . only darkness . . . no understanding . . . only fleeting pictures . . . vague memories that mocked him and ran from him when he sought to catch them like mischievous boys in a royal nursery.

He did not know that his granddaughter, young Charlotte, was dead; he did not know that Charlotte his wife had gone; nor that the Prince of Wales had become the Regent and King in all but name because his father the true King was helplessly insane, living in darkness behind the strong grey walls of Windsor Castle.

He knew nothing – except sometimes, that he was waiting for the end.

Once he had said before he was blind, before the darkness had descended on him: 'I would that I could die for I am going mad.'

He did not say that now. But somewhere in his mind was the longing for release.

And one morning when his attendants came to his room they saw that it had come.

'The King is dead,' they said.

The Regent was confined to his bed with an attack of pleurisy. His doctors had bled him but he showed no sign of improving. His great bulk did not make breathing easy and it was generally feared that he could not live long.

In the streets they were shouting: 'King George III is dead. Long live King George IV.'

'What is it they are shouting?' he asked.

'Your Majesty,' they called him. So at last, he thought, it has come.

All his life he had been bred for this; he had known from nursery days that one day he would be King and he had longed to wear the crown. And now? He was not so sure. He had had a taste of sovereignty as Regent. The people had loved the Prince of Wales better than they loved the Regent. Now perhaps they would prefer the Regent to the King.

The glory had come too late. He was too old and ill for it.

He lay back in his bed and remorse came to him. He and his father had never been good friends. There had been a natural enmity between them. It was always so in the family. It was a Hanover tradition that fathers should quarrel with sons. So many things he might have done. So many little kindnesses.

He wept and they were real tears.

'I should have been a better son to him,' he murmured.

He was in a low state. His spirits would rise when he felt better. He would send for Lady Conyngham to come and talk to him. She would cheer him.

And then he thought: I am King. Then she ... that loathsome woman will be Queen.

Oh God, what will this mean? She will return to England. She will want to be at my side. She was content enough to stay away when she was Princess of Wales. But now she will want to be recognized as Queen of England.

The thought of what this could mean destroyed his peace of mind. No one could comfort him. Not even Lady Conyngham.

There was real anxiety for the state of the King's health. His doctors insisted that he must not dream of attending his father's funeral. Even the people, who had grown to hate him, were concerned for him now. They might taunt him and ridicule him but they did not want to lose him.

His doctors prescribed the air of Brighton which had never failed to benefit him, and as soon as he was able to be lifted from his bed he travelled down to the Pavilion with a few special friends and there he attempted to regain his strength.

At Windsor the old King was buried with the pomp due to his rank. The bells tolled and the trumpets rang out to remind everyone that this was the passing of a king. He had lived more than

171

eighty years – nine of them in a state of insanity. No one could really regret his passing yet many remembered that he had been a man who had always striven to do his duty.

The last rites were performed. A new reign had begun, but how long would it last? was a question on everyone's lips, for the new King was a semi-invalid so swollen with gout and dropsy that it was said the 'water was rapidly rising in him'; he was beset by mysterious illnesses; some even implied there were lapses when he suffered from his father's complaint.

That may have been but he was a King and whatever his ailments, however gross his body had become, he only had to appear in public to dazzle all who beheld him.

A new King meant a coronation. And what of the Queen?

The people were not displeased with George IV; he could always provide diversion.

They were right in this.

Very soon the news spread through the country. Caroline, wife of George IV, having learned that she was the Queen of England was coming home to claim her rights.

She shall be Victoria

Adelaide and William could not stay in the inadequate apartments in Stable Yard and William took her down to Bushy House. The grounds delighted her; so did the house itself which she saw as an ideal country residence, not grand enough for ceremonious living and yet spacious enough to exist graciously.

'It's enchanting,' she told William, who was delighted.

'I always thought so,' he replied. 'Some of the happiest years of my life were spent here.'

She smiled. She had learned not to be in the least jealous when he referred nostalgically to his life with Dorothy Jordan. 'The children always loved it,' he added wistfully. 'They made it their home.'

'I hope they will continue to think of it as such.'

He gave her that dog-like look of gratitude which was often on his face when he regarded her. He wanted to tell her that when he had married her he had seen her just as a vehicle for providing an heir to the throne. Somehow it had become different; and it was due to her. He was well aware of that. He himself was changing. He was no longer the crude sailor he had always fancied himself to be. George had said: 'William, Adelaide is good for you. You've ceased to be a sailor and are becoming a gentleman.'

He felt he must treat her gently – far more so than he had treated Dorothy. There was a fragility about Adelaide; and her pleasant placidity was a great contrast to Dorothy's vitality and quick temper. It was impossible to quarrel with Adelaide. Of course he could not feel for her the wild passion he had felt for Dorothy; he could not in fact understand his feelings. It was almost as though in spite of himself a sturdy affection was becoming the foundation of his family life. He was proud of this quiet pleasant girl who was his wife. She was no beauty it was true, but she had dignity and her charm of manner served her well.

As he crossed the threshold of Bushy House with her he felt a sudden happiness such as he had not experienced since the death of Dorothy. Those rumours of her not being dead or, worse still, dead and unable to rest had worried him.

Now, oddly enough, with Adelaide beside him in the house which had been Dorothy's home, he could find peace.

Everywhere there was evidence of Dorothy. He had planned the gardens with her, and he only had to look back into his memory and he could see Dorothy on the lawn surrounded by the children, sitting there laughing with them as she used to on those occasions when she slipped away from her duties at the theatre to come home. He could see her playing pranks such as those she played on the stage in the role of Little Pickle to amuse the children. It was not really so long ago.

Bushy was haunted by memories of Dorothy but with Adelaide beside him strangely enough they were not unhappy memories. He could imagine himself explaining to Adelaide his feelings for Dorothy. He wanted her to understand the strength of that love which had enabled them to live together so cosily for twenty years and bring up ten children. And he had deserted her in the end and she had fled from the country and died with no one but a woman companion beside her. Poor Dorothy, the comic actress whose life had ended in tragedy.

Adelaide seemed to guess his thoughts.

'Yes,' she was saying, 'the children must continue to think of this as their home.'

'I will tell them what you say.'

William was already making plans for the future. They would live here together – all the unmarried ones – and the grand-children would come and visit them; it would be as he and Dorothy had often planned it should be when she gave up the stage. It had always been a dream of hers to give up the stage and settle down to enjoy domesticity. Only instead of Dorothy presiding over the family, it would be Adelaide, Duchess of Clarence – a title he could never have given Dorothy.

One thing that had distressed Adelaide was the ever-present con-flict which existed throughout her new family. She had heard that the Kents had given themselves such airs since the birth of their daughter that they had alienated the Regent himself and that the Cumberlands and the Cambridges were extremely put out by the fuss that was made of the little girl at Kensington Palace who, because her father was the eldest member of the family to have a young child, was being considered as the future Queen.

'It is not good,' said Adelaide to William. 'And what is that poor woman feeling at Kensington – so recently widowed and the family so much against her. I think, if you have no objection, I will call on her.'

William, who was accustomed to Adelaide's good sense which far exceeded his own, replied that if Adelaide wished to call on Victoria Kent he saw no reason why she should not.

So Adelaide called at Kensington Palace where she was re-ceived by a somewhat suspicious Victoria.

'It is good of you to come,' said Victoria, asking herself: Has she come to gloat? Is she pregnant? If she should have a son that would be the end of my hopes for Alexandrina.

'I wanted to come,' said Adelaide, 'because I was hoping that we might be friends.'

Did she mean it? wondered Victoria. Could she possibly find a friend among the women of her new family?

'You have had such a terrible loss,' said Adelaide, 'but you have the children. They must be a great comfort to you.'

'They are my life,' said Victoria and sensing her sincerity, Adelaide felt at ease.

'It is a blessing that there are young people in the family. I have heard such stories of little Alexandrina. She seems to be a most unusual child.'

Victoria could not hide her pride.

'Drina is adorable. I defy anyone to deny it. Such a bright child! Though a little temper now and then.'

'I should love to see her.'

'Come to the nursery now.'

Adelaide stood over the cradle of the important child and marvelled at the perfection of her limbs. Wide blue eyes stared up at her and the baby chuckled.

'She has taken a fancy to you,' declared her mother. 'I can assure you she does not to everybody.'

'Could I hold her?'

'But of course. Come, my precious. Your Aunt Adelaide wishes to make your acquaintance.'

Adelaide sat with the baby in her arms and thought how happy she would be if she could have a child of her own. She was almost certain that she was pregnant again.

'I hope you will invite me to come often and see little Drina.'

'By the look of it she will be delighted to see you, and I am sure I shall. I cannot tell you how pleasant it is not to have to try to speak English. I am sure I shall never master the language.'

'It is most difficult,' agreed Adelaide. 'But you will in time.'

'We speak German in the nursery, but of course Drina will have to speak English. It will be expected of her.'

Victoria watched for the reaction to those words. It was almost an assumption that Alexandrina was destined to be Queen. She

175

and Edward had been so certain of this that it was only by a special effort that they could avoid conveying their conviction to others.

Adelaide gave no sign that she was aware of the meaning beneath the words. She said: 'Oh yes, it would be well for her to learn English. But it will be easy for her here.'

Alexandrina was allowed to crawl on the floor under the watchful eye of her mother.

'I do not care to leave her to the care of nurses,' she admitted. 'In fact it is my great pleasure – and solace now – to care for her myself.'

Adelaide nodded sympathetically.

'You will understand my feelings when you . . .'

Victoria's eyes were on Adelaide's face. If she were pregnant surely she must admit it now.

'I shall hope to,' replied Adelaide enigmatically.

'You have had unhappy experiences . . . twice,' said Victoria.

Adelaide admitted this and Victoria asked questions about those sad occasions. Twice! she was thinking. It really seems as if she might have difficulty in bearing children.

Adelaide told her of the indispositions which had preceded her two miscarriages. 'The next time,' she said, 'I shall take very special care.'

'We must only hope that the next time will soon come,' replied Victoria insincerely.

Adelaide remained noncommittal and seeing that she would disclose nothing, Victoria suggested that she meet Alexandrina's sister Feodore which Adelaide was delighted to do.

The thirteen-year-old girl promised to be a beauty; she was charming and modest and adored Alexandrina. It was quite clear that everyone in the household was aware of the importance of the little girl.

When Adelaide took her leave Victoria said: 'You have cheered me so much.' And Adelaide promised to come again.

The visit had in truth cheered her for as she remarked to Fräulein Lehzen she was absolutely sure that the Duchess of Clarence was not pregnant; moreover, if she were, she doubted she was meant for motherhood. There was a fragility about her which was a great contrast to the buxom vitality of the Duchess of Kent.

Adelaide was in raptures. There was now no longer any doubt. She told William and he rejoiced with her.

'This time,' she said, 'I must take the greatest care. I am sure everything would have been all right before if I had done that. On the first occasion I caught cold and on the second there was that fatiguing journey.'

'This time you will rest in Bushy; you will sit in the gardens in peace and quiet and the girls will make sure of that.'

The girls, Sophia, Mary, Elizabeth, Augusta and Amelia lost no time in coming to Bushy House, and Adelaide showed such pleasure in their coming that they did not see why they should not regard it as their home. Their brother Augustus, who was the only one of the boys who had not gone into the Army or the Navy, came too. He was only fifteen.

'It is so pleasant,' said Adelaide, 'to have a family. This is too big and beautiful a house not to be full.'

It was clear that she had a talent for motherhood, for in a short time she was presiding over the family as though it were indeed her own. Nothing could have delighted William more. He was at heart, like the King, a very sentimental man.

'When our son is born,' he said, 'I shall be the happiest man in the kingdom. Think, Adelaide, he will be the future King of England.'

'Suppose the child is a girl?'

'Then she will be Queen of England. Ha, ha, that will put Madam Kent's nose out of joint, eh? She is certain that fat baby of hers is going to be the Queen.'

'Poor Victoria! It is sad that she will be disappointed. What a pity that my triumph will be her disappointment. But little Drina is such an adorable creature. I am sure that to have such a child must in itself be such a joy that a crown cannot be of such great importance.'

'You don't know the Duchess Victoria,' retorted William. 'If ever I saw an ambitious woman, it's that one. And she's got it into her head through some prophecy or other.'

Adelaide felt uneasy. She did not believe in prophecies . . . at least she thought she did not. It was disconcerting though that the prophecies of glory for that adorably plump blue-eyed child could only mean disaster for her own.

She would not dwell on them. She longed for her baby. Only when she had a healthy child of her own would she be content. Nothing else would matter than that. She longed for a child with an intensity which was new to her quiet nature.

She made plans for Bushy. She refurnished the nursery. Often she thought of the children who had played here – all those little FitzClarences who had been born and bred here.

They talked to her freely. They had little reticence; they were, after all, the children of an actress.

'We used to look forward to the days when Mamma came,' Amelia told her. 'She was always bringing us presents. I don't remember her as well as the others of course. But she sometimes came at night after the performance, driving down to us without a care for the danger of the roads. Next day she would leave in the early afternoon to do the evening performance at Drury Lane. Sometimes she didn't bother to take off her stage costume but came down in that.'

Adelaide could picture it all – the wild and beautiful actress, so charming, so volatile, enchanting William and her children.

'She used to rehearse her parts here,' said Elizabeth. 'Do you remember, Mary? How we all had to play with her. It was great fun. Papa used to love to play. He fancied himself as an actor.'

'He did act on board ship when he was in the Navy,' Augustus put in. 'They played *The Merry Wives of Windsor* and tipped the fat lieutenant who played Falstaff into a load of rubbish. Papa was always telling us about it '

It was so easy to picture it all – that happy-go-lucky unconventional family presided over by a Duke and an actress; and strangely enough she felt grateful to have been allowed to become a member of it. She never tired of hearing stories of the past. If she had been a fanciful woman she might have imagined the presence of Dorothy Jordan presiding over the house now, as benignly glad that Adelaide had come to Bushy House as Adelaide was to be there.

178

Once when Adelaide went up to the attics she saw a picture there of a lovely woman in a theatrical costume and she guessed at once who it was.

She studied it carefully, looking into the big brown eyes that seemed to speak to her. When she went into the gardens she found Augustus there playing with his dog.

'There is a picture in the attic,' she said. 'It's rather lovely. I wondered about it.'

'I expect it's one of Mamma. People did paint her quite a lot.'

'Will you come to the attic and tell me if it is.'

Augustus expressed himself willing and they went up together.

'Why, yes,' he said, 'that is Mamma. It used to hang over the fireplace in the dining-room. Every day when we came in I used to say "Good morning, Mamma". It was nice when she was playing somewhere and wasn't at home.'

'When was it taken down?'

'When you were coming, of course. Papa said you wouldn't want to see our Mamma there. So it was taken down and put up in the attic. I remember the day they did it.'

'And what did you think then?'

'Well, I was a little sad because after Mamma went I used to think that she was still there. You see what I mean.'

'I do see,' said Adelaide.

William came into the dining-room and stared at the picture hanging in its old place over the fireplace. For the moment he thought he was dreaming. He remembered the day it had been brought home and hung there and how the family had all congregated to admire and criticize it; and how he had made Dorothy stand just beneath it. 'It's not quite like you, Mamma,' one of the children had said, 'It's too . . . quiet. It's like a dead you.'

He often remembered that and told people of it; he had bored people with a repetition of his children's sayings.

He sent for the chief footman.

'Who hung that picture there?' he demanded.

'Your Highness, I did.'

William's face was suddenly purple with rage. 'How . . . how dared you? On whose orders?'

179

The footman inclined his head almost proudly; and he replied: 'It was on the Duchess's orders, Your Highness.'

'The Duchess's orders!' Then he said: 'Oh . . . I see.'

He could not wait to find her. She was in the gardens with Augustus and Amelia. He did not wish to speak to her of the picture when she was with the children; and it was not until later that they were alone together in that very room in which it hung that she herself explained.

'I asked them to bring it from the attic and hang it there.'

'But you know who it is!'

'Yes,' she said, 'the children's mother. Augustus told me. They love that picture.'

'It shall be taken down. We will have a portrait of you hung in its place.'

'I want you to follow my wishes over this,' she said. 'I want that picture to remain.'

'I don't understand you.'

She laid her hand gently on his arm. 'You will . . . in time,' she said.

'But you can't want her picture there . . . in this room which we use so much.'

She nodded. 'I think,' she said, 'she was a most unusual woman, a great woman. And she is the mother of the children. They wish it there . . . and so do I.'

'*You* are their mother now,' he said.

She shook her head. 'I can only take the place of the mother they have lost if they need me and it shall be my pleasure to be that. *She* is their true mother. They will never forget it, nor must we wish them to. So . . . the picture will hang in its old place?'

He took her hands and kissed them. 'You are a wonderful wife to me, Adelaide,' he said. 'I trust I may deserve you.'

There was no secret now of the fact that Adelaide was pregnant. The Dukes of Cumberland and Cambridge could no longer feel they were in the running while the 'plump little partridge' was flourishing in Kensington Palace. But what happened at Bushy was of the utmost importance to the Duchess of Kent.

She could not bear it, she told Fräulein Lehzen, if anything should happen to keep Drina from the throne. She and the Duke had believed so whole-heartedly in the prophecy; and one had already come true. Two deaths in the family, it had said; and they had come, one fast following the other.

Fräulein Lehzen declared that the Duchess of Clarence would never have a healthy child. She knew it. She had a feeling for these things. It was going to be Queen Alexandrina. She felt it in her bones.

'How I hope and trust you are right, dear Lehzen,' sighed the Duchess. 'But we must be watchful. I want to know any news that comes from Bushy. The Duchess is a good woman. I feel for her. She longs to be a mother. It is so sad that if she realized her wish it could be so damaging to our little darling.'

'It is not like Your Highness to anticipate trouble,' said Fräulein Lehzen.

'She has already lost two. Oh dear, and I could quite like the woman if she did not threaten Drina.'

In her cradle Drina slept peacefully, little dreaming that her greatness was menaced.

On a hot June evening of that year a carriage drove into London. In it sat a plump woman with short neck and legs, her face daubed with rouge and white lead, her eyebrows painted deep black and a hat adorned with feathers set on her black curly wig. She was dressed in purple mourning for the late King.

Queen Caroline had returned to England.

'Long live the Queen,' shouted the people; and they laughed and whispered together. Now there would be some fun. Elegant George must be fuming with rage because this painted woman – no longer young – had, in spite of all the stories that had been circulating about her, come back to England to share the throne with him.

Caroline put her head out of the carriage window to wave her greetings. 'God bless you, good people.'

'God bless you, Queen Caroline,' was the reply.

Caroline settled herself against the upholstery. She was smiling complacently. She had come back to take her stand against the enemy.

'There'll be a coronation,' she had said, 'and it's only right that the Queen should be crowned with the King.'

The King was incensed. He wanted to take to his bed and shut everyone out. He wanted to forget the world which contained Caroline.

She had been a menace to his peace ever since he had first seen her. Oh God, he thought, shall I ever forget Malmesbury presenting her to me – that low vulgar woman in that hideous white dress, the daubed face, that unwashed odour. That they could have done *that* to me!

'I must be rid of her. I must, I must, I must,' he cried hysterically to Lord Castlereagh, his foreign secretary.

'Your Majesty, there should be enough evidence to rid you of her.'

'If those who should have served me have done their duty there will be.'

'I think you will find that they have done that, Your Majesty.'

'This man Bergami . . . he was her lover. If we had proof of this I could divorce her immediately.'

'There will be witnesses, Sir. We are bringing them over here in readiness.'

'And I suppose Brougham is with her?'

'He's a good lawyer, Sir, but he can't stand out against the truth.'

'I should think a reasonable court would only have to look at her to know her guilty.'

'It will be a mighty scandal, Sir. She has powerful supporters and many of the people are with her.'

'They would be . . . just to plague me. Oh God, she is so clearly guilty. She was before with that Willie Austin of hers. He's her child, I'll swear it. They say he is repulsive enough to be.'

Castlereagh was uneasy. The Queen was going to be put on trial for adultery and such a case was almost certain to become political. The Tories would stand with the King, the Whigs with the Queen, and one of the most capable lawyers in the country

182

was Brougham who had long ago established himself as the Queen's adviser.

As the weeks passed there was no other topic of conversation throughout the country than the impending trial of Queen Caroline. Before the arrival of the Queen it had been planned that the coronation should take place on the first day of August; quite clearly this would have to be postponed for how could such an event take place when it was not certain whether the Queen, who should take such an important part in it, was on the point of being divorced from the King?

The stands which had been set up in the streets for the spectators of the procession to and from the Abbey, had to be taken down; the people who always enjoyed such ceremonies were not entirely disappointed for the trial was even more of a peep show than a coronation.

They formed themselves into factions – for and against.

'Are you for George or Caroline?' was a constant question, sometimes asked good-humouredly; but quite often there were quarrels which ended in fights and even riots.

When the Queen rode out, which she liked to do wearing the most flamboyant clothes, her carriage would be followed by groups of cheering people, who assured her that they were for her. It was obvious who was the more popular of the antagonists. The cartoons and lampoons against the King increased; there were some ridiculing the Queen but that was to be expected.

In Bushy, taking the utmost care not to exert herself, Adelaide heard what was happening and shuddered. She could not help thinking of the days when war had come to Saxe-Meiningen and she and Ida had made bandages for the wounded.

'Surely a controversy such as this could result in civil war,' she said to William.

William shrugged off such a suggestion. 'Not here,' he replied. 'Not here.'

'I shall never forget when the armies came to Meiningen. All was peaceful before and we would have said: "It could not happen here." But they came and ravaged the land. You can imagine what a town is like when an army has passed through it – hungry for food and excitement. It frightens me . . . this new feeling in the streets.'

'No. This is a battle between the King and Queen.'

'But people take sides. There are riots. Riots can become . . . worse. I remember hearing of what happened in France. That was not so long ago.'

'Don't compare us with the French,' said William almost fiercely.

But William, she had long since learned, was not the most discerning of men; and she was disturbed.

He became tender. 'Nothing for you to worry your head about.' He patted her stomach. 'All you must concern yourself with is the little one, eh?'

Yes, she thought fiercely, whatever happens, all must be well with the little one.

In Parliament the Bill of Pains and Penalties was introduced. This was to deprive Caroline of the 'title, prerogatives, rights, privileges and pretensions of Queen Consort and to dissolve the marriage between herself and the King'. The reason for this was her immoral conduct and a court was set up that she might stand on trial against a charge of adultery with an Italian, Bartolomeo Bergami, who had been the majordomo of her household.

Rarely in the history of any British royal family had there been such a scandal. The King's brothers had been adepts at providing salacious material and two of them had once stood on trial, the Duke of York on suspicion of selling commissions in the Army through his mistress Mary Anne Clarke, and the Duke of Cumberland on suspicion of having murdered his valet. Both of these were scandalous; but for a King – whose own life was scarcely one of moral rectitude – to bring a public charge of adultery with an Italian servant against his Queen, was surely the most scandalous of all.

The King was determined to have his divorce; and the Queen was determined that he should not. Behind both stood some of the ablest men in the country; it was going to be a tremendous battle.

The King did not appear in public. He was overcome with

humiliation and anger; but the Queen could not resist showing herself to the people. She rode out in her feathered hats and tastelessly coloured garments waving to all, accepting their acclamation, glorying in the discomfort she caused the King; confident that she was going to win her case and that adultery could not be proved against her.

The trial began and Caroline drove to the House of Lords to appear before her judges; and one by one members of her household who had been with her during her travels came forward to give evidence for or against her. It was not the first time the King had ordered an enquiry into her behaviour; years ago there had been the 'Delicate Investigation' which had attempted to discover whether or not Willie Austin was her illegitimate child. She had won then; she was confident that she would win now.

Lawyer Brougham was a genius. Deftly he dismissed the witnesses for the prosecution and with a dexterity which was truly marvellous he turned everything to the Queen's advantage.

Not only all over England but throughout the world the case against the Queen of England was being discussed.

It seemed incredible that Caroline could not be proved guilty. She had her enemies, but she also had her friends, and the great unpopularity of the King undoubtedly worked against him. Adelaide was not the only one who feared the unrest in the capital which was being aroused by what was called the King's ill-treatment of his wife.

The Bill of Pains and Penalties was finally passed in the Lords but the majority was the small one of nine. The Prime Minister, Lord Liverpool, was uneasy. On the second reading of the bill the majority in favour had been twenty-eight; such a big drop on the third reading showed clearly that the Bill was losing what little support it originally had.

It was a defeat for the King but only stalemate for Caroline. What did she care? Many people might believe her an adulteress, but while adultery could not be proved the King would not get his divorce and she was still Queen of England.

The King was in despair; but Caroline was determined to accept the result as triumph for herself. What did she care if the world thought her guilty; her behaviour on the Continent pointed to the almost certainty of that; all she cared about was that she had humiliated the King and she enjoyed every moment of that. As for him, he had suffered unnecessarily; he had been the centre of a gigantic scandal and had gained nothing from it.

He was still married to Caroline.

The Duke of York had come down to Oatlands in answer to an urgent message. The Duchess was in bed, her animals slinking about the room as though they knew that they were about to lose their friend and benefactress. In the garden the howl of a dog would now and then break the silence.

The Duke sat by her bed. She looked shrunken in spite of the dropsy which was killing her; she had always been a little woman. Never a beauty, he thought, and now, poor soul, she resembled one of her own monkeys. Tenderness overwhelmed him. He had been fond of her – once he had recovered from the disappointments of early marriage; and he had not been so unfortunate as poor George. He had succeeded in making a friend of Frederica.

'Frederick,' she said feebly, and held out a hand.

He took it. Like a claw of one of her creatures, he thought. What a menagerie she had made of Oatlands!

'My dear.'

'The animals . . .'

'They shall be cared for.'

She was contented. They were her first thought – those bright-eyed monkeys, those mournful-eyed dogs, those cats whose indifference on this occasion seemed assumed.

She closed her eyes for a moment and then opened them. 'Frederick.'

'My dear?'

'It was not so bad . . . our life?'

'We made something good of it,' he said.

She nodded and he gave her a spoonful of honey because her lips were so parched.

As a marriage it was a failure. They had parted. She could not bear a child – the sole reason for a marriage such as theirs. Yet he would never forget how she had stood by him during the Mary

Anne Clarke scandal, and he would always cherish their friendship.

He would miss coming to Oatlands which had been a kind of haven – though a malodorous one. She did not notice the smell of animals. They were her darlings and she preferred them to humans. Poor Frederica, who had failed in her human relationships and had sought the company of her cats, dogs and monkeys. But had she failed? Young Charlotte had loved her; he, her husband, was mourning her now; she had her friends; she had made a life for herself here at Oatlands, an eccentric life perhaps but still one which was pleasing to her.

And now it was coming to a close.

'Frederica,' he said, 'I want to tell you. I grew to love you, you know.'

But it was too late to tell her now.

He sat by her coffin and wept. Now that she was dead he could have explained his feelings towards her as he would never have been able to do in life.

She was buried in Weymouth parish church – a quiet funeral, not in the least royal; and yet those who mourned did so sincerely. The poor of Weymouth would never forget her; she had done so much for them – no one who was poor or old had asked her help in vain. Her servants wept. No longer would she sit on the lawns during summer, her animals around her, while she sewed for the poor; never would she be seen tramping through the grounds by moonlight, her only companions her faithful hounds. Frederica, Duchess of York, was dead, and for those who had served her and depended on her, it was the end of an epoch.

The Duke was unusually thoughtful as he stood by her grave.

So many deaths in the family, he thought. Charlotte – young and vital – had been the first. Then Kent and the King and now Frederica – all in such a short space of time. Who next? he wondered, and shivered. He was feeling his age. George had been so ill at the time of his accession that many had feared he would never live to wear the crown. And if he dies my head will be the one to carry it, thought the Duke.

God forbid! May George live for years yet ... until such a

time as I shall not be the one to follow. He could not think of a world which did not contain his brilliant brother, friend and companion of a lifetime.

But this fearful scandal with Caroline was ageing George. And when one considered the deaths in the family what could one ask oneself but 'Who next?'

The King could find solace from his troubles only with Lady Conyngham; and the reason was that she never talked of them. She was the most comforting of companions because she could make him feel that there was no such person in the world as Queen Caroline.

He never saw Lady Hertford privately now; and if they met in company he was courteous – as he was to all women – but he made it quite clear that there was no special relationship between them.

Lady Hertford pretended not to notice the change. She was not like Lady Jersey, who since she had been discarded by the King – Prince of Wales as he had been then – could never forgive him for leaving her and sought every opportunity of intriguing against him.

Lady Hertford had her dignity; she was an extremely unpopular woman; one of the reasons for the King's disfavour with his subjects was due to her. His carriage had been more frequently pelted with rotting fruit and vegetables when it was outside her house than anywhere else.

Lady Conyngham was not exactly popular but far less disliked than her predecessor. Lady Conyngham was so notoriously stupid that no one could be envious of her.

'The King is growing old,' it was said. 'He needs a brainless creature to look after his comforts. Fat Conyngham fills the bill very well.'

People were amused too to see the haughty Lady Hertford discomfited. Not that she showed it. She pretended to be quite unaware of the fact that there was any change in her relationship with the King.

Her acquaintances could not resist the attempt to plague her.

'What a foolish and vulgar creature Lady Conyngham is!' said one. 'I am surprised that the King seems so interested in her. I saw her in her carriage coming from Ascot. He was quite devoted. I wonder why. Has His Majesty ever discussed the creature with you?'

Lady Hertford opened cold blue eyes very wide and the delicate colour in her cheeks did not change one bit.

'Why should he?' she asked lightly. 'Intimately as I have known him and frankly as we have discussed every subject, he has never discussed his *mistresses* with me.'

This was considered the most intriguing remark of the day. It was discussed and joked over, for everyone knew that Lady Hertford had since the beginning of the Regency been the King's mistress.

But it was characteristic of the woman; and much as she was disliked for her cold, hard nature, no one could but admire the adroit manner in which she refused to admit the relationship between herself and the King.

But it was now clear that the King's devotion to Lady Hertford was at an end and the reigning mistress was Lady Conyngham.

She suited him perfectly in his ageing state.

He could not show his gratitude sufficiently. She might bring all her family to Carlton House or the Pavilion and he would be delighted to see them. Just as previously he had made the Hertfords his great friends, now it was the Conynghams.

Within the peace of Carlton House she sat beside him, plump, handsome and placid.

'My dear,' he said, 'I think the moment now has come to plan the coronation.'

'That will be delightful.'

He did not find her inane. She was perfect. She soothed him and he thought: By God, what I need more than anything on earth is to be soothed.

Dear Elizabeth Conyngham! No one had the power to soothe and comfort him that she had – not even Maria. And when he could say those words 'not even Maria' he knew that he had indeed cause to be grateful.

All through that summer and autumn, while little was discussed but the trial of Queen Caroline, Adelaide lived quietly at Bushy. All was going well. This was very different from the other pregnancies. She sat for hours in the gardens with one or other of the FitzClarence children talking of her life in Saxe-Meiningen and Ida's marriage and the two children she had – William her son and little Louise who as she had begun to grow had shown herself to be a cripple and over whom Ida had suffered much anguish.

'How I long to see them,' she said.

'You should invite them to Bushy,' said Mary.

'Why not?' added Elizabeth. 'You'll be able to talk babies endlessly together.'

Adelaide smiled at her stepdaughter and wondered whether Elizabeth herself would soon be anxious to talk of babies. She was shortly to marry the Earl of Erroll and William was delighted with the match. So was Elizabeth herself.

'Perhaps when my child is born, I will invite her,' mused Adelaide.

'It will be pleasant to have guests,' said Augusta. 'We never did when Mamma was here. People didn't come much, did they Mary?'

Mary agreed that they did not. 'It was because Mamma was an actress and her friends could not mix with royalty – which Papa is of course; and Papa's friends did not want to mix with stage folk. Not all of them, of course, but some. Uncle George was always kind to Mamma. He was fond of her because she was so gay and attractive. He liked actresses.'

'His Majesty would be kind to all women.'

'They say he's not very kind to Lady Hertford at the moment,' said Mary with a giggle. 'Nor was he to Maria Fitzherbert, nor to Perdita Robinson and a whole crowd of them.'

There was no reticence in the FitzClarence family. William had never stood on ceremony and it was unlikely that their mother would.

Adelaide did not wish the subject to turn to the disastrous matter of the King and Queen so she hastily changed the subject to Ida and discussed plans for inviting her to Bushy.

But the most important topic in the household was of course Elizabeth's marriage. Adelaide studied her stepdaughter. She was not exactly beautiful but dazzlingly attractive. So must her mother have been. They had with their usual frankness told her that Elizabeth was more like Dorothy Jordan than any of them.

Elizabeth described her wedding dress which had been presented by Aunts Sophia and Augusta, her father's two unmarried sisters, the royal Princesses.

'Such a dress!' cried Elizabeth. 'A royal dress. Well, we are royal through Papa and no one can deny that. But it was good of the old aunts to present me with the dress. It was a very ceremonious occasion, I can tell you. They sent for me to go to St James's, and there I must wait until their Highnesses were ready to receive me.' Elizabeth began to mime the reception of herself by the royal Princesses and then gave a little sketch of their imparting the news that they were presenting her with a wedding dress.

'A young lady's wedding day is the most important day in her life,' mimicked Elizabeth.

'I wouldn't say that,' retorted her sister Sophia. 'It's what comes after that is important. Don't you agree, Adelaide?'

'I am sure you are right.'

How gay they were! How unconscious of the fact that their father had never married their mother. What did they care that she was an actress? They were as proud of her as they were of their royal connections.

I am happy, thought Adelaide. This is the happiest time I have known. And when the child comes, that will be the very height of contentment. I ask nothing more than to have my child . . . and to live here in this pleasant spot comfortably, at peace, for the rest of my life.

The sound of carriage wheels intruded on the scene.

Augustus jumped up and ran to see who had come. They heard him shouting: 'It's George!'

And there was George FitzClarence coming across the lawn surrounded by his sisters who had rushed to meet him, and young Augustus was leaping in front of him like a jester.

George greeted Adelaide affectionately. They shared a special friendship. Hadn't she spent her honeymoon nursing him!

Like all the FitzClarences he did not stand on ceremony. He

sat beside her, asked after her health not in the most delicate manner. He was very knowledgeable about the birth of babies for his first child – a daughter – had just been born.

He had come to talk of the christening. They had chosen the baby's name.

'What is it?' cried Amelia.

George turned to his stepmother. 'Adelaide,' he said. 'With your permission.'

Yes, she thought. I am happy. I've never been so happy. They have accepted me.

Her eyes had filled with tears. George leaned forward and kissed her.

'Permission granted?' he asked.

And everyone cheered.

She looked across to the flower gardens which they had told her their mother had planned during her brief sojourns between theatrical engagements. She could almost fancy the ghost of Dorothy Jordan looked on, benignly content with the one who had taken her place.

Elizabeth FitzClarence was a handsome bride.

'The image of her mother,' it was whispered. 'The last time I saw *her* was as Lady Teazel in *The School for Scandal*. She was magnificent, but they say it was not one of her best parts.'

'Oh no, you should have seen her when she was young. Miss Hoyden in *The Relapse* was one of her best. I'll never forget her. And the new Lady Erroll is the image of what she was at her age.'

'The Duchess must be near her time. Fancy her coming to the wedding!'

'No doubt she did so to please the Duke. They say he insists on her receiving his bastards.'

'Poor creature. She looks meek.'

Adelaide was aware of their whisperings but they did not disturb her. She was happy. She felt well. In two months her baby should be with her; she was longing for the day, and it was pleasant to be at her stepdaughter's wedding and to see how the bride was aware of her and now and then gave her an understanding look, as though, thought Adelaide, I am indeed her mother.

The Duke was delighted. He made one of his long, rambling speeches which set everyone trying to stifle their yawns; and the Princess Sophia had graced the wedding with her presence.

It was the Princesses' way of letting the world know that they accepted the FitzClarences as their relations. No one was surprised to see her there. There were whispers about Sophia and always had been. The fact that she had remained unmarried did not mean that she had retained her virginity. The scandals of the family were not made entirely by the boys. No one could be absolutely sure that some twenty years before the Princess Sophia had secretly given birth to a child, but many believed this to be so. So there was no reason why she should not accept the results of her brothers' indiscretions. However, her presence at the wedding delighted her brother William.

People were beginning to look with new interest at William. He had improved since his marriage. He no longer used the crude oaths he once had; his manners were changing; and instead of making himself ridiculous by offering his hand to impertinent young commoners who refused it, he had a dignified royal wife, who was very properly pregnant and who had undoubtedly brought some dignity into his somewhat disorderly life. But the main point of interest was his nearness to the throne. There were constant rumours of the Regent's illnesses and the Duke of York did not enjoy good health. If they died, and they were becoming elderly, then this bluff sailor with the pineapple-shaped head and the habit of making endless and entirely boring speeches, would become the King of England, and the insignificant Adelaide the Queen.

There would be a king with ten illegitimate children all of whom were acknowledged by his family – and there would soon be another, legitimate this time and heir to the throne! For there was no doubt that the child the Duchess so proudly and delightedly carried would be the new King or Queen of England.

The Princess Sophia bade Adelaide sit beside her.

'For you look a little tired, my dear,' she said.

'I have been so careful lately,' replied Adelaide, 'that I am unused to functions.'

'You mustn't overtire yourself, my dear,' said Sophia.

'Remember those other two occasions. Women get accustomed to having miscarriages.'

Sophia looked doleful with prophecy but Adelaide refused to be dismayed.

Her child would soon arrive. Only two more months and it would be here.

Sophia was saying: 'I wonder if it will be a little girl or a little boy?'

Adelaide smiled. What did she care? It would be a child – her own child. That was all that mattered.

'I believe the Duchess of Kent is taking it badly,' said Sophia not without a trace of pleasure. 'I for one am delighted. She was beginning to give herself airs and one heard of nothing but the perfections of her little Drina.'

'I hope she will not be too put out,' said Adelaide.

'My dear Adelaide,' laughed Sophia, 'nothing in the world could put her out more. She has already taken on the role of Mother to the Queen, and the child not two years old yet!'

'It is a pity that what brings so much joy to one should bring pain to others.'

Sophia looked at her shrewdly. 'Is that not the way of the world, Adelaide?' she asked.

Adelaide was not sure of this. She tried to dismiss the Duchess of Kent from her mind. This was such a happy occasion; she did not want it spoiled.

A week after Elizabeth's wedding Adelaide's pains started.

She was frightened because they had come six weeks too soon. Terrified, she called to her women who quickly sent for the doctors.

The labour had undoubtedly begun and was long and arduous. Adelaide was in agony; but through it all she reminded herself that anything was worth while if the child was alive and well.

The apartments in Stable Yard were scarcely adequate. How much better it would have been if the child could have been born at Bushy where she had arranged it should be; but how could she have known it would arrive six weeks before it was due?

At length the ordeal was over leaving an exhausted Adelaide

194

more dead than alive, but when she heard the cry of a child and knew it was hers her joy was overwhelming.

'A little girl,' said the Duke, at her bedside.

'My own child . . . at last,' she murmured.

For some days it was believed that Adelaide could not survive, but so great was her joy in her child that by her very will to live for it she slowly began to recover, and a week after the birth she was out of danger and able to sit up and hold her child in her arms. A little girl – a perfect little girl!

'I have never believed such happiness was possible,' she told William.

He assured her that he was as happy. This precious child was the future Queen of England unless they had a boy; but he had suffered so much from her ordeal that he did not want to think of her going through that again.

'What's wrong with a queen?' he asked. 'They say the English have no objection to them and like them better than kings.'

'What shall we call her, William?'

'We'll have to have the King's consent to whatever we choose because she is . . . who she is. It could be Anne or Elizabeth . . . both great queens.'

'Anne or Elizabeth,' murmured Adelaide. 'I should like Elizabeth.'

The King called to see his little niece.

'Perfect! Perfect!' he beamed, as he came to sit down by the bed and study Adelaide. 'And you, my dear?'

'I grow better every day, Your Majesty.'

'Nothing could please me more.'

He looked younger than when she last saw him, Adelaide thought. He wore an unpowdered wig with curls of a subdued nut brown which became him. He excelled on such an occasion as this – benign monarch, loving brother, unselfish in his delight for a brother who had what he had failed to achieve: a loving wife and an heir to the throne.

He leaned over and patted her hand.

'*You* must get well.'

'I am doing so quickly. Happiness is the best healer.'

His eyes filled with tears or perhaps they were not real tears. In any case he flicked his eyes with a scented kerchief.

'Long may it last,' he said. 'Bless you, my dear.'

'We have thought of our child's name and want to know if we may have Your Majesty's consent to it.'

'Ah,' he said, 'that little one can in due course be the Queen.'

'For that reason we should like to call her Elizabeth.'

He smiled. He remembered that the Kents – somewhat ostentatiously – had wanted a queenly name for their daughter. And he had refused. They had to put up with Alexandrina Victoria instead. And serve them right. That woman was too ready to push herself forward.

'An excellent choice,' he said.

Adelaide was delighted. 'And if you would allow us to call her after you – Georgiana . . .'

'On one condition,' he said, with the utmost charm, 'that she is also called after her mother.'

'Elizabeth Georgiana Adelaide.'

'I can think of nothing that would please me more,' said the King.

The Duchess of Kent was frustrated. To think that the Duchess of Clarence – that fragile young woman – should have successfully come through her ordeal and the result should be a daughter!

She went into the nursery where Alexandrina was playing with her bricks, so intelligently, already taking an interest in the pictures and saying 'Mamma'.

To think that that innocent child should be robbed of her birthright! thought the Duchess, and was ready to burst into tempestuous sobs.

'My Drina, my darling child.' She picked up the little girl whose wide blue eyes surveyed her mother wonderingly. She was accustomed to passionate embraces and already aware that she was a very precious person.

'Mamma,' she said triumphantly.

'My angel! Oh, it is cruel . . . cruel!'

Alexandrina's fingers seized the locket which the Duchess wore about her throat. She tried to open it.

'It is your dear Papa, my darling. Oh, if only he were here to bear this with me.'

Alexandrina chuckled and began to pull at the locket so there was nothing to do but sit down and open it and show her the picture.

'Your Papa, Drina.'

'Papa,' repeated Alexandrina. 'Mamma . . . Papa . . .' And she laughed at her own cleverness.

So soft were the flaxen curls, so clear the blue eyes, so soft the pink and white skin; she was the picture of health. What was that other child like, wondered the Duchess. Sickly, she was sure. The bulletins said that the mother and child were progressing well. How well? she wondered.

It would be a great tragedy if anyone stood in Alexandrina's way. And while the Duchess of Clarence was able to bear children there would always be a danger.

Fräulein Lehzen had come into the nursery and Alexandrina laughed with pleasure. Here was another adorer.

'Mamma . . . Papa . . .' called Alexandrina.

Fräulein Lehzen's face was pink with pleasure.

'She is so forward, Your Highness,' she said.

The Duchess nodded, while Alexandrina, having displayed her cleverness, imperiously signed that she had had enough of lockets and admiration and wished to be returned to her bricks.

Her mother put her back on to the carpet and said to Fräulein Lehzen: '*That* child is healthy, so they say.'

'They say these things,' said Fräulein Lehzen a trifle scornfully.

'The Duchess is a kindly woman. I daresay she is beside herself with joy. I could be happy for *her* . . . but when I think of what this means to our angel . . .'

Fräulein Lehzen nodded. 'I heard that His Majesty has called on the Duchess.'

'He did not call on me. He was most *unkind* about darling Drina's name.'

'He has asked that the child be called after him, so I heard.'

'Georgiana!'

'Elizabeth first, they say. Then Georgiana Adelaide.'

'Elizabeth first! But that is a *queen's* name.'

'I suppose that is what they thought,' said the Fräulein gloomily.

'Oh, it is *so* cruel! I wanted Drina to be called that if she could not be Georgiana and he refused. Yet he has given his consent to this child's having it.'

'I never thought the Duchess would bear a living child. She had all the appearance of a woman whose pregnancy was not a healthy one.'

'Do you think . . .'

The two women were gazing at the child on the floor, so beautiful, so perfect in every way. Already a little queen, they were both thinking.

'Alexandrina,' said the Duchess. 'It is not the name of an *English* queen. That was why he wanted her to be called that. And this other child is Elizabeth. She will be Elizabeth the Second . . . if she lives.'

'*If* she lives,' said Fräulein Lehzen.

'Queen Alexandrina! No, it won't do. And what else is there. Victoria.'

'Queen Victoria,' said Fräulein Lehzen. 'It has a ring of dignity.'

'It sounds more like a queen's name than Alexandrina. Lehzen, my dear, we will cease to call our darling Alexandrina. From today she shall be Victoria.'

Fräulein Lehzen nodded. 'Queen Victoria,' she murmured. 'Yes, it is not Elizabeth . . . it is not Georgiana . . . but Victoria.'

'Victoria,' said the Duchess. 'Victoria, my darling.'

The child, not recognizing her new name, did not look up.

But of course she would soon realize that she was to be Victoria.

A visit to St James's

So Adelaide had her baby. She wrote to Ida of her happiness and told her that she looked forward to seeing her and showing her the little Princess Elizabeth who was all that she had ever hoped for. Why should Ida not pay a visit to Bushy House? There she could meet Adelaide's other family – a most amusing family, she did assure her; something interesting was always happening to them; marriages and births, balls and love affairs. 'My stepchildren are the most natural people in the world. I am so fond of them and I believe they are of me. I want you to know them, Ida.'

She particularly wanted to see her little niece Louise who suffered from some mysterious spinal trouble. Adelaide had a special fondness for little Loulou as she was called; and she longed to see her young brother Wilhelm. Please, Ida must come to England with her children soon; and what could be a better time to come than coronation year?

The King was becoming not exactly popular but less unpopular. After all, he was going to provide the citizens of London with a wonderful spectacle in his coronation, which meant visitors to the capital and trade for the shops, besides the excitement such occasions inevitably meant.

They could be sure that the coronation of George IV would be as lavish as any that had gone before. It was not in his nature to give a second-rate performance and at his own coronation he must excel.

So there were fewer hostile shouts when he drove out and he even heard a cheer or two; he was comforted, although Caroline continued to cause him great anxiety. She was determined, she made it known, to be crowned with him; it was no use trying to exclude her for she would not be excluded. The King had tried to prove a case against her and had failed; therefore she was entitled to be treated as the Queen of England.

She had taken up residence in Brandenburg House close to the river near Hammersmith and she made a point of driving out frequently and in such style that she could not fail to be noticed. Her face bedaubed with rouge and white lead, enormous hats adorned by colourful feathers topping her black wig, she would sit in her carriage nodding and smiling to all those who crowded about her carriage. She enjoyed playing the injured wife and loved to encourage the cheers for herself and hostility towards the King.

'It's my coronation as well as his,' she declared to her women. And she intended to make it so.

The King behaved as though she did not exist. Any communication from her was ignored. He could not prove her guilty of adultery but he firmly believed she was and that only an evil fate kept him bound to her.

The Duchess of York being dead, the Queen ignored, the first lady in the land was Adelaide.

The Duchess of York had not mixed in society but this could not be the case with Adelaide, for she was now the mother of the Princess Elizabeth, who might well be a future sovereign.

'You see, my dear,' said the King, 'it puts you in a more prominent position.'

Adelaide saw this and was eager to do her duty. She was often at Court; she gave parties which the King attended – often with Lady Conyngham; she appeared at all important royal functions.

People were noticing her more now than they ever had. She was far from handsome, was the verdict, but she had a charm of manner which made up for her lack of beauty; and her effect on William was miraculous.

She regretted the need for these ventures into society because they kept her from her baby. She felt she would never be accustomed to the wonder of having a child of her own; every moment she could spare from her duties was spent with the child. Queen Charlotte had had a wax image made of her beloved son George – now the King – and she had kept it on her dressing-table that she might see it every day. Adelaide now ordered a sculptor to model a reclining figure of the little Princess Elizabeth.

'I want to have her with me always as she is now,' she told William.

William was ready to indulge her and engaged the sculptor Scoular to carry out the work. The figure of the child was to be depicted lying on a couch, her head on a tasselled cushion; and when Scoular started the work Adelaide occasionally went to his studio to see how it was progressing.

The weather during January and February of coronation year had been mild, but in March it turned suddenly cold; and to Adelaide's consternation the Princess Elizabeth caught a chill.

Going into the nursery one day she found the child uncomfortably flushed and in panic she immediately sent for the royal doctor, Sir Andrew Halliday.

At first he said that the child had merely taken a chill which he expected she would throw off in a day or so, but within a few hours he grew alarmed and sent for Sir William Knighton and Sir Henry Halford.

Adelaide was terrified. How could this have happened so suddenly? A day or so before the child had been quite well. She sent a message to William, who was with the King, to come to her at once.

When William heard that the child was ill he returned immediately. Adelaide met him at the door and when he saw how white she was and how she trembled he sought to comfort her.

'Children have these ailments,' he soothed. 'Why, there are always alarms when they're young. I should know . . . with ten of them.'

But this was not the ten vigorous FitzClarences; this was her precious fragile Elizabeth.

He went with her to the child's nursery and there he was greeted by Sir Henry Halford, who was grave.

'I have to tell Your Highnesses that the Princess has fallen into a convulsion and my colleagues feel that she is very gravely ill.'

William said nothing; he turned to Adelaide who looked as though she were about to faint.

'I will take the Duchess to her room,' he said; and he led her unresisting away.

She lay down as she was bid. She was praying silently. This could not be. She could not know so much happiness merely to lose it almost as soon as it was hers.

'Anything, anything, let anything happen to me but let my baby be well again,' she prayed.

She kept saying the child's name over and over again and in her own ears her voice sounded mournful as a tolling bell and the fear in her heart would not be dismissed.

She must know what was happening. What was she doing lying here when her baby might be needing her?

She left her bed and went to the nursery.

William was there – looking unlike himself, a look of bleak bewilderment on his face.

She knew as soon as she saw him.

'Not . . .' she began, but she could say no more.

William nodded slowly.

'Oh God,' she whispered. 'How could it be!'

She could see the child lying in her cradle . . . white and still.

'*No*,' she murmured.

William had caught her in his arms.

'Help me get the Duchess to bed,' he said.

There could not be such misery. She would not believe it. She did not want to know what was going on about her because everything would be dominated by one tragic fact.

She had learned in these last months that what she wanted more than anything, what she needed, was to be a mother. She was intended for motherhood. Her children would be the very meaning of life to her.

Her little Elizabeth had taught her that, and now she was gone.

She became ill, for she had never fully recovered from Elizabeth's birth and the shock of her death was more than she could endure.

There was only one thing she wanted in life and that was for someone to come to her and say: 'You dreamed this. It is not true. See here is your child, alive and well.'

The FitzClarences came to see her; they sat at her bedside and tried to comfort her. They did to a certain extent; but they were not her own children; and she had learned what it meant to hold her own flesh and blood in her arms.

William came. 'You must get well,' he said. 'There will be others.'

But there was a terrible fear in her heart. Three times she had tried and failed. A fearful certainty had come to her that she would never bear a healthy child.

William told her that her sister Ida had written to say she was coming to England to comfort her, and she was bringing little Loulou and Wilhelm to help her in this.

'You see, my dear, you must not grieve for ever,' said William.

He was right. She had her duty. She must get up, try to live a normal life, try to pretend to the world that she did not believe that nothing would ever be the same again.

'I have a surprise for you,' said William. She tried to show some pleasure because he was so eager to interest her.

He took her into the small room in which she sat when she wished to be alone; sometimes she read there or did a little needlework. In one corner of this room was something covered by a velvet cloth.

William lifted this cloth; and there was the statue of a child – her Elizabeth – reclining on a sofa, with one exquisite little foot exposed; tiny fingers perfectly chiselled, curled about the stuff of the robe. The eyes were closed; the child was sleeping. It was Elizabeth, her child.

She stood staring at it; then she fell on her knees and laid her face against that cold little hand.

She began to sob as she had not been able to since the loss of her child, and the Duke knelt with her and they wept together.

The enormity of her grief swept over her; but in some strange way the cold marble statue had rekindled the life in her.

She was ready to go on.

Ida arrived in England with her two children and the reunion brought happiness to Adelaide. She admired her niece and nephew and they, sensing her genuine affection, were soon returning it. It was characteristic of Adelaide that in spite of her ever-present grief she bore no envy towards those who were more fortunate than herself.

Being with Ida, giving parties for her and introducing her to society helped her a great deal; but what she most enjoyed were the hours she spent alone with the children. The afflicted little Loulou was her special favourite, perhaps because the child

203

aroused her pity; she even felt that in some way her little niece filled a part of that emptiness which had been created by the loss of Elizabeth.

The Duchess of Kent, now that Victoria's rival was no more, was anxious to commiserate with her sister-in-law. Whenever she looked at her sturdy Victoria and thought of what had happened to the child's cousin fear gripped her; and this quickly turned to pity for the Duchess of Clarence for she refused to allow herself to believe – for more than a second or two – that Victoria could possibly be threatened by death. Victoria was the elect, the beloved of the gods; it had been prophesied that she was to be a great queen – therefore fate could not allow it to be otherwise.

'We were foolish to imagine anything could stand in Victoria's way,' she said to Lehzen. 'Oh dear, I am so sorry for poor Adelaide. I have written to her condoling with her and I have told her that I have refrained from bringing little Victoria to see her for fear the sight of the child might upset her.'

'How thoughtful of Your Highness!' murmured Fräulein Lehzen.

Adelaide, however, was soon writing back to her sister-in-law thanking her for her letter and declaring that it would give her the greatest pleasure to see little Victoria, so that if the Duchess of Kent would bring her daughter to her she would be delighted.

'There!' said the Duchess to John Conroy who had become her chief adviser. 'The Duchess of Clarence would like to see Victoria.'

'She will be extremely jealous.'

'They say she is not of a jealous nature – although having lost her daughter and seeing mine . . . I shall go of course. There is nothing else to be done and it is well that Victoria should be on good terms with *all* her uncles – particularly those who might one day wear the crown.'

John Conroy thought this was sound.

'I shall certainly not take her to Bushy. It would be quite *wrong* for her to be near Clarence's illegitimate brood. On no account shall I allow her to see them. So the visit will be paid when the Duchess is at St James's.'

'An excellent idea and worthy of Your Highness.'

The Duchess looked at him fondly; they worked so well together and he had been such a comfort to her since Edward's death. There was always Leopold of course; and he came to Kensington every Wednesday to see her and Victoria; and what she would do without him she did not know. Victoria was so fond of him. The child did seem fond of men. She liked to sit on Leopold's knee, examining his decorations and call him Uncle in her charming baby way.

'I shall take Feodore with me. It is time that child was *noticed*. We shall soon have to concern ourselves with her future. How time flies! She is fourteen, you know.'

'In a year or so . . .' said Conroy.

'And in the meantime she should appear now and then. A visit to the Duchess of Clarence will be a start – after all she is the first lady now the Duchess of York is dead. One cannot count Caroline. I am sure the Duchess will be enchanted with my daughters . . . both of them.'

Conroy assured the Duchess that he was of the same opinion and when the Clarences were at St James's, the Duchess of Kent decided she would pay the call.

Victoria should be dressed in one of her prettiest gowns – soft blue silk with a wide blue sash of a deeper blue and her fair hair curled with especial care. Her little white slippers with the blue bows just showed beneath the draperies of her gown.

'Angelic!' murmured the Duchess when the child was brought to her.

And there was Feodore, looking remarkably pretty. Surely two of the loveliest girls in the kingdom!

Feodore curtsied prettily. It should not be difficult to find a husband for her.

Victoria signified her desire to be picked up by Feodore and Feodore immediately complied with this wish. An enchanting picture, thought the gratified Duchess.

'We are going to see the Duchess of Clarence at St James's,' said their mother.

'Sissi?' asked Victoria, her eyes on Feodore.

'Yes. Sissi is coming with us. Now, I believe the carriage is waiting.'

Feodore handed Victoria to her nurse who carried her down to the waiting carriage. All the way from Kensington to St James's Victoria alternately looked out of the window at the streets through which they passed or bounced up and down on the upholstered seats. *Not* very decorous behaviour for a future queen, thought the Duchess; and it was quite clear that soon Victoria's exuberance would have to be curbed, but for the moment the sheer vitality of the child was such a joy to watch that Victoria might continue to amuse herself as she wished.

No one in the streets gave more than a cursory glance at the occupants of the carriage. They seem to be unaware, thought the Duchess, that their future queen is passing by.

When they reached St James's they were warmly welcomed by Adelaide, who, the Duchess of Kent noticed with pleasure, could not take her eyes from Victoria.

When the children were sent away to play together – poor crippled Louise, her brother William, Feodore and Victoria – Adelaide said to her sister-in-law, 'Your little daughter quite enchants me.'

The Duchess glowed with pride. 'I feared to bring her before...'

'You should not have done. My loss does not prevent my delight in seeing her. She is so full of life; she looks so *healthy*. I trust you will often allow her to come and see me.'

'You have only to ask, my dear,' said Victoria of Kent graciously.

When the children came back Victoria sat on Adelaide's knee and delighted in her admiration while she herself admired Adelaide's rings and the locket which she wore round her neck. It was like her Mamma's; she wanted to see the picture inside which was of the Duke of Clarence.

This delighted her and she spent some time shutting the locket and watching it spring open. Adelaide's heart overflowed with emotion as she watched those chubby fingers at work.

William, having heard that his sister-in-law was visiting Adelaide, called in to pay his respects and Victoria looked at him with delight and holding her arms to him cried: 'Papa! Papa!'

William picked her up and held her over his head so that she shrieked with laughter. Oh dear, thought her mother, this is not very decorous – but I suppose it is all right since he could be

King *if* the present King and the Duke of York died soon.

The result of that visit was that all decided it was a great success; and after that Adelaide took a special delight in the little Victoria and they saw each other frequently.

The charm of the child gave her great pleasure; and she believed if she could surround herself with children she could find some happiness, although she would never cease to mourn for her own Elizabeth.

Coronation – and freedom

The coronation was fixed for 19 July, and as plans went forward the excitement arose.

An important event had taken place that May which in the minds of many predicted a peaceful reign for their new King. Napoleon died at St Helena of cancer in the stomach, and there was no longer any fear that he could escape and cause misery and suffering to thousands as he had from Elba. There was great security in the knowledge that he was dead.

The people felt that they could give themselves up to the pleasure of the grand ceremony and forget wars. It was sure to be a dramatic occasion. They could always trust old George to give them that; and what with the Queen's saying she would be there and the King's saying that on no account should she be, the whole thing would seem like something out of a comic opera.

Lady Conyngham was now constantly in the King's company; she had a house in Marlborough Row and when she wished to ride used a carriage from the King's stables; each day she dined with the King; her daughters were never far off; and the King treated them as though they were his own family, being far more gracious to them, it was noted, than he ever had been to his own daughter, the Princess Charlotte. They received handsome presents from him, and as it was a custom of his to walk through his apartments after dinner displaying the latest *objets d'art* he had acquired, he often did this with Lady Conyngham on one arm and one of her daughters on the other.

The story was told that on one occasion Lady Conyngham gave orders that all the candles in the saloon should be lighted – there were hundreds of them – and when the King entered and seemed a little startled by the brilliant light she said to him somewhat apologetically: 'Sir, I told them to light the saloon as guests were coming.' To which the King replied, taking her arm with the utmost devotion, 'Thank you, my dear. You always do what is right. You cannot please me so much as by doing everything you please, everything to show that you are mistress here.'

Many people heard that and they said that they had not seen the King so deeply in love since the days of Maria Fitzherbert. And he was now a man of nearly sixty, though he did not look it in spite of his great bulk and his constant illnesses, for his charm – aided considerably by that unpowdered wig – helped him to throw off the years.

During the weeks which preceded the coronation the King was aware that his popularity was rising a little. He felt confidence in the future. Napoleon was dead, an era of peace lay ahead, the long-awaited crown was his, and the people were perhaps beginning to appreciate that he wished to serve them well. He had Lady Conyngham to be his constant companion, and he was in love – he could never be happy unless he was in love – so the future seemed fair but for one heavy cloud.

The Queen!

He could not get her out of his mind. What was that dreadful woman planning to do to ruin his coronation.

That was something he would not know until the day.

On the evening of 18 July the King drove to the Speaker's House in readiness for the next day's ceremony. He retired to his room early and sat at his window looking out on the river flowing peacefully by.

'Tomorrow,' he murmured, 'I shall be crowned King.' And he thought of those days when he had been the young Prince Charming and people had said how different his reign would be from that of his father, and had longed impatiently for him to ascend the throne. That was before they had learned to hate him, in the days when he had been a handsome and romantic figure, when he had courted Maria Fitzherbert and secretly married her in the drawing-room of her house in Park Street.

And now here he was an old man, worn out by excesses and a hundred aches and pains, tormented by ailments which were a mystery to him. All this time he had waited for the crown and now that it had come to him, did he greatly want it? There would not be much difference between being a King or Regent and it was ten years ago that he had assumed that title and the responsibilities which went with it.

But tomorrow he must recapture the glory of his youth. He must charm his people with the ease which he had in the past. It was not so easy when one was almost sixty; when one's limbs were swollen, one's girth uncontrollable and one's subjects had been making sly jokes at one's expense for thirty years, so that they had built up an image of him which they could not admire. How did they see him? An ageing voluptuary? No doubt they were right. Perhaps he had pandered to his sensual appetites and it was certain that they had been prodigious. Everything would have been different if he could have openly married Maria; he had always believed that. If she had not clung to her religion ... if ...

But what was the use?

He was nearly sixty and tomorrow he would be crowned King of England. He had to forget the past and look to the future – what there was left of it. Sometimes he thought there was not much.

He smiled suddenly. Tomorrow he would put on his coronation robes; he would play his part magnificently in the Abbey ceremony. He was a great actor, and he performed the parts he assigned to himself with as much verve now as he had at twenty.

Tomorrow at least his people should not be disappointed in him.

Nor were they. He might be old, fat and ill; but he was magnificent. Nothing could detract from his dignity and in every word and gesture his charm was evident. He even looked handsome.

From the moment the women with the herbs – following the

old custom of strewing them along the route the King would take – appeared, all the spectators knew that with George IV as the central actor the play was going to be a grand one.

Of course he looked splendid; of course he looked all that a King should look; and of course his coronation was a superb glittering colourful spectacle.

But the Queen had made up her mind to share it. She had no sense of propriety, no decorum; she was all that the King was not; but one thing they shared and that was determination: his that she should *not* share in the coronation, hers that she *should*.

While the King was making his way from the Speaker's House to the Abbey the Queen left Brandenburg House for the same destination.

She did not notice that the cheers for her were less fervent than usual. She had believed that when she rode out the crowd would follow her to the Abbey and force an entrance with her, if need be. But she did not know the English. They reviled the King; he was an old roué; he had behaved badly to Mrs Fitzherbert; his debts were enormous; he lived in extravagant splendour while there was great poverty in the country. But this was his coronation and he was playing his part with a flair that they admired. He might be an indifferent ruler; but he was a superb actor and to-day's affair was a pageant. They were not going to have it spoilt, and the Queen was wrong to try and force herself where she was not wanted.

That was the verdict of most of the crowd. They were not looking for trouble today, but spectacle. They had come to cheer the King not to boo him. Whoever heard of a king being booed during his coronation when they were all going to get drunk in the taverns shortly drinking his health.

So Caroline rode through silent streets to present herself at the Abbey and be refused admittance – on orders of His Majesty. Nothing deterred she presented herself at another door, only to be once more prevented from entering.

In her tawdry finery she looked vulgar, decided the people. How different from their glorious King who at this moment, under the canopy of State, was receiving the orb and sceptre.

'Go home,' shouted a voice; and others took up the strain.

Caroline was bewildered. It was the first time she had received such treatment from the people.

She could not storm the Abbey; she would only wait disconsolate; and at last she gave the order to drive her back to Brandenburg House.

The King was pleased with his people and they were not ill-pleased with him. Today they had not failed him but had helped to drive the wretched Caroline away from the Abbey.

He was benign and regal and his charm was touching said all who beheld it. He presided with kingly dignity over the coronation banquet and when the long exhausting day was over he was cheered on his way to Carlton House.

The cheers of his people were the sweetest music in his ears.

He would have a portrait painted of himself in his coronation garments; it would serve to remind him of this triumphant day.

King George IV! An old man, he thought; and who is there to follow me but Frederick who is even more ill than I and may not live much longer; or William who is getting old, too; and then that precocious infant at Kensington Palace. But he should not misjudge the child; it was the mother who irritated him, not the little girl.

But who knew, there might be someone to displace her yet. Adelaide might bear a child. He himself might become the father of one if he could rid himself of that woman.

But what was he thinking of? He was too old now. He did not want to go through the ridiculous farce of marriage, even if he could ... and then find he could not get a child.

He was content with dear, delightful, not exactly intellectual, Lady Conyngham with her beautiful motherly bosom and her handsome looks. She reminded him very often of Maria – but without Maria's temper.

Ah Maria, he thought, what are you thinking on this day?

He could not know. And did it matter?

He was tired; he wished to rest. He would send for them to get him to bed.

It had been an exhausting day.

*

The King decided a few days after his coronation that he would visit different parts of his realm so that he might have the experience of speaking personally with his subjects. His intention was to go first to Ireland, and preparations were immediately begun.

People continued to discuss the coronation, the splendour of which would be talked of for months to come; those who had not witnessed it listened to accounts of it in the taverns and wherever people congregated. The manager of Drury Lane decided that instead of a new play he would put on the Pageant of the Coronation which should be like the real thing in every detail.

It seemed to be an excellent idea and when the curtain rose on the Abbey scene there was a hushed silence in the house and everyone joined in the ceremony, cheering and calling God Save the King.

No play could succeed as this spectacle did, and the theatre was crowded night after night.

The Queen heard of what was going on and thought that if she attended no one would be able to ignore her this time.

So she dressed herself in odd vulgar clothes – too short in the skirt, too low in the neck, with the feather and diamond head-dress waving over her wig – and appeared in the royal box.

She had been ill for some time, refusing to be treated by doctors and successfully hiding her affliction, dosing herself with lauda-num which brought her the solace of sleep; but as the time had gone on she had found it necessary to increase the doses and thus caused alarm to some of her ladies. They had found it useless to dissuade her. She had to give herself relief from pain; she had to be able to feel alive – and mischievous again; she had to paint her face more brightly with rouge and plaster it with white lead to get the startling contrast.

She would laugh as she did so and say to her most intimate lady-in-waiting, 'Now my love, what would they think of me if they saw me without my warpaint, eh? They'd think I'd come from the grave instead of from Brandenburg House. We don't want to give the good people a shock or His High and Mighty Majesty so much pleasure, do we?'

They, who knew how ill she was, were anxious for her. In her

212

way she had been a good mistress. Kind, friendly – in fact over-familiar calling them 'my love' and 'my dear' in front of the lower servants. But if they were in trouble she would be the first to help; and in spite of her eccentricities, which at times seemed to border on insanity, they were fond of her.

Painted and glittering with jewels, the plumes waving in her hair, she set out for Drury Lane.

She was going to win back the popularity she had lost. The King had won the battle of the coronation; it was after all *his* coronation, though she ought to have shared it with him; but he was their King and she but the Queen Consort. She granted that. It was for this reason that the people had been lukewarm to her; it was because he was after all the King that they had not forced an entrance for her into the Abbey.

Never mind. The coronation was over. Now they would be sorry for *her*. The first skirmish would be in the Drury Lane where they would cheer her and feel it was a shame that a queen had to witness a mock coronation from a box in a theatre when she had been excluded from her own in the Abbey.

When she entered the theatre the people rose and cheered her. Grinning wildly, bowing so vigorously that the feathers were in danger of being dislodged, she responded to the greeting and the pageant began. Before it was half way through, the effects of the mild dose of laudanum she had taken to enable her to visit the theatre began to decline, and her lady-in-waiting looked at her in some alarm.

'I think . . . I should leave the box . . . for a moment,' she said faintly.

She sent one of her attendants to tell the manager not to interrupt the show simply because she wished to slip out for a few moments.

So she left the box while the stage coronation continued; and after more sips of the laudanum she was able to return. But not all the artificial colour on her face could disguise the fact that she was ill.

As the audience sang the national anthem, glancing up at her box, she bowed but was forced to grip the front of the box as she did so.

Wildly they cheered her, and she tried to respond; but she could only murmur: 'Get me to the carriage.'

'The Queen is ill,' it was whispered. 'The trouble has been too much for her.'

She was led out to her carriage and was swiftly driven home. Her ladies took off the clothes that were always too tight for her gross body; they lifted off her wig; they removed the rouge and lead from her face and revealed a tired old woman with the marks of a ravaging disease clearly defined.

Lying in her bed she said in an almost jaunty way: 'Something tells me I shall never get up again.'

The King on his way to Ireland for the first State visit of his reign was aboard the royal yacht at Holyhead when the news was brought to him.

The Queen had died less than a fortnight after that visit to the theatre.

Free! he thought. At last! For twenty-six years he had been bound to that loathsome creature and now he was free! Never again would she have the power to plague him. Never again need he wonder what she would do next.

He stood on the deck of the *Royal Sovereign* and savoured the breezes from the sea.

For years he had been in the thrall of his father and almost immediately he had been tied to that woman. This was his first real taste of freedom. He was King, the ruler of his country, and best of all he was a free man. No longer need he be tormented by the most vulgar woman in the world to whom ironically he, the most exquisite gentleman, had been married.

Free . . . at fifty-nine. It would soon be his sixtieth birthday.

Too late, he thought sadly. Ah, too late.

But was it? He had overcome his melancholy. I'm free, he kept telling himself. She can plague me no longer. There was no need to look for evidence for divorce. Fate had stepped in with the most final of all separations, the most conclusive of all divorces.

'Your Majesty will wish there to be a period of mourning?' he was asked.

214

He was not going to pretend. Some might have expected him to play the part of bereaved husband but he was too good an actor for that. It would be a part which no one would believe in. So since it would be ridiculous to play the mournful widower, he would be the widower who was too honest to pretend to anything but the relief Caroline's death had brought him.

The Court might have six weeks mourning. That would be expected; but it would be foolish to make it longer; as for him, he was on a State voyage; he was going to visit his Irish subjects; he wanted them to like him. They would not care for a miserable man.

He remembered how he had always loved the Irish. He hoped *they* would remember it now. His greatest friend had been Richard Brinsley Sheridan who had died some four or five years ago – a witty Irishman if ever there was one. Why even his present dearest friends the Conynghams were Irish. He anticipated a happy time.

And how could it be otherwise? If he exerted all his prodigious charm they could not fail to succumb; he was already rehearsing what he would say to them. 'I feel I have come among my own people,' he murmured.

He dressed with the utmost care in blue – blue neckcloth, blue breeches, blue coat – all of course of the most exquisite cut, and blue was the colour which suited him perhaps best of all. The only contrasting colour was the yellow of his coat buttons – quite dashing while they detracted not in the least from his general air of elegance.

He would speak to them from the heart as though the words came naturally. They would never guess what careful thought he had given to them. If his English subjects rejected him, that should not be the case with his Irish ones.

He was not disappointed. His emotional approach, his sentimental words were exactly what fitted the occasion best. Crowds had come to cheer him and escort his carriage to the Lodge in Phoenix Park.

There he addressed the multitude – a grand, imposing and decidedly regal figure.

'This is one of the happiest days I have ever known. My heart

215

has always been Irish. I have always loved Ireland and now I know that my Irish subjects love me.'

He was going to drink their health, he told them, as he hoped they would drink his. It would be in Irish whiskey punch.

How they cheered! How they loved him! He had the gift of words. He must have kissed the blarney stone. He knew exactly how to win their hearts.

A real fellow of a King, they said.

And so began his first State visit. Nothing could have been more successful. They loved their King; he loved his subjects. It was so long since he had heard such cheers.

A beloved monarch. A free man. If he had been twenty years younger how happy he would have been! But even in the midst of his triumphs a voice within him kept reminding him, 'Too late. It has come too late.'

Other people's children

Victoria was growing up. She was almost three. She chattered constantly, mostly in German; but as Uncle Leopold said, it was essential that she speak English equally well.

Victoria was intelligent and was already aware that she was important not because of her charm and beauty but because of Another Reason, which was most intriguing. Mamma did not speak of this Other Reason. It was something she must not know of yet because she might in a moment of indiscretion betray that she knew to someone like Uncle Frederick, Uncle William or Aunt Adelaide, which would make them very cross – although she could not believe that Aunt Adelaide could ever be cross; and Uncles Frederick and William were most benevolent whenever she saw them.

There was another uncle – the most important of all: Uncle King. She saw very little of him, although sometimes she had been held up to see him pass by in his carriage. He was an enormous, glittering being who thrilled Victoria merely to look at him. She respected Uncle Leopold, of course; she adored Aunt Adelaide and she loved Mamma, Sissi and Charles dearly, but for Uncle King she had a feeling of reverence. It would be a glorious day when *he* joined the band of Victoria worshippers. But he never came to Kensington Palace, nor was she invited to Carlton House. The oddest thing about Uncle King – in Victoria's opinion – was that he seemed unaware of Victoria.

Sometimes she forgot him when she was playing with her dolls. She loved her dolls. People knew this and were constantly giving them to her. Sissi helped her dress them and knew all their names. Aunt Adelaide, dear gentle Aunt Adelaide, had just sent her a beautiful big one – the biggest she had ever seen, almost as big as Victoria herself and dressed in a blue silk dress with a sash, like Victoria's.

'She could be called Victoria,' she had told Sissi, 'but then who would know whether she was being called or I was.'

Sissi covered her with kisses and said she was the cleverest little girl in the world and thought of the most *sensible* things.

Of course she must be sensible because of That Reason; and there could not be three Victorias in the family; there were already Mamma and herself.

As it was a Wednesday afternoon Uncle Leopold left his beautiful house at Esher – Claremont which Victoria and her Mamma visited now and then – to come to Kensington Palace where he spent a long time talking to Mamma; and Victoria could not help knowing that she was often the subject of their conversation. She would be brought in to stand before Uncle Leopold and answer his questions while Mamma looked on, never missing any little lapse of good conduct, of which Victoria would be told afterwards. She must always be careful to behave as one in her position should. One in her position! It was a phrase she was constantly hearing; and she did not fully understand it except that it was involved with That Reason.

Uncle Leopold was asking her questions – in English, which he spoke differently from the people of the household, and she answered in English, now and then bringing in a German word, which made him frown.

'She has not started lessons yet?' he asked Mamma.

'A little. She is learning to read. But she is only three.'

'So young,' said Uncle Leopold tenderly picking up one of her curls in his hand and twirling it.

She leaned against his knee examining his odd boots; they had thick soles so that when he took his boots off – she had once seen him do this at Claremont when he had come in on a very wet day – he sank down and became a much smaller man.

Uncle Leopold liked to talk of his ailments.

'My rheumatism has been more painful even than usual this last week. It's the damp weather.'

Sometimes it was the hot weather that did not agree with him and gave him headaches; the cold got 'on to his chest' and made him suffer 'agonies'. Poor Uncle Leopold, and he was so good looking that she liked to watch his face while he talked. His hair was a magnificent mass of curls. Victoria, watching it, touched her own smooth locks, which Fräulein Lehzen spent a long time inducing to curl. They all said she had pretty hair, but it was not grand and glorious like Uncle Leopold's. His was not always the same either – the colour varied, which made it even more interesting.

When she asked Sissi about it and Sissi whispered: 'It's a wig,' that seemed even more clever – to have hair that came off and could be put on a stand at night.

Of course, she had been *very* young when she thought that. Now she knew lots of people had wigs. Uncle King's mass of nut-brown curls might well be one, she supposed. But perhaps a King could command hair to grow. She had asked Sissi this and Sissi had laughed and said she thought of the funniest things.

But here was Uncle Leopold, studying her intently, asking her questions and telling Mamma what she should do.

Then he lifted her up on his knee. How were the dolls? Would she show them to him? And was she speaking English *more* than German? Yes was the answer to the two last questions.

'Now,' she told him; and he went with her to the nursery where the dolls all sat obediently awaiting their orders from her.

'They obey your orders, I hope,' said Uncle Leopold jocularly.

'Oh yes, you see I am the Queen.'

Uncle Leopold and Mamma exchanged a somewhat odd glance – as though she had said something alarming.

While they were looking at the dolls Aunt Adelaide arrived and they went back to the drawing-room to receive her. She often called and Victoria knew why. It was to see her.

'Do you wish I were your little girl?' Victoria had asked her.

And the answer had been a fierce hug which had been very gratifying. And the big doll was from Aunt Adelaide – her favourite among them all. There had never been such a doll. How I wish she could be named Victoria, thought Victoria. That was the only name for such a big fine doll.

Aunt Adelaide had a look of happiness about her. Victoria presumed it was because she had come to see her. She threw herself at her aunt – forgetting Mamma's instructions but Aunt Adelaide did not mind at all; she picked her up and kissed her many times and Victoria put her arms round Aunt Adelaide's neck.

'And how is my *dear* little Victoria?'

'Victoria is well . . . and so is the Big Doll.'

'She has no teething troubles that Big Doll?' asked Aunt Adelaide.

Victoria laughed gleefully. 'No, they have all come through now.'

The Duchess and Leopold looked on in some exasperation. Adelaide seemed to forget decorum in the presence of the child. She was so besotted about Victoria that she behaved like . . . The Duchess sought for words but could only think of A Common Person. Of course life with Clarence might be responsible for that. And where had she come from? A little dukedom! She would not pursue that because Meiningen was very similar to Leiningen – both small insignificant principalities. But at least the Duchess of Kent was aware of her position. To think that if two very likely events took place this Adelaide might be Queen of England.

Two Queens! thought the Duchess, good humour restored as she looked at the Duchess of Clarence talking animatedly to Victoria. The only occasions when she seemed animated were when she was with the child.

Victoria wanting to show Aunt Adelaide how the Big Doll was settling in with the others, had taken her hand and was attempting to drag her across the room. Really, Victoria! thought the Duchess of Kent. But perhaps since Adelaide could well be a queen it was permissible. Two queens! What a pleasant thought.

'Victoria,' she said in a tone of mild reproof, 'I daresay your Aunt Adelaide would wish to stay here and talk with Mamma and Uncle Leopold.'

Adelaide would clearly greatly have preferred to go with Victoria but there was nothing to do but remain and talk to the adults. So she inquired politely after Leopold's health and as this was one of his favourite topics he kept it going for some time.

When they talked of the King's State visits, Victoria listened avidly. She loved hearing anything about Uncle King. She would keep so quiet that Mamma would forget she was here. It was the best way of learning that which they might not wish her to know.

'I believe the Irish visit was a great success,' said the Duchess of Kent.

'William has heard from His Majesty that he enjoyed it. The Irish adored him.'

'And of course he is feeling his *freedom*,' said the Duchess of Kent who, in all matters not connected with her daughter's accession to the throne, could be a little indiscreet.

'It was a trying situation,' admitted Adelaide.

Leopold looked a little supercilious. He had never been on easy terms with his father-in-law and in fact the King made no secret of his mild contempt for Leopold. He had never wanted Charlotte to marry him and would have much preferred the Prince of Orange as a son-in-law. Leopold's abstemious habits and his somewhat pompous manners made him in the King's view a dull fellow.

'Rarely could a man have been so relieved to be free from the bonds of matrimony,' said Leopold.

Victoria wished they would not use such long words. But she remained very still watching Mamma's glorious curls bobbing up and down as she spoke and all the frills and ribbons on her gown; and Uncle Leopold's thick soles and curly wig and Aunt Adelaide who looked so simple beside them, but so kind. And I love her, thought Victoria.

'Heaven alone knew what she would have done next . . . if she had lived.' The Duchess of Kent shuddered. 'And it would serve His Majesty right after the way he has treated her. The investigation . . . the trial . . .'

Leopold threw her a warning look.

'It is all over now,' said Adelaide. 'William is relieved, of course.'

'And now,' went on the irrepressible Duchess, 'he is on the Continent and I hear he is making a great impression everywhere he goes. Of course he could always *talk* people into admiring him.'

'He has great charm,' said Adelaide.

'If his own people made as much of him as the foreigners do he would be a contented king, I doubt not,' added the Duchess of Kent.

Leopold thought: I must impress on her the need to curb her tongue. The King already dislikes her. Heaven knows what he might do. What if he made some law which would enable them to pass over Victoria?

To change the subject he said: 'I have heard that the King has been to see his nephews – the two young Georges who are named after him, Cumberland and Cambridge. They're just about Victoria's age.'

The Duchess of Kent laughed scornfully. 'They will never have a *chance*.'

'The King has always had a great respect for his brother Ernest,' said Leopold. 'It would not surprise me if Cumberland did not return to England now that the old King is dead.'

'Let them come,' said the Duchess of Kent recklessly.

Leopold frowned. But after all it was only Adelaide. She would not report anything, nor see any evil in it.

'You are looking in exceptionally good health,' said Leopold to Adelaide.

'I am very well, thank you.' Adelaide had flushed slightly.

Oh God, thought the Duchess of Kent. It can't be. I couldn't bear it.

But she must know. The suspense would be unbearable if she did not. And if it were so? No! Fate could not be so cruel. There had been three failures. There could not be another attempt.

She was aware of Victoria quietly leaning against Adelaide playing with the rings she was wearing.

'My stepdaughter, Lady Erroll,' Adelaide said, 'is very happy. She is expecting a child.'

'Excellent news,' said the Duchess of Kent. Was that a certain lilt she heard in Adelaide's voice? What did it mean? Was it possible?

'If it is a girl she wants to call it Adelaide.'

'And you will allow this?' asked the Duchess of Kent whose manner always grew cold when the FitzClarences were referred to.

'I shall be delighted.'

The Duchess of Kent could restrain herself no longer.

'You yourself look much happier than you have since . . . the tragedy. Is there any reason?'

There was a tense silence in the room. Victoria listening intently wondered what it could mean.

'I have hopes again.'

Hopes! Oh God! thought the Duchess of Kent. It is as I feared.

They could not talk in front of the child, of course; but it was clear enough. Adelaide sitting there, quiet, serene, *smug*! thought the Duchess of Kent. I cannot bear it. It was like the distant funeral bell tolling dismally. The birth of Adelaide's 'hopes' could only mean the death of her own.

Adelaide begged that Prince Leopold and the Duchess of Kent would excuse her. She wanted to pay her respects to the dolls before she left and she was going to ask Victoria if she might do this.

Victoria was taking her aunt's hand, forgetting the strange conversation she had not understood, and together Adelaide and Victoria went to the nursery while back in the drawing-room Leopold was trying to restrain his sister and begging her not to have hysterics until *after* the Duchess of Clarence had left.

*

Adelaide grew happier as it became certain that her hopes were well-founded. She would take care, she promised herself; everything that could be done to achieve a safe delivery should be done. She kept reminding herself that but for that bitterly cold day her baby Elizabeth would have lived. She could bear a child – and a healthy one.

Elizabeth Erroll's baby was born and like the daughter of George FitzClarence was christened Adelaide. William was delighted both to be a grandfather and that his son and daughter should have wanted to name their children after their stepmother.

At least, thought Adelaide, I am surrounded by babies. And that made her very happy. Not only was she constantly with her step-grandchildren but there was her niece Victoria too. She never lost an opportunity of visiting Kensington Palace and she and Victoria were the best of friends. But she must be careful for she sensed that the Duchess of Kent was a little jealous of Victoria's love for her.

But however much she might enjoy the company of other people's children, desperately she wanted her own. Only when she had her own child would the pain of Elizabeth's loss begin to fade.

As the time for her confinement drew near she stayed at Bushy; she was very large and believed that presaged a strong and healthy child.

The FitzClarences were constantly with her, George's wife and Elizabeth – mothers themselves – giving her advice, the rest cosseting her.

And then came the day when her pains started . . . far too early. She was hurried to bed to have a miscarriage.

She was desperately unhappy. It seemed a double misfortune since there had been two babies and she could not help picturing herself with her twins, one in each arm.

Had any woman ever longed for a child as she did? she wondered. Had any ever been so heartbreakingly disappointed.

William came and sat by her bed. He wept with her.

'My poor, poor Adelaide,' he said. 'But I still have you.'

And that was some comfort.

He had written to the King, he said, to tell him the sad news.

His Majesty, now at Brighton, feeling far from well, would be desolate.

William was right. The King sent his deepest condolences. He was genuinely sorry for he was disliking the Duchess of Kent more than ever; the airs she gave herself were intolerable to him and he would very much like to see her relegated to the background by the birth of a child to William and Adelaide.

William himself had no liking for the lady who had been extremely rude about his dear sons and daughters. Why should this upstart Duchess imagine herself too good to know *his* children? A most unpleasant woman! he decided.

Adelaide, however, was fond of young Victoria so she continued to visit Kensington Palace. He did not wish to spoil Adelaide's pleasure so he did not suggest she should forgo these calls. But it was galling when the haughty Duchess refused to come to Bushy because she feared she might come into contact with some of the FitzClarence family.

Adelaide was delicate for some time after the miscarriage and William believed a holiday would be good for her.

'Let us do a bit of travelling,' he said. 'We will go and stay with Ida and perhaps look in at Würtemburg to see my sister. She would be delighted and you two were fond of each other.'

Adelaide agreed that she would enjoy a continental tour! Not that it would make her forget. Nothing could do that; but William was obviously elated at the idea; and who knew, there might be hope yet of realizing her greatest dream.

So they made plans to leave and it was with some sorrow that she discovered she would not be in London to celebrate Victoria's birthday.

She wrote to her before she left:

Uncle William and Aunt Adelaide send their love to dear little Victoria with their best wishes on her birthday and hope that she will become a very good girl, being now three years old.

Uncle William and Aunt Adelaide also beg little Victoria to give dear Mamma and dear Sissi a kiss in their name; and to Aunt Mary, Aunt Augusta and Aunt Sophia too, and also to the Big Doll.

Uncle William and Aunt Adelaide are very sorry to be absent on that day and not to see their *dear, dear* little Victoria, as they are sure she will be very good and obedient to dear Mamma on that day and on many, many others. They also hope that dear little Victoria will not forget them and know them again when Uncle and Aunt return.

So for Victoria it was a birthday without the presence of Uncle William and Aunt Adelaide. She missed Aunt Adelaide very much indeed. But her mother was by no means displeased.

Victoria was growing far too fond of Aunt Adelaide, who spoiled her in any case. Why, there were times when the Duchess of Kent believed that the child – *her* child – was more anxious for the society of her Aunt Adelaide than that of her own dear Mamma.

Shortly afterwards on a sunny June day the *Royal Sovereign* carrying the Duke and Duchess of Clarence left Walmer for Flushing; the holiday had begun, but as the yacht left the Downs it struck rough weather and most of the passengers were ill so it was a great relief when the coast of Belgium was sighted and they came to Antwerp.

Adelaide was delighted to be on dry land again and after a short stay at Antwerp they went on to Ghent to see Ida and her family.

What a joyful reunion and how delighted was poor little Louise and her brother Wilhelm!

'Children always love Adelaide,' said William rather sadly; and Ida went on quickly to talk of how they had enjoyed their stay in London and were all hoping to come again.

'We'll be glad to see you at Bushy whenever you care to come,' replied William. 'And I know I speak for Adelaide, too.'

The time in Ghent passed too quickly. There was so much to tell Ida. At first it was not easy to talk of her disappointments but in time she was able to and Ida's ready sympathy was comforting.

'You will have a healthy child one day, Adelaide,' said Ida. 'I am sure of it.'

'How I wish I were! I believe though that the Duchess of Kent is fearful.'

'Oh, that woman. *I* believe she is very ambitious.'

'It is natural that she should be. Little Victoria is the most

225

enchanting creature whom her mother has quite made up her mind is going to be the Queen of England. I wish that the Duke of Kent had been older than William, then she might not have been so fearful.'

'Adelaide!' cried Ida aghast. 'You don't think that she *ill-wishes* you.'

Adelaide smiled. 'Dear Ida, she is not a wicked woman, and I so well-wish myself that I am sure the fervency of my wishes would outweigh hers.'

'I am not so sure,' said Ida. 'Ambition is a frightening thing.'

'Then don't let's talk of it. Tell me about Louise and Wilhelm, and all that is happening here.'

'Oh, we get along well. I am always hoping to find a doctor who can do something for Louise. And we are not rich, you know. I did not make a grand marriage as you did.'

'It was a happy marriage, Ida. What could be better than that?'

'And you are not happy?'

'But of course I am. William is kind and he is really a good man, Ida.'

Ida looked a little sadly at her sister. Her marriage to the ageing Duke could scarcely be called romantic; and she was still childless after several attempts.

So, thought Ida, I would still say 'Poor Adelaide'.

It was very pleasing to the sisters to feel that no great distance separated them. When Adelaide left Ghent it was after having received a promise from Ida that she would visit her next year.

They then proceeded with their journey, calling on Elizabeth, the Landgravine of Hesse-Homburg, and her rather odd husband, with whom Elizabeth declared herself well pleased, although she admitted that he had to be asked very persuasively to bath. Then to Saxe-Meiningen where Adelaide's mother and brother, the Duchess Eleanor and Duke Bernhard, were delighted to see the visitors.

But the Duchess was disturbed by her daughter's misadventures in childbirth. 'Dearest child,' she asked, 'do you take the greatest care?'

'The utmost, Mamma,' replied Adelaide.

'You were always a little delicate,' sighed the Duchess. 'Not like Ida and . . .'

She did not add that Ida's husband was young and vigorous and that the Duke of Clarence was scarcely that. What a pity that the Duke of Saxe-Weimar was not the Duke of Clarence and vice versa. It was far more important for Adelaide to have children than for Ida; and yet ironically – one might say mischievously – it was the younger daughter who was productive when the elder one could have given birth to a monarch.

But what concerned Duchess Eleanor as a mother was the health and happiness of her daughters. She need have no fears for Ida – but Adelaide. Adelaide so deserved happiness; and there was a haunting sadness about her which the Duchess knew was due to frustrated motherhood.

Still, she was having her effect on William. He was far less crude than he had been at the time of their marriage. When they parted the Duchess Eleanor gave her daughter injunctions to come again soon and declared what happiness it was to her to know that she could see all her family from time to time.

And after that followed a brief visit to the Queen of Würtemburg who welcomed her brother and sister-in-law with great warmth. They were shocked by the sight of her, for her body had become not only gross but oddly shaped. She had the family tendency to grow fat and unlike her brother, King George IV, she had never corseted. Her face had grown so large that eyes had sunk into flesh; she was an extraordinary sight and scarcely human, but she was kind and felt very friendly towards Adelaide and was full of commiseration over the loss of her children. Adelaide was sorry to leave her sister-in-law but she was beginning to feel an eagerness to be back in the peace of Bushy with her younger stepchildren where the elder ones called frequently bringing the children which they knew made them exceptionally welcome.

Back in England, settling happily at Bushy, visiting Kensington Palace, seeing how the little Victoria had grown, was certainly very pleasant.

The Duchess of Kent though was decidedly jealous, for on Adelaide's first call after the return to England, Victoria so far forgot her good manners as to fly at her aunt and put her chubby arms about her knees and bury her face into Aunt Adelaide's gown in an excess of affection.

'Victoria!' cried the Duchess of Kent in an angry voice.

And Victoria, flushing with shame, withdrew herself and curtsied to Aunt Adelaide in the manner laid down in the nursery.

Adelaide laughed and picked up the child in her arms.

'Oh, we are too good friends for ceremony, my precious.'

At which Victoria chuckled with relief and putting her arms about Adelaide's neck gave her a resounding kiss.

We must put a stop to this, thought the Duchess of Kent.

'I must apologize for my daughter's behaviour,' she said to Adelaide.

'I like it,' was the reply.

'So,' complained the Duchess of Kent afterwards to John Conroy, 'shattering all the good sense I have been trying to instil into the child. But what can you expect of a woman who receives those dreadful FitzClarence bastards as though they are her stepchildren.'

'And how is the Big Doll?' Adelaide wanted to know.

'She is very well, Aunt Adelaide. And she will be pleased to see you. She has missed you. She told me so.'

Victoria must be taught not to tell lies, thought the Duchess of Kent.

'And may I see her?'

'Oh, please come, Aunt Adelaide. And I have some more dolls. Aunt Augusta gave me one dressed like Queen Elizabeth. And Aunt Mary has promised me another.'

'That is a lovely idea. Perhaps you will make a collection.'

'What *is* a collection?'

The Duchess of Kent watched in exasperation while they looked at the dolls and the Duchess of Clarence behaved in what she could only call a most *infantile* manner.

Now, she thought, she will be calling often; Victoria will be visiting St James's – but not Bushy, never Bushy, that is something I will never allow – and Victoria is growing up. She is advanced for her years. She picks up things quickly ... sometimes, I think, too quickly. We shall have to be very watchful.

Adelaide was telling Victoria about the dolls she had seen on the Continent and she must look about and see what were to be had here. They must really start their collection.

Really, thought the Duchess of Kent, I would say it was time that woman had a child of her own – *if* it would not be so disastrous if she did.

A glorious thing had happened. Adelaide was once again pregnant.

This time, she told herself as she had on every other occasion, I shall succeed.

When Adelaide wrote and told Ida of her hopes Ida wrote that Mamma had suggested she come over to England and look after Adelaide during her pregnancy. Did Adelaide feel it would be a good idea? Adelaide's reply was that little could delight her more and Ida said she would prepare to leave at once bringing the children with her.

'It would be pleasant,' Adelaide said to William, 'if when we entertained we could do so in London as well as at Bushy.'

'The apartments at St James's are hardly big enough for that. We should need a bigger house. Really it is ridiculous that we have no place in London but these dismal rooms. I'll choose a moment to speak to George about it. He is constantly adding to Carlton House and the Pavilion; and now he has notions for Buckingham House. He was telling me about them the other day. I don't see why we shouldn't have a house of our own.'

'It must either be that or we shall have to refurbish these St James's rooms,' said Adelaide. 'But there is always Bushy. Ida and the children will stay there of course. But it would be convenient if we could be in London now and then.'

'Leave it to me,' said William.

It was a great joy to see Ida very pleased with herself, and looking extremely well.

'You've put on weight,' said Adelaide.

'It's not to be wondered at,' retorted Ida. 'There will be two of us.'

'You . . . again.'

'Oh, come, I only have my two. Three will be a pleasant number.'

'Ida . . . when?'

'October.'

'I'm so pleased that we shall have our children together.'

'That's what I thought and that's why I came. I'm to take the greatest care of you. Make sure you don't tax your strength. I have orders from Mamma.'

'Oh, it's wonderful to be together again.'

'The children think so. Loulou adores you, you know.'

'As I do her.'

'When she heard we were coming to stay with you her face lit up with joy. Poor darling, I fear life will not be very good for her. She looks so sad sometimes when she sees other children running about.'

'We must try to make her happy.'

'You do, Adelaide. You always do. You have a way with children. They all seem to love you.'

Adelaide sighed and Ida wished that she had not said that for she had reminded her sister of her losses.

But this time it was going to be different.

Alas, this was not to be.

It was the familiar pattern. Weeks before the child was due, Adelaide felt the warning pains; and all the attention of the royal physicians and her sister Ida's care could not save her from the inevitable miscarriage.

With each one she grew more and more desperate. It seemed to her that she was incapable of bearing a child that could live. And the fact that there were ten healthy FitzClarences to prove that the fault did not lie with William made her all the more depressed.

'Our marriage is pointless,' she told Ida, 'for it was solely to provide a child that it was arranged.'

'That may have been,' retorted Ida, 'but it is not so now. William relies on you. He was quite distracted when you were so ill. Whatever the original reason for the marriage, now it is based on true affection. He relies on you. He needs you. That has to be your consolation.'

There *was* some consolation in the thought.

In October Ida gave birth to a son – a healthy boy who was christened Edward and in caring for him Adelaide found much comfort.

William went down to see the King at the Pavilion, whither he had gone after his very successful tour of the Continent which had followed that of Ireland.

The King was not in good health and William was shocked at the sight of him. The coronation and the State visits which had followed had given him an interest which had temporarily rejuvenated him but now he was back in England and his people showed quite clearly that they had recovered from the excitement of the coronation. They did not like their King now that it was over any more than they had before it had taken place. The spate of lampoons was growing and they were getting more and more unpleasant.

By God, he has changed! thought William; and remembered how awkward he had always felt in glittering George's presence. The King still retained his charm and when he displayed it one forgot his unwieldy body, but he felt that unless he were firmly corseted he could not possibly appear in public and to be firmly corseted had become an agony.

He was pleased to see William as he always was to see any of his brothers, and commiserated with him immediately about the loss of the child.

'How I would have delighted if all had gone well! Not only for dear Adelaide's sake and yours, William, but to put an end to the vanities of that absurd woman at Kensington Palace. I hear *that* infant thrives.'

'Adelaide tells me so. She is very fond of her. She is embroidering a dress for her now.'

'Adelaide is a saint.'

'I know.'

The King looked as though he were about to launch into an account of his own matrimonial disasters from which release had come too late. So William said: 'Adelaide feels we should have a place in London. Those St James's quarters are cramped and uncomfortable.'

'So you should,' said the King. 'Why don't you get a London house?'

'For the usual reasons,' said William. 'Money.'

'My dear fellow, I am sure that could be arranged.'

So that was settled, and now the King could talk of his own troubles.

He had felt damned ill when he returned from his travels and had had to be bled even more than usual.

'And those damned scribblers! By God, if this is not a libel I don't know what it is. You know what they were suggesting, William? That my illness was *mysterious*. That I had to be shut away from my subjects. And the reason because I was suffering from the same trouble as our father did.'

'What rubbish!'

'That is how it is, William. It will never be forgotten that our father was *mad*. They are going to watch us very closely and if we show the slightest sign of eccentricity there will be those to whisper against us.'

'It's monstrous.'

'I thought so, William, and that is why I wished to sue for libel. But you know what happened when Peel raised the matter. The Attorney-General was against it. It would have meant one of those interminable cases and so, I was told, whatever the verdict, the rumours would remain. You see what I have to suffer, William.'

'I am glad that you have dear Lady Conyngham to make life easier for you.'

The King looked sad, but decided not to make a confidant of William.

The truth was that he was discovering he had no great confidence in Lady Conyngham. He was not such a fool as not to know that her affection was rather for the King than for the man. She was no Maria Fitzherbert. How he wished that Maria were with him now. But it was many years since they had been together. He wondered whether she ever thought of him now. It was when he had become Regent that they had parted and she would have grown accustomed to being without him; she had devoted herself to her adopted daughter Mary Seymour and he had heard from time to time that she had derived great happiness from the girl. He could recall times when Mary Seymour had been a very little girl and used to climb on his knee and call him Prinney – and they had been like a happy family – the three of them. That was how it should have remained.

But he had left Maria. No, no, he would not have that. Maria had left *him*. But it was due to his friendship with Lady Hertford. And what happiness had that brought him? And now Lady Hertford had gone and Lady Conyngham was the companion on whom he relied.

But she was weary of him. He knew it. She did not want to be a nurse to a tired, sick old man. She wanted a king who could give her diamonds and sapphires and at whose side she could appear on glittering occasions.

But he was ill and tired – mad, his enemies tried to say, like his father; and life had not gone well for him because he was lonely and he must cling to Lady Conyngham because there must be some woman in his life. She did not want him and through his own folly he had lost the one whom he had truly loved and who had truly loved him.

She was not very far away in distance but too many years, too many quarrels, too many humiliations separated them.

So, tired, old and ill, he must be lonely too.

And while Lady Conyngham continued to be with him and he bribed her with his kingship and the jewels she so loved and the honours she demanded for her family, he knew that he did not care for her; he only wanted not to be lonely.

And the name that most constantly was in his mind was Maria.

When Ida said she should return to Ghent to join her husband, Adelaide was melancholy.

'I can never tell you,' she said to William, 'what it has meant to me to have my sister and the children with me at this time.'

'You've grown fond of the little ones,' said William. 'Particularly Louise.'

'I am so sorry for the dear child. She is a brave little thing for I know she suffers pain.'

'I sometimes think she cares for you more than she does her own mother.'

'That's not true. But Ida is so gay and full of life. Perhaps her mother makes her realize more fully what she has missed than I do.'

William was thoughtful and later that day he went to Ida's room and asked if he could have a word with her.

'You'll be leaving soon,' he said. 'Adelaide is going to miss you very much.'

'As I shall miss her.'

'You will go back to the gay life of Ghent. You have your husband and your children . . .'

'Oh dear, how I wish Adelaide's child had lived.'

'And how I wish there was something I could do to make her see this is not quite so important as she thinks. If we cannot have a child there is no use brooding on it. We should forget it and enjoy life. A trip on the Continent, I always say – and go on hoping. But one thing did strike me. You have to go but why shouldn't Loulou and the baby remain?'

'My children!' cried Ida.

'It would comfort her. Let them stay on. She'll have little Louise to care for and that will comfort her for the loss of her own. Ask Louise if she will stay and if she wishes to, let her. And the baby too. That is what Adelaide needs at this time – a baby to care for.'

Ida looked in astonishment at William. How he had changed since his marriage! He was developing a little imagination and had grown thoughtful. He did indeed love Adelaide.

Of course, this was Adelaide's influence on him. She was thought to be quiet and perhaps insignificant. It had always been so; but this was not true. It was people like Adelaide who had a stronger influence than frivolous people like herself.

And Louise? She had to admit that there were times when she was impatient with Louise, when she could not suppress her irritation with the child, when the sight of a crippled daughter depressed her; and she saw now that Louise, perhaps made more sensitive by her affliction, was aware of this.

But Adelaide would feel only love for Louise and the love would be greater because of the child's disability. Adelaide would never flare into sudden temper; she would be equable, able to bring Louise out of *her* fits of depression; she would make her believe that there were compensations in not being able to dance and play games that other children could.

'You see what I mean,' persisted William. 'Think about it, Ida. And if you agree, tell Adelaide.'

Thus it was that when Ida left for Ghent she left behind her baby and the crippled Louise. The latter, when questioned by her mother, had admitted that she would prefer to stay in England with Aunt Adelaide than return with her mother to Ghent.

That was enough for Ida who told Adelaide that Louise wished to stay.

Adelaide could not disguise her pleasure in the fact that although her sister must go she was not going to lose her little niece and nephew.

Could Ida bear to part with them?

Ida said she could and since the baby had been born Adelaide had done far more for him than his mother had.

'He would be lost without you,' said Ida. 'Let them stay on until I have settled in; and then I will come again and take them home.'

So Ida left and the parting was not so desolate as it might have been: for Adelaide had the children to look after and if they were not her own – well, they were the next best thing.

William was in excellent spirits for he had chosen a site for his new House which was to be built in St James's.

'I shall call it Clarence House,' he said, and Adelaide agreed that it was as good a name as anyone could wish.

With the approach of Christmas came an invitation to join the King at Brighton.

Adelaide was a little uneasy as the death of the Queen and the

Duchess of York had put her in the position of first lady, which meant at Brighton where the Court was she would be constantly called upon to do her duty in that role, for where the King was there must be a certain amount of ceremony and she would be often at the King's side.

She was aware that she lacked the handsome looks of many of the women with whom the King surrounded himself. Lady Conyngham who was always very prominent at all functions might be considerably older than Adelaide, but she knew how to be beautiful by candlelight at least, and she rarely appeared in the bright light of morning. Nor did the King, who was growing more and more conscious of his ageing looks; and all the glittering ornaments and decorations he could put on to his beautifully cut garments could not hide the fact that his body was becoming a grotesque travesty of what it had been in his youth. The swelling in his neck necessitated a neckcloth so vast that it almost suffocated him; there were times when his gout was so painful that he could not put his foot to the ground. But for Christmas he needed to charm his guests, so he was bled – not too profusely this time – and lived very quietly for a few weeks in readiness for the festivities.

Adelaide was a little overwhelmed by the Pavilion – as indeed everyone was who entered it. It changed continuously for the King could not conquer his passion for beautiful *objets d'art*, nor for building, so there was always something new to be admired and the King took an almost childish delight in his treasures.

The newest acquisition was the wonderful bathroom the pipes of which were connected with the sea. This enabled him to enjoy the sea-water baths which had so delighted him in the days of his prime. When he had first discovered the spot and transformed little Brighthelmstone, the tiny fishing village, into royal and fashionable Brighton, he had taken his dips in the sea attended by old Smoker – the dipper who respected no person, not even the Prince of Wales, and who had been christened by the Prince himself, the King of Brighton.

Those days were over. The Prince of Wales had become Regent and then King and as he passed from one glorious role to the other he had shed his youth and handsome looks. He had been too fond of indulging his tastes – too much rich food, too much good wine. And women? No, not to excess. He had had many mistresses but he had always deceived himself that he was in love with them. And one thing he had never lost throughout his life was the power to deceive himself.

Adelaide found the ordeal less trying than she had feared, for the King exerted all his magic to make her feel at ease; and since she was at his side so often he had the opportunity of charming her.

Lady Conyngham was very sure of her position, flashing the new sapphire which the King had given her and which was reputed to be part of the State jewels. She was a little arrogant because while she enjoyed occasions like this and, without doubt, the gifts and honours she received as the King's mistress were well worth having, the King's growing desire to live in retirement was very tiresome, and there had been times when she wondered whether the disadvantages did not outweigh the advantages.

The fact that the King needed her more than she needed him gave her a sense of such self-importance that being a rather foolish woman she could not help showing it.

She was extremely unpopular among the King's enemies who looked upon her as a royal extravagance and by his friends who regarded her as a harpy.

Adelaide did not like her, although Lady Conyngham considered Adelaide too insignificant for her notice.

As the days passed Adelaide thought longingly of the simple life at Bushy with the children she had staying with her. Louise must be missing her, though the baby was too young to do so. Perhaps the noisy FitzClarences discussing their always interesting affairs missed her too.

The Pavilion was almost unbearably hot, being overheated because the King felt the cold. In the evenings there was usually a concert in the Music Room, and there the King liked to lie on a couch and listen; consequently the guests were expected to do the same.

The Music Room during a concert, thought Adelaide, with its

oriental decor, its almost suffocating heat, its occupants stretched out on sofas, was like a room in a Sultan's palace. And there, benign, enormous, in complete harmony with the surroundings he had created, lay the Sultan himself – King George IV.

Yes, it would be a great relief to go back to family life at Bushy.

One step nearer

It was not to be expected that the ambitious Duke and Duchess of Cumberland had cut themselves off from affairs in England. Though it was true that since Queen Charlotte had ordered them to leave the country, they had done so, they had watched what was happening with the greatest interest.

'Soon,' Ernest told Frederica, 'it will be necessary for me to go back.'

'We have lost the throne for our George,' replied Frederica sadly. 'That fat child at Kensington Palace seems as healthy as a child could possibly be.'

'She may not always remain so.'

'That's true. And Adelaide is not going to produce – that much is evident.'

'I hear that George is very ill. In fact no one would be surprised if he went at any moment. And Frederick is not much better. They are both puffed up with dropsy.'

'There's still Clarence.'

'Curse Clarence! He's the stumbling block.'

'No. It's that fat child, Victoria they are calling her now. And I believe her dear Mamma is giving herself such airs that the family is a little put out with her.'

'One thing,' put in Ernest, 'I shall be a king before I die. King of Hanover. Little Victoria cannot have Hanover. Thanks to the Salic law they'll not have a woman ruler – not even darling little Victoria.'

'I'll swear that infuriated Mamma Kent.' The Duchess's lips

tightened. 'And to think that our beautiful George would be King of England were it not for that girl. It's maddening.'

'Quite maddening,' agreed Ernest.

'And is there nothing that can be done about it?'

They looked at each other cautiously. There *were* means of preventing precocious children from coming to the throne. There were methods which were unmentionable – even to such as they were; not exactly for moral reasons but because they could never be sure who might overhear them. Besides, such ideas were futile at the moment. That was the point. At the moment.

Kent, Clarence and then Victoria – and if they all failed to reach the throne, Ernest, Duke of Cumberland – with his son George to follow.

It was a brilliant prospect – if it were not for the lives between.

'The time will come,' said his Duchess, 'when it will be necessary for us to go to England.'

'In due course,' replied her husband.

And he saw himself – as she saw him – the crown on his head. King of England. And why not? Only two ageing brothers stood between him – and a plump, spoiled little girl, of course.

Adelaide and William had settled down to a quiet domestic life. They had travelled once more on the Continent. She had kept Ida's children with her and Ida made no complaint; with them and the FitzClarence family she felt that she was indeed a mother. Louise relied on her, was unhappy when not in her company and was even resigned to her affliction for she was sure that it had brought her and Aunt Adelaide closer together.

The romances of the FitzClarence girls – always confided to Adelaide – were a source of continual excitement. Mary was now married to Captain Fox of the Holland family, and Sophia, the eldest of the girls, had announced her engagement to Sir Philip Sydney; only the two younger girls, Augusta and Amelia, were not yet engaged, and they were only twenty-one and eighteen.

'My word,' said William, 'if Dorothy could see her family now, she would be delighted. And there is one thing that would please her more than anything else and that is to see how fond they are of their stepmother.'

Dear William. He might be tactless but he had a good heart; and she must be grateful for it.

He had a great liking for card games and in the evenings would sit playing Pope Joan with Adelaide, Louise and any members of the FitzClarence family who happened to be available. He would chuckle when he won, although the stakes were never more than a shilling a night. How his brothers George and Frederick would have laughed at his simple pleasure. But Adelaide found it endearing.

And from her place on the wall Dorothy smiled down on the woman who had taken her place in Bushy House.

The King's health was deteriorating; he had gone to his cottage at Windsor and was living there in as much seclusion as was possible. He suffered acutely from gout and dropsy and there were times when his legs and feet were so swollen that he could not put them to the ground.

He occupied his time by planning the restoration of the castle which at that time could only be lived in if one was prepared to face the utmost discomfort. The constant interviews with the men he had selected to carry out the task, the vision of what the castle would be like when restored by him, sustained him considerably and made him forget his pains.

But it was not a very happy existence. He hated to be seen by his subjects. Such ridicule had been heaped on him and he had to admit that even the most elegant clothes could do little for the mass of flesh he had become. The desire not to be seen became an obsession. He had trees planted around The Cottage so that no one could see any part of it; and he always had servants stationed at certain spots to prevent any trespassers invading his privacy. He even had certain glades in the forest shut in for his special use; and when he rode back and forth to Brighton and London he did so in a closed carriage, so determined was he not to be seen by his subjects; only his friends, his ministers and those who could not be prevented from seeing him, were allowed to do so.

Art, music, literature still delighted him; and when he was at the Pavilion there were many concerts in the Music Room where he and his guests lay on sofas and were entertained by the greatest musicians of the day. He could be momentarily happy on such occasions and relied on his innate elegance and charm to carry him through; but when he reached the privacy of his apartments and saw his reflection he would be overcome by depression.

Only the thought of beautiful things could give him pleasure, and he could only soothe himself by planning fresh alterations to the Pavilion and Carlton House. But, he thought, shall I be here to enjoy them? Not for long, he feared. But the restored Windsor Castle, the glories of Carlton House and his magnificent Pavilion would be his epitaph. In the generations to come people would say: 'His subjects reviled him but he was a man of exquisite taste.'

He was worried about Elizabeth Conyngham. She had been acting rather strangely lately. The fact was that he had seen little of her. He had been spending so much time in bed, not rising until the afternoon, and then driving out into the secluded glades of the forest accompanied by very few people; sometimes she was there but not always. And when he questioned her absence he heard that she had a headache, or she was slightly unwell.

When he expressed concern she would visit him and explain that it had only been a slight indisposition and she was well again. But she had changed; and he was alarmed.

He knew her very well. She was a stupid woman really. It was six years since he had deserted Lady Hertford for her and he was not sorry to have parted with that lady; but he had now to admit that the relationship with Elizabeth Conyngham was not what he had hoped for.

He sighed. He needed women – or rather one woman over whom he could sentimentalize. It had always been so, all his life; and now that he was forced to spend so much time incapacitated and could brood on the past he saw so clearly how different life would have been if he had never parted from Maria Fitzherbert. She would have remained faithful to him. She was faithful by nature. It was Maria's religion which had come between them.

'Ah,' he moaned, 'I never should have parted with her.'

He became morbid picturing how different it would have been if Maria was here in The Cottage now; he could imagine the pleasant domesticity. She would talk to him *intelligently* – something Elizabeth could not do if she tried – and they would discuss her adopted daughter Minney's affairs, for Minney would have been his daughter as well as Maria's. What a comfort she would have been when he had lost Charlotte.

Once he had thought that if he could be rid of Caroline he would be perfectly happy. And now he was – and he was far from content.

Elizabeth Conyngham was handsome; he did not deny it. She had great feminine charm – but she was a fool.

Yet he could not lose her, for if he did he would be without a mistress. Oh, there might be others who would be willing, but he was too romantic to accept what could not at least appear to be romance. What woman could be expected to fall in love with a mountain of flesh that was in a state of rapid decay merely because it wore a crown?

The worst of being intelligent was that one had to face moments of truth like that. And here he was, tired, old and alone – with the truth.

No, his only hope of a little comfort was to keep Elizabeth – at least outwardly – as his mistress. Even if there was no woman to love him, he must delude himself now and then into believing that there was.

Oh, Maria . . . how different if you were here! Maria was not the woman to turn away because her husband had grown old and ill. That was the difference. He was Maria's husband and nothing could alter that. Why didn't Maria realize it? Why didn't she come back?

It was time to rise. His attendants had come into his bedroom to ask his pleasure. Yes, he would get up.

Later that day he found himself in the company of Madame de Lieven, the wife of the Russian ambassador, a lively woman who although far from beautiful was decidedly fascinating. He was attracted by her and even as he talked to her and considered the defections of Elizabeth Conyngham he was wondering whether it might not add some spice to life to begin a courtship of her.

That of course would infuriate Elizabeth and it would give him some pleasure to do that.

Madame de Lieven, who loved gossip, had noticed that the relationship between the King and Lady Conyngham was a little strained and she thought how amusing it would be to discover the truth of the matter and to pass it on to her friends. She loved writing letters and was proud of her reputation for having intimate knowledge of scandals, royal and otherwise.

She it was who brought up the subject of Lady Conyngham.

'I see that she is not present this evening, Sir.'

'I believe her to be suffering from some slight indisposition.'

'Is that so? I saw her but yesterday and she seemed extremely well.'

'Then perhaps her health has deteriorated since then.'

'She was most animated,' went on Madame de Lieven, 'and greatly enjoying the company.'

There was an insinuation in Madame de Lieven's manner which made the King feel that he must pursue this.

'It was excellent company, no doubt.'

'The most excellent . . . at least so much was evident from Lady Conyngham's manner. Lord Ponsonby, you know, has returned from Corfu. He was present. I believe that he and Lady Conyngham were once old friends.'

Lord Ponsonby! thought the King. He had heard when he had first become friendly with Elizabeth that Ponsonby had been one of her lovers. He had not paid a great deal of attention. A woman like Elizabeth would be certain to have had many lovers.

And Ponsonby was back in England and Elizabeth was suffering from constant minor ailments which prevented her from sharing the King's company as frequently as in the past.

'Ponsonby is a most handsome man,' went on Madame de Lieven mischievously.

'I have heard that opinion expressed before. Was his wife with him?'

'No. She was not present on this occasion. So . . . he had more opportunity of renewing his acquaintance with old friends.'

Stupid Elizabeth, he thought. Did she think he would not

hear? And if she wanted to go ... let her. She was a foolish woman in any case.

'He is a clever fellow, this Ponsonby.'

'He is said to be.'

The King was silent for a while and then he went on: 'Madame de Lieven, I can talk to you very confidentially.'

'Sir, I am honoured.'

'I have always respected your intellect, Madame de Lieven, which is a great attraction when one is surrounded by somewhat stupid people.'

'Stupid people, Sir?'

'A stupid woman,' said the King in a sudden anger against Elizabeth Conyngham because his gout had started to be very painful and Elizabeth did not care and he should never have allowed Maria Fitzherbert to leave him.

'Your Majesty cannot be referring to ... Lady Conyngham?'

'I am,' said the King shortly.

'But ... she is Your Majesty's very good friend. I believed ... and so did others ...'

'Things are not always as they seem. I find the woman a stupid bore. She is handsome, physically attractive but mentally she is an ignoramus; she bores me with her chatter. I am tired ... tired ... tired ...'

'Your Majesty!'

He laid his hand over hers. She *was* an attractive woman. She was a woman of the world. She did not possess the fair good looks which he had always admired, but her conversation and wit would make up for her lack of beauty. Not that she was an unattractive woman by any means. There were rumours of her very romantic relationship with Prince Metternich. She was elegant and worldly.

Yes, he would be pleased to replace Lady Conyngham by her.

Madame de Lieven was alarmed. She had merely been maliciously amused by the King's mistress who couldn't make up her mind what to do – stay with the King and enjoy the glory or leave the King and enjoy herself. The silly empty-headed creature had been debating that for some time; but she would not do so much longer because the handsome Ponsonby, romantic figure from the past, had come forward to make up her mind for her.

Poor King! thought Madame de Lieven. But no woman in her right senses would agree to become his mistress just because Elizabeth Conyngham had decided she was bored with the job. And that it was indeed boring Madame de Lieven was well aware. He was leading the life of an invalid – bed till the afternoon, a little drive in the forest, cards. Ugh! thought Madame de Lieven.

'I have long admired your elegance and wit,' said the King.

'How gracious of Your Majesty to say so.'

'I have often thought how delighted I should be if ours were to become a closer relationship.'

'Your Majesty does me too much honour.' She had skilfully removed her hand. What a scene, she thought. She would embellish it a little (writer's licence) and tell her Prince, in one of her amusing letters, all about it.

But how to extricate herself? It should not be so difficult with the King as with some men. He was so quick to catch an inflection of the voice, the meaning behind the words. He had had many adventures with women, although it would be a rare occurrence for him to be told that he was not wanted.

'We must talk of this,' he went on.

'I had meant to tell Your Majesty that I may be obliged to leave Court for a few weeks.'

He had taken the hint. He had withdrawn but with the utmost ease. He would never forget his courtly manners.

'Your Majesty will understand how exacting it is to be the wife of a diplomat.'

Of course she was not going to leave Court. She would merely keep clear of him for a few weeks. She could not openly refuse the King's advances but at the same time she need not accept them.

The King began to talk of his building plans. They were most intricate and he was eager to see them put into practice. One day when she *returned* to Court he would *arrange* for her to see them.

His Majesty was indeed gracious, said Madame de Lieven.

When she left the King she could not wait to pick up her pen. What a story! The King was tired of Conyngham; he thought her a bore and a fool. He had sought to replace her – and by none other than the wife of the Russian ambassador!

How fascinating! And how delightful to tell it. The Prince would realize what a *femme fatale* he had for a friend.

That night the King felt very melancholy.

Madame de Lieven had told him quite clearly that she would not consider being his dear friend.

He pictured himself making advances to attractive women who would imply politely that they had no wish to share his life. Who would have believed it in those days when he was merely Prince of Wales and he only had to signify his desire to speak to a woman and she was ready to give all he asked.

And now he was a king. But of what importance was rank when one had lost youth.

He must not lose Elizabeth.

He sent for his foreign secretary.

George Canning was a man who had once been a supporter of Caroline, but the King had learned to trust him.

He said when he arrived: 'I heard Ponsonby is back from Corfu.'

'That is so, Your Majesty.'

'A clever fellow, I believe.'

'I have seen no evidence of it, Sir.'

'But somewhat personable. How old is he?'

'Oh ... in his early fifties I should think.'

Younger than I, thought the King.

'It seems to me that he has the necessary qualifications for service abroad. Good ambassadors are not easy to find.'

Canning knew, of course, of Lady Conyngham's interest in Ponsonby. The King's affairs were common knowledge. He was not at all sure that he approved of selecting the country's ambassadors in order to remove them from the field of the King's amatory adventures. But the King was sick and in need of the comfort a woman could give. Lady Conyngham was not the person best suited to minister to the King, but he had chosen her; and it was important to keep the King happy.

Canning thought: If he dies there is York, who sometimes

seems even more of an invalid than the King; and then Clarence whom everyone knows is a fool – and he is not very young at that. And after him . . . the child Victoria, who must be just about seven years old.

No, the King must be kept happy.

'We could use Ponsonby in South America,' he said. 'I will sound him.'

'Offer him an attractive post.'

'Your Majesty may rely on me.'

So it was arranged tactfully.

All through the year the King alternated between dangerous illness and recovery. He could on occasions appear at functions charming everyone, laughing, quipping and consuming large quantities of wine; then he would go to Brighton and shut himself away, not leaving his bedroom for several days. He would have to be wheeled from room to room and it was reported that the water was rising in him and he could not last much longer.

The Duke of York suffered from the same complaint. He too was said to be near to death on more than one occasion.

In the fashionable clubs bets were taken. Would the Duke of York ever be King of England? One day the King was said to be the 'favourite'; the next the Duke.

William had decided to take his wife abroad again that year; and he took some of the family with him. All the old haunts were visited; they called on Adelaide's mother, on the Queen of Würtemburg and Ida at Ghent. William found it most enjoyable and he believed that the waters at the spa of Ems were good for him.

When news reached him about the illness of the King and the Duke of York the enormity of what this could mean was brought home to him. He discussed it with Adelaide.

'You see?' he said. 'I always thought that Fred would be King if George went. And there is not much difference between our ages. Two years to be precise. But if they *both* went . . .'

'You would be King, William.'

'King William,' he repeated.

There was a strange look in his eyes. He was realizing that he was ambitious.

'I'd never really faced the fact that George could die. He's been there all my life. The first person I was aware of was George. We are great friends, Adelaide.'

'I know of your fondness for the King.'

William nodded. 'Oh yes, George has been a good brother to me.'

'And still is.'

'But he's a sick man, you must realize. He can't live for ever and Fred is a sick man, too ... and if he goes ... By God, Adelaide, *I* shall be King.'

It seemed strange that he should react in this way. He had always known that there was a possibility that one day he could be King. But it was coming nearer and now it seemed almost a certainty.

'You see, Adelaide, they're both *ill*. They're both sick men. At home ... they are asking which one will die first. You see, Adelaide ...'

She was alarmed by the excitement in his voice; and she noticed the wild look in his eyes.

'It could come ... soon. Perhaps even now ... Adelaide, perhaps even now ...'

'If it were so you would hear quickly,' she told him calmly. 'The King has been ill for so long and recovered so many times. And so has the Duke of York.'

'But they say ... Just fancy it, Adelaide, King William.'

'You would be desolate if George died,' she said. 'And so should I. He has been a good brother to us both.'

'Yes, yes, yes. I'm fond of George. But ...' Then he smiled slowly. 'Adelaide,' he went on, 'I think this is a time when we should be in England.'

She could only agree that this was so, but a strange uneasiness had come to her. She had never seen him quite like this before. She knew him well – a simple man, caring for his family at Bushy, living rather humbly for one in his position, playing Pope Joan for small stakes. That was the life which suited him.

248

She thought: If it ever happened that he should wear the crown I should be uneasy.

When they returned to England it was to find the state of affairs much as it had been when they left. The King had been ill and was better; the Duke of York had been near to death several times but lived on and was building a new home for himself in St James's.

William did not seem depressed by the news. He was remembering, Adelaide hoped, that he was fond of his brothers.

All was well with the family. Sophia, Lady Sydney, had named her daughter Adelaide – so three of William's grandchildren now bore this name. It was a pleasant tribute to Adelaide.

The affairs of the FitzClarences could always absorb William, and Adelaide shared his enthusiasm for the family; she was delighted, too, that William had ceased to brood on the possibility of being King.

The winter was bitterly cold; and in January the Duke of York became very ill. He was swollen so with dropsy that he could not leave his chair; and one day, clad in an old dressing-gown of a drab grey colour which for the last weeks he had worn all the time, he sat in his chair and appeared to sleep. When his attendants, alarmed by his long silence, came to see if he needed them, they found that he was dead.

When the news of Frederick's death was brought to the King he lapsed into deep melancholy. Frederick had been his favourite brother and memories of nursery days came flooding back. It was Frederick who, in the days of their youth, had aided him in his assignations with maids of honour in Kew Gardens; it was Frederick who had stood watch on Eel Pie Island when he had been there with Perdita Robinson. Frederick had supported him through all the trouble with Maria. No two brothers had ever been closer.

And now, Fred had gone first although he was a year younger. It was a melancholy occasion. He talked constantly to Lady

Conyngham who listened sullenly. She was sulking because Lord Ponsonby had been sent to Brazil.

The day of the funeral was the coldest even in that cold spell. The King was clearly genuinely grieved; but it was noticed that the Duke of Clarence was in a state of great excitement. He had of course taken a very close step to the throne and was the heir apparent and it really seemed, by the appearance of the King, that his accession would not be long delayed. But, said the spectators, surely he might have had the decency to restrain his excitement.

'By God,' he said in an audible whisper, 'the cold goes right through your boots.' And turning to the Duke of Sussex he continued: 'This should mean a difference in the way I'm treated now ... You too. It will make a difference ... no mistake about that.'

Peel, the Home Secretary, whispered to a colleague who was blue with the cold: 'Take off your cocked hat and stand on the silk round it. It'll give you some protection from these icy stones.'

'This,' whispered Clarence, 'is going to lay some of us up. There'll be some deaths after this, you see. This cold is ... killing.'

Was he looking hopefully at the King? people asked themselves.

What had happened to Clarence? He had been thought to be a kindly simpleton but was the glitter of a nearby crown blinding him to all family affection?

The King wept openly; but then he had always wept easily. Yet these were genuine tears and as the bells tolled he covered his face with his hands.

'I feel as though nails are being driven into my heart,' he told the Duke of Rutland. 'He was my dearest friend as well as my brother. In our youth we were inseparable and when my father sent him to Germany we were desolate. We considered it the greatest tragedy of our lives; and when he came back it was just as it was before he went away. A world that does not contain Frederick has little charm for me.'

As soon as the funeral was over he drove immediately to

Brighton, for, as he explained, he wanted to shut himself away from the world and he could best do that there.

At Windsor the bells would go on tolling as they would in London. He could not bear to hear them.

In Kensington Palace the Duchess of Kent summoned her daughter. Victoria was growing up. She would be eight in May. Old enough, said her mother, to be aware of her enormous responsibilities.

The tolling of the bells filled the apartments and Victoria told her dolls that it was because of the death of poor Uncle Frederick.

The Duchess thought this preoccupation with dolls a little childish. She had said so to Fräulein Lehzen, but the Fräulein in her devotion to her charge was not always ready to agree with the Duchess. A disturbing element, but the Duchess had to admit that however mistaken Lehzen might be she had the good of Victoria at heart and was assiduous in her care of the child. She also had a method of teaching which was unrivalled and Victoria was not naturally brilliant at her lessons; she was bright and intelligent, precocious even, but sitting down at a desk and learning from books did not appeal to her.

Lehzen believed that as a future Queen the most important subject she must study was history and as Victoria refused to assimilate cold hard facts and dates, Lehzen turned historical facts into exciting stories which she told to Victoria while her maids were dressing her.

The child was too exuberant and apt to gossip too freely in front of servants and this served a double purpose, keeping her from uttering indiscretions and at the same time teaching her what it was essential for her to know. Victoria actually enjoyed these stories.

Fräulein Lehzen was strict in the extreme; she laid down a set of nursery rules from which she would not allow Victoria to diverge; and yet at the same time she managed to inspire in the child a great affection.

The Duchess was well aware of this and so although at times she had her differences with Lehzen, she appreciated her worth.

She had said to that worthy woman, 'We must now double our

vigil. Who knows, the great day may come sooner than we think.'

One of the obstacles – for that was how she thought of those who stood between Victoria and the throne – had been removed.

'My child,' said the Duchess when Victoria came in answer to her summons, 'you know what has happened?'

Victoria said she did and wondered whether Mamma wished her to look sad or gratified. It was not always easy to know; so she compromised and looked half sad, half expectant.

'Poor Uncle Frederick has passed away.'

'Yes, Mamma.'

'And of course we are very sad.'

There was the cue. They must look sad for a moment.

'He was very kind,' said Victoria. 'He gave me my donkey and my lovely Punch and Judy Show.'

The Duchess looked at her daughter in a manner which implied that this was not the time to talk of donkeys and Punch and Judy Shows.

Of course, thought Victoria, I hardly ever saw him. I hardly ever see *any* of the uncles. Uncle William doesn't come with Aunt Adelaide. Uncle Adolphus is always going to Germany. Uncle Ernest is *in* Germany; and Uncle King is too busy being King to see me. She was regretful about that because of all the Uncles she would have liked to see more of Uncle King. There was Uncle Leopold who came on Wednesdays and talked to her very seriously but kindly. He was always very melancholy and there was something going on of which Mamma did not approve. Something to do with an actress who was a friend of his, Victoria believed; she kept her eyes and ears open and liked to hear what the servants had to say. Visits to Claremont were some of the happiest times of her life although there Uncle Leopold was more melancholy than ever, but she could enjoy Uncle Leopold's melancholy because she was sure he did. He told her about Cousin Charlotte and showed her her bedroom and told her of the things she had done and said. Cousin Charlotte had been very gay and a little wild and had shocked people, in the nicest possible way. Strangely enough had she lived she would have been Queen and that would have meant that she, Victoria, would have been more like an ordinary little girl and what she did and said would not have been so important. Victoria did not think she would have wished for that. Sometimes life was very restricting and she was impatient with it; but in her heart she knew that she would not have it different. She was Victoria with a great future – and that was how she wanted it to be. Louisa Lewis who had been dresser to Charlotte and who was an old, old woman still at Claremont, was very fond of Victoria. I believe, thought Victoria, she sees me as Charlotte sometimes. Louisa Lewis told stories of Charlotte – how she was always tearing her clothes – and she spoke as though there was some virtue in it, at least in the way Charlotte did it. 'She was the sweetest, most loving creature that ever lived,' declared Louisa Lewis. Then she would cry and Victoria would wipe away her tears. 'Never mind, Louisa,' she would say. 'It was God's will.'

That was a pleasant thought. It was God's will that Charlotte had died so that Victoria should be the most important little girl in the kingdom.

'You are not paying attention, Victoria,' said the Duchess severely.

'I am now, Mamma.'

'You will have to be more *serious* now. You understand what the death of your Uncle Frederick means?'

'Yes, Mamma, it means that he is dead and we shan't see him again.'

The Duchess looked exasperated, but affectionately so.

'It means this, child, that you have come a little nearer to the throne. Your Uncle George, alas (such a gratified smile for Mamma made it clear that she did not love Uncle King) is a very sick man. If he died tomorrow your Uncle William would be King.'

'Aunt Adelaide would be Queen. I think, Mamma, that she will make a very good Queen.'

Mamma ignored such an idle observation. 'And if they do not have a child, do you know what would happen if Uncle William died?'

'But Uncle William is not going to die ... and Aunt Adelaide ...'

'Aunt Adelaide has nothing to do with this. Uncle William

253

is not immortal. We all have to die and he is not a young man. If Uncle George died and William died, you would be the Queen of England.'

Victoria clasped her hands and raised her eyes to the ceiling, an expression of ecstasy on her face.

The Duchess was pleased. 'I see that you realize your *responsibilities.*'

Victoria had not been thinking of those but of a glittering crown on her head and a cloak of purple velvet edged with ermine.

'We must bear them in mind,' said the Duchess. 'We must be less frivolous. We must prepare ourselves.'

'Yes, Mamma.'

'We will speak of this on a more *suitable* occasion.'

She meant, of course, when the bells had ceased to toll for Uncle Frederick because funerals were supposed to be sad times and how could one be sad when one contemplated being a Queen.

'You may go now, Victoria.'

She curtsied prettily and went to the nursery. She had an urge to play with the dolls. She loved them; she talked to them; they all had names; and most of them represented famous people. Fräulein Lehzen had made some of them herself; she was very good at it, and she would make sure of getting their costumes right. There was Queen Elizabeth who had been a prisoner in the Tower of London before she was Queen and Mary Queen of Scots who had lost her head. She wanted to know all about the dolls and what had happened to them before they had become members of her family. Fräulein Lehzen knew many stories of them all and they were all fascinating. There was the dashing Earl of Leicester who might have married Elizabeth for he wanted to but he had a wife, Amy Robsart. She had always had rather a fancy for Amy Robsart because her story was so sad and she was one of the prettiest of the dolls. She would never really *like* Elizabeth because of Amy Robsart.

She picked up Elizabeth and straightened her ruff with impatient fingers.

'Untidy again!' she said severely. 'And I really believe you had a hand in murdering Amy.' Then she took Amy and kissed her.

'There! A consolation for being pushed down the stairs.'

What exciting dolls they were! Not all famous. The Big Doll presented by Aunt Adelaide was just . . . the Big Doll, bigger than the others and like a baby. She loved the Big Doll but the others were more interesting. They were a worthy collection for a girl who might one day be a Queen herself.

'Listen to the bells,' she said to them. 'They are tolling for Uncle Frederick and because he is dead I am nearer to the throne. One day I shall be a queen.'

She was thoughtful. One day she would be like one of the dolls – Queen Victoria – made of sawdust with a wooden face and a mantle of purple velvet and ermine and a crown on her head.

How strange to think of herself as a doll? But one had to live first of course – and the exciting future lay before her.

Ernest Duke of Cumberland heard of the death of his brother Frederick with undisguised pleasure. There was after all no need to conceal from his clever Duchess that which seemed to him a perfectly natural emotion.

The Duchess had softened a little since the birth of their son. She doted on young George who was a bright boy, and handsome too. Her greatest ambition would be fulfilled if she could see him attain the throne of England.

And to think that there was that smug fat child at Kensington Palace standing between her and her desires was more than she could endure.

She knew that Ernest felt the same; though he was perhaps thinking more of getting the throne for himself than for George.

George would inevitably follow his father – and as usual their ambitions were identical.

'George cannot last much longer,' Ernest was saying. 'It's a miracle that he's held out so long. He's a mass of disease and has to be wheeled about most of the time. Frederick has been removed. And that leaves only William.'

'William is in moderately good health.'

'Is he? Wasn't he at Ems taking the water for something or other? I was thinking more of his *mental* health. I've heard that he has been behaving very strangely. Of course there is the example of our father, so no one would be exactly surprised.'

Frederica raised her eyebrows. 'That might apply to any member of the family.'

'Only if he showed tendencies.'

'It has been said of George.'

'Well, George has behaved somewhat madly now and then. Now, listen, if George died and William went off his head . . .'

'There still remains Miss at Kensington. The little horror seems to be full of health and vigour. How do you propose to remove her from your path?'

'It is something which would have to be considered very carefully; and it would hardly be possible to do that from such a great distance.'

'I see, so you propose going to England?'

'It's the only thing to do. I shall leave almost immediately. There may be little time to lose.'

'And your son and your Duchess?'

'Will follow me, of course. It is important that George be brought up in England. We must show the people that he is as important as his girl cousin of Kensington . . . and far more suited to become their ruler.'

'Will they accept that since he is the son of a younger son?'

'That is what we have to discover, my dear – a means of making the desirable event acceptable to the people of England.'

'There is only one thing that would make them accept it – the death of Victoria.'

'Don't look so despondent, my dear. You sound as though you think the child immortal.'

She laughed.

'So, you will go to England to find a way?'

He nodded thoughtfully.

'I agree,' she said. 'It *is* a matter of urgency.'

Victoria and Uncle King

The King lay in bed in that house in Windsor Park which was called – with mock modesty – the King's *Cottage*. He wore a rather grubby silk jacket and his nightcap of peacock blue satin was a little greasy. He was becoming so blind now – for he had lost the sight in one eye – that he was for great periods of time unaware even of what he looked like.

One of the actresses from Drury Lane sat at his bedside reading to him. He did not go to the theatre now. How could he face his people? But his love of the drama had not abated and it consoled him to have a woman with a beautiful voice to read to him, particularly as she could inject life into the parts as she spoke them. Miss Elizabeth Chester read most days until commanded to stop, although he never allowed her to tire her voice; he might be old, almost blind; he might even forget to be aware of his appearance, but he never forgot the courtesy due to a woman.

Now she was reading *The Winter's Tale*. He had asked for it specially. What memories it conjured up; and as he listened he was no longer an old man lying in his bed but a handsome young prince in a balcony box at Drury Lane Theatre and on the stage was Perdita Robinson – as exquisite a woman as ever graced the theatre of her day – or for that matter anyone else's day.

He closed his eyes and it was Perdita's voice he heard but not her face he saw, for he could not clearly remember what she had looked like; it was Maria's, for hers was one that was engraved on his memory for ever – Maria with the fine eyes and the unpowdered golden hair and the finest of fair skins to put all others to shame, for it had never needed artful aids. Her nose, he thought tenderly, was aggressive enough to add character to her beauty – the imperfection which was more fascinating than perfection could ever be.

So he lay dreaming of the past and Miss Chester's lovely voice was Perdita's and Florizel's in turn. In those days they had called him Florizel and Mary Robinson had been Perdita ever since. But he was no longer Prince Florizel.

He sighed and Miss Chester paused to glance at him.

257

'You read beautifully . . . beautifully . . .' he murmured.

'Thank you, Sir.'

'And perhaps now you are a little tired?'

'No, Sir, if it is Your Majesty's wish that I continue.'

'I must not be selfish.'

She thought how charming he was – even lying there in his bed, without an elegant neckcloth to hide his swollen neck, a mountain of flesh under the silk coverlet; his voice was musical still and he had the power to make any woman feel she was important to him.

'Have I Your Majesty's leave to retire?'

'Please do, and come again tomorrow.'

When she had gone he dozed a little and was startled to be awakened by a servant at his bedside.

'Sir, the Duke of Cumberland is here.'

'Cumberland! From Germany? Where is he?'

'He is in the drawing-room, Sir. I have told him that I will acquaint Your Majesty of his arrival.'

'Bring him in. No, wait.' His fingers touched the silk coat he was wearing. Cumberland must not see him like this for the first time after so long. 'Bring me my robe. And my wig. The nut-brown one.'

He was helped out of bed; he looked different and felt different in wig and robe. He only needed the clothes and he was every inch of him a king. He peered at himself in the looking-glass. He looked pale and it had never suited him to be pale.

'A touch of colour in the cheeks,' he said.

'Yes, Sir.'

There, that was better.

'I will go into my dressing-room,' he said. 'Bring the Duke of Cumberland to me there.'

They faced each other. He did not wish Ernest to know how bad his eyesight had become and that his brother was a blurred figure to him. Ernest looked astonishingly sinister, but he always had; it was due to having lost an eye.

'Ernest, my dear fellow.' He held out his arms and they embraced.

'George! You're looking better than I was led to believe.'

'Oh, these rumours. It is good to see you. I did not know you were in England. Tell me, how is Frederica? How is my young namesake, eh?'

'Well, and they send their respects and affection to Your Majesty. They have made me swear that I shall ask you to receive them . . . soon.'

'They are here?'

'Not yet. I came on in advance. I had heard such tales of your illness. It seems so long since we had been in each other's company. I thought that now that Frederick had gone . . . you might have been feeling the need of a little brotherly companionship.'

'I miss him sorely. We were devoted as you know.'

'Ah, it was always you two. I'll confess now, George, I was always a little jealous.'

'Not you, Ernest!'

'Oh, I know I didn't show it. I was proud. I was arrogant. But I had such a high opinion of myself that I couldn't understand why you had selected Fred as your favourite brother.'

The King laughed. He was feeling better. Family friendships were good. He had always wanted to be on the best of terms with his brothers. He had never had much to do with Ernest, but that was doubtless because Ernest had not been much at home. After that disastrous affair in his apartments when the valet had committed suicide – for that was what had happened in spite of attempts by the press and Ernest's enemies to blacken his character and make him out a murderer – it was to Brighton he had come to recuperate, at his brother George's request. The only brother the King had not liked was the Duke of Kent; and that was largely due to the fact that he believed he had been instrumental in exposing the scandal about Frederick and his mistress Mary Anne Clarke which had upset Fred so much and resulted in his losing command of the Army.

'Well,' said the King, 'Fred and I were of an age. Only a year between us. We were in the nursery together. You're a little younger.'

'Six years.'

'So I was quite a big fellow when you came along.'

'Indeed you were. I remember first being aware of you. I thought you were the most important person in the world.'

'I am sure I would have agreed with you,' said the King with a laugh.

It was easy, thought Ernest; there was no resistance to friendship. George had become rather pathetic. He was still George, of course, larger than life – in more senses than one – but what was he doing here in the Cottage ... living a life of seclusion? It was not like George to hide himself from the world of fashion. But he could no longer compete with the dandies, and he kept away from the wits and the adventurers because he was old and tired and constantly ill.

Poor old George, thought Ernest. I'd only give him a year or so at the most.

'Do you propose to stay in England?' asked the King.

'It depends on your wishes.'

'Mine?'

'I've been thinking. We're a family. Fred has gone, we're all getting older. It seems a pity we were not more together. I shall delay my decision to return until you have had a chance to see a little of me. If you find me a bore and a nuisance, you only have to say so.'

'My dear Ernest, as if I ever should! It would be pleasant if you stayed here.'

'It was what I was hoping you'd say. I have not allowed myself to remain ignorant of what has been happening while I have been out of the country. I shall be able to discuss affairs with you if you wish me to ... oh, only as a figure in the background.'

'It would be a comfort. It's always advisable to discuss matters with friends outside the government.'

Ernest nodded. He was longing to take part in affairs, to offer advice to the King, to guide him, to lead him; to be the King in the background until he could step forward and wear the crown openly.

'I have been thinking of William,' went on Ernest, 'and wondering how he is. I have heard some rather disturbing reports.'

'About William?'

'You know what rumours are. I heard he had been acting in a

strange manner – showing unbecoming hilarity, even at Frederick's funeral. I don't believe it, of course. But I've heard it said that Frederick's death has gone to William's head. He's almost calling himself King William.'

'It's nonsense. William is too fond of me, I'm sure. I flatter myself I mean more to him than a crown, and by God, Ernest, I can assure you of this: Shakespeare was not far wrong. Uneasy does lie the head that wears a crown. If I thought there was anything in these rumours about William I'd let him know that . . . quickly.'

'Poor William, he was always a bit of a buffoon.'

Ernest was watching the King closely. How fond was he of William? How far could he go in his criticism?

The King was smiling affectionately. 'William ought to have some recognition of his position certainly,' he said. 'I have been discussing with Canning the possibility of reviving the title of Lord High Admiral. Why not? It would suit William. He always fancied himself a sailor.'

Lord High Admiral? thought Ernest. That was a good idea. It would keep William occupied in a sphere that interested him; and no doubt give him plenty of opportunities to make a fool of himself. That was what he wanted William to do – make a fool of himself again and again and again. And then in due course he could be shown to be suffering from his father's malady. They had taken King George III's throne from him, so why not William IV's – if he were to get it?

And then . . . that child Victoria. All his plans were foiled by her.

'I think that would be a highly suitable post for William.'

The King nodded. 'I remember how he was whisked away from us all at Kew to join the Navy. He was only thirteen or fourteen. I can see his face now – woebegone and wretched. Poor William!'

'But he enjoyed life afloat. He likes to think of himself as the Merry Tar.'

'He'll enjoy being Lord High Admiral. And he can plague them at the Admiralty.'

That was just what he would do, thought Ernest. And it would not be difficult for William to prove himself a fool.

'Do you see much of Edward's wife?'

'I can't bear the woman. I never did like the Coburg family. I find Leopold a bore. It surprises me what that actress sees in him. She's a charming woman, I hear. It's amusing though to find that Leopold is human after all.'

'And what of Madam Kent?'

'I call her the Swiss Governess. She's an intolerable woman. She guards Victoria like a dragon.'

'Do you see much of the child?'

'No, but I should and I shall. I shouldn't blame her for her mother's sins.'

'I hear she enjoys robust health.'

'I believe so. She's healthier than Charlotte ever was. My daughter suffered from constant ailments – although people forget it now. From what I hear of our young princess it is quite another matter.'

Ernest forced his lips into a smile.

'I should like to see the child. I suppose I might pay my respects at Kensington Palace.'

'Certainly you should. And you remind me of my duty. She is a very important little person and we shouldn't forget it.'

'It is indeed good to be home,' said Ernest smiling malevolently. 'I feel I am once more in the heart of the family.'

The Duchess of Kent summoned her daughter to her presence, and as soon as Victoria lifted her eyes to her mother's face, having given her a deep and respectful curtsy, she saw that Mamma was excited.

'His Majesty, the King, has invited you to call at Windsor Lodge.'

'Oh, Mamma, so I am to visit Uncle King!'

'Pray do not use that ridiculous appellation when referring to His Majesty.'

'No, Mamma.'

'You must behave perfectly. His Majesty is very particular about good manners. He will be watchful of you, and if you behave badly in the smallest way I have no doubt that he will be contemptuous of you.'

Victoria was apprehensive. She had always found Uncle King – on the few occasions they had met – particularly charming and not in the least prone to find fault. But perhaps she had been younger then and not so much was expected of her.

'I think,' went on the Duchess, 'that this is an occasion to remind you of the importance of your position.'

'I had not forgotten it, Mamma.'

'Pray do not interrupt, child. You will see that His Majesty is a very old man and *you* are old enough now to know that if he should die only Uncle William stands between you and the throne. And Uncle William is an old man, too. Keep that in mind.'

Victoria was puzzled. Must she while she was with Uncle King keep remembering that he soon must die? She must be very careful not to mention it, for, as dearest Louisa Lewis at Claremont said, she was like Cousin Charlotte in that her tongue was apt to run away with her.

'Pray don't frown,' said the Duchess. 'It is most unbecoming and leaves lines. Now go along and they will prepare you. I have given instructions as to your costume.'

When Victoria had gone the Duchess sent for Fräulein Lehzen.

'This visit to Royal Lodge,' she said. 'Of course it is right and proper that she should go, but it is a somewhat unusual household.'

Fräulein Lehzen raised her hands to the ceiling. Like the Duchess she wondered greatly at the manner in which the English conducted their affairs. Sometimes she thought they were completely lacking in discipline. That was why she was most anxious that Victoria should be brought up in the Teutonic manner. The Duchess and Fräulein Lehzen saw eye to eye on most matters; they were two Germans in an alien land.

'That woman is living at the Lodge, although they say that she would rather not be there.'

'What is so shocking, Your Highness, is that her family should be there too.'

'It is disgraceful! Lady Conyngham, her husband and children, all living there under the same roof with the King! I consider it most improper. If he lived openly with her at Court that would be another matter. But he shuts himself away and lives alternately, they say, between the *squalor* of the Cottage, where he spends most of the time in bed, and the oriental splendour of the Pavilion or Carlton House like some . . . some Sultan.'

Fräulein Lehzen cast down her eyes. One did not join in criticism of the royal family even when it was by the royal family, unless specially asked to do so.

'And it is to this . . . this household . . . that Victoria is going!'

'I trust, Your Highness, that Lady Conyngham will be absent.'

'That would be a great relief.'

'Do you wish Victoria to be warned?'

'I have been considering the matter. Perhaps, on second thoughts, it would be wiser to say nothing. I shall do everything in my power to protect her; and for that reason I am arranging for her sister to accompany us.'

'She will of course grasp the situation,' began Fräulein Lehzen.

'Feodore is eighteen; she is worldly enough to be aware of what is going on and she is devoted to Victoria. But I shall be there to keep my eye on the child. Will you send her to me? I wish to see that she is dressed as she should be and to give her some last-minute warnings.'

Victoria enjoyed riding along in the carriage with Mamma and Feodore; she almost forgot in the excitement of looking out of the windows that she was going on a great adventure: to meet Uncle King.

She must remember to call him Your Majesty and Sir, not Uncle King. She must only speak when spoken to; she must be very careful of her curtsy; it must be a very special curtsy and she had practised it until she was weary of curtsying, but Mamma still said it left something to be desired.

A visit to Windsor Lodge! What a prospect! She would sleep in a different room and the dolls would all have to stay at home in Kensington. Poor dolls! Mamma could say it was foolish for one of her age and responsibilities to play with dolls and pretend that they were people, but she didn't care. She was going to keep on loving her dolls. What defiance! She giggled to herself. Then she remembered that she was on the way to Uncle King and set her face into a serious mask because Mamma was watching.

Feodore caught her eye and smiled. How pretty Feodore was! She looked rather like one of the dolls. Darling Sissi! She had heard that Sissi might go back to Germany to get married. She hoped not. Wouldn't it be fun if some handsome prince came and married Feodore, an *English* prince so that she did not have to go away. Perhaps dear Lehzen would make up a story about it and they would make it go on and on together until Feodore and her prince had many adventures and lived happily ever after. But of course, Lehzen's stories – apart from historical ones – did not have happy endings unless the people were *good*. Only virtue was rewarded. There always had to be a moral because they were for improving the mind.

They had arrived at Windsor Lodge and the great moment had come.

Mamma was tense. She could feel it. Now they were going to be ushered into the presence of Uncle King. Victoria's eyes were dancing with excitement, which must not show of course. One must be demure and respectful – but at the same time showing dignity remembering that the day would come when she would be a queen and every bit as important as a king.

He was large and his body was a queer shape; his face was enormous, but his cheeks were quite prettily pink and his hair was a mass of nut-brown waves.

She approached and swept the most practised curtsy, more aware perhaps of Mamma's critical eye even than the figure in the chair.

Then the King said: 'Give me your little paw.'

Paw! she thought. That was funny and she laughed. He laughed too. All ceremony was over because there was nothing terrifying about him.

'It's a very pretty little paw,' he said.

'Paw,' she said, 'is a funny word to use for a hand.'

'I often take liberties with the language,' he replied.

She didn't exactly understand but she laughed; and he went on: 'It was good of you to come to see me.'

'It was all arranged,' she told him.

'And you did not object?'

265

'Oh no. I wanted to see you, Uncle King.'

There! She had said it. Mamma must be very angry; but he did not mind at all. He liked it in fact. She knew he did because he said: 'And Uncle King wanted to see his little niece and now that he has he is charmed with her.'

Oh yes, she thought, she could *love* Uncle King. He was not in the least strict or stern or critical. He just smiled and his eyes filled with tears and he said that she reminded him of the days when he was her age.

'That,' she remarked, 'must have been a *very* long time ago.'

'Alas,' said the King. 'A very long time.'

She could not take her eyes from the diamonds on his fingers. They sparkled and glittered more than any diamonds she had ever seen. A king's diamonds, she supposed.

'You like jewellery?' he asked.

'When it shines and sparkles it's very pretty.'

'You must allow me to give you something to wear.'

'To wear?' she asked; and she was aware of Mamma, very alert and anxious. Oh dear, she thought. I am not doing it at all as we had planned. But then Uncle King was so different. She had not expected him to behave as though he were a true uncle. He made one forget that one must be on one's best behaviour more so than anyone else did ... except young people like Feodore. He was not as solemn as Uncle Leopold, for instance, so it was difficult to remember that he was the King.

'My dear,' he said to the plump and handsome lady who had been seated by his side, 'bring the trinket.'

The trinket was a miniature of the King set in diamonds.

'Do you like it?'

'It's pretty.'

'A good likeness.'

'Oh, is it you?'

There was silence. Having to be so careful all the time one developed an extra sense which made one aware of false steps. This was a bad one and everyone was very shocked except Uncle King. But he was a little hurt and she hated that because he was so kind.

'You are much smaller there,' she said consolingly.

266

He leaned forward and patted her shoulder which was a way of telling her not to worry.

'Pin the miniature on her dress, my dear,' he said to the plump lady. 'I am sure it will be most becoming.'

So the lady – Lady Conyngham she learned later – leaned forward and, smiling, pinned the miniature to her dress.

'There now, you look very grand,' she said, 'with His Majesty gracing your shoulder.'

'Thank you indeed for such a lovely gift,' said Victoria. Then with a rush of affection: 'Whenever I see it I shall remember your kindness to me.' That was genuine at least; for she *would* remember this occasion, she was sure, for as long as she lived.

'Am I to have a kiss in exchange for the present?'

She laid her hand on that enormous thigh and lifted her face; but he could not stoop to her nor could she reach to him so that the obliging Lady Conyngham had to lift her up and set her on his knee.

What a strange face – all lines and pouches; and close to she could clearly see the paint on his cheeks. What a strange body; it was so fat; she felt as though she were sinking into a feather bed.

Now what she had to do was kiss that painted cheek. It was not really an ordeal because although he looked so odd and very old so close, he was kind. She knew that if she said something of which the others did not approve, he would understand; she knew that he was not putting her to a test; he was really interested in her; he liked her because she was young and she liked him because he might be old but he was kind.

That was it, she thought: He is kind.

At that she put her arms about his neck and kissed him.

It was wrong and not what was expected. It should have been a quick respectful peck upon the cheek and done in a manner to show that she appreciated the honour of being allowed to kiss the King's cheek. But she had kissed him as though she wanted to ... not because he was a king but because he was a kind old gentleman and she liked him.

He liked the way she did it. An arm hugged her momentarily and he said in a voice slightly shaken with emotion:

'Thank you, my dear.'

Then she was lifted down and Feodore was being presented.

This was far more formal, but it was quite clear that the King liked Feodore. A chair was brought for her and he would have her sit beside him and talk of Germany.

The King was laughing and looked very pleased with Feodore.

Victoria thought in some astonishment: I do believe he likes Feodore better than he likes me.

When the presentation was over and the Duchess was in the room which had been assigned to her she was very uneasy. She wished that John Conroy was with her so that she might discuss the occasion with him.

In the first place, why had the King suddenly commanded them to come to Windsor? Did he have some plan to take Victoria away from her? That was her constant fear – that Victoria would be taken away from her. If the child were removed she, her mother, would have no say in her upbringing. She would be reduced to a mere nobody. And what would they teach Victoria? To be as they were – dissolute, pleasure-loving, incapable of ruling, to lead an immoral life, to run into debt, to gamble. The Duchess of Kent shuddered.

And he had gone out of his way to charm the child which he had done easily for Victoria, being very young, was naturally susceptible. One could not blame the child, although she had thrown her teaching to the winds and responded to him in what could be called a somewhat unbecoming manner. He, being the man he was, had been charmed by her natural manner, and that was to the good, because the King undoubtedly liked her. But it was a tricky situation and she could not help being full of misgivings.

And what if they were to kidnap the child?

She went to Victoria's room; the child was drowsy. It had been a day full of excitement.

'My darling,' said the Duchess, kissing her forehead.

'Hello, Mamma.'

'You are very sleepy, my dear.'

'Oh yes.'

'You will have to be careful. You must remember that your

Uncle George is the King. You should let me know at once if he makes any suggestion and asks you if you would like to live at Windsor . . . or . . .'

Victoria's lids had fallen over her eyes. She was asleep.

She looked so young – little more than a baby, thought the Duchess tenderly. Oh, my precious lovely child, may God preserve you and bring you safely to your crown.

She leaned over and kissed the smooth brow. Victoria opened her eyes and said: 'I think he liked Feodore . . . very much.'

And that gave the Duchess something further with which to concern herself.

The King was restless that night. Sleep had deserted him. The child with her youthful freshness had been charming. How delightful was youth! He had not seen her very clearly until she was set on his knee and put her face close to his while she kissed him. Then he had been aware of a smooth unblemished skin, a delicate pink in the cheeks, the clear wondering eyes. Oh, how beautiful was youth – and only appreciated by the aged! And that little one would one day be the Queen – providing Adelaide didn't have a child which was becoming more and more unlikely with every passing week.

No, it was almost a certainty. And one day that fresh pinkness would fade and she would be a mass of corrupting flesh like the great bulk which lay in this bed. But perhaps not so; perhaps she would lead a different life. I am so because of the way I have lived, he thought.

His fingers closed about the miniature of Maria Fitzherbert which he wore round his neck.

It could have been different.

Thinking of Maria he remembered the charm of Victoria's sister. What a little beauty – eighteen years old! There were days when he felt well enough to marry again.

Someone young and luscious like Feodore would make him feel young again. Why not! He would discuss it with Ernest who had now settled at Windsor and was in his confidence.

Marriage – with a beautiful young girl like Victoria's half-sister Feodore.

It was a happy note on which to fall asleep.

Lady Maria Conyngham – Elizabeth's daughter – and Lord Graves, on the orders of the King, had brought a pony carriage with four lively grey horses to the door of the Lodge. They were going to take Victoria for a drive to the Sandpit Gate.

Lord Graves explained that the King had thought Victoria would be particularly interested in the animals for he had set up a zoo there.

Victoria was wild with delight but the Duchess of Kent was displeased because Maria Conyngham was going with them and she thought it was most unseemly that the daughter of the King's mistress should be in Victoria's company.

Victoria enjoyed the animals very much, particularly the giraffe and the gazelles, and she thought how wonderful it was to be a king and own a zoo.

She said so to Lady Maria who laughed and replied that the King would be delighted that his animals had given the Princess Victoria such pleasure.

'I shall tell him myself,' said Victoria and wondered why Lord Graves looked so sad. Later she learned that it was because his wife was having a love affair with the Duke of Cumberland – another uncle of whose wickedness Victoria was in time to learn a great deal.

It was a very pleasant day and Victoria was tired out when she returned to Windsor Lodge and her anxious Mamma.

The next day she was walking with Mamma and a few attendants when the King drove up in his carriage. She was enchanted by the speed with which the glittering equipage galloped towards them and the suddenness with which it pulled up. It could not be mistaken for anything but a royal vehicle.

Her mother grasped her hand firmly, but the King called a greeting; then his eyes rested on her and he smiled as though they were old friends.

'Pop her in,' he shouted.

Victoria felt Mamma's hand tighten on hers and for a moment she thought Mamma was going to refuse to let her go. Then she was lifted up and put between the King and Aunt Mary, the

Duchess of Gloucester, who was the only other occupant of the phaeton.

They whisked away, leaving Mamma standing there looking somehow forlorn, but she soon forgot them because there was no doubt that it was very exciting to be in the company of the King.

Aunt Mary was kind too and asked her how she was enjoying her visit to Windsor; and she very quickly found that in the company of Uncle King one could forget what should be done and do and say what came naturally. She told him this and it amused him.

'It's far more comfortable here than in Kensington,' she said. And she added, 'You *are* a comfortable person in spite of being a king.' Which made him and Mary laugh.

He seemed much younger than he had when he sat in his chair. His body was more like a body and his cheeks were a less painted pink. He really looked very fine, if you did not look too closely; and although he was so kind and said such funny things, he always seemed like a king – but in the nicest possible way.

He could imitate people in a manner which made her laugh; and because it made her laugh he did more and more of it.

Riding in the King's carriage with him and Aunt Mary, who clearly loved him dearly and thought he was wonderful, was even more enjoyable than visiting his menagerie with sad Lord Graves and flighty Lady Maria.

They drove round Virginia Water and then the King said he would take her to his Fishing Temple; here they went on a barge and she sat beside the King while he fished and the band played, starting off and finishing with 'God Save the King'. The Duke of Wellington was there and the King presented him to her. A very important gentleman and, thought Victoria severely, very much aware of it and anxious that everyone else should be too. He was by no means as charming as Uncle King – but then no one else could be as charming as that.

When they arrived home Mamma must be told all that happened. She listened avidly and wanted to know everything the King had said to Victoria and what Victoria had replied. It was not easy to satisfy Mamma's demands, for when one was enjoying oneself, as she pointed out, one did not think what one was saying nor did one make a point of remembering what others said.

'I think, Mamma, that Uncle King is the most charming gentleman in the world.'

The most charming gentleman in the world! thought the Duchess. He is setting out to win her. For what purpose? What but to take her away from her mother because charming as he might be to Victoria and correct in his manner towards the Duchess, that did not entirely hide the fact that he did not like her.

Oh, to be back in the comparative safety of Kensington Palace! Now that Victoria is growing up there are dangers on every side.

The wicked Duke of Cumberland was the King's confidant. He was capable of anything. A rogue and a roué ... and even worse, a murderer!

What plans were being made for her precious Victoria?

The King was determined that Victoria's visit to Windsor should be a memorable one. They must, he said, think up amusements for her. What would be most likely to entertain a child? Something gay and colourful; music, dancing.

There should be a party in the conservatory. Troupes of dancers should be engaged. Victoria should sit beside him and he would make sure that she enjoyed the entertainment.

She did. It was wonderful. Now and then she laughed with delight. The King watched her with the utmost pleasure. He had not felt so contented for a long time.

She loved the band. She thought: When I'm Queen I'll have a band in all my houses; and they shall play all the time. One thing she had learned from the visit was that it was very exciting to be a ruler. Everyone wished to please you, and you could make everyone so happy by giving them rides and parties.

He was leaning towards her.

'I believe you are enjoying the music.'

'I am, thank you, Uncle King.'

'It's a custom in our family. Even my father loved music.'

Even? thought Victoria. Why even? His father was her grand-father but she heard very little about him. He had been the King when she was born so it was not so very long ago. She must remember to ask Fräulein Lehzen why she did not hear more of King George III. At least now she knew he liked music.

'But he would listen to nothing but Handel. Handel has always been a great favourite in the family.'

She was aware of that for she too had been taught to like Handel – only they called it appreciating it.

'Now tell me,' he said, 'what would you like the band to play? They shall play whatever you wish.'

She smiled at him, loving him dearly because he was so com-forting to be with.

'I should like to hear it play God Save the King.'

The King was a shade more pink. She had made the right choice, she knew; and she was very happy.

'The Princess Victoria will ask the band to play what she most wants to hear,' said the King; and everyone waited for her to speak.

'God Save the King,' she said in a very clear voice.

The King leaned towards her and pressed her hand.

'That, my dear,' he said, 'was a very charming thought of yours.'

There was amusement throughout the conservatory.

'The Princess Victoria is a diplomat already,' it was whispered.

The wonderful visit had to come to an end.

There was the final leave-taking which was rather like the opening ceremony. There was the King seated in his chair with Lady Conyngham beside him. There was Victoria making her curtsy.

'Now tell me,' said the King, 'have you enjoyed your visit?'

'It was the most exciting visit of my life,' replied Victoria truthfully.

'Tell me which part you enjoyed most?'

She did not have to think long. 'The best part,' she said, 'was when I was walking with Mamma and you came along in your splendid carriage and you said "Pop her in".'

'Did I indeed say that?'

'Yes indeed you did. "Pop her in", you said, and I was popped in.' She laughed and he laughed with her. 'And we went riding off to Virginia Water and we drove faster than I have ever ridden and the harness jingled and it was *such* a splendid carriage and we talked and laughed – and that made it the best part of the visit.'

There was no doubt that Victoria knew how to charm the King as readily as he knew how to charm her.

Lord High Admiral of England

William had been acting oddly since the death of Frederick; he was making the most indiscreet comments and it was quite clear that the fact that he was the heir apparent to the throne had gone to his head. He talked freely of what he would do when he was King; he was continually inspecting the house which was being built for him; and would drive back and forth from Bushy every other day to see how it was progressing. He was enchanted with it; it was going to be a novel building with its Ionic and Doric columns and its three impressive storeys.

He dreamed of a house even more grand than Carlton House, but he would have no oriental touches in his house. It should be a fine house; a magnificent house; but a sailor's house.

The only subject which could lure his thoughts from the royal grandeur which he was sure would soon be his was the affairs of his children. Augustus had just taken Holy Orders and he was a little disturbed about this.

He discussed the matter with Adelaide who was only too pleased to be able to talk of something other than his accession to the throne.

'Augustus has not the temperament for a priest,' he said.

'I am sure he will make a very good one,' insisted Adelaide. 'After all, one does not need to be melancholy to be a man of the church. And if Augustus's approach is a little light-hearted, that is better than being sorrowful.'

'My dear Adelaide always sees the brightest side,' said William.

'I am sure you are not blaming me for that.'

'Only admiring you, my dear, as ever. But one must visualize all possibilities. When you consider the state of the government now and what would happen if the King were to die . .'

Adelaide said quickly: 'I am a little worried about Amelia.'

'Amelia. What's wrong with Amelia?' The very thought of something being wrong with one of the children could drive everything else from his mind.

'I fancy she has been a little preoccupied recently.'

'Preoccupied. What do you think. You think she has a lover?'

'It is not the only possibility.'

'I'll speak to her.'

'Perhaps it would be better if I did?'

It seemed strange that Amelia might be able to talk more easily to Adelaide the stepmother than to her own father, but William was fully aware that this was so.

'Yes, speak to her,' he said.

If there was anything wrong he wanted to know.

Amelia was tearful when Adelaide questioned her.

She was in love; she wanted to marry; and she was sure that her choice would not be approved of.

'But why ever not?' Adelaide wanted to know.

'He is a widower. He has children. He is years older than I am.'

'None of these are insurmountable difficulties. Your father is years older than I am.' She might have added: And if he was not a widower when I married him, it might have been more respectable if he had been.

'But, you see, Horace is poor.'

'Horace?'

'Horace Seymour.'

'He is one of the Hertford family?'

'Yes, he is.'

'Well, then I am sure that there will be no objection to your marrying into such a family.'

'But he has no money. He has settled everything he had on his children. I am *sure* there will be objections.'

'We might first discover if there will be before we assert so strongly that there are.'

'Adelaide . . . will you speak to Papa?'

'But of course I will.'

There was nothing that pleased William so much as to be called in to deal with family affairs.

So Amelia was in love, and she was afraid to tell her father. She had had to get her stepmother to approach him. It both pleased him that Adelaide should have his daughter's confidence while it hurt him that she could not have come to him.

But, as Adelaide said, as long as she came to one of them what did it matter?

The facts were that Amelia was in love with a penniless widower, and a daughter of the Duke of Clarence could not marry into poverty. All her brothers and sisters had done well for themselves; Amelia must do the same. And if she were so much in love with this man that she wanted to marry him – money or not – some means of providing money must be found.

William believed the solution lay with Lord Hertford, the head of the Seymour family. He would, therefore, write to Hertford explaining that his daughter Lady Amelia FitzClarence wished to marry Horace Seymour and that he would give his consent to the marriage providing Lord Hertford made an allowance to Horace which would enable him to marry the Duke's daughter. He confidently expected Lord Hertford to express his immediate willingness. After all, Horace would be marrying into the royal family – albeit from the wrong side of the blanket.

Lord Hertford was one of the proudest peers in the country. He had become friendly with the King – then Prince of Wales – at the time of the Mary Seymour case when he had, as head of his family, taken charge of the little girl, who was after all his niece, and placed her in the hands of Mrs Fitzherbert, which had been done entirely to please the Prince of Wales. As a result Lord Hertford's wife had become very friendly with the Prince and had remained on intimate terms with him during his Regency until she had been replaced by Lady Conyngham. That intelligent, fastidious Lady Hertford should have been replaced by stupid Lady Conyngham was not likely to endear the Hertfords to the royal family.

. Moreover, Lord Hertford did not consider an illegitimate daughter, even of a royal Duke, worthy to marry with a Seymour and he replied bluntly that he intended to do nothing to further the match.

William was astounded. When he received Hertford's letter he read it to Adelaide and then began to rave against Hertford.

'How dare he *slight* the connection? Does he realize that Amelia is *my* daughter. Does he despise a link with the King.'

Adelaide said: 'Perhaps he does not wish to put up the money.'

'Not wish to put up the money. Why, he is one of the richest men in the country. No, this is an insult to *my* daughter. Let him wait. I'll not forget this. Let him wait . . . it will only be a few months now . . .' Adelaide listened in horror as his voice rose. He was back on the old subject. 'I shall soon be King now.'

She sought to soothe him and she did to some extent, but he still went on talking of what he would do when his brother was dead and he was the King.

There was poor Amelia to be soothed. Poor, pretty, melancholy Amelia! Adelaide did her best; she told Amelia that she was young; perhaps her happiness with a man so much older than herself might not have been of long duration. Let her wait a while and if in, say, a year she was still in love with Horace Seymour . . . well, there were still means.

So it was Adelaide who comforted Amelia, but as she did so she was thinking of William.

Change was fast approaching. The peaceful days at Bushy were coming to an end. The simple country entertainments could not continue. There was little time to spend with their neighbours who had called during Dorothy Jordan's reign and William's nautical friends with whom he had kept in touch. How different they were from the fashionable crowd that circulated in Court circles. They were more simple in their tastes; they were more genuinely friendly. They talked of crops, the weather, their gardens and family affairs. Then there had been frequent visits of the married FitzClarences with their children; and in the evenings perhaps a small dinner party or no visitors at all and a simple game of Pope Joan.

But that was in the days before William saw himself as a king.

George Canning called at Windsor Lodge to discuss the Duke of Clarence with the King.

Canning was a man for whom the King had a great respect in spite of the fact that he had at one time been a firm supporter of Caroline. He had come to power very recently when Lord Liverpool had had a stroke, and the King believed that the government was in firm hands.

But Canning had not come to discuss high politics but this purely domestic matter of the post which should be given to the Duke of Clarence.

Canning came straight to the point.

'There has been an addition to his income, Sir; but he needs a position of some authority. We must not forget that the unfortunate death of the Duke of York has placed him in a very important position.'

'From what I hear,' said the King, 'he is becoming increasingly aware of it.'

'It is natural that he should,' replied Canning. 'He is the heir apparent and although we hope that he will retain that title for many many years, it is one nevertheless to which some dignity should be attached. So far His Highness has not been very much in the public eye. He has lived an astonishingly obscure life. It is my belief – and I know Your Majesty shares this view – that he should be brought into prominence.'

'I do agree,' said the King. 'And you are referring to the post of Lord High Admiral. Now, is it possible to revive this office?'

'As Your Majesty knows, it was abolished with Prince George, the husband of Queen Anne. I see no reason, and I am sure Your Majesty's cabinet will not either, why this office could not be reinstated.'

'In that case let us reinstate it. I will be perfectly frank though,' went on the King. 'My brother has had no experience of office of this kind. He is apt to be a little . . . excitable.'

'I had thought of that, Sir,' said Canning. 'The title of Lord High Admiral is not meant to carry any arduous duties with it. There will be a Board set up at the Admiralty which will undertake such work. In fact such a board has already been assembled under Sir George Cockburn. His Royal Highness will merely be an ornament to the Navy. The title will give him the standing he needs; it will bring him out of the somewhat provincial life he has been leading for so many years which, admirable as it may be, is not the way of life expected of the Heir Apparent.'

The King nodded. It was not one of his good days. At such times death seemed very close; and when he felt thus a great sense of responsibility came to him. He wanted to ensure that the House of Hanover continued to rule – and rule well. But when he thought of all the pitfalls which loomed under a monarch's feet he shuddered for William. Still, he had nice sensible Adelaide at his side. A good wife was so helpful and the people like a cosy domesticity – as he had learned to his cost.

And Canning was there. He looked at the man – brilliant statesman, one of the great men of the day – but by God, he thought, how ill he looks! A fine pair to be discussing the affairs of England – a couple of death's heads.

He told Canning that he would leave the appointment to him for he knew it would be in the most capable hands.

They then began to discuss more important matters of State than the Duke of Clarence's appointment to the sinecure of Lord High Admiral of England.

William strutted before Adelaide in his Admiral's uniform, his eyes gleaming with happiness, his face grown youthful so that he resembled a boy with a toy which he has coveted for a long time.

'Lord High Admiral, Adelaide. Think of that! It's something I used to dream of in those early days on the *Prince George* and the *Barfleur*. I was a midshipman then. Plain William Guelph. It was my own wish that I should be known by that name. And it wasn't easy, Adelaide, for the son of the King to become a common sailor.'

'I can well believe it was not.'

'Oh no. But I accepted the discipline. I forgot my rank. I became one of them and I learned to love the sea and ships. By God, it's a fine thing – the British Navy. It's the finest institution in the world. But there is room for improvements. By God, yes! And there will be improvements. They have got a sailor at their head now ... a sailor who started at the bottom and rose to his present position through his own determination and ...'

Adelaide was not listening to the words. She was alarmed by his excitability. He was constantly making long speeches as though he were addressing the House of Lords.

'I am sure it is realized what an asset you will be to the Navy, William,' she said quietly. 'It is for this reason that you have been offered the post.'

'There'll be jealousies,' went on William. 'By God, I'm not sure that I like that fellow Cockburn. Seems to think he's in some superior position. Talks about the Board. "The Board", I demanded. "What of the Board? The Lord High Admiral of England does not need a *Board* to tell him what to do. Let me tell you, sir, that the Lord High Admiral of England was a sailor which is something this *Board* could never be!" I said to him ...'

His eyes grew wild, his cheeks flushed with excitement.

'William,' said Adelaide gently, 'remember your asthma. You won't want to provoke another attack.'

But William could not be calmed. He was Lord High Admiral and he intended to make his presence felt.

They were scarcely ever at Bushy now. There was no time for the old peaceful life. 'I have my duties,' said William. 'Navy affairs must come first.'

He was not content merely to wear a uniform and appear at naval functions which was what Canning had planned for him. He wanted to be responsible for reforms, he wanted to make speeches. The latter was easier than the former and he plunged into this on every occasion; he made the mistake of thinking that he was a master of oratory; his voice sounded magnificent to himself; he could laugh at his own words and when the occasion demanded it be intensely moved by them. Unfortunately they did not have the same effect on his listeners, who had difficulty in suppressing their yawns and whispered comments. The result was ridicule in the press.

William did not care. He was going to hoist his flag and go to sea. For this purpose he determined to take the *Royal Sovereign* yacht at the head of a Squadron. Excitedly he discussed the project with Adelaide.

As she dreaded going to sea she was less happy. She was almost always ill; and this was not like a Channel crossing; William planned to stay at sea for more than a week.

'William,' she said, 'I cannot come with you. I should be violently ill.'

His face fell childishly.

'Don't forget you will soon be Queen of England.'

'I beg of you do not speak so loudly of such things.'

'Why not?' he roared. 'It's true.'

'It sounds as though you almost *want* your brother to die.'

'Old George has had his day. To my mind he's not all that anxious to cling to life. It's inevitable. Fred's gone . . . and Fred was younger. Oh, the day will come soon and I see no reason to pretend otherwise.'

'It might not be considered seemly, and a king has to consider his words.'

'That's right, that's right,' said William. 'A king has his responsibilities.'

'And often has to act with discretion.'

William laughed. 'You'll make a good queen, Adelaide,' he roared.

All the same she could not go with him, so she compromised. He was calling at ports along the south coast. Very well, she would travel overland to all those ports and when he docked she would join him in the *Royal Sovereign*. This would prevent her suffering from seasickness, which in any case would have rendered her incapable of doing her duty; she could help him entertain in the ports and be on board with him when the ship was in dock and while it was at sea she would have an opportunity of visiting some of the noble families who had country estates in those ports.

It would be, she said, a sort of royal progress.

A royal progress! The phrase appealed to William.

Trust Adelaide to think of the right thing. How she had developed under his guidance. To think that when he married her he had believed that the alliance with the House of Hanover might have gone to her head. No, she was steady and reliable, his Adelaide; and he couldn't have had a better wife.

He was very pleased with life. But he would be more pleased when the crown was placed on his head and he was proclaimed King of England.

The Duchess of Cumberland had joined her husband and his son George was with her. George was immediately taken into Adelaide's circle of young people and the boy was charmed with his aunt. He was given presents and made to feel very welcome and his parents looked on with amusement.

They were staying at Windsor where the Duke of Cumberland had become the closest confidant of the King. The Duchess too was often in his company: he found her clever and amusing.

Lady Conyngham was not very pleased with the Cumberlands. She had been contemplating leaving the King and would have done so if she could have found a means of effecting it easily; but now that she saw her place being usurped by the Duchess of Cumberland she was angry.

The King was very old, she reasoned. He could not live much longer. She should remain with him until the end now. There might be quite a few perquisites to fall into her hand for the King was very lavish with his jewellery and who would be able to say whether such and such a piece had been given to her or not.

No, she was going to stay to the end and she was not going to be pushed out by the Duchess of Cumberland.

The Cumberlands carried a sinister aura wherever they went. No one could quite forget that during their past they had both been suspected of murder.

They had a standard of morals all their own. They were undoubtedly allies, yet that did not mean that they were faithful to each other.

The Duke of Cumberland was known to be engaged in a liaison with Lady Graves; the Duchess did not object in the least; and in fact had the King not been so old and incapable of such conduct, she would most certainly have attempted to become his mistress.

They understood and they had one aim which made any other desire that might come to them of the greatest insignificance. They wanted the throne of England – first for the Duke and then for their son George.

The situation amused them. An ailing king with clearly a short time to live and when he was dead between them was merely William (Silly Billy as they called him) and Victoria.

If the situation had been straightforward, if there had been no lives between, they could not have experienced the same stimulation and exhilaration which the present state of affairs gave rise to.

When they were together they discussed the way things were going.

'William,' said the Duke, 'is playing straight into our hands.'

'Trust William.'

'Behaving like an idiot. He can scarcely open his mouth without showing his impatience for George's death.'

'That may upset George, but however upset he is he can't alter the succession.'

Her husband's eyes narrowed. 'Successions can be altered.'

'What have you in mind?'

'Our father was put away; he went into retirement and George became King – in all but name.'

'You can't mean they would put William away?'

'Why not . . . if he behaved like a madman?'

'But he's just a fool.'

'There is a very fine line between folly like his and madness.'

'You would never get others to see that point.'

'Then, my dear, it will be my job . . . our job . . . to make them.'

Frederica laughed. However much she might be attracted by

other men and Ernest by other women, they still found each other the most exciting person in the world.

'A terrible misfortune has come to the country,' said the King, holding a handkerchief to his eyes. 'I have just had word that Canning is dead.'

Lady Conyngham was scarcely listening. She was bored with politics; but she was glad of course that the King was confiding in her instead of in the Cumberlands. He had just received the news and was very upset about it.

He rambled on: 'Of course there was a time when I was set against him. He was very friendly with the Princess of Wales.' (He never thought of Caroline as the Queen; to him she remained the Princess of Wales.) 'At the time of the Delicate Investigation he was visiting her frequently; and when the Bill of Pains and Penalties was brought forward he was on her side. Some said he was her lover. Who knows? With that woman one could never be sure of anything. And when he became my Foreign Secretary I don't mind saying now that I could not endure the fellow. But that changed. He had such good taste; he was the sort of man with whom I could find an understanding. No, I cannot believe that he could ever have been the lover of that creature. One did not have to spell things out with him. He had a quick mind; a great eloquence; he was one of the most brilliant men of our day.'

Lady Conyngham yawned and wondered whether to have her sapphires reset with the new diamonds the King had given her, or wear them as they were. Canning's death meant nothing to her.

'And now he is dead,' went on the King. 'I have lost a good friend as well as a great minister. And what can I do but ask myself what would Canning have *wished* me to do in such sad circumstances? He would have wished me to send for men whom he trusted. That is so. Don't you agree with me, my dear?'

'Oh yes, I agree,' said Lady Conyngham.

In accordance with what Canning would have wished the King sent for Lord Goderich and offered him the office of Prime Minister.

But it was soon clear that Goderich was no Canning; the

choice was a bad one and 'The Goody' as the press called Goderich was soon in difficulties.

A few months after his appointment he called to see the King and in tears informed him that he could no longer carry on.

'My dear fellow,' said the King, 'then you must resign.'

With that he passed Goody his handkerchief to dry his eyes and decided that there was nothing to be done but call in the Duke of Wellington.

One of the most romantic men in the country was Arthur Wellesley, Duke of Wellington. After the battle of Waterloo it was inevitable that he should be the country's hero. Who had rid them of the enemy Napoleon, the villain who had cast a shadow over Europe for so long? The answer was Wellington. Nelson had beaten the Corsican at Trafalgar but he was still able to plague Europe for ten long years after that. But with Waterloo came the eclipse of the arrogant conqueror. Everyone must admire Wellington if he were the most ill-favoured man in England. But he was not. Tall and spare of figure, with aquiline nose and keen grey eyes, always immaculately dressed, he was not only handsome but, also romantic.

He was married, and the story was that he had married out of chivalry. As a young man he had fallen in love and the lady of his choice, Kitty Pakenham, had declined his offer of marriage at which he had gone away and devoted himself to his career in the Army. When he had gone Kitty regretted having let him go and decided to mourn her loss for the rest of her life. Some years later the news of this reached him and being the romantic man of chivalry he wrote to her and asked her to marry him.

'I have been a victim of the smallpox,' she wrote. 'I am very different from the girl you wished to marry. I have lost my looks and you would be shocked if you saw me. Do you still wish to marry me?'

There was only one reply a chivalrous man could make and he made it. It was not for her beauty alone that he had wanted to marry her. So they were married and he was soon regretting his impulsive action; and when the war was over and he came into politics and made the acquaintance of the fascinating Mrs

Arbuthnot he was more in the latter's company than that of his Duchess. But so discreet was he that although it was considered appropriate when inviting the Duke to invite Mrs Arbuthnot too and to place them side by side at dinner, no one was absolutely certain whether or not she was his mistress.

There was Mr Arbuthnot, that very respectable Tory gentleman, who was one of the Duke's greatest friends, and surely this could not have been the case if the Duke had taken his wife?

Of course Mr Arbuthnot was years older than his beautiful wife; and she was a strikingly intelligent and intellectual woman. Mr Arbuthnot himself said that ministers discussed State affairs before her – not only because they could trust her discretion but because she often had valuable advice to offer.

So it was with the Duke. He could talk to Mrs Arbuthnot; he enjoyed her company as he could no one else's; and the poor doting Duchess, who had been married for chivalry, must accept this and make the best of it. She was half blind in any case and declared often that she could not see her husband's 'precious' face as clearly as she would like. She had her sons whom she adored and who treated her without respect, obliging her to fetch and carry for them and generally making a slave of her. But all this she accepted as she did the Duke's attitude towards her, for he, accustomed to commanding an army, liked to issue orders as to how the house was to be run and the guests entertained.

It was to Mrs Arbuthnot he turned when he was selected as Prime Minister.

She was delighted, of course, and certain of his success.

'A Ministry with Wellington and Robert Peel as its leading lights,' she cried, 'is certain to be a great one.'

William was delighted at the appointment of Wellington.

'A great hero,' he told Adelaide. 'I have always admired him – almost as much as I did my dear friend and colleague, Nelson. The talks we had! There was a man! One of the greatest England has ever known. I was at his wedding. Ah, he thought he'd done a very fine thing when he married Frances Nesbit. It was one of the few mistakes he ever made.'

'He was openly unfaithful to her,' said Adelaide.

'Ah, but with a fellow like Nelson you have to make allowances. He was not a promiscuous man. And Lady Hamilton was a fascinating woman . . . fascinating! The greatest sailor . . . and Wellington the greatest soldier! Mind you, I never thought the Army was so important to the country as the Navy.'

'Spoken like a sailor,' said Adelaide with a smile.

'A great fellow for reforms, Nelson. He was one of the few commanding officers who spared a thought for the men. He used to say, "Look after the men and they'll look after England." It's true – and by God, Adelaide, that's what I intend to do. Now I think promotion should be given by merit. There is too much command given through influence. Nelson was against it. He would talk for hours about the disaster that sort of thing had brought to the Navy. I want to pension off some of the older men so that I can have a chance of bringing the younger ones forward. That's how it has to be. This means money but I shall put the plan before the Treasury.'

'I am sure,' said Adelaide, 'that you are going to reform the Navy.'

William was delighted. He saw himself as the great reformer.

Admiral Sir George Cockburn was scarlet with rage.

'Look at this,' he said. 'Our Lord High Admiral going over our heads to the Treasury. Promising pensions without consulting the committee! What does he imagine he is? Dictator of the Navy? Why does he think the Board has been set up? To take orders from him?'

The Board agreed with Sir George.

'Doesn't he know why this office has been created? It's to give him some standing in case – which God forbid – he should inherit the throne! Reviewing the Navy in the *Royal Sovereign*! Harmless in its way but unnecessary expense. But when he sets up his own rules and attempts to carry them out without referring to the Board, that, Gentlemen, is something we cannot endure. Now he has set up a commission on gunnery – about which we have not been consulted. I think we have him here. He has far exceeded his power. I shall have to inform him of this and humbly – I suppose – beg His Royal Highness to toe the line.'

287

Sir George was not a humble man. He was a sailor and accustomed to speaking his mind.

'The fellow's crazy,' he said. 'Ever since the death of the Duke of York the possibility of his own position has gone to his head. Gentlemen, it is agreed that I write to the Lord High Admiral and convey to him the displeasure of the Board and inform him that he must desist from taking any action of importance to the Navy without consulting it?'

This was unanimously agreed.

The fact that William was at loggerheads with the Board of Admiralty was soon common knowledge.

The Duke of Cumberland, meeting Sir George Cockburn, casually alluded to the matter.

'Trouble with my brother William, I hear?'

'His Highness is over zealous,' said Sir George with a rare caution.

'Oh, you call it that. I have heard it said that William is just a little mad.'

Sir George relaxed. 'It might seem so from his actions.'

'We have to watch William,' said the Duke confidentially. 'We have often said – in the family – that we feared he might go the way of his father.'

Sir George was pleased. By God, he thought, Cumberland is right. And we don't want a madman running the Navy . . . or trying to.

When William received Sir George's letter he was furious.

'Upstart!' he cried, forgetting Sir George's long record. 'Who the hell does he think he's ordering? I'll have him know that the Lord High Admiral is not taking orders from him!'

He hoisted his flag on the *Royal Sovereign* and set off along the coast to continue his grand tour which had been interrupted by the death of Prime Minister Canning; and in this again he was defying rules, for he should have asked the Board's permission before taking the *Royal Sovereign*.

Once again there came a letter of protest from Sir George.

Now the battle had begun in earnest.

He rapped Sir George across the knuckles in a manner which the Admiral found intolerable.

Your letter does not give me displeasure but concern to see one I had *kept* when appointed to this situation of Lord High Admiral constantly opposing what I consider good for the King's service.

It was too much to be borne. Here was this *fool* – for Sir George could call him nothing else – who had been given this office simply because he was the heir apparent, believing that he could come in and take command over experienced sailors. Now he had had the temerity and insolence to tell Sir George Cockburn that he had *allowed* him to remain, as though he, occupying the sinecure – for it was nothing else – of Lord High Admiral had control over all the British Navy!

He was indeed a madman.

There was only one action to be taken. Sir George must appeal to the Prime Minister, with whom William was already in correspondence demanding the dismissal of Sir George Cockburn. He wished, he said, that Rear-Admiral the Honourable Sir Charles Paget be appointed in his place.

There was nothing Wellington could do but lay this letter before the King, who was extremely irritated by his brother's folly.

It was inevitable that Cumberland should be at hand when the letter arrived. He had been expecting it. He believed that his pointed observations towards Cockburn had strengthened him in his determination to stand no nonsense from William – not that he would not have stood firm in any case; but the fact that one of the royal brothers believed William to be suffering from a touch of the late King's malady was added support.

William could not have played better into Cumberland's hands. But then, it was because of William's nature that the idea had come to deal with him in this manner.

'You look weary, George,' said Cumberland. 'Disturbing news?'

'It's William.' The King passed the Duke of Wellington's letter to his brother.

'Conflict between Sir George and our Lord High Admiral, eh?'

'William has no sense,' said the King.

'A very true statement, alas.'

'Sometimes I wonder what he'll do next.'

'What's going to happen about this?'

'I hope Wellington will be able to sort it out. William can be stubborn as a mule. I shall have to write to him and explain, I suppose. Oh, what a bore.'

'And so unnecessary when there are important State matters with which to concern yourself.'

'He's a good fellow, William. He just has a genius for being ridiculous. It was always the same. That long affair with Dorothy Jordan meant that she kept him in order; and now Adelaide does much for him. He is lucky with his women.'

The King sighed – ready to begin an account of his own misfortunes in that direction. But Cumberland was not interested in that. This affair between William and Sir George Cockburn was not over yet. It must become common knowledge. It must be discussed in public. The press would use it, of course. He must make sure that they did so in the correct way.

William is going mad, that was the theme. Who but a man who was not quite balanced would behave as he did? People only had to remember his ridiculous behaviour in the past; his attempts to get married; his long, rambling speeches in the House of Lords; and now he believed, because some high order had been pinned on him, that he could command the dismissal of George Cockburn, the King's own Privy Councillor, himself appointed to give advice to the Lord High Admiral.

Like the late King, William was capable of the wildest actions.

There were new stakes in the betting clubs. They concerned the Duke of Clarence.

What were the odds against his being in a strait-jacket *before* George's reign was over?

And then . . . the little Princess Victoria.

Yes, thought the Duke of Cumberland sourly, and then the Princess Victoria.

*

Those were days of speculation.

The King was not expected to live, but he had been in that state for several years. He had the constitution of an ox, it was said. No other man could have endured all the dosing and bleeding he had suffered and still be alive. He had led a life of indulgence; he had eaten unwisely and drunk too much; he had kept late hours; he had burdened himself with debts and they must have caused him anxiety; his adventures with women were notorious. He had married Maria Fitzherbert morganatically and his marriage with Queen Caroline had been the most extraordinary in the life of British royalty. He ought to have died years ago – but he still lived on, near death one day and the next in excited consultation with architects planning improvements to Carlton House and the Pavilion, Buckingham House and Windsor Castle, in addition to which he was conferring with Nash whose Regent Street, Carlton House Terrace and terraces of Regent's Park he declared to be some of the finest architecture in the world.

But in spite of all this – he could not live long.

And then what?

The rumours persisted that if George should die William would go completely off his head.

He was behaving oddly now. There was all this controversy with the Prime Minister over his office of Lord High Admiral. The grave for George; the strait-jacket for William.

And Victoria? The child was rarely seen in public.

Someone had heard from a friend who knew someone in the Duke of Cumberland's household who had said that the Princess Victoria was a very delicate child. She had a disease of the bones which would not allow her to stand and she was obviously destined for an early grave. Perhaps even before George found a haven in the tomb and William was constricted in his strait-jacket the nation would be mourning the death of little Victoria.

The next in line was the Duke of Cumberland – Ernest with one eye and the scarred face. Battle wounds it was true; but he did have an evil reputation. It would be a long time before people forgot the Sellic case. And there was some dark history connected with the Duchess.

Still, he was a strong man; and what the country needed was a strong man.

In the clubs bets were being taken. There seemed to be a fairly even chance that the next King of England would be King Ernest.

John Conroy wanted to speak to the Duchess of Kent confidentially.

She received him graciously; she was very fond of him, because, she assured herself, a woman needed a man whom she could trust.

He was carrying a newspaper and she saw from his expression that he was disturbed.

'I want Your Highness to read this,' he said, 'and tell me what you think of it.'

She read it. It was an account of Victoria's weakness. The disease of the bones from which she suffered prevented her from walking. She suffered from other ailments and there was great anxiety for her health in Kensington Palace.

'But this is a monstrous lie!' cried the Duchess.

'Of course it is, Your Highness. But there is a purpose behind it.'

'Who could find such satisfaction in pretending that a healthy child is an invalid?'

'Those who want her out of the way.'

The Duchess stood up, her curls quivering, her hands clasped to her buxom bosom. But she had grown pale. Her Victoria in danger!

'Want ... her ... out of the way!' she repeated.

'I think the Duke of Cumberland has very decided views as to who should inherit the throne.'

'It is no use his having views. He cannot meddle with the succession.'

'Not by constitutional means.'

'What do you mean?'

'By saying Victoria is a weakling he may have some plan in view.'

'How do we know *he* has said this?'

'Madam, this is a matter of the utmost importance. That child who is so dear to us both may well be in acute danger.'

The Duchess's expression was bewildered. 'But I don't understand.'

'We have to conjecture, Madam. We have to be a step ahead of our enemies. We may be wrong, but we have to consider all possibilities. There have been rumours that the Duke of Clarence is going off his head. It may well be that they have been started by the Duke of Cumberland with the hope that he will be set aside.'

'Well?' said the Duchess.

'The Princess Victoria would still stand in the way of . . . the Duke of Cumberland and his son.'

'You terrify me.'

'Madam, I feel it is necessary to do so.'

'What do you think he plans for Victoria?'

'How can I say? But someone is telling lies about her. Preparing the people to accept . . . something.'

'They are such foolish lies. One only has to look at her to see how healthy she is.'

'At the moment . . . yes.'

'What *do* you mean?'

'I cannot say. There may be some plot. Don't forget the Duke's valet was found in bed with his throat cut. It was *said* to be suicide.'

'But . . . I cannot believe that here . . . in Kensington Palace . . . my own child is in danger.'

'We do not know, Madam. But this could be a warning.'

'What do you suggest we do?'

'The first thing is to show these rumours to be lies. The Princess must not be shut away from the public view. She must be seen to walk perfectly, to be in good health. That is the best way of foiling the devil . . . or devils . . . who may be working against us.'

'I will take her for a walk myself . . . this very day. I shall not let her out of my sight. She shall be guarded. I shall tell Lehzen right away. We must be watchful. Oh dear, how you have alarmed me!'

'I am glad, because although I hope that my zeal for your

welfare and that of the Princess may have let my imagination run away with me, at least there are these lying rumours to show us that something sinister may well be afoot.'

'I shall send for Fräulein Lehzen at once. I shall take her into my confidence. The Princess Victoria is to be watched night and day.'

Victoria walked with her mother out of the gates of Kensington Palace.

'Oh, Mamma, are we really going into the park?'

'It is time you appeared now and then in public.'

'Oh yes, Mamma. I enjoy it.'

They walked as far as the Duke of Wellington's house. Now and then someone called out: 'God bless the little Princess!' Which greeting Victoria prettily acknowledged.

She enjoyed it and told her mother so.

'I am glad, because from now on we shall be taking walks such as this.'

'It is pleasant to see something of the people,' said Victoria.

'And very pleasant that they should see you,' retorted the Duchess.

She was delighted when Conroy brought a paper to her in which Victoria was mentioned. The little Princess had at last come out into the open. She appeared to be a healthy young person and the rumours about shaky legs were clearly false. The implication was that in future the public would like to see more of Victoria.

Children always had the power to win public approval quite effortlessly and when they were as fresh, charming and healthy as the Princess Victoria, it was a pity to keep them shut away.

'I am sure someone is feeling a little put out by this,' said Conroy.

'How grateful I am for your care, my dear friend,' said the Duchess tenderly. And added fearfully: 'But we must be watchful. No harm must come to Victoria.'

William was astounded.

'It seems,' he told Adelaide, 'that Wellington is on that fool

Cockburn's side. Look at this. Read it. He says he's sure I am too well acquainted with military discipline not to know that I can't hoist the flag without the consent of the Admiralty Board. He thinks the differences between myself and Cockburn should be settled and forgotten because they are causing annoyance to His Majesty. I shall write to him at once and tell him that I don't agree.'

Adelaide tried to soothe him. 'William, perhaps it would be better if you did forget this affair.'

'And allow Cockburn to insult me?'

'It seems that he thinks you have insulted him.'

'Who the hell does he think he is? I happen to be the Lord High Admiral and the heir apparent to the throne. Is this the way to treat his future King?'

'Oh, William, please do not talk of that. With the King still with us . . .'

'He won't be for long and then what is Master Cockburn going to say, eh? I'm surprised at Wellington. I thought he would be on my side.'

A further communication had arrived. This time it was signed by every member of the Board. If Sir George was asked to resign, it stated, they would resign too . . . in a body.

'Let them,' cried William. 'We can manage very well without them.'

He left Adelaide to return to the *Royal Sovereign* to continue his tour. He would meet her at his next port of call. He was taking no notice of Wellington's warning that he had no right to go to sea in this way without the Board's consent.

Wellington went to the King.

He was very disturbed, he said. The Lord High Admiral was acting in a very strange way and the Admiralty Board had threatened to resign in a body. Something would have to be done and as the Duke of Clarence seemed disinclined to listen to the Prime Minister he must appeal to a higher authority. Would His Majesty consider letting his brother know what a serious position he had put himself in?

The King sighed. Really William was a fool. Didn't he realize how he was making himself ridiculous? But when had William ever understood how foolish he looked? Of course, he was pleasing quite a number of the junior officers by boasting of the better conditions he proposed for the Navy and talking of giving promotion where it was deserved. But he was going to disrupt the entire service in bringing about his reforms, which in any case were going to be expensive in some cases and this would mean heavier taxation – a subject the public was not very happy about at the moment.

'Your Majesty will write to the Duke of Clarence?' asked Wellington.

The King said that he could see that it would be necessary for him to perform this unpleasant duty.

William! he thought when he was alone. What a stubborn fellow he could be! But he was fond of him all the same; he and his brothers had at least been devoted to each other – some more than others. Frederick . . . ah, how he regretted the loss of his favourite brother! But Ernest was always with him now. Secretly he could not be very fond of Ernest; there was a barrier between them which the King was too tired to think about. He couldn't see very well and sometimes when he looked at the blur which was Ernest's face it seemed quite malevolent. This was merely due to his loss of an eye and the scars, and one must remember that these were worthy wounds won in battle.

But there was something strange about Ernest. He implied that he had come to stay whether the King wanted him or not.

'Ah, we know too much about each other, eh, George, not to work together.'

What a cryptic remark for one brother to make to another. To what was he referring? What did Ernest know of George? That he was in truth married to Maria Fitzherbert? It was common knowledge – or was it? There had been some to doubt it. But his affairs had always been so public; it had been impossible for the Prince of Wales or the Prince Regent to do anything without having the full glare of publicity turned on him.

What secrets did Ernest have which he would not wish betrayed?

Little secrets of the private apartments; the carefully applied rouge, the fear of corseting which was becoming too painful to be endured. The humiliating results of undignified illness. Were those the secrets? It might well be, for he would rather the public heard of his secret marriage than some of the tricks it was necessary to perform to make an old man presentable.

No! He was imagining it. It was Ernest's way of talking. He should be grateful for Ernest's advice . . . Ernest's help. And his Duchess was a fascinating woman. In her way she was a little alarming too. The little hints that were dropped, the innuendo which might have had nothing behind it at all. She was a damned attractive woman, though the antithesis of Maria.

Ah, Maria! He grew tearful at the thought. Where are you now? Living in Brighton. Sometimes in London. Why are you not here to keep these people from me? How different everything would be if you were.

What had made his thoughts run on in this melancholy way?

It was William. He had to write to William and explain that he would have to behave. William was a good fellow, an affectionate brother. It was true that at times he seemed to be waiting for the King's death so that he could step into his shoes but who could blame him? Poor William, who had always made such a fool of himself. Naturally he wanted to be King.

He sighed and took up his pen.

My dear William,
My friend, the Duke of Wellington, as my first minister, has considered it his duty to lay before me the whole of the correspondence which has taken place with you upon the subject relating to yourself and Sir George Cockburn. It is with feelings of the deepest regret that I observe the embarrassing position in which you have placed yourself. You are in error from the beginning to the end. This is not a matter of opinion but of positive fact . . .

It was true. William must be made to see this. If he were ever King of the Realm he would have to learn how far he could go in his treatment of men in high positions. Yet he could not keep an affectionate note from creeping in. He did not love William any the less because he was a fool.

You must not forget, my dear William, that Sir George Cockburn is

the King's Privy Councillor, and so made by the King to advise the
Lord High Admiral . . .'

He wrote on, trying to explain even more clearly, hoping William
would accept the fact that he had erred and make some apology
to Sir George Cockburn who was, according to Wellington,
exceedingly put out.

Am I to be called upon to dismiss the most useful and perhaps the
most important naval officer in my service for conscientiously acting
up to the letter and spirit of his oath and duty?

Poor William, he would think he was very harshly treated. He
would say: 'My own brother is against me.' The King wanted
William to understand that he wished to help him, that he would
have preferred to be on his side; but William must see reason.

. . . I love you most truly as you know and no one would do more or go
further to protect and meet your feelings; but on the present
occasion I have no alternative. You must give way and listen to the
affection of your best friend and most attached brother.

G.R.

The King sighed. The little effort of writing had wearied him
considerably. And when he thought of all the letters he had
written in the past it seemed astonishing that such a short epistle
could have this effect on him. Letters! he thought, and remembered those he had written to Perdita Robinson and which had
cost a small fortune to retrieve; and all those he had poured out
to Maria when he was entreating her to come to him.

And there he was back to Maria. It seemed that everything he
did led back to her – even William's affair with George Cockburn.

When William received his brother's letter he was truly dismayed.

It was delivered to him when he came to port where Adelaide
was waiting for him.

'Read this,' he cried. 'What nonsense! That fool George Cockburn the King's most useful and important naval officer! How
could that be? That conceited jackanapes . . . "the King's most"
. . . Upon my word, I never heard such rubbish.'

298

Adelaide said quietly: 'William, remember those are the King's words.'

'King's words or not they're nonsense.'

'Please, William.'

'What do they expect me to do, eh?'

'Couldn't you make friends with Sir George and then perhaps gradually introduce all the reforms you have in mind?'

He looked at her steadily. She was a clever little woman, his Adelaide. No one would think it. She was so quiet, often one would think she hadn't a thought that didn't concern the children. But it wasn't so. There was a lot of deep thought going on behind that plain little face.

'That fool Cockburn would be completely outwitted.'

'I'm sure he would. And you have to consider the King's letter.'

'I'm surprised Wellington went to the King. It wasn't a matter for my brother at all.'

'But now that he has gone to the King and you have this letter, it will be necessary to carry out your brother's wishes.'

'Yes,' said William reluctantly. 'I'll write to Cockburn and tell him that if he retracts I'll forget all about my orders to dismiss him. He may stay in his post if he'll retract all he's said and done so far. That's all I ask.'

'But . . .' began Adelaide; but William tweaked her ear.

'Don't you give it another thought. I shall say to him: "Sir George, we will try to work together. I have plans for the Navy. They are excellent plans. As my late lamented friend Lord Nelson said to me . . ." '

William was off on one of his long speeches; he stood rocking on his heels and Adelaide was sure he saw a great assembly before him as he talked; he certainly spoke as though he were addressing a large gathering.

But he did not understand.

Adelaide sighed. They were back where they started.

How right she was! Sir George Cockburn's reply to William's magnanimous offer was that he could in no circumstances retract. He would stand by all he had said and done and if His Royal

Highness acted in any way similar he would continue to raise his voice in protest.

'There, you see,' cried William. 'There is no placating that man.'

But the Duke of Wellington was determined that there should be peace between the two antagonists and arranged a meeting at the Admiralty. There he pointed out how damaging it was to the Navy and the country to continue in such a dispute. So eloquently did he talk that at the close of the interview William, who was always ready to be moved by patriotism, was prepared to shake hands with Sir George and let bygones be bygones.

The Duke trusted that His Royal Highness would in future remember that while it was no doubt an excellent exercise to visit the various ports with his squadron of ships, these exercises must have the approbation of the Admiralty Board – which he was certain that Board, under the most excellent command of Sir George Cockburn, would not withhold.

There must be friendship within the service. War was to be practised among enemies only and amity must prevail.

That, thought Wellington, was an end of the matter; but he deplored Canning's lack of foresight in bestowing the office of Lord High Admiral on the Duke of Clarence.

William was gleeful. 'Such a bother,' he said to Adelaide. 'All a matter of form, of course. That fellow Cockburn has really been put in his place. He'll know better than to interfere again.'

Adelaide looked dismayed. 'But you have agreed to settle your differences.'

'My dear Adelaide, the heir apparent does not make bargains with naval officers.'

He was growing excitable again. Sometimes she feared where these moods would end. He had always been subject to them but since the death of Frederick they had increased alarmingly. He must calm himself; he must stop talking so freely. Otherwise she could not imagine what would happen.

She could not dissuade him from setting sail once more and on a warm July day he sailed out of Plymouth Hoe on the *Royal*

Sovereign dreaming of Drake going forth to fight the Armada, George Cockburn and the Admiralty Board taking the place of the Spaniards in his mind. It was the same thing, he reasoned. He was defending freedom just as Drake had.

What a sight with *Sovereign* at the head of the accompanying squadron! The *Royal Sovereign*! What an apt name for his ship! He would soon be the Royal Sovereign himself.

With him watching the receding land was his eldest son, George. George was a bit of a rebel himself and had applauded his father's tussle with the Admiralty. George, like the rest of the family, was very much looking forward to the day when his father would be King, for there could be no more indulgent parent in the world.

'This is the life,' cried William. 'The fresh sea breezes in your face and a rolling deck beneath your feet. My only regret is that your stepmother is not with us.'

It was a happy ship – the *Royal Sovereign*. William was the most thoughtful of commanders; and there was not a man on board who did not know that they were defying the Admiralty and it was exciting to take part in the famous quarrel.

Wellington called a Cabinet meeting. The Lord High Admiral was on the High Seas. For what purpose? Was it some secret mission? Why was Major George FitzClarence present? Who had authorized the mission?

The Prime Minister called on the King, who was suffering from one of his more painful lapses and was unable to leave his bed.

'In spite of everything he has gone off again?' cried the King. 'I fear so, Sir.'

'He must be recalled at once. It must be made clear to him that if he will not obey the laws of the country he will be dismissed.'

That was what Wellington needed.

'Leave this to me, Sir.'

The correspondence had started again. William returned like a conqueror in the *Royal Sovereign*; it had been an exhilarating trip – he and George together and his ship's company delighting to serve under him; he had forgotten all about exacting people at home. But when he came into port again, there were letters and messages awaiting him.

The most important was from the King himself. He deplored his brother's conduct. It might well be that he had a very short time to live and William would then be his successor. William must remember that the first duty of a king to his country was to obey the laws laid down by the Parliament. No king – or any other man – could be a law unto himself.

When he read this letter William saw that there was only one thing he could do.

He resigned the office of Lord High Admiral.

Menace at Kensington Palace

They were at Bushy again leading a quiet life for a while. It was very necessary for the Affair with the Admiralty had upset William more than Adelaide cared for people to know.

He brooded on it; he went about mumbling to himself; she would go into a room where he was alone and find him talking to an imaginary Sir George Cockburn or Duke of Wellington, or perhaps to his brother the King. He would be somewhat incoherent and there would be a wild look in his eyes.

'You need rest,' said Adelaide fearfully; and she wished that her mother-in-law Queen Charlotte were alive so that she could have confided in her. Was this how William's father had behaved in those weeks which had preceded his attacks?

She tried to interest him in the laying out of new gardens; such matters were very soothing to him. The children helped and they were constantly calling at Bushy. He was a little worried though about Amelia's broken romance with Horace Seymour and he was not sure that the Church was the right vocation for young Augustus.

Adelaide persuaded him to play Pope Joan in the evenings and to retire early to bed.

302

Sometimes he would look at her with tears in his eyes and say: 'What should I do without you . . . you and the children?'

Then she would feel that he was moving away from this threatening shadow, for then he was seeing things as they were. It was when he pictured himself as the great Drake defying tyranny in the form of Cockburn and the Admiralty Board, when he saw himself as the great King of England that she feared for him. The quiet family man at Bushy remembered that he had had nothing but kindness from the brother who now lay close to death; and who was not so much a King with a crown to pass on but a friend and brother.

'Oh, my dear wife,' he said, 'what I owe to you nobody knows!'

Adelaide embraced him and said: 'Never forget that I shall always be at your side.'

And so William passed out of danger and settled down to enjoy the quiet life of Bushy.

There were children on the lawns. Poor crippled Louise was there with her brother, and the FitzClarence grandchildren looked upon Bushy as their home.

Adelaide was happiest when surrounded by the children but she often confided to William that there was one member of the family whom she missed. It was Victoria.

'She's guarded like the crown jewels,' said William.

'I think of her often,' said Adelaide. 'Poor child, hers is not a very natural childhood, I fear. She seems to me such a grown-up little person. The only childish characteristic is her love for her dolls.'

And as she could not see Victoria as often as she would like, Adelaide started to embroider a dress for her in coloured wools and as she worked she thought of the child and selected the colours which she believed would please her best.

Peace was restored to Bushy.

The danger, thought Adelaide, was past. But like all such dangers it could return.

Was this how Queen Charlotte had felt? Was it some strange presentiment which had made her feel drawn to the mother-in-law who seemed to be out of sympathy with almost everyone else? It was an alarming thought.

A tragedy had occurred in Court Circles. Lord Graves had committed suicide, and there was no doubt of the reason. The Duke of Cumberland had seduced his wife, and so rendered his life no longer worth living.

Because Lord Graves had been a kindly man and popular, a wave of disgust for the behaviour of the Duke of Cumberland swept not only through the Court but throughout the country.

Cumberland had become a bogy man. His very appearance was evil. No one could trust him; and it was said that his grotesque looks fascinated some people, particularly women as in the case of Lady Graves. His attitude to life was cynical, as was that of the Duchess. Old scandals were revived. They had both been implicated in mysterious deaths which could have been murder.

Cumberland was shunned in some society; but most people were a little afraid of him. They remembered that he was a younger brother of the King and there were only two lives between him and the throne. It was true one was an ageing man, and not a very stable one at that; but the other was a young girl who had been proved to be in glowing health. There had been rumours about her delicate state, but those had been false for she was seen walking in the park with her mother almost every day, sturdy and intelligent. There was nothing wrong with the Princess Victoria.

The people cheered her. They were pleased with her. This pleasant little girl was not only destined to be their Queen, she was also a bulwark between the throne and the evil Duke of Cumberland.

The Duchess of Cumberland was a little exasperated with her husband.

'This Graves affair is most annoying,' she said. 'It has focused attention on you. Was it necessary?'

'Quite unnecessary. Why did the fellow want to kill himself so publicly?'

'And he gave no indication that he was about to act so maddeningly?'

'My dear,' replied the Duke coldly, 'don't you think that had he done so I would have prevented him at all costs?'

The Duchess replied that she hoped it would be a lesson and that in future he would choose women with less *mischievous* husbands.

'What's done is done,' he said. 'No useful purpose is served by recriminations.'

'But it has drawn attention to us. It has revived old scandals. And what of the Princess Victoria? They are saying now that she is a healthy child and the rumours about her delicate health were false. Soon they will be asking who started these rumours.'

'Not they. They'll have forgotten them.'

'And William?'

'I've kept a watch on William. He would have been in his strait-jacket now if Adelaide had not cosseted him and kept him quiet at Bushy.'

'We have to watch Adelaide. I don't trust those quiet people. So self-effacing! Always working for the good of others! She's devoted to Victoria as well as William. The *good* woman is in fact a universal mother. She's even taking our own George under the maternal wing. He dotes on her.'

'Adelaide is of no importance.'

'She could in a few weeks' time be the Queen of England.'

'Let us leave William and his pretensions alone for a while. He's old and probably on the verge of madness. It's the child who is important to us.'

'And now we hear nothing but reports of her good health. No one believes that she is a delicate child and if she were suddenly to go into a decline suspicions might be aroused.'

'She's guarded like a prisoner. Her mother scarcely lets her out of her sight.'

'What do you expect after those rumours? It was too early to start them.'

'Perhaps. But if Victoria were taken from her mother's care . . .'

'There would be an outcry.'

'Not if there was a very good reason for her being taken away.'

'What reason could there be for removing the child from her mother.'

'The Princess Charlotte was prevented from seeing her mother during the Delicate Investigation. Why? Because Caroline was suspected of immorality.'

'The Duchess of Kent is no Caroline.'

'Who said she was? But Caroline is not the only woman who has strayed from the paths of virtue. Imagine our Duchess – not so old, luscious, alone. What would be more natural than that she should take a lover?'

The Duchess began to laugh.

'I see your reasoning.'

'And you find it worthy of me?'

'Completely worthy.'

'There is a ready-made situation.'

'And the gentleman in the case?'

'Surely you don't need to ask. John Conroy – her controller and adviser – such a handsome man! I believe the Princess Sophia finds him most attractive. The Duchess of Kent certainly does. Now you must admit that it would not be proper for our future Queen to be brought up in an *immoral* household.'

'You will have to act more subtly over our immoral Duchess than you did with her delicate daughter.'

'You will see,' said the Duke, smiling his evil smile.

It was pleasant riding one's pony through the grounds at Claremont; in fact Claremont, thought Victoria, was one of the most lovely places in the world. Here, Cousin Charlotte had walked with Uncle Leopold. She supposed that Charlotte was her aunt in a way, because she had married Uncle Leopold; but royal relationships were so complicated. People could be cousins and aunts at the same time.

Here Charlotte had made plans about her baby. Oh yes, it was having a baby which had killed her. Louisa Lewis had let that out. Mamma would be cross if she knew, for Victoria was not supposed to know anything about having babies.

She was watched all the time. It was very strange that they allowed her to ride her pony alone. But then she was only in the *grounds* of Claremont. And I am thankful for a little freedom, she thought.

Something strange was going on.

Feodore had left her and she was sad because Feodore was so pretty and charming and they had always been together. Feodore had been one of her admirers. But Feodore herself was admired – by men. Which, said Mamma, was dangerous. So Uncle Leopold, who always seemed to decide what should be done, had said that it was time that Feodore was married. So poor Feodore, weeping in bed at nights and hugging Victoria and saying that she never never wanted to leave her little sister, had to prepare to leave Kensington and go away to marry the Count Hohenlohe-Langenburg. Poor Feodore. How frightened she had been!

'Lucky Victoria,' she had said, 'when you marry you won't have to go away . . . and you will be a Queen who will chose your husband.'

Yes, thought Victoria, she was very lucky.

But sad as Feodore's going had made her, her sadness had nothing to do with the strangeness.

And Lehzen had now become a Baroness. She supposed they thought a mere Fräulein was not good enough to be the close companion of a Queen.

But it was nothing to do with that either.

No, the strangeness was in Kensington Palace. Mamma had taken to sleeping in her room which was odd; and before Mamma came to bed the new Baroness sat there doing her needlework.

'Why do you sit there?' Victoria wanted to know. 'I used to be all alone in my room.'

'Do you not wish for a companion?'

Victoria was usually precise. 'I was not thinking of whether I liked a companion but asking why it was thought necessary to give me one.'

'Her Highness the Duchess has asked me to bring my needlework in here and sit until she comes to bed.'

'I see,' said Victoria, 'that it must be because she does not wish me to be alone.'

'The Duchess thinks constantly of what is best for you.'

'I know,' said Victoria.

'And knowing it, it would be wise to accept it without question.'

How could one accept anything without question? Victoria wondered. For if one did, how could one expect to discover what everything was about?

But it was very pleasant at Claremont – Charlotte's Claremont, where she might have had her little baby and if he had lived – for Louisa Lewis had let out that the child was a boy – Victoria would not have been as important as she was at this moment; in fact there might not have been a Victoria at all. What a gossip Louisa was! She loved to tell stories of the family; so Victoria knew of all the urgency of getting her uncles married when Charlotte had died, including her own Papa.

A world without Victoria? Impossible! she thought. So poor Charlotte had to die.

It was hard to imagine death in Claremont; but death could be anywhere ... even in Kensington Palace. Death! Mystery! Something strange was happening and it was all about her. It concerned her.

She was suddenly alert. She had seen a figure moving among the trees. Who was it? Not Mamma, for Mamma was seated on the lawn; she knew exactly where Mamma was. Someone was watching her.

Her heart began to beat faster. Who was watching her? And why? And all this mystery was a little frightening. It made one wonder if something really dreadful was about to happen.

She could ride quickly back to the lawn and Mamma – or she could go closer to the trees and look. She hesitated for a second. She was on her pony; she could always gallop away or call for help.

She galloped over to the trees.

'Who is there?' she called.

She was relieved yet a little disappointed. It was only a young woman who stepped out from among the trees.

She curtsied as Victoria pulled up.

'Who are you?' she asked.

'I am Dr Stockmar's niece.'

Victoria knew Dr Stockmar; he was Uncle Leopold's physician

308

and Uncle Leopold was very fond of him and talked to him for hours of his rheumatism.

'Are you staying at Claremont?'

'Yes, Your Highness.'

'It is very beautiful, do you think?'

'Very beautiful.'

'I haven't seen you before.'

'No, Your Highness.'

'I suppose you know my Uncle Leopold?'

'Yes, Your Highness.'

'Do you know who I am?'

'Certainly. Everyone knows the Princess Victoria.'

'That is a remark which gratifies me,' said Victoria. 'What is your name?'

'Caroline Bauer, Your Highness.'

Victoria wrinkled her brows. 'I have never heard of you although I know your uncle ... well.'

'There is really no reason why Your Highness should hear of me,' was the answer.

And at that moment the Duchess of Kent appeared. Hearing the sound of voices and recognizing one as that of her daughter, she had come hurrying to see with whom Victoria was conversing.

The effect on her was startling. She gave the girl a withering look and said: 'Victoria, ride at once to the stables. I shall expect to see you in your room in fifteen minutes.'

Victoria, who had been about to present Caroline Bauer to the Duchess, hesitated, thinking that her mother could not have been aware of the young woman's presence.

But the Duchess said coldly: 'Pray go at once.' And as Victoria went she noticed her mother turn away and sweep back to the lawn, just as though the girl were not there, and someone Victoria had imagined.

Life was really growing very strange.

The Duchess looked reproachfully at her brother.

'Really, Leopold,' she said. 'A most distressing occurrence. Victoria came face to face with Caroline Bauer in the gardens.'

'I am sure Victoria must have been enchanted.'

'We are not all as besotted as you. And besotted you must be to keep your mistress here . . . where *Victoria* is likely to meet her.'

'My dear sister,' said Leopold, 'I doubt Victoria would have thought anything amiss if you had not walked off in a huff and left Caroline standing there.'

'So that unfortunate creature has been carrying tales of what happened?'

'You can hardly call it tales.'

'But, Leopold, is it wise? Think of Victoria.'

'Victoria will have to learn something of the world one day.'

'Not such immoral details, I hope.'

'Well, if she is going to learn the history of the world she will discover much of what you are pleased to call immoral. And she won't have to go farther than her own family either.'

The Duchess shivered. 'Leopold, I sometimes wonder what has come over you. You used to be so different! Here . . . in this house where you lived with Charlotte.'

'Charlotte would understand,' he said. 'It is twelve years since she died. She would not begrudge me this friendship . . . as you appear to.'

'I was thinking of Victoria.'

'An occupation of us all – thinking of Victoria. I must say the child is exceptionally bright.'

He looked at his sister quizzically; he had succeeded in changing the subject. The accomplishments of Victoria were an irresistible bait.

He added: 'She will make a great Queen.'

'I pray nothing will interfere with her accession to the throne.'

'What could?'

'I am afraid. All these rumours. I sense danger . . . and I am not sure from where it may come. I never like the child to be alone.'

'You are fanciful.'

'It is a great responsibility.'

'Of course it is, but you have me to help you.'

'If you can spare the time from . . . your mistress!'

'Oh, pray don't be tiresome. Caroline has nothing to do with this. You ask me why I keep her here in Claremont. Do you ask

310

yourself *why* I should be in Claremont? I might be in Greece. Did you know the Greeks had offered me the crown? Did you know that I had declined and the reason I had done so?'

'Because, my dear brother, you did not want the Greek crown.'

'Because, my dear sister, I preferred to stay in England. I wish to be at hand to stand with you when you need me. And believe me, you will need me, when Victoria is Queen and you are Regent, for she will not be of age, I am certain, when the crown is hers.'

'You think Clarence will not live another eight years?'

He put his head close to hers. 'I think Clarence may well be put away. You have heard the rumours?'

'What if they are but rumours . . . like those about Victoria?'

'I don't think they are but rumours. Clarence is unbalanced to say the least. It could happen . . . this year, next year. This *week*. What then? Where would you be without your brother Leopold?'

'I admit it is a comfort for me to remember that you are here.'

'Then allow *me* my comforts, sister. And where is my little niece now? Why is it that you have allowed her out of your sight?'

'Because she has gone to her room and Baroness Lehzen will be there. While she rode in the gardens Lehzen would have been watching her from the window. We never let her far out of our sight.'

'Little Victoria is safe . . . with such watch-dogs.'

The Duchess was not sure that she liked the term watch-dog which was somewhat undignified; but she needed Leopold and so she must accept his ways.

John Conroy was delighted with the situation. He was becoming indispensable to the Duchess of Kent who discussed everything with him. The Princess Sophia, who since the death of Queen Charlotte had made Kensington Palace her home, was rather taken with him too.

'I have a way with the royal ladies,' he told his wife. She was a meek woman and thought him exceedingly clever; she was ready therefore to allow him to go to work in whatever way he considered best. He had now become Sir John, which pleased him. With Lehzen a Baroness it was only fitting that he too should have a title.

He was indisputably head of the Duchess's household and since her fears concerning the Princess Victoria he had become even more important to her. In her anxiety she depended on him almost as much as she did on Leopold; and now that Leopold did not seem to be completely trustworthy, she leaned towards him more and more.

He would have liked to discuss his cleverness with Lady Conroy, but she was too stupid; so all he could do was continue in it. One day he would be a rich and powerful man. If George died and William either followed him or was put away, Victoria would be Queen and her mother Regent, and who would be her chief counsellor? Sir John Conroy. One might say brother Prince Leopold of Saxe-Coburg, but would Leopold stay here? Sir John, who flattered himself that he had a finger in foreign affairs, did not think so. Already Leopold had toyed with the idea of accepting the Greek throne and although he declared that he had no intention of taking it, that was not true. He had considered the proposition very seriously. And no wonder. What was he doing here in England? He was at loggerheads with the King and his brothers; he was accepting a pension from England, grudgingly given, he was living at Claremont which must be full of memories of his brief but blissful life with Charlotte; and it was clear that he was only waiting for the right opportunity to leave.

It would come; and then Sir John Conroy would be the power behind the Duchess of Kent and that would be the power behind the Queen.

All he had to do now was wait – and in the meantime he must make the Duchess understand how close were the bonds which bound them, that he was her trusted friend, her tender friend; and that nothing could make him swerve in his loyalty towards her and her daughter.

The affairs of royalty were discussed everywhere in the Capital where men congregated together. Servants of the royal family confided in servants of others and news seeped out to be garnished according to taste.

'How could one expect a woman like that to live the life of a nun?'

'She is a handsome woman . . . and not young.'

'Ah yes, and they say he's a very fascinating man. Why the Princess Sophia is in love with him too, I hear.'

'Sophia! She's a bit long in the tooth.'

'Maybe, but some of them are never too old.'

Long-ago scandals were revived about the Princess Sophia. Wasn't there talk of a child she had had years ago? He must be a grown man now. These things did happen in royal circles.

It was not long before many people accepted it as a fact that the Duchess of Kent was the mistress of Sir John Conroy.

The Duke of Cumberland sat by the King's bedside. He had a somewhat arrogant habit of presenting himself without permission, which the King half resented. He implied that he came as a brother, and therefore, out of affection, dispensed with ceremony.

The King smiled faintly, feigning pleasure. There was always the vague threat conveyed in Cumberland's manner. Yet he was so affectionate, so determined to do everything he could to help.

'Well, George, and how are the pains today?'

'Agony at times, Ernest.'

'My poor brother, if the people only knew what you went through.'

There it was. The King shuddered. If the people could see him now in his somewhat grubby silk coat which he wore in bed and the crumpled nightcap hiding his wigless head, what would they say? He thought of cartoons, newspaper comments and shuddered again.

Ernest should have warned him that he was coming; then he would have arisen and have been made presentable.

'The latest gossip concerns your Swiss Governess.'

The King groaned. 'That woman! What has she been doing now?'

'She's having a love affair with that man Conroy.'

The King laughed. 'I wish him joy.'

'Do you think he finds it?'

'She's a handsome woman. She might not irritate him as she does some of us. I think she was quite attractive before she became Victoria's mother. The fact that she has the child has given her false ideas of her own grandeur.'

'The Princess is a precocious child.'

'A delightful creature.' The King smiled. 'I should like to see more of her. I shall never forget a very enjoyable ride to Virginia Water.'

'You *should* see more of her. After all, she is the heiress to the throne.'

'Don't harp on that. You make me feel I have to apologize for having outstayed my welcome.'

'For God's sake don't say that, brother. I often wonder what would happen . . . if you . . . I can't speak of it. It affects me too deeply.'

The King wrinkled his eyes in an effort to see his brother's face. He could not believe Ernest would be greatly affected by his death – at least by affection – but when a man was old and sick and had as he had said 'outstayed his welcome' he wanted to believe that when he died there would be some to regret him. And whom could he expect to do that but his own family?

'And there is William,' went on Ernest. 'When I remember our father I tremble.'

'William is recovered now,' said the King. 'It was a momentary lapse. That unfortunate affair of the Lord High Admiral and the fact that Fred's death put him next in the line went to his head.'

'I know. To his head . . . to his weak and foolish head! Things went to our father's head.' Ernest came closer to the bed. 'It would not surprise me if he went the way of our father.' He raised his eyes piously to the ceiling. 'Thank God, there are heirs. And that child Victoria would then be the next. She must be prepared for her great position. It occurred to me to ask this question. Should the heiress to the throne be brought up in an immoral household?'

The King was astounded. Ernest of the evil reputation, who had recently been involved in a scandal with a married woman

314

whose husband had committed suicide; who was suspected of practising every vice ever heard of and had been concerned in a violent killing, which could have been murder; Ernest to talk of an immoral household – simply because the Duchess might be having a love affair with a member of her household!

The King, who had also been guilty of many an immoral act, was a little shocked that Ernest could have spoken in this way of the Duchess of Kent. He did not like the woman, but he understood her position. She was a widow, not old, she had an attractive controller of her household. It was in the King's view inevitable that she should take a lover; and if he had not felt so tired and ill he would have defended the Duchess and asked Ernest why he had suddenly decided to become so virtuous, because it did not become him.

He merely said coolly: 'I find the Duchess an extremely exhausting woman; her type of looks do not appeal to me, but I certainly would not think of her as an immoral woman.'

One could go so far with the King and no farther. Cumberland knew that. Every action he had to take must be subtle; and the King was no simpleton.

But how could he realize his ambitions while that fat smug child lived on and flourished in Kensington Palace? and how could she cease to do so when she was guarded day and night by her fatter and even smugger mother?

He must be careful though. This was not a matter which could be hurried.

While Adelaide worked in gay-coloured wools on the dress she was making for Victoria, enjoying the peace of Bushy, she was thinking that this could not last. There was change in the air. She could sense it.

One did not need to have special powers to do that. The King was critically ill. The fact that he kept recovering a little because of his strong constitution did not mean that he could go on doing it for ever.

King George was going to die soon and then there would be King William and Queen Adelaide.

But would there?

During the last months she had suffered a terrible fear. She had believed that William was going mad. And yet when she considered his behaviour it was eccentric more than anything else. It had been exaggerated; the rumours had done that.

And who was responsible for those rumours?

Whenever she was in the presence of the Duke and Duchess of Cumberland she felt uneasy. Was it the Duke's appearance? That scarred face; that void where an eye should have been? Sometimes he wore a patch over it and that gave him a sinister look. It was absurd to judge him by his looks. He had been wounded in the face like many soldiers.

But had he been involved in the Graves' affair? What had the Duchess of Cumberland thought of that? She gave the impression that she did not care.

She was embroidering the last of the flowers on the dress. This blue would bring out the colour in Victoria's eyes, she thought. Dear child! She wished that she could see more of her. She feared that the restricted life she led at Kensington Palace was not right for a little girl. There was too much emphasis on etiquette and decorum. Victoria should be allowed to run wild like the FitzClarence grandchildren. Adelaide smiled to think of the pranks they got up to.

Victoria was now spending a few weeks by the sea. The Duchess had decided that she would take her there that she might be seen making the journey; and when she came back she would be so full of good health that the Duchess would wish the people in the Park, where they took their walks, to see it too.

There had been such unpleasant rumours about her health.

Victoria was an interesting child. Such a grown-up letter she had written for Adelaide's birthday, accompanying some charming presents. Of course it would have been the Duchess of Kent who had chosen the presents, but they had come in Victoria's name.

Victoria was one of the band of children with whom she had had to compensate herself for having none of her own. The FitzClarence grandchildren, the Cumberlands' George – a delightful boy – and the Cambridges' George too. She loved them all, although of course the Duchess of Kent was most insistent that Victoria should never meet any of the FitzClarences which was tiresome and meant that Victoria was often excluded from parties which she would have enjoyed.

Victoria was on her mind today, and when she had finished the embroidered flowers she went indoors out of the hot August sun to write to her.

She sat at her desk and wrote thanking her for the well-written birthday letter and the gifts.

It gives me great satisfaction to hear that you are enjoying the sea air. I wish I could pay a visit there and see you, my dear little niece . . . Your Uncle desires to be most kindly remembered to you and hopes to receive soon also a letter from you, of whom he is as fond as I am. We speak of you very often, and trust that you will always consider us to be among your best friends.

God bless you, my dear Victoria, is always the prayer of your truly affectionate

     Aunt Adelaide

She sealed the letter and sent it; but she could not get Victoria out of her mind.

She could not talk to William of this sudden fear which had come to her. It obsessed her. And it concerned William too.

It was true that William had been over-excitable; it was true he made long, rambling speeches, that he was eccentric; but there was a long step between such conduct and . . . madness.

It was always as though there had been a force at work which was trying to send William mad.

There! She had faced it.

A force? She might go farther and bring out what was truly in her mind: the Duke of Cumberland.

It was so clear, so simple. The motive could not have been plainer. There was a crown and the Cumberlands wanted it — first for themselves and then for their son. Poor innocent young George, that charming boy whom she loved. God preserve him from the influence of his parents!

They shall never drive William insane, she thought. I will prevent that. I will stand between him and them. I will nurse him. I will not let it happen. It need not, I know — and yet the alarming thing is that it could.

William is safe . . . with me.

And Victoria?

Oh God, she thought, the child is in danger. Those rumours of her illness. What could they mean?

Whenever she thought of Victoria she saw a great shadow hanging over her, and she was afraid.

The Duchess of Kent and her daughter were back at Kensington Palace after the seaside holiday and Victoria, blooming with health, took her daily walks with the Duchess as far as Apsley House and back and the people cheered her as she passed.

Adelaide called at Kensington Palace. She had brought the dress she had been embroidering for Victoria who was enchanted with it. She must try it on at once, she declared.

'You shall,' said the Duchess. 'Go and do so now and your Aunt Adelaide and I will have a chat while we await your return.'

As soon as she had left Adelaide looked over her shoulder furtively.

'Is anything wrong?' asked the Duchess.

'I have been waiting for an opportunity to talk to you. Perhaps I am being foolish but I feel this is of such great importance to us all. Forgive me if I am stupid, but it is out of my love and concern for the child.'

'For Victoria!' cried the Duchess.

Adelaide nodded.

'Pray go on.'

'I am anxious. I believe that there is some . . . evil at work. I cannot forget those accounts of her weakness which were so false.'

The Duchess had turned pale. 'Nor can I forget them,' she said.

'Who started those rumours? Who saw that they were circulated?'

The two women looked at each other and it was Adelaide who spoke first. 'I believe it to be the Duke and Duchess of Cumberland.'

'My dear Adelaide . . . sometimes I am terrified.'

'I too. And there is William. Those reports about him. Oh, it is so *clear*. They want William put away.'

'And Victoria?' said the Duchess.

'I don't know, but I fear some evil. I beg of you, never let the child out of your sight. Keep her with you or that good woman Lehzen . . . all the time.'

The Duchess had put her hand to her heart. 'Oh God, it is a terrifying thought.'

'It is not, alas, so unusual. Crimes have been committed for a crown before. How I wish we were not so close to it. I can see great danger.'

'I shall see that the child is guarded night and day.'

'My thoughts will be with you.'

'My dear, *dear* Adelaide!'

'You know I love her as though she were my own daughter.' The Duchess nodded. 'If you should discover anything . . .'

'Never fear, it is my concern too. Both for William and the child.'

'They shan't succeed.'

'No,' said Adelaide firmly. 'We shall protect them and there is none who could do it as we can.'

'She is coming back now.'

Victoria came in wearing the dress with the hand-embroidered flowers.

'It is most becoming,' said the Duchess.

Victoria turned round smiling, but she was not thinking of the dress so much as she pretended; she was wondering what they had been discussing while she had been out of the room. It was something frightening. She could see it in their faces. And she believed it concerned her.

Yes, there was certainly something mysterious going on.

They were afraid for her. It was obvious. If when she was riding her pony in the park she tried to stray a little from her attendants they were immediately beside her.

Orders, she thought.

And then Mamma's sleeping in her room; and the Baroness'

sitting there until Mamma came. That was the most unusual thing of all.

Could it be that she was in danger?

She thought a great deal about the Princes in the Tower. They had been kept there and suddenly they disappeared, stifled in their beds and their bodies were buried under a stair.

What if someone was trying to murder her?

She told it to her dolls; she wondered whether Lehzen could make the little Princes for her. Mamma said she was getting too old for them, but they were not ordinary dolls. They had been with her so long; they were her family; besides, many of them actually represented her ancestors.

Thinking of her dolls she decided to visit them; and she rose and went to the head of the stairs. The apartments occupied by her mother's household were on two floors and the staircase which led from one to the other was a spiral one. She had always felt it was rather an exciting place because it twisted so and if anyone were coming up and you were going down, if they were silent-footed you would suddenly find yourself face to face with them.

You could stand on the staircase and look right up to the little window in the roof at a patch of sky; she had always found that fascinating.

But now as she started down the staircase she was thinking of the little Princes in the Tower. Under a stone stair, she had heard, they found their bodies years later. What had they felt when they woke up in the night and saw murderers at their bedside? Did they scream out? Or were they too terrified to open their mouths? Or were they just suffocated in their sleep?

Poor little boys! Had they any suspicions on that last day when they heard the hammering going on close by that it was their murderers preparing the secret hiding-place which was to be their grave?

They were murdered because someone wanted what was undoubtedly theirs – a crown. It was that same crown which would be Victoria's one day if no one took it from her.

Why was she standing here, looking up at the skylight? She was trying to frighten herself.

And then . . . she thought she heard a step on the stair behind her. She caught her breath and gathering her skirts in her hand she sped down the stairs.

At the foot of the staircase she almost fell into the arms of Baroness Lehzen.

'What has happened?' demanded the Baroness.

Victoria was too frightened to pretend.

'I . . . I thought someone was coming after me . . . on the stairs.'

'Nonsense,' said the Baroness. 'Who would want to come after you on the stairs?'

But they could not deceive her. The Baroness was frightened . . . even as her mother was.

And after that there was a new edict.

Victoria was not to go up and down the stairs alone. Someone must go with her. The Baroness Lehzen, if possible, or the Duchess's own lady-in-waiting, Baroness Späth.

'Not to go up and down stairs without someone to hold my hand!' cried Victoria.

'That,' replied the Duchess coldly, 'is exactly what I said.'

'So now I know,' Victoria told her dolls, 'that they are afraid someone is going to kill me and the reason is the same one that brought death to the little Princes in the Tower.'

She could not really believe it would happen because it was impossible to imagine a world without Victoria.

The Duke of Cumberland was thinking a great deal about his niece. William was not so important. William would provide his own evidence he was sure; and in any case his brother was six years older than he was and suffered from gout and asthma, and these in addition to his mental aberrations made the Duke of Cumberland feel confident that he could not long stand in the way.

It was different with Victoria, the precious child who was hardly allowed to put one foot before another without someone to stand on guard.

It had been a mistake to try to make her out to be delicate. Madame Kent had soon put an end to that by parading the healthy little brat for all to see. He knew from friends in the

Kent household that the child was never in her bedroom alone and that now a rule had been made that she was not even to walk up and down stairs on her own.

It was clear that she must be removed from Kensington Palace and the eagle eyes of her mother and that other watchdog, Lehzen.

He was determined to get her away from her guardians and he saw a way of doing it.

The rumours about the Duchess and the Controller of her household, Sir John Conroy, must persist; but it might be that he would not succeed in persuading the King through them, though they could serve to convince others.

With the King he had another method.

When they were together he talked often of the Princess Victoria.

'I have seen that the child made a deep impression on you, George.'

'I found her amusing.'

'You should see more of her.'

'Yes, I should like that.' But would he? What would a mass of corrupting flesh look like in the clear sighted searching eyes of youth?

'I think it is not good that she should be brought up in the way she is. A household of women . . . German women. There is her mother who can scarcely speak English and Victoria speaks German to her. And then there are the Lehzen and Späth creatures. All German. I believe she speaks English sometimes, but I have heard many people murmuring about that household. There seems to be a barrier between you and the child.'

'There is no barrier.'

'How often do you see her? She should be here at Windsor. She should be your close companion. Why, you hardly know the child.'

The King was thoughtful.

'I believe,' said the Duke of Cumberland, a nerve twitching in his cheek, 'that you are considering having Victoria brought to Windsor.'

*

The Duchess of Kent was in a panic.

She sent for Sir John Conroy. 'What shall I do? The King has made no commands yet, but I have heard that he intends to. He wants Victoria to go to Windsor.'

'You must resist at all costs.'

'I know. I know. But what if he should command? And at Windsor is . . . Cumberland.'

'The child must not go. You must have a breach with the King rather. I would not answer for her life if she left Kensington. Here we can protect her, but she must not leave us. The Princes who were murdered in the Tower were taken from their mother. It must not happen to Victoria.'

'It shall not. I'll take her out of the country rather.'

The Duchess of Clarence called. She embraced the Duchess of Kent fearfully.

'You have heard the rumours,' said the Duchess of Kent.

Adelaide nodded. 'She must not go. You must not let her out of your sight.'

'I have determined not to. Anything . . . anything . . . rather than allow it. I am so terrified.'

Adelaide said: 'When William comes to the throne she will be safe. He will be King and I know he will protect you. But . . . now . . . it is Cumberland they say who rules, for the King is so ill he hardly knows what is going on about him. I know him for one of the kindest of men. I am sure he would be horrified if he knew what was in our minds.'

'It is as though an evil familiar has taken possession of him.'

'It is exactly so. I do not know the source of Cumberland's power over him, but it exists and while he lives we shall have to fear Cumberland.'

'My dear Adelaide,' said the Duchess, 'I live in terror. What if the King should send for her?'

'I think it is a matter for the Prime Minister. I will approach him and see what can be done. I will tell him that you will never give up Victoria and I am certain that the people would be on your side.'

'You will speak to the Prime Minister?'

'I do not like him. He treated William very brusquely over the

Lord High Admiral affair but I believe him to be an honest man and that he will do what he believes to be right.'

'Oh, Adelaide, you are a great comfort to me. I know why Victoria loves you so dearly.'

Adelaide had shed her meekness. One of her children was threatened and she was going to save the child.

The most angry and frustrated man in England was the Duke of Cumberland.

The Duke of Wellington had called on the King that day and had a meeting with him alone. Had Cumberland known that the Duke intended to call he would have made sure that he did not see the King; but Wellington had called unexpectedly and it was not until after the interview had taken place that Cumberland learned what had happened.

The King had invested his brother with the office of Gold Stick which meant that he had great authority at Windsor and no one was allowed to write to the King unless their communications passed first through his hands.

'I have the authority of His Majesty,' he announced; and indeed it seemed that Cumberland was in all but name the King.

Wellington had known this. It was his reason for coming unannounced.

Cumberland lost no time in discovering what had been the purpose of Wellington's call.

'It was just the matter of Victoria's leaving Kensington,' said the King.

Just the matter! It happened to be one of the most important matters in the world to Cumberland.

'The Duchesses of Kent and Clarence have heard that we had a mind to bring her here. They are very much against her leaving her mother.'

Cumberland laughed shortly. 'Of course they are. They are a couple of foolish women.'

'I do not think they are foolish. In fact I believe Adelaide to be a most intelligent woman. She was very insistent. She said that it would break Victoria's heart to leave her mother. They are devoted.'

'She does not realize that the child must be brought up to be the Queen . . . which she may well one day be.'

'I do not wish her to be unhappy.'

'She would be completely happy here.'

'*Here*, Ernest? What are you thinking of? In the Lodge? In the Castle? In the Cottage? It is no place for a child.'

'By God, George, this is no ordinary child. It is the Queen.'

'That is what people forget of royal children. They are destined to be human beings as well as kings and queens. I remember our upbringing. I think it was responsible for my wildness as a young man. No. The child is happy. She shall stay where she is.'

'George, you should consider . . .'

There were times when the King could be very regal. 'I have discussed the matter thoroughly . . . with Wellington, who is of my opinion. Victoria shall stay at Kensington.'

'I am sure when we have discussed the matter . . .'

The King was peevish. 'My dear Ernest, I have already told you that the matter is settled.'

There was no arguing with him. Wellington had convinced him and they had decided this matter so vital to Cumberland's plans without him.

Rumour had defeated him. The order should have been given, the child removed before anyone knew that it was his intention to bring her to Windsor.

Another plan foiled.

But there would be others.

The King is dead

The King's health had deteriorated rapidly. As many as eleven leeches had been applied to his leg at one time; punctures had been made in his thighs and ankles to draw off the water; he had grown enormous with dropsy. It was evident that he could not live long.

The news spread all over London and down to Brighton. The King is dying.

Mrs Fitzherbert, now living in Brighton, wept when she heard the news. It was long since they had met but she had always regarded him as her husband; she had always hoped that some time before the end they would come together.

He had loved her, she was sure, as deeply as he had been capable of loving anyone; it had not unfortunately been deep enough to keep him faithful; and she had overlooked so many infidelities. He had learned too late that they should never have parted. But there were two great barriers to the happiness of their life together: his crown and her religion. He dared not admit that he, the King, had married a Catholic; and she could never renounce her faith.

Ill-starred lovers, she thought; and yet there had been happy years.

The happiest of my life, she thought.

And now that he was dying did he think of her? Did he remember the day forty-five years ago when in the drawing-room of her house in Park Street they had taken their marriage vows? They had been in their twenties then – she twenty-nine and he some years younger. She was seventy-four now. An old woman; but not too old to forget and not too old to hope that now that he was leaving this life he would want to go with his hand in hers.

She could not stay in Brighton, so she travelled up to London. Who knew? He might express a wish to see her and if he did she must be on the watch.

She waited for some sign; none came, and at last she could not resist taking up her pen and writing to him.

After many repeated struggles with myself, from the apprehension of appearing troublesome or intruding upon Your Majesty, after so many years of continual silence, my anxiety respecting Your Majesty has got the better of my scruples and I trust Your Majesty will believe me most sincere when I assure you how truly I have grieved to hear of your sufferings . . .

It was true and she could not see the page because the tears blurred it.

So many wasted years, she thought. I should have been with him. I am his wife. Why could he not have been true to our marriage? If he had, what misery we should have been saved.

But they had parted. He had always said it was not his wish, but he would not give up Lady Hertford for her sake. And when he had left Lady Hertford it had been Lady Conyngham, the harpy, who cared more for diamonds and sapphires than she did for the King, and made no secret of it.

Oh, the folly of it!

And now it was too late. But at least he should know that she thought of him.

She went on writing and when she had finished she sent for a messenger to take her letter to the King.

He could not see very clearly. The faces about his bed seemed to be floating in space. He was not even sure where it was.

He heard them talking. 'We should give it to him. Mrs Fitzherbert . . .'

Her name roused him. He cried: 'What is it?'

'It is a letter, Sir, from Mrs Fitzherbert.'

He smiled. 'Give it to me.'

She had not forgotten him. She had written to him. He held the paper in his hand. Her paper . . . her writing. Maria, he thought. So you did not forget. All those years you remembered and at the end you wrote to me.

He could not read what she had written. It did not matter. She had written. He put the letter under his pillow. It gave him great comfort.

Mrs Fitzherbert stood at her window, waiting. Surely some messenger would come? He would wish to see her to say a last farewell. He must. He could not die without seeing her once more. She had made it clear in her letter that she longed to see him, to hear him say his last farewell to her. Perhaps to tell her that he had never forgotten, that she was the one he had always loved.

If she could see him, she would treasure the memory for the rest of her life. It would not be long before her turn came.

He must send for her. He *must*.

She lay on her couch listening. The sound of carriage wheels on the road? No, they had gone right past.

All through the night she lay fully dressed, waiting for a summons that did not come.

And he was sinking fast; one thing he remembered was the letter under his pillow. Her letter. She had written to him at the end.

Maria, Maria, he thought. We should never have parted.

And Maria was waiting through the night for the message that would never come.

He was dead – George the King, who had shocked the country with his scandalous adventures; who had been known as the First Gentleman of Europe; the elegant dandy, the man of exquisite taste, who had enriched the land with magnificent buildings, who had given them Carlton House, the Pavilion, Nash's terraces and Regent Street; who had turned Buckingham House into a Palace and had made Windsor Castle habitable. Prinney, who had been loved in youth and hated in his middle and old age, the incomparable George.

No one mourned as Maria Fitzherbert did. She was so ill that she had to keep to her bed. She was sad thinking of what might have been, and bitterly hurt because he had not answered her letter.

That was until she knew. And then they told her that he had worn her picture about his neck at his death and in his will he had left the instruction:

I wish that the picture of my beloved wife, my Maria Fitzherbert, may be interred with me, suspended round my neck by a ribbon as I used to wear it when I lived and placed upon my heart.

They would carry out his wishes.

And in death, she thought, we shall not be divided. She heard of his inability to read her letter; she was told how he had seized it and kept it under his pillow.

So she knew that at the last he had been thinking of her even as she had been thinking of him.

And then – Victoria

King George was dead. There was a new King and Queen to rule the land. King William IV and his Queen Adelaide.

Lady Conyngham was busy packing her bags; she wished to get out as quickly and with as much as possible.

The King's doctor, Sir Henry Halford, hastened to Bushy to call on the new King who must of course be the first to hear the news.

It was early morning but William was up while Adelaide still slept.

William knew as soon as he saw the doctor.

His hand was kissed; he heard the magic words: 'Your Majesty.'

'So he has gone,' said William. 'Poor George, he found it hard to die. Now we must tell the Queen.'

He sent one of the servants to waken Adelaide and as soon as she saw William she knew.

'Your Majesty,' said Sir Henry.

And she stared at him blankly and said: 'So it has come,' and there was great sorrow in her voice.

William, however, could not pretend to grieve for his brother, because through his death he had realized his great ambition. The crown was his.

'Go back to bed,' William told her. 'And I will join you.'

'I could not rest . . . now.'

'Go back, nevertheless,' said William, 'and I'll join you. I've never yet been to bed with a Queen.'

The new King was popular. He was so different from his brother. He went among the people freely; he had no airs and graces. He was the rough sailor.

He was soon in conflict with his brother Ernest, for Ernest was certain that soon the King would be in a strait-jacket and then there would be a Regency for Victoria and he would be a member of that Regency and then there should be no obstruction to his plans.

The first friction came when William discovered his brother's horses in the Queen's stables at Windsor.

'Remove them,' he said. 'That's the place for the Queen's carriage.'

'I'll be damned if I'll move them,' retorted Cumberland.

But William was the King and not to be defied; so the horses were removed and Cumberland's office of Gold Stick taken from him.

'I *am* the King,' said William, 'and I'll *be* the King.'

It was Cumberland who had started those rumours about himself, and Adelaide had told him some nasty stories about his designs on Victoria.

'By God,' he said, 'I am the King and all here had better remember it.'

He took the first opportunity of showing his intentions towards his brother when at a dinner where Cumberland and several others were present the King rose to give the toast.

'The land we live in and let those who don't like it, leave it.'

His eyes were on Cumberland when he said that, and he meant: I understand you, brother. There is not room at this Court for you and me. And as it's my Court and I am the King of it, there is no room for you.

At Kensington Palace the Duchess of Kent rejoiced. 'He can't harm her now,' she told Lehzen. 'His power is broken.'

'But Your Highness will wish to guard her all the same.'

'I do not forget how precious she is, Baroness. Nor must any of us.'

So she continued to sleep in her room and Victoria must not descend the stairs alone. But the tension was lifted. They could breathe more freely in Kensington Palace; and the Duchess of Kent must impress on her daughter more firmly than ever that one day she would be the Queen of England. And that day was not far distant, she was sure.

It was more like a holiday than a day of mourning. On that beautiful July day the sun shone warmly and it seemed that all the inhabitants not only of Windsor but the surrounding country had come out to see the last of George IV.

He was buried in the royal vault with the miniature of Maria Fitzherbert over his heart. And the new King could scarcely contain his exuberance, so delighted was he to have the crown in his grasp at last.

The gentle Queen whispered to him that he must hide his pleasure. It was hardly seemly to show such delight in the death of a brother.

William was puzzled. He had loved old George. But he loved his crown better. He would explain to Adelaide when they were alone.

The bells were tolling; they were firing the salute; even if few cared that this was the funeral of the late King it must be a royal funeral.

It was more than that. It was the passing of an age.

The great Georgian era was at an end. It was William's turn now – William's and Adelaide's – and in the apartments at Kensington Palace the Duchess of Kent put her arm about her daughter and led her to the window.

'All your life,' she said, 'you will remember – this day.'

Victoria had wept; she had been fascinated by Uncle King. But it was long since she had seen him; and she knew what this meant.

One day – and perhaps quite soon – there would be another royal funeral – and a new sovereign would mount the throne.

And then . . . Victoria.

Jean Plaidy
The Plantagenet Prelude 80p

The first book in her magnificent Plantagenet Saga by one of England's
foremost historical novelists.

A king, a queen and an archbishop – three figures who dominated the
dawn of the Plantagenet epoch ... Eleanor of Aquitaine – romantic and
beautiful, Queen of the 'Courts of Love'; Henry Duke of Normandy,
great-grandson of William the Conqueror; Thomas à Becket, the
merchant's son who rose to become a saint and a martyr, beloved and
hated in turn by Henry his king.

The Revolt of the Eaglets 80p

The second book in the Plantagenet Saga.

The murder of the sainted Becket had earned Henry Plantagenet the
condemnation of all Christendom. His queen, Eleanor of Aquitaine,
hated him after her discovery of his infidelity with Rosamund Clifford.
Like an ageing eagle he held the throne of England, under constant
attack from three of the eaglets he had nurtured, while a fourth waited
for the moment of utter defeat to pluck out his eyes ...

The Heart of the Lion 80p

The third book in the Plantagenet Saga.

The death of Henry II brought his son Richard to the English throne –
his destiny was to be one of the greatest warrior kings of the
medieval world, to ride against the Saracen at the head of his army of
Crusaders, sworn to win back the holy city of Jerusalem for Christendom.
At court, Berengaria, Richard's queen, struggled to hold the place in
his life that was ever beyond her reach, while his treacherous brother
John cast greedy eyes towards England's crown ...

The Prince of Darkness 95p

The fourth book in the Plantagenet Saga.

The untimely death of Richard Coeur de Lion left his nephew Arthur and his younger brother John in contest for the English throne. Reluctantly the barons chose John – and brought years of evil upon the realm; his unbridled sensuality and terrible temper, his cruelty and idleness made King John hated and feared. Men came to believe the House of Anjou was tainted by the Devil's blood ...

The Battle of the Queens £1.25

The fifth book in the Plantagenet Saga.

The first half of the thirteenth century was dominated by two women, as proud and ambitious as they were beautiful, yet totally different in all other qualities.

Isabella, flamboyant and passionate, wife to King John and mother of Henry III ... Blanche of Castille, serene and virtuous, Queen of France, wife to Louis VIII and mother of Louis IX .. The two women hated each other on sight. Isabella would stop at nothing, not even murder, in her passion to destroy the French Queen.

The Queen from Provence £1

The sixth book in the Plantagenet Saga.

Marguerite, eldest daughter of the Count of Provence, had married a king of France. Her beautiful sister Eleanor was determined on as grand a match. Good fortune and cunning brought her Henry of England for husband – a weak king, he ruled a nation that still remembered cruel King John, his father. Henry's extravagance forced him to levy ever greater taxes, until the spectre of revolt loomed. For the adventurer Simon de Montfort, the hour of destiny was at hand ...

Elizabeth Byrd
The Flowers of the Forest £1.50

Edinburgh in the year 1513 – the bloodstreaked year of Flodden Field.
Against the setting of the teaming capital of Scotland, plague-ridden
and aflow with riches and squalor, this vivid novel follows the fortunes
of two women: Bess Andersen, the spirited country girl, seduced and
scorned, turning to prostitution and wedlock to a weakling; and
Margaret Tudor, the princess who became Queen of James IV, seeking
in vain for love and affection . . .

'Full-blooded stuff' SCOTSMAN

Maid of Honour £1.50

Lady Mary Seton, maid of honour to ill-starred Mary Queen of Scots,
followed her queen through tempestuous and tragic years, to the
corrupt and elegant court of Henry II of France and to a world of danger
and intrigue in Scotland. Passionate and pious, timid and courageous,
how could she condemn her queen for adultery when she herself had
fallen in love with a priest?

'One of the best historical novelists' YORKSHIRE POST

Immortal Queen £1.50

Her magnificent novel of Mary, the tragic Queen of Scots. On a chill
morning, February 1587, in the Great Hall of Fotheringay, an elegant
and beautiful Queen prepared to die as bravely as she had lived. On a
black scaffold, clad in red and gold, she faced the last link in a chain of
destiny . . . from Catherine de Medici and Elizabeth of England to
Bothwell – whose name was the last word on her lips as the headsman's
axe-blade fell.

'A joy to read' DAILY EXPRESS

Laura Black
Castle Raven £1.25

Katie was ill-suited to the elegant world of Ravenburn Castle. Her stepmother and uncle were trying to turn a tomboy into a Cinderella. But with their neglect she was free to roam the Highland wilds, coming across the ruined castle buried amid the heather of Eilean Fitheach island. On this enchanted island, shunned by the locals, she would meet dramatic and terrifying events, the truth about her parents, and a sudden deadly peril . . .

Jean Stubbs
Kit's Hill 95p

Set in the bleak, harsh countryside of Lancashire on the eve of the Industrial Revolution, this is the fascinating story of the Howarths; of Ned, the rugged Yeoman farmer, consumed with a passion for a girl above his station; of Dorcas Wilde, the beautiful and spirited girl who married him in the face of family hostility. We share their joys, fears and heartbreaks, from a splendid country wedding feast to the devastation of cattle-plague and the horrors of primitive surgery.

David Toulmin
Harvest Home 95p

These stories bring to vivid life the world of the Buchan farming folk of half a century ago. John Rettie, doctor to man and beast, whose pony brought him safely home sober or no . . . Maggie Lawrence who found a suicide deep in her well . . . Jotty McGillivray, the fiddle-playing blacksmith, and Souter Duthie, whose shop was the place for news and a blether and smoke thick enough to cut with a scythe . . .

'A born writer who recreates . . . the incredibly hard, rough life of farm workers in north-east Scotland . . . moving, tender, astonishing, funny and grim' SUNDAY TIMES

Barbara Whitehead
Quicksilver Lady 85p

In the heady years after the victory at Trafalgar, London is the only place of fashion in which to choose a husband. So to London Arabella must look, and she persuades her sister Caroline, Mrs Richard Welby, to winter there as her companion. The Prince of Wales's star is in the ascendant, and London is a whirl of coffee houses and countesses, balls and beaux. Impetuous and warm-hearted Arabella will find more than enough sentimental intrigues and romantic escapades to test her constancy to the last.

Juliette Benzoni
The Lure of the Falcon £1.25

Gilles Goëlo watched the soldiers who sailed from Brest bound for the Americas with longing and excitement. To follow them over the ocean was his escape from the gloomy seminary to a land filled with adventure. Setting out from France, Gilles was destined to serve General Washington in the soldier's trade, to face danger, torture and death, to meet the Indian girl whose beauty might tempt him to forget the faithful Judith . . .

The first in a magnificent new saga of romantic adventure.